A NOVEL

JOHN BANKS

₁8₉
819 Publishing

This book is a work of fiction. Names, characters, places and incidents are either the product of the author's imagination or are used fictitiously.
Copyright © 2017 by John Banks
All rights reserved. No part of this work may be reproduced or transmitted in any form or by any means, except by reviewers who wish to quote brief passages.
Published by 819 Publishing
1004 Harvest Time Way
Greensboro, NC 27410
Excerpt from "Gisli Sursson's Saga" (translation by Martin S. Regal), taken from *The Complete Sagas of Icelanders,* is reprinted with permission of Leifur Eiriksson Publishing Ltd.

Printed in the United States of America
Library of Congress Control Number: 2017914764
ISBN: 978-0-9833334-1-8

To Bonnie and Lucinda

...Skeggi the Dueller suggested to Thorbjorn that their families be united: "I'll marry your daughter, Thordis," he said.

But Thorbjorn did not want the man to marry his daughter. Thordis, it was said, had since become friendly with Kolbjorn. Suspecting this was the real reason his proposal had been rejected, Skeggi went to meet Kolbjorn and challenged him to a duel on the island of Saxo....

After three nights had passed, Gisli went to meet Kolbjorn and asked him if he was ready for the duel.... "I don't think I'll fight Skeggi to win Thordis," said Kolbjorn.

Gisli told Kolbjorn he was the greatest scoundrel living – "And though it shame you forever," he said, "I shall go instead."

Gisli went to the island of Saxo with eleven men. Skeggi had already arrived at the spot where the duel was to be fought...but he could not see his opponent nor anyone to replace him.

There was a man called Ref, who worked for Skeggi as a carpenter. Skeggi asked him to make wooden effigies in the likenesses of Gisli and Kolbjorn.

"And one shall stand behind the other," he said, "and those figures of scorn shall remain like that forever to mock them."

Gisli, who was in the woods, heard this and answered, "Find some better employment for your farmhands. Here is a man who dares to fight you."

– *Gisli Sursson's Saga* [translated by Martin S. Regal]

1

W,

All I hear is your crying. It isn't like when you were a kid and you cried all the time. This is heartbreaking and I am helpless. And it was the last time I'll ever hear your voice (most likely), so I'm doomed to replay that call in my head forever. I suppose I should be grateful for it, though its purpose was not pleasant. It was obviously important to you that you call – when was the last time we actually *talked?* – but I think I can be certain that you were also unaware at the time that we would never speak again, correct? So what happened? As excruciating as the entire incident was to you I know there must have been more. Why now, Will? After we had all successfully endured the worst? It doesn't make sense. Please help me figure it out. So do you mind if we go over it one more time from the top?

Of course, I almost had to drag it out of you. Were you just being Southern Diffident or were you having second thoughts about calling me? Did you think I would criticize you? I hope that wasn't the case. You know how proud of you I always was, right? How much I admired you and everything you did? When you finally got around to telling me, the last thing I was thinking about, believe me, was chastisement. Jeez, when you said he had a gun your voice cracked as if the word *gun* itself was a little bullet that had grazed you. And to sucker-punch you in the gut after he had already taken what he wanted? I'm sure you would have happily handed over your wallet if he had asked nicely. No one would blame you for being irate, of course, but there was more than just anger in your voice – there was *betrayal*. Didn't he know you had dedicated your life to helping those just like him? Where was his gratitude? Oh Will, this is but one of the many ways I failed you. This is where I actually had some useful instruction to impart to you. This is the lesson I never taught you – we are in no position to ever expect gratitude from them. And unfortunately we are quickly putting ourselves in a position of not deserving gratitude from anybody – but that's another sermon for another day.

I understand why you didn't want to tell Mom, but your decision has made my position rather untenable. She sees no reason – except maybe Pop – why you might have wanted to do this. But I heard it in your voice, I understood your anguish, your deep guilt, your self-loathing and shame – I understood it all too well. But I chose many years ago to turn this knowledge and new self-awareness into cynicism and acceptance. Can I be forgiven if it didn't occur to me that you would choose a different way to express your grief? Not that Pop wouldn't be a good enough reason, but that was all about Pop – this was all about you. It was a startling revelation, wasn't it, Will, when you realized that you and Pop had something in common after all? He was a disorienting, nauseating, concussive blow to the head to be sure, but this was visceral; this was a kick in the balls. And of course, because of Pop, there's a whole different layer of speculation I have to deal with, but your assailant didn't broach that particular subject, did he?

I know the fact that you were robbed wasn't something you would dwell on. And I know that being punched in the stomach wasn't an unforgivable offense either – certainly not to you. I wasn't too concerned about it either, after you assured me you were unhurt. But still, I was surprised, to say the least, when you said that wasn't the real reason you called. What could possibly be more troubling than having your life threatened by a thug at gunpoint? But then you started crying. Will, your tears are killing me. What can I do to make them stop?

But it all made perfect sense after you finally fessed up; it was almost predictable, though I was still a bit stunned that you would do such a thing. What I told you at the time is definitely true – you shouldn't blame yourself for all the crap Pop forced down our throats – it was bound to come back up eventually – but what I should have said also is this: It may have taken a lot less than a physical assault to elicit from me a similar slew of unexpurgated insights and incongruous feelings regarding racial harmony. I'm not proud of it – quite the opposite – but I long ago accepted this congenital, constitutional racism as a part of me and a part of America, as bred into my bones and swirled into my system as sugar into sweet tea. Would it have helped to have heard that from me? It may have made things worse, if I implied that you had failed at some essential southern task. But I have the rest of my life now to regret my ironic detachment, my lack of empathy, and my unwillingness to join hands in a shared confession of sins. But I couldn't help it – you were so distraught by this. If you hadn't been suffering so much obvious grief, I would have been tempted to laugh. Damn Will, do you really think you are that pure of heart? That you are that different from me and every other damn white person I know? Are you really that Great White Hope that good old Jerome insisted was purely mythical – a non-racist cracker? Well, obviously not. In the end, you turned out to be not very different from any other unreconstructed rage-filled Southerner; but very much unlike them you looked in the mirror and were sickened by what you saw.

Should I have asked more questions, prodded you to tell me what else was going on? Well, only in hindsight. At the time it was clear you had been put through enough for one day. And you seemed okay when we hung up. I even got you laughing a little. Jesus, thank God your car windows were rolled up. Seriously, it filled me with fear all over again to think about how close you undoubtedly came to getting your head truly bashed in if someone – *anyone,* in that neighborhood – had been an audience to your performance. But really – and I'm going to have to insist that I bear the brunt of responsibility for this – there is no excuse for your naiveté at your advanced age. "Is it really that close to the surface? Still? Even after all this time?" Those questions, Will, mixing with your tears, will echo in my ears forever. And you thought we had banished that word forever from our vocabularies when we were still kids.

You did a better job than most, but I guess it's just like riding a bicycle, isn't it? So, welcome to the Great American Dilemma, little brother. You came a bit late to the party, and you decided not to hang around to help collect all the empties, but here's the question we must ask ourselves: How are we supposed to get rid of all this shit that's inside of us?

You called to confess your unpardonable sin – the sin of failing to rise above your raising – and I ended our call believing I had given you the absolution you needed, but three days later you're dead and I'm left helplessly wondering if my words were ever any benefit to you at all, or if they were the cause of any of your pain. Perhaps I was incapable of understanding your pain. Or maybe, despite all the tears, we never even got around to discussing it.

ON THE ISLAND OF GOTLAND there once lived a man named Thorbjorn who had amassed great wealth through the capture and selling of slaves. He had two sons, Thorstein and Ketil, both of whom were loyal sons and good traders. Though loyal to their father, they were not always loyal to each other. A great rivalry existed between them, which their father did nothing to discourage since their rivalry served to bring him greater wealth. Thorstein went on many successful summer raids throughout the lands to the west of Gotland; Ketil preferred to go east, to Gardariki. During one such trip, Ketil captured many slaves, including many women. There was one woman in particular, however, whom Ketil fell in love with. It is difficult to paint pictures using words, but suffice it to say there was something within the features of her face – some combination of nose, mouth, eyes, cheeks, and skin – that made him happier than he could remember feeling at any other time. He knew immediately that of all the slave women captured for this journey she was the one he would treat differently – perhaps he would even take her for his wife.

"I almost wish I hadn't captured you," Ketil said to her, "for I foresee you bringing me a great deal of trouble."

"You have the power to set me free," she said.

"Yes, but I don't foresee that happening," Ketil responded. "I also don't foresee wanting to sell you. Taking a slave for a bride will not make my father happy, however. We'll see what happens, won't we?" Ketil smiled. "Good luck has always been my best friend, and I have no reason to doubt it will remain by my side."

As Ketil made his way toward Miklagard with his slaves, he was many times made excellent offers for the one slave that was more beautiful than the others. He refused them all, however. The men interested in buying her then made even larger offers, which were also refused. "I don't foresee selling you, my dear," he repeated often. Unlike all the other captured slaves whom Ketil treated indifferently or harshly, he did not mistreat her in any way. Food was taken from other slaves to ensure that she did not go hungry. He had his way with the other female slaves, but not so with her, for he wanted her to remain chaste until they were married, which, as the days and weeks passed, seemed more and more likely to happen. One day, however, a man from the East offered Ketil twice as much gold as anyone previously had offered. Ketil considered the offer briefly and then accepted it. The beautiful woman was heartbroken because she had grown to love Ketil even though she was his slave. She had begun thinking of herself as his wife, who would return to Gotland with him to live in wealth. "How can you do this, Ketil?" she implored. "You said that you would never sell me."

"You are mistaken. I said I didn't foresee selling you, but I didn't foresee being offered a fortune for you, either. My father will be immensely proud of me for making such a good bargain and my brother may actually die of jealousy. I hope this man treats you as well as I have." Ketil gave her to the other man and continued his yearly journey to Miklagard, amassing riches along the way.

Thorstein had many adventures on his raids as well. This same summer Thorstein had pledged his support to a Dane named Harald Thickskin, who promised in return for Thorstein's help in battle the opportunity to capture and sell many slaves. It was said of Harald that in all his battles he had never suffered so much as a scratch, which is how he had earned the name Thickskin. Thorstein fought many bloody and exciting battles with Harald and was rewarded well with slaves and much other booty. Harald, however, though generous with those who offered their support, was merciless to those who failed to display proper loyalty and courage. To one man who appeared to be less than courageous, Harald said, "If you are not going to use your arms to fight for me, then I consider them to be useless." Harald then took his sword and severed both of the man's arms just below the shoulders, bleeding him quickly to death. To another he said, after a hard-fought battle had concluded, "You did not come running to me when I requested your aid, so what good are your feet to me?" This man, though afterwards unable to walk without great difficulty, lived many more years and was called Thorolf Three Sticks.

After their summer raiding, Ketil and Thorstein returned to Gotland with more wealth and glory to bestow upon their father. Ketil eventually married a woman from Gotland named Gudrun and she gave him a son, whom he named Thorbjorn in honor of his father.

Thorbjorn grew into a healthy young boy, but showed little of the adventurousness of his father or uncle. He dreamed of glory in his sleep, however, and on particularly stormy nights his mind would drift to the stories about Gotland sinking under the sea that had terrified him since he first heard them. He imagined running to the shore and bravely unmooring the boats in which to rescue everyone. During the day he played alone among the rauks in the waves, chasing himself through all kinds of adventures. He gazed for hours at picture stones and was content to make no marks of his own on them. As Thorbjorn grew older, this strange child became fascinated by the silver hoard his grandfather had amassed. But when he wanted to see the hoard and to play with it, he had to sneak underground because his father forbade him access to it. "It will anger the gods," he said. But that made no sense to Thorbjorn. This silver was here for the afterlife – it belonged to his family, for eternity, not to the gods. The real reason his father refused to allow him to see the hoard, he thought, was his fear that he would steal some of it. But he had no interest in removing any of the silver. He only wanted to admire it, hold it, turn it over in his palms and study its contours and mysterious engravings.

When Thorbjorn came of age it was time for him to embark on his first summer raid across the sea. He chose to go east with his father. Ketil said he was getting too old for raids and wished next year to remain at home with Gudrun and hoped that Thorbjorn would prove himself to be as brave and successful as he and Thorstein had been. Thorbjorn did not lack courage, and was very successful in fighting and capturing men and women who could be sold as slaves. However, in the business of trading, his love of all the beautiful qualities of silver proved to be a great disadvantage. He was once offered two dinars for one of his slaves.

"Do you have that amount in dirhams?" Thorbjorn asked.

"No – it's much easier to carry two of the one rather than forty of the other. Wouldn't you agree?"

"I will only take dirhams."

"You'll refuse an honorable transaction in gold because I don't have the equivalent in silver?"

"Yes."

"Your future as a trader does not look promising."

Thorbjorn saw many other things that summer that made him doubt that he could make his family proud of him as a slave trader. One man captured more slaves than he thought he could transport. Rather than sell them at lower prices, or set them all free, this man invented a game whereby he offered gold as a prize to whoever in his service could be most ingenious in the killing of a slave. There were many men loyal to him eager to take up an axe and to play the game and many slaves lost their limbs and lives in this manner.

It also happened this summer, just as it had happened to Ketil many summers ago, that Thorbjorn fell in love with one of the women he had captured. She was called Yelena. Unlike his father, however, Thorbjorn could not be induced by greed to sell her. "I wish to take Yelena back to Gotland and marry her," he announced to his father.

"I understand that desire," Ketil said, "but I fear your

grandfather may understand it less so. We'll see what happens, won't we?"

Though despairing of ever becoming a successful slave trader, Thorbjorn was excited, however, about travelling to Miklagard with his future bride. He had heard the tales from Ketil of the fire-breathing dragons that the Greeks had captured to use against their enemies and wished to see one of these dragons in action. His wish was granted, as a great sea battle took place in Miklagard at the time he was there. Unfortunately, he and his father were not involved in the battle, but they watched it unfold from the harbor shore. Great bellows of fire poured forth from the dragons' jaws and put to fire not only the enemy ships but the very water upon which they were sailing. Only a dragon's magic can set water aflame, thought Thorbjorn. He was disappointed, however, in his inability to see any of the dragons, for they were much too distant to see upon the ships in the sea, though he saw clearly enough the fire issuing from their mouths and the destruction that they wrought.

Ketil and Thorbjorn returned safely to Gotland with Yelena. As expected, the elder Thorbjorn did not approve of her. "You may marry her if you wish, but I will never have a slave for a granddaughter," he said, adding, "I am disappointed in you, Thorbjorn. You brought a whore back from Miklagard, but not much else. You have much to learn about being a trader, that is, if it is possible to teach you anything. Ketil," he said to his son, "you should have given my name to someone more worthy of it."

Filled with shame, Thorbjorn decided that he and Yelena should leave Gotland and make a life for themselves elsewhere. To this end, he built a ship – for he was an excellent craftsman – and on a morning when the wind was in their favor, they braved the sea between Gotland and the western mainland. They landed safely on one of the Small Lands of Geatland where Thorbjorn built a longhouse for himself, Yelena, and their future family. He thrived as a farmer and fisherman.

Yelena bore Thorbjorn three children, one of whom was called Thorstein, in honor of Thorbjorn's uncle. Thorstein, like most children, was restless at home and eager to roam as far as his luck would take him. He left Geatland and became a great warrior in the service of King Gorm of Denmark.

After many years of fighting, Thorstein married a woman called Eydis and settled in Denmark as a farmer. He named his son Thorbjorn, in honor of the boy's grandfather. Thorbjorn was a difficult child. He cried relentlessly and neither Eydis nor Thorstein could do anything to soothe his crying. It was only when Thorbjorn was outside that his crying ceased. His parents soon learned to take him outside whenever his crying began, which was always soon after returning indoors. Eventually, his parents decided to leave him outside at all times. Other families looked down upon them for allowing a child to remain outside during rainstorms and blizzards, but they had little choice, as Thorbjorn would bolt for the door as soon as he was brought inside, regardless of the weather. Despite his dislike of being enclosed, Thorbjorn otherwise appeared to be a happy child. As he grew into a young man, Thorbjorn no longer felt a need to remain close to his house and his parents' supervision and began to roam the forests and remained gone for days at a time, returning only long enough to soothe his mother's fears for his safety. By this time, Thorstein had given up all hopes for Thorbjorn and allowed him to remain away from home for as long as he wished. Thorbjorn began thinking of himself as being more bear than human. He learned to hunt and to subsist as a bear and to find whatever pleasures in the forest that exist for bears. He often wished he had been born a bear and eventually he stopped regretting his inability to live indoors. All the inhabitants of Jutland learned to recognize Thorbjorn in the woods and left him alone to live the life of a bear. Everyone soon began calling him Real Bear.

Real Bear had been the first child born to Thorstein and Eydis, but they also had a daughter named Thordis. Thordis grew up to be beautiful like her mother, but she was too stubborn, according to both her parents. One example of her stubbornness was her refusal to stop visiting her brother Real Bear in the forest. Some days she could locate him; other days she could not, but her parents insisted that a girl should not spend hours alone in the forest. They could not convince her otherwise. On the days when she could locate her brother, she tried to persuade him to come back home. "Perhaps you can live indoors now," she would say.

"Thank you for your concern, dear sister," Real Bear would reply, "but outdoors is where I belong. The very thought of a roof over my head causes me great discomfort. I cannot breathe indoors and I feel as if I'm being strangled by Thor himself. I know it is inhuman to live such a life as this, but there is no other choice to make."

"Well, then, will you at least promise to leave with me when I get married? Mother and Father have given up on you, but I haven't. You may certainly remain outdoors, if that is your wish, but I want you to live where I may look after you."

"I think I can promise you that much, but no more. When you marry and wish to leave, I will go with you."

Thordis's parents also thought her stubborn in her choice of suitors. Many young men of Denmark asked to marry her. Thorstein had strong opinions about all of these men, but the final decision, as always, came down to Thordis. Against her father's wishes, she chose to marry a man named Arnthor, who was a wealthy trader from Norway. "Why would you choose to marry a Norwegian when so many wealthy Danes have proposed to you?" her father asked. "It is as if your decisions are determined entirely according to what I would desire least."

"It is disrespectful to argue with one's father, so I will let you have your say."

"Yes, it is convenient for you to show your respect for me in that way, but much less so than by obeying me. That would show much greater respect, don't you agree?"

"As you say, Father. I love Arnthor and we will make a good family together, regardless of where we live. And I will continue to look after Real Bear, since you and Mother can no longer be troubled to do so."

Thordis and Arnthor went into the forest to look for Real Bear. Upon finding him, Arnthor said, "A family is a remarkable thing. The most beautiful lady upon Earth and this wild animal, sprung from the same source. I will say to you, Real Bear, if you are still capable of understanding human speech, that you are the luckiest beast in the woods in having such a sister."

"And I will say to you, Arnthor, that your luck is twice that of mine, for Thordis had her pick of men wealthier and wiser than you. Indeed, she is much wiser than I, for she sees something admirable in you that I so far fail to see, though, for her sake, I will continue looking for it."

Thordis stepped in between the two most important men in her life and said, "We begin a long voyage together tomorrow. This is not an auspicious beginning."

They sailed the next morning for Norway.

DEAREST CONSTANCE,

Greetings, my love. I now have been in the town of Omaha for one week, and when not purchasing supplies and equipage, and making other necessary arrangements for a long journey by "prairie schooner," I have been in a state of joy because of your letters! I was eager to the point of impatience to arrive in Omaha, knowing that I had asked you to post your letters to this location – but you can imagine my happiness when the postmaster delivered into my hands a veritable armful of letters from you! There seems to be one for each day I have been absent from your arms. What a glorious little thing you are! I am happy to hear that your mother is improving, of course – that would be good news at any time. However, such tidings make me miss you all the more, since, had she been in a likewise favorable condition when I departed, then perhaps your sense of duty would not have implored you to stay behind with her. How I miss you so, my darling! My loneliness is made only worse by the haste of my departure from you and my worry that you may have become angry with me in my absence. How your letters lighten the weight I have borne! I hope that I may rest assured as well that you understand the force of necessity I felt bearing down so hard upon me – a force I feared you had not an adequate understanding of.

Charleston has gone mad, and what once I would have

dismissed as an impossibility has transformed into a certainty. I am speaking now not just of the present fate of our state, which I need not explain to you, but also of the present state of my mind. Though shackled, like its slaves, to this wicked, malevolent institution, Charleston was my homeland and, years ago, I would have judged the act of forsaking it as an abomination to my conscience. How many times throughout history have men been faced with the choice that is now confronting all of us? How often have good men – wise men – chosen to remain by their hearths to contend for what they know to be right, even if doing so insured the destruction of their homes and families? As a hurricane approaches the shore, a man can be blamed neither for battening himself behind his doors nor for running to higher ground – but he cannot do both. And how can one be certain which is the wiser course? I cannot speak for others, but I felt for many long months incapable of making any decision whatsoever. The tug of war taking place in my mind admitted of no resolution. You remember well the horrible throes of indecision I labored under! And also you must remember well the moment I told you that we must go. You thought I was being so suddenly rash, but is the sun behaving rashly as it bursts forth from behind a cloud? Such decisions, my dear, are not made using Aristotle's analytics. And once made, they brook no delay. Although we were in no immediate danger, I felt as if your house were aflame and I were trapped with you within it, and our lives could be saved only by my brave and swift action. And I do indeed esteem this action I have taken to be an act of bravery, though you tell me of those others who see it quite differently. We should try not to concern ourselves too much with their base opinions, but I do fear that I have but little defense against their condemnation of me as a coward – for how often is courage associated with taking flight?

Perhaps I should have agreed to wait for you. Please forgive me, darling, if you ever believe that I have acted unwisely or foolishly, but I feel truly as if I had little control over my decision. And, as I am not the first Charlestonian to follow this path, neither will I be the last, so I am confident that as soon as

I am safely settled, you will have no trouble finding a family or two whom you can accompany west. We must put the past behind us to the extent allowed by the present perilous circumstances of our country, and look forward only to our wonderful future together! To this end, I shall put an immediate stop to these rueful ruminations and describe for you the preparations I am eagerly making!

Omaha is the "jump off" point which will mark the beginning of my odyssey overland to Oregon. After weeks spent as passenger on assorted trains and steamers, amid varying degrees of luxuriousness, I am now prepared to begin what undoubtedly will prove to be the most difficult portion of my journey. Indeed, though I have been traveling for weeks and have traversed approximately two thousand miles, I cannot help but have the emotions tonight of one who is freshly packed and preparing to depart the station, and who is ready to take his first steps toward his destination. I am no stranger to steam trains; boats offer a pleasant diversion; within and upon these you are transported as a guest; I do not expect to experience such solicitude on the trail.

The most significant difference between stepping off a train platform, stepping onto the stage of a steamer, and "jumping off" onto the westward trail – that is to say, before any journey properly can be said to begin – is in the fact that prior to embarking on a train or a steamboat, the only required purchase is that of a ticket. Yet I have been in Omaha for no less than seven days, and I am only now satisfied that I have purchased all that I shall require on the trail. I must admit, darling, to great feelings of trepidation after I crossed over the Missouri to Omaha, and began to realize what lay before me. My first task was to obtain lodging. In such a small town as Omaha – if one can properly attach to it the appellation of "town" – this is not a difficult thing to do, provided that one does not expect too much. I have enjoyed my sojourn at the Herndon House, not because of what type of lodging it is, but rather because of what type it is not. How marvelous it is, sweetheart, to have a proper bed and bath, rather than a cramped berth on board some type of portable conveyance! But please, my darling, do not permit your mind to imagine the Charleston as you visualize the room I occupy currently. I daresay you would be disappointed! But I have learned to value comfort over any other possible amenity, so I can state unequivocally that this hotel meets this modest standard.

After securing my lodgings, many other rude messengers of alarm announced their arrival. Here I was, darling, alone, staring westward out along the horizon, and I realized that I had not a clue as to how to continue. So many questions sprang into my mind: What shall I purchase? In what quantities? From whom shall I make these purchases? From what location does the trail begin? At what time? There is no depot here, my dear, and no timetables. The *town* is the depot; the sun appears to be the only timetable; there is no porter to shout, "All aboard!"

I do not believe it is possible to succeed along life's journey without some modicum of good fortune. And if the subject is a lonesome traveler, without necessary knowledge and supplies, then the good fortune must take the form of another person, who, with patience and a good heart, decides to reach out and offer his assistance. In my particular case, this fortunate person (fortunate for me, certainly, although not, perhaps, for him) is named Jason Sanders, who, with his wife and small child, is in Omaha also in preparation for the journey to Oregon; whereupon arriving and building a cabin, Jason is hopeful of finding a rich vein of gold from which to dig a lifetime's worth of wages within whatever amount of time is required to discover it. This scheme, repeated now tens of thousands of times by tens of thousands of similarly hopeful nomads, is tempting to contemplate, but I believe it is the duty of every man to earn his living, rather than stumble upon it. However, it is easy to forgive a man for succumbing to such an alluring temptation, as long as he does not allow the sin of greed to overshadow his duties to God and family. Since I have alluded to the subject of the folly of greed, I am prompted to say that I miss sincerely the company of Mr. Carlyle and the many wonderful stories he told on board the steamer. Have you received those letters? If not, I promise you will enjoy reading my relation of the misadventures of Burt Humphrey, Joe Clark,

Dirk, &c., as much as I enjoyed hearing Mr. C. tell of them. His gregariousness transformed what otherwise would have been an interminably monotonous riverboat journey into a grand pleasure which I was saddened to have to terminate.

But to return to my new friend Jason: unlike your beloved correspondent, J. took adequate time, before departing his home city of Philadelphia, to plan and to learn of all the things he would need to know for the successful completion of this portion of his journey. I met J. when speaking to a hostler regarding where one should go to purchase a horse. J. had completed the same transaction earlier, as well as that of the purchase of a team of mules, and was making the necessary arrangements with the hostler for their upkeep until such time as they would be required. Upon learning the few small details of my circumstances, that were possible for me to impart during such a brief conversation, J. immediately offered to adopt me, as it were, into his family, for the duration of our mutual journey. I was overwhelmed by the generosity of his offer; so much so that I was quite speechless for a moment. What prayers of thanks do we owe to God for the presence of such goodness in the world! However, after expressing my heartfelt gratitude to J. for his selfless offer, I declined to accept it. I refuse to be a burden to any man, even if, as in this case, the burden is freely offered to be undertaken. J. insisted that I reconsider his kind offer, but, as you know well, I am capable of great stubbornness when the occasion calls for it! I was, however, more than willing to accept his subsequent offer of friendship and advice. J. has seen to it that I am well equipped for the journey ahead, including the purchase of a "prairie schooner" that I can now call mine! J. attempted to dissuade me from making such a costly – and, in his view, superfluous – purchase, but I once again declined his proffered generosity. My wagon may not be so full by half as those of the large families I will accompany, but, if for no other reason than to serve as a replacement upon the misfortune of someone else, then my purchase is justified.

As with the hotel décor, my sweet, I believe you would disapprove of the daily fare upon which we would dine, if I had the pleasure of your company for the duration of this voyage. I have purchased a cask each of beans, bacon, and flour – that is correct, my dear – enough victuals to feed an army, but bought for consumption by a solitary person! J. assures me that this is the barest minimum I should wish to procure; that even this incredible quantity is no guarantee against all contingencies.

I asked J. about the dangers posed by the Indians along our route. The fear of Indian attack, although remaining largely unspoken by everyone – as if the mere mention of scalps and tomahawks and bows and arrows is enough to conjure them up out of the morning mists! – is certainly on the minds of anyone preparing to undertake this journey. Perhaps I am relying too heavily on J. for information that he has received at second- or third-hand as well. There have been times this week when I have all but forgotten that J. is as much a "greenhorn" as I. However, J. assures me that with the military escort we will have – and of which I was entirely ignorant – the Indian threat should be negligible.

I hope that I have safely put to bed many of the worries you must have, Constance. I believe I have laid in supplies enough to stave off starvation; I have my wagon and mules; I have a rifle and a revolver, with ammunition sufficient to kill many an outlaw or "injun" if called upon to do so; I have additional protection being provided by the U.S. Army; and, of equal importance, I have obtained the advice and encouragement of a good friend. If, however, the prospect of my difficult journey has you in a gloomy mood still, please remember that the most important protection I have is the merciful oversight of a kind Providence.

I shall post this letter tomorrow, and then I believe my journey westward will recommence within the next few days. Your letters will keep me company along the way! Please continue writing, and send everything to Fort Laramie, Nebraska Territory. Please do not delay in writing and posting your beloved letters! I am fearful that my mules may outpace the postal service and I may be beyond Fort Laramie when your letters arrive!

WILL,

Have you had time to watch the news lately, or have you been too busy saving the world one freeloader at a time? (Sorry – channeling Pop there.) Portland is all over the news and, for the first time, it has nothing to do with hippie angst of one form or another – unless, of course, you wish to paint a picture of the Vikings as this country's original long-haired, hedonistic vagabonds. This is really amazing stuff. As if those damn commie socialist pothead Scandinavian bastards weren't already head-and-shoulders above us in everything else, now they could probably make a legitimate claim to taking over the whole country. After all, our whole basis for claiming Oregon in the first place was prior settlement. Who knows, this could turn into the Republicans' worst nightmare – Norwegian nanny-staters trying to cash in a thousand-year-old claim.

Frozen mountain corpses are becoming a hot new item around here, like the latest flavor from Ben & Jerry's – Yummy Mummy or Brownie Bigger Mortis. But seriously, I've been thinking about this – growing up where we did, we didn't have much of a reason to contemplate the significance of mountains, but I've learned to appreciate them living out here. Mountains can be many things – sources of inspiration, recreational challenges, obstructions to progress. And now that all the snowcaps are melting like mad they are forcing into our awareness other things they have always been as well; namely, deathtraps, graveyards, and history lessons. Nearly every month now a long-lost mountain climber is discovered – in the original *OED* sense of that word – *uncovered* after years or decades of ice-bound anonymity. And occasionally, the melting mountains give up more surprising secrets – ancient Indians, woolly mammoths, old fur traders from the days of the Hudson's Bay Company.

And to think it all came about because of a little trinket. Something called a *mjolnir* – Thor's trusty hammer, worn in miniature replica by fashionable folk throughout the Viking Age. It was amazing enough that, based upon the rotting furs, moccasins and other sartorial clues, the dwindling snowcap apparently had delivered up another fine specimen of

Northwestern Native American. But then the *mjolnir* was spotted hanging out within the desiccated chest cavity of our unfortunate, belated guest of honor. So the great question became: how does an ancient Indian – on the west coast! – come into possession of what, for him, would have been a contemporary article of jewelry manufactured halfway around the world at a time when no European was even aware of this continent's existence?

And then the radiocarbon and DNA tests came back and things became REALLY interesting. But I'm sure you're up-to-date on all of this. They do have cable up there in the pine barrens, right?

I wonder if the local archeologists – trained as they undoubtedly are to look for all things Chinook – understood at first the significance of the lonely little *mjolnir*. To me, it looks like a ship's anchor, or an anvil, or maybe even a Christian cross. Of course, there weren't any native inhabitants here during that time period who would have known what an anchor or an anvil was, even if – God forbid – it hit them on top of the head. And the idea that it represents a cross is an equally absurd conclusion to draw, but, then again, since it's Christians we're talking about, we'll see how many of them try to claim that first-millenium Oregonians were actually good rosary-rubbing Catholics.

But we all have our obsessions and delusions, don't we? While the Christians may focus on the cross, academics such as myself will focus on a different metaphor and talk about what this poor thawing Norwegian means to America. Does it make sense that the Vikings would simply stop at Newfoundland? Throughout their history, they continually pushed westward, pillaging and genociding along the way, not letting anything stand in the way of their progress. Sound familiar? Maybe this poor Viking was just waiting on us – waiting to confirm what we knew had to be true all along. After all, look how long the world had to wait for L'Anse aux Meadows. But the meaning of this mummy doesn't stop there – that is only the beginning. It can be used to confirm not only what we always have known about the Vikings, but what we always knew about ourselves.

Bold, restless, ruthless, searching, seeking. We look at the icy Viking and contemplate how he came to be in Clackamas County, and as he stares back at us through the centuries we know that we are looking at ourselves.

Yes, these are fascinating times to live in Oregon and exciting times to be an American. What we thought was merely an American Century just may have turned out to be an American Millenium, all because of one frozen old man and what he will come to mean to us.

THORDIS, ARNTHOR, AND REAL BEAR sailed to Norway to live on Arnthor's father's land. Real Bear continued to live in the forest, but enjoyed sitting outside Arnthor's longhouse and speaking and laughing with his sister. These were troubled times, however, in Norway. King Harald was intent on conquering all of Norway and forcing Christianity upon all his subjects – both of which greatly angered Arnthor. He decided to follow many of his countrymen westward to Iceland to escape the oppression of King Harald and his brothers. Thordis, of course, wanted Real Bear to accompany them, but he refused. "I know nothing of Iceland, but it doesn't sound like a good place for bears. I am happy here in Norway. King Harald's misdeeds, as far as I know, do not extend to the harassment of bears. I will be fine in my woods."

Thordis begged her brother to reconsider, but Real Bear was as stubborn as his sister. "I now understand the anger Mother and Father felt toward me," Thordis said through her tears, "your refusal to obey me is breaking my heart, Real Bear." Real Bear, however, had no desire to sail to Iceland, and so he and Thordis had a tearful farewell. She never saw her brother again and the fate of Real Bear is unknown, as it is for most bears.

Thordis, Arnthor, and their three slaves sailed safely to Iceland. Upon sighting it, in the tradition of his countrymen, Arnthor tossed his high-seat pillars overboard. Upon searching the shoreline, the pillars were located within a small fjord which was mostly barren of woods. "I must admit that your brother was right," Arnthor said, "this is no place for bears, nor perhaps for people."

"We can search for a more suitable location," Thordis suggested.

"No, it is here that we will build, for the pillars have spoken. It is not ideal, but circumstances seldom are. We can be as happy here as elsewhere." Arnthor and his slaves worked quickly to build a longhouse and it was not long after this that Thordis was with child. Her pregnancy, however, was a difficult one. "This is a rambunctious child," she said to her husband, as the infant kicked within her womb, "it will either make us very proud or be the death of us." It also was going to be a large child, as Thordis's belly grew and grew. When the time arrived, it became clear why her pregnancy had been difficult. Thordis gave birth to twin boys. The first-born was called Gudmund; the second boy was called Thorbjorn, in honor of Thordis's grandfather and her brother. Arnthor spent much of each year abroad on trading journeys, leaving the upkeep of their homestead to Thordis and their slaves.

Gudmund and Thorbjorn were best friends as brothers, though of course they each had moments of selfish anger toward the other. Gudmund was the larger and enjoyed playing roughly with his brother. They engaged in wooden-sword battles that often ended with Thorbjorn wiping blood from his face. Thorbjorn, on the other hand, displayed a precociousness that may have precipitated much of Gudmund's violence. From a very young age, Thorbjorn expressed his desire to be a skald to a king and annoyed his brother with his attempts at poetry. "Your war-wand waves at brother bear, but no battle-wine is wasted," Thorbjorn would recite; or "Gudmund-gutter flashes fiercely. War-water drips from his helmet-house."

The *godi* in this part of Iceland was called Freystein. He visited Thordis often to check on her welfare and promised to provide whatever assistance she may need in Arnthor's absence. Freystein's wife had died recently and, since he was the most powerful man in the region, it was assumed he would soon remarry. The first summer of Arnthor's absence, Freystein visited Thordis occasionally, but more often than not he sent one or two of his men to check on her. In subsequent years, however, Freystein visited Thordis more and more often. Naturally, rumors began circulating about them, though nothing was said openly. Freystein offered to foster Gudmund and Thorbjorn – his resources, he said, would allow him easily to foster both boys. Thordis was happy to allow him to foster Gudmund, who was hard for her to handle, but said she would be too lonely with both her boys gone, and so she chose to raise Thorbjorn at Arnthorsfjord. The twins were unhappy about being separated, but still managed to spend much of their time together. Gudmund always accompanied Freystein on his many visits to see Thordis, and Thordis sometimes allowed Thorbjorn to visit his brother, though not often enough to please Thorbjorn.

One winter, after Arnthor had returned from abroad after a successful season of trading, he became aware of the rumors concerning his wife and Freystein the *godi*. He asked Thordis whether or not the rumors were true. Thordis replied, "Arnthor, I suppose you have a right to ask me that, but I have two questions for you in reply. First of all, would you not expect me to become lonely for companionship during all those months you are gone each year? And secondly, have I ever asked you how you pass your time when you are away striking bargains? You are welcome to answer those questions if you wish, but I have no more to say on the subject." Arnthor struck Thordis across the face. She said nothing to her husband and expressed no anger at being hit, though she did turn away and walk by herself down to the edge of the fjord, where she remained for several hours.

One year, when the boys were nine, a great storm blew up all along the Icelandic coast, which damaged or destroyed many boats. During this storm, one boat which was blown off-course wrecked within Arnthorsfjord. Thordis saw the boat and she and Thorbjorn ran to see who was aboard and to offer assistance. There were two men aboard the boat. They were unharmed, but their boat was severely damaged. The men were called Halle and Odd. "We are priests from Norway sent here to help bring Christianity to Iceland," Halle explained to Thordis.

"You are welcome to stay here with me and my son for as long as you need to repair your boat. I will be grateful to have your company. My husband is a trader and will not return for several months."

"And we will be eternally grateful to you for your hospitality. Are you a Christian? I know they are not unheard of here."

"We are worshipers of Thor, but you are welcome here nonetheless. You are lucky, however, that my husband is not here, nor my friend Freystein, the *godi*. They would not treat you as kindly, I daresay. I will also predict that you will not be welcomed as warmly as you were here, as you travel from hof to hof."

Thordis was happy to have Halle and Odd staying with her and Thorbjorn. They not only repaired their boat but made many neglected repairs to Thordis's longhouse as well. She also appreciated having them to talk to, though their Christian proselytizing was quite annoying. "Why do Christians insist that there is but one god?" Thordis asked. "It makes no sense to me that one god is solely responsible for everything that has been created. It is not the proper way of the world. It is not unlike your king insisting that he must rule over all Norwegians. You will discover that the people of Iceland believe much differently."

"You are kind to us, Thordis, but what you speak is blasphemy and I fear that you will be punished for it."

"Perhaps so, but as I know my neighbors very well, I suspect that it is you who should be prepared for severe punishment, though I certainly don't wish for it."

Thorbjorn enjoyed having the two men around as well. Halle and Odd were not playful with him, but they were friendly. Thordis was careful, however, that the two men's preaching was not taken to heart by her sons, for Halle and Odd had visited Freystein's longhouse as well and told Gudmund stories from their religion. She gave to each of her sons Thor's hammer to wear around their necks at all times.

As Thordis predicted, Halle and Odd were treated rudely as they attempted to convert the Icelanders to Christianity. Their lives were threatened more than once. They enjoyed returning often to Arnthorsfjord, for they knew they would be welcomed there. As it happened, the two priests were with Thordis when Arnthor returned home late one autumn. After Thordis had explained the reason for the presence of Halle and Odd in his house, Arnthor said, "My wife is a much better host than I. I am happy that she was hospitable to two shipwrecked men in need of help, and I must say that these walls are in much better repair than when I departed, but you are not welcome here any longer. After I depart, I have no control over my wife's actions, for she is a stubborn woman, but I will not welcome you here as a corrupting influence on my children."

Halle and Odd returned to Norway to pass the winter, but sailed once again for Iceland in the spring. Though they had not been welcomed by the Icelanders, such behavior among pagans was not unexpected and the priests were courageous and optimistic for their ultimate success. They heard that Arnthor was away again making his trading rounds, so they paid a visit to Thordis and Thorbjorn. Nothing had changed throughout the winter, except that Thorbjorn had continued to grow like a bean sprout. The priests reported to Thordis that they expected to have more success this year than last in their mission to Christianize Iceland. "I am not happy to hear that," she said, "but I am glad that you two are safe." When Arnthor returned home, he asked Thordis whether those priests had returned to visit her. "Yes, Arnthor, and I welcomed them as friends; but have no fear, the boys and I are still safely pagan, as the Christians like to call us."

"Do you enjoy acting contrary to my wishes? I believe you must, since you indulge in it so often."

"As you say, Arnthor, but you should be grateful that my ears remain closed against their teachings. Halle and Odd reported much success this year. It appears that stubbornness is often rewarded."

Arnthor paced the room and then exploded with rage at Thordis, though he did not hit her this time. "Do not let those men visit here again!" he shouted. "Can you not obey one single demand I make of you? Do I have to have a wife who refuses, apparently on principle, every request I make of her?"

He sat down, though his anger remained unabated. "We were forced to leave Norway because of Harald and his priests! My ancestral home! How far do I have to go to be rid of these infernal Christians?" Rather than returning to a calm state and expressing his happiness to be home, as was usually the case, Arnthor seethed silently for many days and sank into a sullen mood, which lasted all winter.

In the spring, after Arnthor departed, Thordis said that she had an announcement to make. Freystein was present, along with Gudmund. "Gudmund and Thorbjorn, you are old enough now to understand what I am going to say to you. I have decided to divorce your father and to marry Freystein. I understand that I am a difficult woman to live with, but your father is worse – that is, when he is even here at all. He is jealous whenever Halle and Odd spend time with me, even though my friendship with them is innocent, and he is immensely jealous of my relationship with Freystein, the details of which are none of his business. He struck me once because of Freystein, and, if I didn't have reason to divorce him before that occurred, I certainly do now."

Gudmund loved his foster-father, with whom he had spent more time than with his father, and was made very happy by Thordis's announcement. However, Thorbjorn was unhappy with leaving Arnthorsfjord and was worried about the feelings of his father. Arnthor, however, took the news of his divorce better than expected and soon remarried. He seemed happy to be married to a woman less stubborn than Thordis who would do as he wished. Thordis, Gudmund, and Thorbjorn lived with Freystein, and all appeared to be very happy.

One day, three years after Thordis had married Freystein, it happened that Gudmund approached his mother and announced that he and Thorbjorn were leaving Iceland and sailing to Greenland. Thordis said, "It is to be expected that young men will want to leave their homes for a time and visit some faraway land. It is the Viking way. You have my permission to do so. When shall I expect your return?"

"It may very well be a short visit, Mother, if Luck does not follow us there. However, you should prepare yourself for perhaps never seeing us again. We are bored with living in Iceland and wish to leave permanently."

"We look at our luck quite differently, then. I would think it was very bad luck indeed if I never saw you again."

"Yes, you would have been luckier to have given birth to sons with less wanderlust than Thorbjorn and I."

"It is my fate, apparently, that the men I most love in life would prefer never to see me again, given a choice. My brother Real Bear had that choice, and he chose it. And now my sons would make that choice as well, if it means not having to live out their lives by my side."

"As you say, Mother. It is not in my heart to argue. We are set to leave tomorrow. But it is not as bad as you say. You will always be in our hearts and, if we are lucky, there will be opportunities to visit you."

"Don't tell me how bad it is! What do you know of heartache? Your heart is filled with the joy of youth, while mine may never know joy again because of this. May you two never know this kind of sadness."

"Do you not want us to be happy? You speak of choices, but which choice would you have us make? To make you happy by remaining here, or to make ourselves happy by leaving?"

"Go on! Go to Greenland! You have too much of your father in you. If those are the only two choices you can offer me, then motherhood is a curse and I want no more of it."

Gudmund and Thorbjorn left the following morning for Greenland, aboard a ship filled with other settlers.

BABY BROTHER WILLIAM,

I am addressing you from the freedom of college. While you are still a slave to the schedules and routines of a seemingly endless adolescence, I, your esteemed and far more worldly sibling, am enjoying the fruits (and other just desserts) of a decadent, succulent, and transcendent university experience. I pity your provincial, coastal-plain existence and all its high-schoolish, mom-and-poppish regulations and circumscriptions. Your life is a veritable hell-hole. But don't despair! In three short (unbearably long) years, all that I am now experiencing can be yours – keeping in mind that your life will never be as good or interesting as mine.

In the meantime, here are some things you are currently missing out on, and perhaps will never have:

1. I stay up as long as I want. Every night.
2. I sleep as late as I want. Every morning.
3. I'm allowed to skip class if I want to (within reason).
4. I do nothing within reason.
5. Instead of stumbling sleepily into our kitchen at 3:00 a.m. and looking into an empty refrigerator or into almost-empty cabinets and being damn lucky to find some pop tarts, I stumble (perhaps drunkenly) at 3:00 a.m. into an always-open cafeteria where I have my choice of cake, ice cream, or any number of delicious goodies, which, because I have no limit on my meal card, I can eat until I throw up.
6. I have cool friends. (Sorry, this one may always elude you).
7. I'm a long way from home in a completely unsupervised environment.
8. All the girls are beautiful and want to have sex with me.
9. I have sex at least three times a day.
10. I can exaggerate with impunity.

I will continue to add to this list as circumstances warrant.

Despite the unenviable predicament you find yourself in by merely being alive, I hope you are doing well, although I really don't give a crap.

And speaking of crap, let's talk about poop, shall we? Always a popular (or poopular) subject. Or more precisely, let's talk about the place one goes to poop. Which here is a huge shower room with several shower stalls on one side and toilet stalls and urinals on the other. In other words, one side is for external cleansing and the other side is for all of your internal cleansing needs. (Yes, they do have indoor plumbing in Texas, which came as quite a surprise to me.) This one room with all its showers must accommodate a whole hall-full of sweaty college boys. It's much more pleasant, however, to contemplate all the college girls who are showering, even as I write, on the hall right below all the sweaty guys. I'm telling you, Will, the guy who invented co-ed dorms was a fucking genius! There should be a national holiday for that guy!

Although they do now have indoor toilets here in Texas, they still have yet to master the fine art of plumbing. After you conclude your aromatic business in the toilet you are required to yell, loud and clear – FLUSH!! I kid you not. The flushing takes all the cold water away for a moment. You shower at your own risk! I've been scalded a couple of times by the lazy murderous Bastards Who Don't Yell FLUSH!!

So why am I telling you all of this? I know you're saying right about now, "That lucky bastard is 2,000 miles from home, surrounded by beautiful girls, no doubt having the time of his life (all of which is true, by the way), while I'm stuck here in this hell-hole (also true), and all he wants to talk about is flushing the fucking toilets?" Patience, mein amigo. There is a method to my madness. I have brought you here into this steamy, stinky shower room to demonstrate to you that your brother is not only a brilliant musician, which you already knew, but also a brilliant fucking poet, which you probably didn't know, but will shortly.

These toilet stalls have been here approximately forever and are covered with all kinds of graffiti. I won't bore you with examples, except for one. Some guy, thinking himself no doubt brilliant, scrawled the following:

> Here I sit in my lonely stall,
> Reading these numbers I should call,
> I recognize one from down the hall,
> Oh my God, it's my roommate Paul!

Well, not bad compared to all the others, but considering how much time I am doomed by Mother Nature to spend in this little cell, with nothing else to do, then surely I can do better! And thanks to one inspired, albeit constipated, visit to the loo, I believe I have. Check this out:

There once was a girl from Denton,
Who farted each time it went in;
There was such music exiting her ass,
With woodwinds and lots of low brass,
That she sounded a lot like Stan Kenton.

You had no idea I was a poet, did you?

      Your humble and obedient servant (i.e., master),
                        Josh

P.S. If you dare show this letter to Mom or Pop, I'll kick your ass and then kill you.

THERE WAS A MAN living in Greenland named Einar Gunnarsson, who was also called Einar Pigshitsson, though he was rarely called this latter name within his hearing. Einar had been teased throughout childhood because of the manner in which his father had died. A warrior strives to die as gloriously as he lived, but if a humble farmer's death is the most memorable event to occur in his life, then it is merely sad. But such was the case for Gunnar Bjornsson. Gunnar had asked a seeress if she could foresee his fate. After spending a suitable amount of time with him and chanting her songs, she took Gunnar aside and said, "This is not the type of news I enjoy reporting, but I foresee for you, Gunnar Bjornsson, an early death."

"That is unfortunate, but acceptable, as long as it is an honorable death."

"That I cannot say. But you are a farmer and you shall die as a farmer, surrounded by many of your animals. I foresee that it is one of these animals that will be the cause of your death."

"Thrown by one of my horses, then? That is not how I would prefer to go, but accidents do happen and cannot always be avoided. I will continue to ride without fear."

"Horses are not part of my vision, but I see you surrounded by piglets."

"Did I hear you correctly, old crone? What did you just say?"

"Piglets."

Gunnar spewed forth his wrath upon the seeress. "After I have invited you into my home, shown you the finest hospitality, honored you with many costly presents I could scarcely afford, and provided you with a feast that will now cause my family to go hungry, this is the gratitude I receive from you? To be the butt of a joke? Do you enjoy playing your patrons for fools? Get out of my sight and take all your useless songs with you!"

After the seeress left and Gunnar's wrath subsided, he was able to think more clearly about her prediction. He did not believe it, yet he also knew that it would be unwise to disregard it completely. He had known men who had choked on thick bites of meat, so he became very careful to chew all his pork thoroughly before attempting to swallow it. His wife wondered at this and said to him, "You are like a cow chewing upon its cud. What are you thinking about?" He told her the seeress's prediction, and she said that Gunnar was wise to chew his pork thoroughly.

Five years passed, during which time Einar was born. Einar's father, however, did not forget the seeress's dire prediction, though he did not tell his children of it. He raised many generations of piglets. When a new litter was born he would laugh and say to himself, "So, which of you little snorting shitheads will have to courage to attack me? While I sleep, which one of you will pulverize me with your evil little hooves? Or will one of you wrap your curly tail around my throat and snap my neck in two?" He roared with laughter. But perhaps he should have asked which piglet would defecate on the large stone in its pen and create such a slippery surface to walk upon. Gunnar was discovered one morning with his forehead resting on that same stone, his blood mingling with the murderous pigshit.

As he entered adulthood, Einar became determined to be remembered as someone other than Einar Pigshitsson. Leif the Lucky had become renowned for his discovery of Vinland to the west. Einar, wishing to escape the land of his father's ignominy, thought to himself, "If Leif the Lucky can sail west to find fame, then there must be something there for me to find as well." He was a capable sailor and had no trouble recruiting men to accompany him to Vinland. The twins Gudmund and Thorbjorn were among those who believed that a voyage to Vinland would be a great adventure.

After three days at sea, Helluland was spotted. Continuing to follow the route of Leif and Karlsefni during their voyages, Einar ordered his ship to sail southward toward Markland and Vinland. Einar was hailed by the men aboard his ship with loud cheers, happy as they were to be within sight of land and headed to the warmth and bounty of Vinland. However, as the ship approached the southern point of Helluland, he ordered the ship to be sailed westward, into an icy sea. "This is not the way to Vinland!" Gudmund shouted. Many other crewmen echoed Gudmund's statement.

"Are you as good at pulling oars as you are at stating the obvious?" Einar yelled at his men. "If so, then we have nothing to fear."

Gudmund said to Einar, "We are not opposed to this new sea-path you have ordered us on, Einar Gunnarsson, but we are angry for being lied to. Did you think we were too cowardly to undertake this adventure otherwise?"

"That remains to be seen," Einar said, gruffly. "I have lied to no one. I promised you an adventure to Vinland and that is where we shall drop anchor."

"You are taking us around the stern to reach the bow, Einar, at much greater risk. What is your plan?"

"My plan is to make people forget Leif the Lucky."

"I believe your plan is to make people forget Einar Pigshitsson."

"How dare you utter that name aboard my ship! If you continue to insult me I'll make you into my skraeling bitch!" Gudmund dropped his oars and stood, ready to challenge Einar, but Thorbjorn stepped between the two men and calmed his brother.

"Perhaps I spoke too harshly, Einar, but we are still waiting to hear what plans you have for us."

"Are we not in agreement that these new lands are islands,

just as Iceland and Greenland are islands; just as Faroe, Ireland, and Britain are islands, as is every new land discovered in this vast ocean? Why should we be satisfied with exploring only one side of this great new land, as Leif and Karlsefni were? The east coast of Greenland is vastly different from its western shore. So what great discoveries await those who have the courage to search for them? Leif and Karlsefni were cowards compared to me! They returned to Greenland when events went against them and ran away like women in fear of a handful of puny skraelings!"

After hearing this speech, Thorbjorn said a poem to his brother:

> Madman mounts his sea steed,
> Tricking twin battle trees.
> Sails seas with unknown names
> Fighting father's pork-shame.

Einar's ship had been in open water, but soon was nearly surrounded by sea ice. All of Einar's skill as a sailor was required to maneuver through the narrow channels provided by the ice. To make matters worse, a thick fog soon enveloped the ship. This fog was thicker than anything ever seen before by these experienced seamen. "This is not a good omen, Einar," Gudmund said. The fog was so thick that an oarsman could not see the man sitting on the bench in front of him. It was as if each man were alone on the ship. "I agree with Gudmund," another man said, though he could not be identified through the fog, "it is not propitious to be surrounded by icebergs in a fog thick enough to chew as if it were meat."

"It was my belief that I had selected a group of brave men to accompany me, rather than a shipload of superstitious cowards!" Einar shouted. "Haul down the sail!" he ordered. "Use your oars to fend off the ice!"

With neither sail nor oars, the ship drifted with the current. When the fog lifted, Gudmund said, "I am grateful that our good luck protected us from the ice, but can anyone tell how far we have drifted? The fog made it seem as if my eyes were closed. I feel as if I have awakened from a bad dream, Einar. I hold you responsible for this."

"Will you also hold me responsible for all the glory you will soon know?" Einar responded. "Thorbjorn, your brother complains more than a woman. I hope you are preparing your verses to praise my name when we discover warm water and a bountiful new land!"

After three days of sailing and drifting through icy water and fog, with land always visible to port whenever anything at all was visible through the fog, an opening to the south was seen and cheered by everyone aboard. "There, Einar, is the way to Vinland," Gudmund announced. "You will not need to order us twice to sail southward."

"You are cheering me now, men, and you will have even more reasons to cheer before this journey is over," Einar said.

They continued sailing south for many days, but Einar grew unhappy. "The sea is too calm for the open ocean. We will not reach Vinland along this coast, I predict. Is it possible that we have discovered a cove the size of a sea? What other strange wonders do we have to look forward to?" Einar ordered the ship to turn to starboard, away from shore.

"If I didn't believe you to be mad before, you have now given me a reason to have no doubt on that score," Gudmund said.

"Gudmund," Einar said, "you have your good luck to thank that you are such an excellent oarsman; otherwise, you would make Markland your home and have to swim to get there."

The men were exhausted and their provisions were running low, yet Einar refused to allow his crew to row toward shore. Gudmund said to his brother, "He fears mutiny, and for good reason. I foresee that this voyage will not end the way Einar Pigshitsson envisions." Thorbjorn responded with another poem:

> Brave sword-stalks, bound in blood,
> With battle-branches stood.
> Pricked, the pig's son bellows.
> He snorts and shame-wallows.

They sailed for five days and nights and the ship made good progress. Neither Einar nor the men were content to let the sail do all the work, and so the men pushed themselves and were pushed harder by Einar to row until all their strength was depleted. The crew was desperate to find a shore on which to land, in order to forage for food and water. Einar knew also that the success of his mission depended on a healthy crew, though he feared what would happen once they came ashore.

When land was at last sighted, the men's relief was mixed with anger and disappointment, for the land they had discovered was not to their liking. It was land, rather than sea, but that was all anyone could think of to say in its favor – barren as it seemed to be of trees and life. "Einar Gunnarson," Gudmund said, "is this the discovery for which you expect to be hailed? If so, then I suspect that your expectations are set too high."

"Gudmund, I am too tired and thirsty at present to deal properly with your insolence. Let us look for fresh water and meat to put into our bellies. Perhaps this land that you are so quick to condemn, and are so ungrateful to have found, will nonetheless prove adequate to save your life." Though the land was boggy and desolate, rivers did abound which contained fresh water and many kinds of fish. Soon, a great white bear was spotted, which proved to be no match against the men's well-thrown spears. "Men," Einar said, "we shall remain here only long enough to rest our bodies, to repair our ship to the extent we can, and to restore our provisions. And Gudmund, to respond to your insolence from earlier, it is obvious this is not the land destined to make me famous, but merely a stopping point along the way. I shall name this land Bogland, as a warning to others who may wish to settle here."

Gudmund whispered to his allies seated around him, "Do any of you expect to set foot on any rock or soil that offers an improvement over this wasteland? Einar Pigshitsson must not be allowed to sail us into an icy oblivion. Are we in agreement on this?" Everyone nodded their assent and agreed as well that Gudmund Arnthorsson possessed the greatest leadership qualities of all the men aboard the ship and that his suggestions should be obeyed. "As soon as we find a clear way east," he continued, "I believe a change in command will be required if we are to find our way home. I will see to it that that is accomplished."

The ship sailed north along the coast of Bogland and the crew asked Einar if they could turn their prow to the east, if for no other reason than to lose sight of Bogland, whose barrenness caused them to feel nothing but sadness. "We shall maintain our present course," Einar answered. "When we lose sight of Bogland it will be because Bogland is no longer there and our passage will be open to the west and to glory! Then I promise you all of your sadness will be forgotten!"

Upon hearing this, one of the crew said to Gudmund, "Is this not as good a time as any other to change command of this ship, as you have promised to do?"

"Any time would be a good time to feed Einar Pigshitsson to the bears, but this is not the best time to do so. Winter is approaching. I predict that the ice we were lucky to escape from many days ago is making its way steadily south and will soon intercept us once again. I am afraid that Einar's ill-advised ambitions have condemned all of us to a long season of cold and privation. There will be bloodshed when I take over the ship, for there are always men who will support even the worst of leaders in a crisis. So it is best to bide our time, for we must all cooperate if we wish to survive the winter in Einar's glorious Pigland."

Soon enough, Gudmund's prediction proved true as the ship sailed into icy waters and was quickly surrounded by ice. "Einar, I believe you and I should be in agreement that it is foolish and dangerous to continue sailing in these conditions," Gudmund said. "I believe that this is the best weather we can expect. If we are lucky to survive the icebergs today, it will only become worse tomorrow and even worse after that."

"Gudmund, your impertinent suggestions are as offensive to me as your farts, and once again you believe yourself to be wise when you are merely stating the obvious. I have already begun plans to go ashore and make winter quarters. Come spring, we will continue our quest for glory!"

The bog on which they landed was now frozen over. Einar and several crew members went on a search for seals and bears, and in a blinding snowstorm they stumbled upon a winter dwelling occupied by skraelings. Einar, followed by his crew, crawled through the entrance of the underground home. The skraelings were sleeping and unprepared for battle, so, taking them by surprise, the Greenlanders roared and bloodied their swords on the unfortunate occupants, all of whom were easily killed. "Men!" Einar exclaimed, "Courage and luck will always be our greatest allies. We have traded the lives of a few worthless skraelings for a winter's worth of warmth!" They returned to their ship and turned it upside down upon a platform of rocks they had built. In this way it would provide additional shelter and storage.

Einar's men spent several months in their winter quarters. As spring approached and the ice surrounding them began to melt and move away, Gudmund gathered the men he knew to be loyal to him and said, "The time has come to feed Ham Hock to the bears. I have a plan that will avoid all bloodshed, except, of course, that of Einar's worthless pig-blood. I will lure him away from our camp, alone, so that when I skewer his little pork-belly there will be no witnesses. I will then return to camp and announce a horrible accident – that Pigshit fell through the melting ice and that I could not save him. In this way, there will be no accusations of mutiny, and I daresay that no one will have the courage to challenge the truthfulness of my tale. If anyone takes notice of the blood dripping from my spear, I will say that it is from a seal that I wounded, but which escaped under the ice. Or, if I am lucky, I will indeed bring a seal back to camp as a souvenir. I will consider that to be a very good bargain struck – to trade a pig for a seal." Gudmund's men laughed heartily and all agreed that his plan was a good one.

Gudmund approached Einar and said, "I foresee the approach of spring and that we have but a few weeks to remain here before resuming our journey."

"Your prediction is remarkable, Gudmund. Tell me, what do you attribute it to? Could it be the ice that is melting all around us? Or the ice that is receding daily from the sea? Perhaps you attribute it to the bright rays of the sun, which are so much warmer now than last week. In any event, your powers of perception are unmatched."

"Einar, because of this good mood I am in, rather than challenge you to a duel because of your insults I daily endure, I am prepared to challenge you merely to a friendly wager. And I'm sure you are not too cowardly to accept it."

"Name your game, Gudmund. Whatever it is, I have no doubt that I will make you regret it."

"I propose one final seal hunt. I have been lucky this winter in killing a number of seals, so I doubt that I'll need much time to prove myself victorious. However, if you are more fortunate today than I, and are successful in killing a seal before I do, then I will proclaim to all the crew your superiority in seal-hunting."

"Will you also proclaim to the crew that the sky is blue? Will you mount the mast and proudly announce that fire will burn your fingers and that ice is cold to the touch? Everyone knows I am the superior seal hunter. I have proven it throughout the winter. If Luck is your companion today and I come back to camp without a seal, and I proclaim your superiority, then the crew will laugh and know that I am joking. I cannot take your wager seriously, and in proposing it you are setting yourself up to look like a fool."

"That is a risk I am prepared to take. I am also prepared to say that there will be more than one crewman who will think you a coward for refusing to take up an honest challenge."

"Point those men out to me and they will feel the cold end of my sword."

"Calm down, Einar. Pig's blood comes to a rapid boil, doesn't it?"

At this, Einar drew his sword. "That is the last insult I'm going to take from you! Are you prepared to meet a real challenge? It is no longer merely seal's blood that you will see spilled! I challenge you to a duel, Gudmund Arnthorsson!"

"And I will gladly accept that challenge, Einar Gunnarsson – but perhaps you should consider three things. Firstly, how will your name go down in history if you are a rotting carcass in a desolate, forgotten bog, victim to a superior swordsman? If I am victorious, Einar, your shame will be greater than even that of your shit-stained father. Secondly, if you are victorious, you will sorely miss the strongest oarsman aboard your ship, who, I should point out, has the allegiance of most of your crew. They will not take kindly to my death by your hands. And thirdly, after such a peaceful winter camp, will the gods deem it propitious for our journey to resume after our blood has been shed?"

"You are a fool. You give me reasons why I should rescind my challenge that do nothing but antagonize me further. First, you insult my father, and then you threaten me with mutiny. If I did not want to kill you before, I most certainly do now. And your superstitions only make you more of a fool. I have nothing to fear from Thor."

"Be that as it may, I suggest you discuss the matter with those few men who still counterfeit a trust in you. You seem willing to risk everything you wish to accomplish merely because of a foolish jest on my part."

"Enough talk. Will you have a joke ready at my expense as my sword slides across your entrails? Oh, how my blade aches to become acquainted with your bones!" Einar set the time for their duel and allowed Gudmund to select the location. Gudmund parted from Einar, disappointed that his plan had not succeeded. He went immediately to see Thorbjorn.

"What news do you bring, brother?" Thorbjorn asked.

"It is not as good as I had hoped."

"Did you not set the pig-snare as you had planned?"

"No, I did not. My foolish tongue has shown itself again to be more my enemy than my friend. Einar has challenged me to a duel."

"I'm sure that is worse news for him than it is for you."

"Indeed. I don't fear his sword. But you can never predict which side Luck will choose. I would feel better about our chances of seeing home again if this duel did not take place, but there is nothing to be done. Porkskin was greatly offended by my jest. I don't believe he will be amenable to *holmgang*.

He wants me dead, I have no doubt. He will insist upon *einvigi*."

"In which case, brother, you will slice him unmercifully and the bears will feed upon pork cutlets. My advice to you is to anticipate this day as a glutton looks forward to a feast."

"I have heard this from you since we were children, with sticks for swords. You encourage me to fight until your skin suffers a scratch. Then you start spouting poetry and try to talk your way into a truce."

"Don't belittle these talents of mine. In fact, after you hear my plan, you may wish to praise them. Listen to what I shall do, since you question the wisdom of fighting. I will go to Einar. I will flatter his vanity. I will sing praises to his courage. I will remind him that every great man deserves a skald to memorialize his achievements. As such, I will offer my services to him. He knows I am the only one aboard his ship capable of composing verses commensurate with his greatness, as he imagines it. But I will also remind him that he cannot expect encomiums from me if he takes the life of my brother. This, I am sure, will induce him to accept the strictures of *holmgang*. You can thank me later, brother, after my plan plays out perfectly." Thorbjorn then recited a poem:

> Venom-gate loudly gapes.
> Out pours warm word-poison.
> Poet's praise-sieve must save
> Salty slander-salmon.

2

W,

When it rains, certainly it pours, but what am I to do about this deluge? I am singularly unprepared to withstand this onslaught. Luck has been my faithful friend but now I have been betrayed. I need your help, Will. I never asked for your guidance before, but I need it now. Mom thinks it's sad that I send you emails. But what is sad is that I didn't speak to you like this before. You haven't replied to anything yet, but take your time. With all these signals floating through the ether maybe something will get through. Maybe our old analog souls are now being digitized. Maybe the afterlife is the universal operating system. . . . iHeaven. . . . It's nice to think about, at least. You never understood why I refused to join the atheistic orthodoxy and that is one reason, among many others, I believe I have failed you.

Just in case you're interested, here's a rundown of the current situation. The cops are officially flummoxed. No gun was found at the crime scene and there was evidence of robbery, so the circumstantial facts point to foul play; but the science points to suicide. The powder residue is consistent with a point-blank (i.e., self-inflicted) gunshot, and the configuration of the entry wound is also highly suggestive of self-infliction. (I'm sorry I sound so clinical, Will – it's the only way I can talk about this. To think of that head – that fell asleep next to mine a thousand times, that I can still smell the sweat of after a long day's play, and that hair – so smooth even as you grew older, and forever dripping water from our summer swims –

clotted with blood and brains, those lively eyes staring dead to the world. My God, it's unbearable.) In other words, the bullet went in at an upward angle. So despite the evidence of suicide, or until the cops are willing to charge either a small child or a midget with murder, your case, brother, remains a mystery.

For Mom, the fact that you were apparently robbed is the most relevant one, but that's not the real reason she rules out suicide. "How can anyone think William killed himself?" she asks. Notice the form of that question. She's not asking for a show of evidence. She's accusing someone of doubting your strength, of disputing your energy and idealism, of believing you succumbed to the distress we all felt after Pop was arrested. And of course I can't tell her everything I know because you didn't tell her when you were alive, so I'm certainly not going to tell her now that you're dead. Maybe you were murdered. I'm okay with Mom believing that, and I'll gladly toe the party line. But I wish I could have Mom's unwavering confidence that you would never "do something like that," because she didn't hear your anguish like I did and she wouldn't have understood it like I did. And then there's the big fat bigoted elephant in the room that Mom is never going to mention. We were cursed with a distinctive last name – plus you're also a doctor, so I'm sure *Dr. Kinninger* rang a lot of angry bells among your clientele. And I can't tell Mom the reason why there appeared to be a robbery, but wasn't, and I'm not telling the cops, either. The guy who actually did rob you had your wallet so it's easy to imagine that upon seeing your name (or upon some female in his life seeing your name and making the connection), he decided to carry out his idea of vigilante justice. I mean, if Mom is right about the murder, can it really be just a coincidence that you were targeted for violence twice within three days after living and working in that area for how many years without suffering so much as a stolen hubcap? But then again, like I said, when it rains it fucking pours. But I'm not going to the police with this information or these conjectures because you didn't want to report the robbery. God Will, I'm so angry at you for that decision. I bit my tongue at the time, but maybe I shouldn't have. Sure, it's unlikely they would have put many man-hours into investigating what amounted to a mugging, but this will gnaw at my soul forever. And why didn't you report it, you idiot? Because you felt so guilty about your little verbal rampage that you now felt as if you retroactively deserved to be robbed and beaten up? Yes, well, I guess if that had happened to somebody else I would have called it poetic justice, since I've been railing for decades about how white people won't take responsibility for their actions.

But in spite of all this talk of murder and motives for murder, I can't help but believe you took this upon yourself, Will. The fact that there was no gun where it should have been doesn't concern me – handguns are a necessary commodity on the streets so I have no trouble believing someone reached into your car and took it, probably shortly after hearing the gun blast, though it would have been ill-advised in the extreme to risk being apprehended holding a gun that's literally smoking. Maybe you were slumped over in that empty parking lot for hours before anyone approached close enough to see you. It's also possible that the gun recoiled out of your window and was on the ground – easy pickings in that case. Your window being rolled down, however, is not conducive to suicide, apparently – it seems that most people who do this sort of thing in their automobiles prefer to do so with some semblance of privacy. And of course the whole robbery thing is a red herring, though only you and I know that. So I don't know, Will – help me out here. Since you're left-handed, maybe you needed that extra arm-room an open window would provide, or maybe you wanted to be discovered as quickly as possible, or maybe you were hoping someone would see you and try to stop you, or maybe you just didn't give a shit about the fucking car window. Or maybe, after all, some ten-year-old gang-banger initiate came up to your car as you were getting ready to go home after another long day of making a difference in this world, and he knocked on your window and because you only wanted to help you rolled down your window which turned out to be the last thing you ever did. God Will, it makes no sense – nothing makes sense anymore and I'm drowning in grief and I feel I may be losing my grip on whatever sanity I have left. I don't know why you would do this, but I'm trying to convince myself it was a suicide because then it would be something you chose of your own free will to do. It's your murder I can't accept, the idea of someone making that decision for you. Mom on the other hand needs someone to blame, and since she can't bring herself to blame you, or Pop, it's imperative there be someone out there running the streets who needs to be brought to justice.

To end on a positive note, I have at least discovered the solace of poetry. It helps to lighten my grief to write these little stanzas to you, about us. They're not much, but I like them. Here's one about something we used to do every day during all those interminable summers:

> I push you off then take a step back,
> My arms over my head just to catch you.
> I wonder if I can make you go all the way
> Over? Laughing high and hard, it's fun
> To have someone to play with. My turn.

AFTER GIVING GUDMUND the details of his plan, the following day Thorbjorn went to see Einar. He was at the shore directing his men in the repair of his ship. Thorbjorn approached him and began to speak:

> Courageous coast-comber!
> Great glory awaits you!
> I shall fan your fame-flames.
> Odin's ardor alights!

"What's this?" Einar asked. "Has Gudmund sent his little brother on an errand? Is he such a coward that he must send an emissary to beg mercy for him?"

"Einar Gunnarsson, I beg of you, hear my poem. It is only to increase your glory that I say:

> Finder of far-off lands,

Searcher for secret strands,
Same-mother man knows not
My passion for praising you.

On the icy island,
Erik's error, greenless,
Was born Gunnar's sole son,
Who dreamed to discover.

Master of sail-saddles,
Tamer of wind horses,
At what young age did you
Foresee your future fame?

At five did you decide
To ride upon tide-trails?
Were you at six transfixed
By wave-steeds sailing west?

At seven did you sleep-see
Visions of unseen Vinland?
Were you eager at eight
To leave Greenland for good?

Salt air your sustenance.
Sip sea foam from your ale.
Sea-spears from gunwales thrust,
To slay distance-dragons.

You surpass Erik's son.
You conquer Karlsefni.
Your deeds I gaze upon
As into a looking-glass.

Listening for your call
My ears heard *Thorbjorn.*
Seeking a kindred heart,
Your lips said *Thorbjorn.*

I too was precocious,
Envy's target from birth.
Taunted for my talents,
Bloodied for having brains.

I too dreamed of escape
On the backs of sea-mares,
To make sea-hills my home,
To farm ocean-valleys.

I too have sought greatness,
Left home behind to be
A hero, to leave my name
On lips of tomorrow.

But in my bones rest not
Skill to wave-horse wander,
Nor strength of war branches
To win eternity.

But I have Aesir's ale
Malting within my mouth,
Torrents of tongue-glory
Gushing through my word-gate.

But as you call upon
Courage only for fame,
I require greatness to
Reflect upon greatness.

Lord of lands undisclosed,
King of islands unknown,
I am your mirror to
Reflect your fame forever.

To be worthy of praise
By men was what you dreamed.

I dreamed of praiseworthy men.
We are as ship and sail.

These icelands where I dwelt,
Kingless to shower praise,
What are poets to do
When heroes are no more?

My mouth empty of praise,
My tongue poetry-parched.
But you called *Thorbjorn*.
Now a word-river runs.

My trouble-twin slanders
Out of envy, not scorn.
He goes to war with words,
But fights with a false sword.

We look like mirror-men,
But we are night and day.
I speak with great meaning,
He means not what he speaks.

He I did not follow.
You are why I am here.
If not for your glory,
I would be farming rocks.

But he is my brother.
Our blood is one river.
Sinking in slander-stream
He pulls me under too.

You must save both twin-men.
Your mercy saves Gudmund,
Your glory Thorbjorn.
Thus I begin your praise.

Einar listened to Thorbjorn's poem and replied, "I am indeed lucky to have you with me on this journey, Thorbjorn Arnthorsson. Your verses bring joy to my heart. If you will promise to remain by my side and immortalize my name in verse, then I will promise to show whatever mercy I can muster to your worthless brother, though I cannot promise that the path of my blade will be to his liking."

Thorbjorn replied with this verse:

Hero's fame runs beside
Poet's boundless praise-path.
Glory is guaranteed
For eternal Einar.

At the time appointed for the duel, Gudmund and Thorbjorn, and Einar and his second, rowed out to a small island. The winter's ice was receding, but still covered much of the ground. A square was staked out with damaged ship timbers and a cloak placed on the icy ground for the participants. The duel began. Gudmund lunged to deliver the first blow. He thrust his sword forward, but Einar deftly parried the blow with his shield. Einar then quickly struck at Gudmund, but to no effect. The two sides exchanged another round of ineffective blows. On Gudmund's third thrust, Einar's shield shattered and Gudmund's sword bit into Einar's arm, and his blood began dripping onto the cloak under his feet, thus ending the duel. "Let this be a lesson to you, Einar," Gudmund proclaimed, "there is no dishonor where none is intended. Your skin is too thin, as you can see from the torrent of blood pouring from that little scratch I inflicted."

"You should appreciate the reprieve you have been given," Einar said. "If not for my love for your brother, and my promise to him, you would have a wound less superficial than mine." Einar studied Gudmund's face as he said this, and then said, "I believe I have been made a fool by both of you. I expected you to deny knowledge of your brother's involvement, Gudmund, but your face has told me the truth. Thorbjorn, you have betrayed me. My arm aches much less than my heart at this news."

"Einar Gunnarsson, you dishonor my brother," Gudmund said. "He and I disagree on many things, including the wisdom of your command. I am not surprised that he went to you behind my back. I have never listened to his advice and he doesn't take orders from me. Whatever arrangements were made by you for my benefit are between you and my brother, and I want no part of it. Your mercy means nothing to me. I neither requested nor required it."

The two combatants returned to their winter camp, both displaying inscrutable faces, but each hiding much different emotions. Gudmund strode proudly to the ship and joined the other crew members as they prepared the ship to resume its journey. Einar, however, crawled into the warmth of the captured skraeling dwelling, where he nursed his wound and remained for several days. Meanwhile, Gudmund continued to boast of his victory. One of his friends said to him, "Gudmund, it is well and good that you pricked Einar's skin, and deflated his pride in the process, but frankly, you would have more to boast of if your blade had bitten somewhat harder. We are waiting patiently for you to make good on your promise to remove him from command. We are all homesick and wish to sail east."

"You may have reason to regret such impertinence toward me, after I have run Einar through and made a pork skewer of him. I have not forgotten my promise to you, and am looking forward to its fulfillment to a much greater degree than you will ever know. The next time I find myself alone with Chitterlings, he will die."

Einar eventually left the skraeling-house early one morning and went searching for Gudmund. Upon finding him, Einar said, "Gudmund, I fear that I have lost the respect of many of my crew as a result of our duel. It was an honorable outcome in your favor, but I cannot bear to lose. You must allow me a chance to regain a modicum of respect before we push my ship back into the waves."

"Einar, it's difficult to regain something you never possessed, and I am in no mood to relinquish the upper hand I now have in our dealings, so I doubt if you have any offer to make that I will be inclined to accept."

"Be that as it may, I seem to remember several days ago a proposal from you involving a seal hunt. Can you now refuse to accept your own proposal?"

"I most certainly can refuse to accept it, without a loss of honor, if you have changed the terms of the offer."

"The terms remain the same. If I win, you must proclaim me to be the superior seal hunter."

"And how do you expect to salvage your dignity on the basis of such a meaningless victory, notwithstanding the fact that your victory is rather unlikely? I suspect that you have something else planned for me out there on the ice."

"So you refuse? In that case, I will prepare to erect a shame-pole, which will make clear to all who is courageous and who is a coward."

"I will never back down from any challenge issued by you, Einar Pigshitsson. We both have our spears at hand. I have no more to say to you, since that would be time wasted on talk when there are miles of ice awaiting me and seals in need of air." The two men disappeared into the distance, the distance between them increasing with each step taken.

After several hours, as darkness descended, Einar came back to camp and announced, "Gudmund Arnthorsson is dead. I heard a loud crack and saw him disappear under the ice. I ran over to rescue him, but the current had carried him away."

Thorbjorn, holding back tears, said, "Einar Gunnarsson, you are a murderer. There is blood on your spear – the blood of my brother."

"Thorbjorn, I will forgive your false accusation as you are no doubt grieving your lost kinsman. But let it be known, this is the blood of a seal, which I wounded but was unable to secure before it slipped under the ice. Is there anyone else here who doubts this? If so, you will not live long enough to regret saying so. Einar Gunnarsson is no liar and is no murderer. The ice is thin and rapidly melting. Seal-hunting is a dangerous endeavor at this time of year. Soon, the way will be clear for us to resume our journey westward, where we will find great glory." Einar walked away and Thorbjorn recited the following poem:

> Farewell, my father's son.
> My life is lopped in half.
> No contentment complete,
> All my doubts are doubled.

As soon as enough ice had melted away, Einar ordered his ship to be reintroduced to the sea. As they rowed to the north, Gudmund's friends said to Thorbjorn, "What are we to do now? I don't see any leaders among us, unless you can fill your brother's shoes."

"Gudmund had a warrior's spirit. I can only fill the air with useless words. If one of you wishes to take on the challenge of overthrowing Einar, I will support you with my feeble arms, but I am like a ship adrift without sail. I care not in which direction we turn our prow. To go home without my brother is not to go home at all."

They continued sailing northward for many days until an opening was sighted to the west. Einar exclaimed, "Thorbjorn, let us have a poem to commemorate this auspicious occasion!"

Thorbjorn recited:

> A poem to proceed
> Further from Gudmund's grave?
> Will you also ask me
> To make a swine's tail straight?

"Be careful the words you choose, Thorbjorn!" Einar shouted. "My patience with your grief is running short, and I will not brook your anger toward me. Do you still believe I murdered your brother?"

"I believe you wanted him dead."

"It is true that my grief for Gudmund was short-lived, but if you had seen me running toward the ice-hole where he had fallen, and the efforts I made to save him, then you would see that your words are as shameful as they are false."

"As you say, Einar. I will sing your praises when my heart tells me to do so, but no sooner."

Einar steered his ship on a torturous course westward, continually dodging ice, now forced to drift sail-less through fog, now forced to steer north or south for long periods of time. Many months passed and it was feared that another long winter would have to be spent on frozen, barren ground. The crew was despondent, yet Einar refused to believe that his fate would be any different from how he imagined it. They survived on seal-meat and the only pleasure they found was in making bets on the killing of skraelings. These creatures, who displayed wonder at the sight of the Greenlanders' ship, would bring their small skin-boats as close to the ship as they dared come. The crew tied ropes to the end of their spears and had contests to determine who could kill a skraeling first or from the greatest distance.

It then happened that what appeared to be open sea was sighted ahead as they sailed to the west, and as they proceeded into this sea Einar noticed the land falling away to the south as far as his eyes could see. He then discerned more land ahead to the west, but at a great distance from them. "This appears to be the mouth of a stupendous river. Yet we are still sailing with the current, though it swirls mightily. Everything in this country is strange and beggars belief. I don't know what this means, but we shall surely find warmer air to the south." They sailed south for three days with no indication that this enormous river was becoming any smaller. The disappearance of all sea-ice, combined with the eagerness of the crew to make landfall and Einar's growing excitement led to his decision to sail up a fjord and to finally drop anchor, after many months among the ice and seals and skraelings – months that seemed like years.

"Have we arrived in Norway?" Einar exclaimed incredulously. "I am sure we have sailed half-way around the world, but have we not sailed more? I pronounce to you all, this is the most wondrous land I have ever beheld! It cannot be Norway, but do any of you have eyes that have seen anything as similar or more breathtaking? Thorbjorn, does not this beautiful land shake loose your grief-stricken tongue? Can your mistrust of me compete with these mountains and this fjord? Come, Thorbjorn, I have tolerated a mute skald long enough!"

Thorbjorn spoke:

> West wasteland wanderer,
> Bane of seals and skraelings,
> Lucky to have found land
> Before our bones were bare.
>
> Up fjord's familiar lane
> Hurry homesick sailors,
> Who call Nowhere Norway
> And mistake hope for home.
>
> Shall I sing to skraelings?
> Proclaim your fame to fish?
> Tell your story to trees?
> These rocks will worship you.
>
> Brave at every oar-bench
> We longed to see Leif's land.
> You scuttled our sea-dreams
> On skerries formed of lies.

"Enough!" Einar interrupted. "What good are you to me, Thorbjorn? At least Gudmund was a strong oarsman. And his insults were made in jest, while you are nothing but earnest. I'm beginning to believe that the wrong brother fell beneath the ice." He paced from one end of his ship to the other. "So, am I to be my own skald as well? Then so be it!" Einar began climbing the mast. "Behold this marvelous land!" he shouted. "It is I, Einar, who brought you here! To a paradise unknown until I have disclosed it to the world! Who would know of this place if not for me? It will now be home to thousands of our countrymen – men who will owe their future wealth to my courage and vision!" Everyone cheered heartily, except for Thorbjorn, which did not go unnoticed by Einar. Now that he had delivered them unto this land that teemed with fish and game to fill their bellies and fresh water to quench their thirst, they forgot their former mutinous feelings toward Einar. "What shall we name this land, men? There is no need to lie to convince men of its bounty, as this land far surpasses anything claimed by that fraud Erik Thorvaldsson! Therefore, under the eyes of Aesir, I proclaim this land to be New Norway, and its discoverer to be Einar Gunnarsson!"

WILLIAM THE CONQUERED,

I'm curious about something. Has there been much conversation around the house about my roommate? I called Pop last week and told him about my new roomie. He took the news pretty well, which surprised the shit out of me, but I wondered if the fireworks started flying shortly thereafter. If so, I'm sorry I wasn't there to witness the spectacle. (Yes, I'm being sarcastic. Why the fuck would I want to be back home?) So I'm assuming you know all about it, unless Pop decided he would rather take this information to his grave. In which case, here's a clue – his name is Jerome. That should give you all the information you need.

Jerome is actually the second new roommate for me since the semester started. My roomie last semester – whom I never saw much of anyway – dropped out of school for undisclosed reasons, and the new guy who moved in just last week is now gone as well – expelled for selling the demon weed. The first day I met him last week he initiated me into his evil ways by immediately stuffing towels under the door and lighting one up. He invited me to join him. At this point, little brother, my narrative must break off so as not to give you any ideas which may sully your innocence or which may implicate me in any expellable offenses. But, suffice to say, only a couple of days later he and his luggage were gone. Classes had not even begun yet! It seems that he has performed the remarkable, if not unprecedented, feat of ending his collegiate career before officially beginning it. (And no, it was not I who alerted the authorites, though I'm sure you would have – which explains why you don't have any friends.)

So, I was now left roomie-less for the second time. My RA suggested I move in with Jerome who – for reasons which will soon be made obvious – also has had trouble retaining roommates. Now, if you haven't already guessed it, Jerome is of African slave ancestry (surprise!). And at first, I was absolutely thrilled by the idea of having a "Niggro" roomie, as Pop would say (when he's trying to be polite. We know what he would usually say). But, man, this dude is going to be hard for me to live with. I feel like I've gone from living with Pop to living with the exact opposite. If I sometimes talk about Pop like he's the Antichrist, then Jerome's the Anti-Pop. I never thought that blacks could be as racist as whites, but I'm reconsidering that. To give an example: He has already called me on various occasions either Whitey (can you imagine what would happen if I called him Blackie?), or Honky (or Honkey, or Honkie – I don't even know how to spell that stupid word. And I really have no fucking idea what it means. I guess it's supposed to be their equivalent of me calling him a you-know-what, but I fail to see what I'm supposed to be offended by. Does it mean that white people honk their car horns too much? Do we blow our noses excessively?), or my personal favorite – Cracker (I don't know what the black equivalent would be. Burnt Toast? Pumpernickel?)

I am still so excited and relieved to be away from home – or more specifically, away from Pop (I actually kind of miss you, you big lug). And just to think that I could make a lot of black friends through Jerome, maybe even have a black girlfriend if I wanted to (a very intriguing possibility!), made me feel so free and happy. It felt like being released from bondage – a special kind of bondage that only white folks like you and me, living in the South, can understand. And I told that to Jerome the first day I met him, when I moved in. I wanted him to like me and to feel comfortable with me as a roommate, and to understand that I wasn't in any way a racist, especially after I told him I was from South Carolina. I said to him, "I think I understand how the black man felt after he was freed from slavery." Well, let me tell you, Will – he gave me a look like I was Jefferson Davis, George Wallace and James Earl Ray all rolled into one.

He yelled, "You don't know shit about slavery, white boy! That's just like you honkies! Daddy pays for yo college and yo high-school prom and buys you a Beemer on yo birthday and then you say you feel like you escaping from slavery? Because you had to put up with your old man's *mouth*? Did you have to put up with his bullwhip, too, white boy? Did you have to put up with the auction block? Did you put up with the middle passage when you drove yo Beemer to Texas?"

But wait – there's more: "If yo Daddy's such a racist, why did you take his money? Why did you take the Beemer he gave you? Why was you still living with the racist son of a bitch? You ain't no slave! You could have walked away from that plantation you live on any time you wanted to. You think the slave had that option? You crackers own the whole fuckin' world and then you talk about bein' freed from slavery! Well, we still in slavery, white boy! We ain't free yet! So what you doing to help free the black man now?" His tirade went on a little bit longer, until he realized I guess that at some point even the slave driver has to stop beating his poor bleeding slave. Man – how would you like to have been subjected to that? And that was just one example. I did try to fight back a little, but, to be honest, I was afraid to fight back much – Jerome's a big bad dude! I don't know if he could possibly be any madder at me, but I didn't want to find out. I told him that, as a matter of fact, I owned an old beat-up LTD and took the Greyhound to Texas. He just laughed and said, "You think that makes any difference? Did you set in the front of the bus or did the man make you set in the back?" Jesus, Will, this motherfucker is relentless. I told him that he had me all wrong – yes, my dad is a big racist, but for that very reason I made sure I wasn't one. He said, "If yo daddy is a racist, then you are too." Can you believe he actually said that? Isn't that the most racist thing you have ever heard? That's exactly the way Pop thinks – that you judge a man not by the content of his character, but by the color of his skin. You think maybe I should get another new roommate?

Well, this letter is a lot longer and a hell of a lot more serious than I intended it to be. But never fear – the Shithouse

Shakespeare is here! I've added another masterpiece to another toilet stall:

There once was a girl from Dallas,
In whose mouth was often a phallus;
But she employed so much friction
That it caused a strange affliction,
On her lip you could see a small callus.

Enough for now. Take it easy.

Signed elaborately,
Joshua A. Kinninger

P.S. Don't forget – this letter is for your eyes only, if you plan on keeping your eyes.

"MR. CARLYLE, MAY I MAKE USE of this wondrous morning as an opportunity to remind you of the promise you made to relate to me the circumstances surrounding your most famous case? I will make a most appreciative audience, I assure you, if presently you are in the mood for storytelling."

"Yes, suttonly, with great pleasure. Take a seat, Cunnel, and I'll tell you everything you may wish to know and probably a dun sott more. Fust of all, I would most lockly ratha choose the wud *infamous* to descrobb those events, just to get us off on the rot foot. I must declare that I have a penchant, as befitting my profession, for making shaw I employ the rot wuds in all the proppa places. So Cunnel, just to set the scene, the whole miserable spectacle had its origin one Sunday monnin in chutch, which location and the fact that I was present to be a witness to it is a fonn illustration of a fust-rate irony because unda nommal succomstances whateva transpodd in that or any other place of worship would have done so without my fust-hand knowledge of it. But as fotchin would have it, that Sunday monnin was one of those rare toms when I periodically retunned to the fold, howeva briefly. And my attendance, on this and every other occasion, was at the behest of my beloved woff Guttrude. Guttrude, you see, will suffa these spells from tom to tom, lock any other woman would come down with the grippe or whatnot, but with her it is invariably a case of the hellfire premonitions – and they don't strock her on *her* account – no sir! – she will succumb to these premonitions entolly on *my* behalf. She is the pusson suffering the affliction, but invariably I am the one made to suffa the cure and compelled to swalla all the dun snake oll. Yes sir, Cunnel, when I hud Guttrude wailin' in her sleep, and her nott shut became soppin' wet with pussporation lock she was outsod unda a cloudbust, and she woke up with her bones rattling – well, I knowed then that come Sunday I'd be fossed out of bed as ully as a dun roosta and handed my chutch clothes to slod into.

"Going to chutch, in my experience, is not dissimila to attending a theater puffomance, though I'm unsutton as to whetha the chutch-goa represents a memba of the audience or one of the pussons on the stage. I was suttonly delivering a bravura puffomance, Cunnel, I can assure you of that. It's hodd wuck trying to put yourseff across as rotchess and pure and requires as motch talent for impussonation as your average thespian possesses, I'm shaw. And I can most suttonly attest to the fact that there were many fonn puffomances that Sunday monnin, wuthy of any accolade you could bestow – because I knowed those dutty dogs constituting half the congagation, and those vommits were so uttally convincing in their roles as uprot paragons of moral rectitude that they were dun near onrecognizable!

"But now, Cunnel, if you want to see some truly fonn acting – some *real* theater – then train your eyes on the Posson up in his puppet gesticulating and orating and salivating and putting on what I would call a *real show*. But I'll grant that what he's preaching in his summon is suttonly true enough. Yes sir, we are all poor miserable sinnas and the good Posson was up there doing his dundest to convince every last one of us of that one obvious, ondeniable fact. Of coss, afta a few prom examples from his big Bobble he was waving around all monnin, of what we can expect in the aftaloff for all our transgressions, one would think the Posson had succeeded in getting his point across. Guttrude suttonly had enough tears streaming down her face to put out a raging broshfire, though I'm shaw she was convinced all that watta was washing away *my* sins ratha than hers. Apparently, howeva, the Posson was unconvinced of his success in demonstrating the erra of our ways, for he continued with his hellfire summonizing and waving his Bobble and th'owing up his feet and contotting his whole body without any apparent fatigue, and without any apparent satisfaction either that any of his summon – not one wud of it – was achieving its desired end. It was as if the Posson was reduced to *pleading* – to *begging* his assembled congagation to heed his wuds, as if any amount of reasoned dis-coss, no matta how small, was uttally useless or perhaps even countaproductive to his puppose. Cunnel, I am entolly of the opinion that a Sunday summon is by far the best example known to mankond of *beating a dead hoss*. Or are we so hodd-headed as a species that even afta voluntolly removing our hats in odda to be hit ova the head with a hamma for several hours, we are still unshaw of what it is we are supposed to be lunning? The Posson suttonly seemed to be unda the impression that the only effective path to enlottenment for such a pack of dun ignorant fools was to hold us unda the watta all monnin ontil we all desodded to grow gills. Or Cunnel, are we so starved and hongry for spectacle and divusion that we are willing and eagga to be mesmerized by the Posson or any other cha'latan passing through town waving something shonny in our faces? Or perhaps we are just gluttons for punishment? We must be loathsome crittas indeed if we feel the need to subject ourselves to sotch intumminable flagellation every dun Sunday.

"So Cunnel, as I said, the Posson was in the puppet putting on his puffomance, if you'll podden all that onnecessary alliteration on my pot. And of coss, every wuthwhile puffomance has to build up to something, a grand climactic moment – I'm thinking of those fonn Elizabethan plays where everyone feels compelled to stab each other to death by the tom the cutton drops. But what the Posson was building up to was – well, his sole puppose throughout his entire summon was to make every man in the dun chutch feel as low about hisseff as a dun snake, and feel the hellfire breathing down his neck and stotting to womm up the soles of his feet – but now afta wucking so hodd to make everyone feel immeasurably *bad*, he now tries his dundest to make some poor broke-down old hoss feel even *wuss*. It's not enough that this poor critta has finally come to feel the hellfire bunning his ommhairs and the suppents crawling up his trouser-legs, but he is fossed to putticipate in the spectacle that the Posson is putting on. No sir, it is insufficient melly to confess your sins in the manna and the privacy of a confessional booth, popish and heretical as that is, where whateva business you may have to negotiate with the Lodd is just between you and the interested potties. No sir, that would allow a man to maintain a little pinch of dignity, and we can't have that – no sir! He has to bawl lock a heffa and rut lock a hog and crow lock a roosta and slobba lock a bud dog. It's bad enough to feel so low that you're grobb'ling in the dutt without having to add a copple more layers of soll to it by acting lock a dun fool.

"So anyway, Cunnel, the Posson is up there impussonating a fisha of men, casting his hook, line and sinka, and then reeling them in and proclaiming that we are nothing but uth-wumms wiggling on a hook and that Satan is a big ol' sea suppent just waiting to gobble us all up, and meanwhile, I'm taking out my watch every dun minute wondering how motch longer I'm going to be fossed to set here till Guttrude and I can retunn to the comfutt of our home and I can pull myseff out of this infunnel stotch shut and have tom perhaps before dock to rod down to the riva and do some *real* fishing. And just then, with the Posson still grappling with that demonic sea suppent, as if on cue somebody rose rot up and snatched his *bait*. Yes sir, this gentleman in the back pew stotted in to hollering louda than a whupped docky and braying lock a billy goat and screeching lock a tomcat and th'owing hisseff down on the floor and tossing hisseff around lock he was mopping up a puddle of watta and he was the dun *mop*. He was setting in the back of the chutch at fust lock he had just walked in on the Posson's puffomance, but he was now dettumined to take over center stage. And unlock all the rest of us poor sinnas who were just playing our pots and melly acting as if we wanted to be there – including probably the Posson hisseff – this poor critta's puffomance was undottedly, onmistakably *real*.

"I had never seen this man before so I knowed he must have been a roustabout coming in off the riva and feeling motty sorry for all the *fun* he was having. And he was suttonly dressed for the pot as well. No stotch Sunday shut for him, and the hair on his head was shooting out in every direction on a compass rose and then some. And the way the dust and dutt rose off him when he th'owed hisseff down on the floor lock a rag-mop made him look lock he was a smoldering campfire or an Indian making smoke signals.

"Well Cunnel, after this poor vommit had stopped howling lock a woof and th'owing hisseff around lock a bear with his leg caught in a snare, the Posson instrocted him to come up to the front of the chutch. By this tom both of them, the Posson and his new disopple, were wimpering and sobbing lock a copple of hysterical old mammies. The disopple dragged hisseff up to the puppet where the Posson was writhing and groaning as if *he* were the one headed straight to damnation – well, maybe he knows something we don't, Cunnel. In any event, with the Posson still flailing his omms and gyrating his hips and exhorting him on to salvation, this new disopple of the Lodd tunned around in the puppet and *rot in front of the Posson*, stotted proclaiming that he was a new man now and that all the gold in O'gon was nothing but dutt as far as he was consunned and he kept th'owing in 'I'm renouncing my claim! I'm renouncing my claim!' wherever it seemed to fit, as if it were his own vusion of 'Hallelujah, Praise the Lodd!' and that he was here now by the grace of God to claim something of a much greata value he reckoned. And rot about now I realized that instead of being near the conclusion of the Posson's puffomance, and that motch closer to dinna tom, I was now being fossed to set plum still for anotha whole dun *summon*! And the poor Posson, upstaged in his own chutch, had no choss but to either jonn the rest of us sinnas in the pews or to juck the reins hodd on this here renegade hoss.

"Well now, this *new* Posson, which is what I mott as well call this fella, he regaled us with this tale about going out to O'gon and fonding exactly what he was sutching for, or what he *thought* he was sutching for – which was gold. About how he secured his claim and then headed back up the Columbia and about how he almost got drownded, not just once, or twoss, but three toms before he got back to St. Louis and now he was here to renounce his claim in front of the good Lodd and everybody – to renounce his claim not only to the gold he found but to renounce any claim he ever had to being a deserving human being or any claim he ever had to deserve salvation or to deserve anything but etunnel hellfire and damnation.

"Now Cunnel, there's one fascinating little detail I've omitted, consunning what happens when people hear the wud *gold*. As soon as this old prospecta fust uttered that infunnel wud, why sir, every ear in the chutch just pucked rot up and stotted hanging on every wud he uttered as if it were the Summon on the Mount. And all the generalized exhorting that they were doing at fust to udge him on toward his etunnel salvation soddenly became a bit more specific in nature. At fust you hud rot many *Praise the Lodd*s and *Amen*s and *Preach It, Posson*s mixed in with the Posson's general bellowing and blowing, but afta the wud *gold* was introduced into the proceedings, then I hud *What pot of O'gon?* and *How far from the Columbia?* and *Who else knows about the claim?* Yes sir, their consunns over the fate of this here sinna's etunnel soul soddenly took on a motch more uthly characta. And Cunnel, you should have seen their eyes! He provodded some answers to their inquiries consunning the general location of this here claim and everybody's eyes stotted bouncing off each other lock billyad balls and the whole dun chutch tunned into one big billyad hall, with the eyeballs bouncing and careeming off each other – with the Posson hisseff now looking lock nothing else but the *cueball*. His eyes would bounce off one memba of his congagation and then anotha, and stare at one and then glare at anotha, as if he were sizing up a kiss shot in the conna pocket. By the tom the old prospecta had concluded his summon – which had tunned soddenly into a lesson on the geography of eastun O'gon – the Posson had dun near ron the table."

"Did they determine where the gold was located in Oregon?"

"Well, I reckoned they mott could fond it, as long as they knowed their ABC's – but pussonally I wouldn't place a wager on them knowing motch more of the alphabet than that – 'cause I knowed these fellas and book-lunning wasn't their potticula specialty. And as it tunned out, I was rot.

"So here's the pitcha I'm attempting to draw for you – at least the pot of it I fond most satisfying. Here's this old prospecta who had belly escaped being drownded three toms on his way back from O'gon and had dodged Indians and starvation and miscellaneous other misfotchins – and all he wanted now was to give his poor buddened soul ova to the Lodd and renounce his wuddly possessions, and most especially that infunnel gold monn he had stombled upon. So he belly makes it off the riva still breathing and comes limping and wobbling and quivering into the chutch for the sole puppose of convutting to the Gospel – and so he jomps up and takes the Posson's bait and stotts in with his own summon – and here's the most savory pot of this whole delectable mess, Cunnel – a summon about *staying away from gold!* About *the sin of cupidity!* About *the sin of greed and avarice and the love of uthly wealth!* I try to imagine the profound disappointment he must have felt when he realized that his hotfelt, inspodd summon was only going to succeed in compelling the whole congagation to act in the exact dun *opposite* manna for which the summon was intended. So Cunnel, it just heps to prove the fact, that there is at least one wud more powerful by far than the wud of Almotty God – and that's the wud *gold*.

"But you wanted to know, Cunnel, where that vein of gold was located. Well, I've neva been to O'gon, or any point west of Omaha as a matta of fact, and it's neva been one of my ambitions to set one foot ova the frontier eitha. This country was lodge enough for the Pilgrims and lodge enough for the Indians and it's lodge enough for anybody who's dun fool enough to come here in the fust place I reckon, but these dun fools want to fott the Indians and the Mexicans and the rattlesnakes and cross the dun desert lock Moses in the Bobble just to get their hands on something they soon enough will regret ever touching. So I'm content to stay rot where I am. So I can't tell you for sutton, Cunnel, where that gold was located. But the one clue that the old prospecta gave to the congagation that I could make any sense of was that it was located unda a big dobble-u."

"Pardon me. W? The letter W?"

"Yes, sir, that's the one. He said that vein of gold ore was in the rock face of a hillsod that had some natural mockings that looked to him lock a big ol' dobble-u. It would be hodd to fond at fust, he said, but you couldn't miss it if you were looking in the rot place to stott with. And Cunnel, you should've seen those billyad ball eyeballs go bouncing off one anotha. It looked lock someone had racked the balls up and said *Break!* and bosted them up real good! So, as I remocked before, he must have been solly disappointed to see all of his hotfelt summonizing have the advuss effect of insotting the exact behavior he had come crawling into chutch to etunnelly renounce. So much so, in fact, that by the tom he got around to descrobbing the big dobble-u to them, they had succeeded in cajoling him to do everything but draw up a dun map. And the Posson by this tom had suttonly moved the saving of souls a bit futha down on his list of prio'ities.

"By this point the congagation had received all the enlottenment it deemed necessary from the old prospecta, and one by one a man would grab his woff and try to slink out the back of the chutch without the Posson becoming aware of their absence. But soon enough he could see that half the dun chutch was empty and even stotting to *echo* a little, so he didn't even bother with the benediction. He shook the old prospecta's hand, grabbed his big Bobble, and then he was gone with the rest of them, leaving me and Guttrude and a few others looking around at each other and one old widda up front still holding on to the proceeds from the collection plate. So Cunnel, it was a memorable summon, I must admit. And for most of the men in attendance it was undottedly the fust tom they had reason to be grateful for being drug out of bed by the woff and fossed to spend Sunday in chutch."

"So what became of all the men, and the Parson, who went looking for the gold?"

"Well now, I can suttonly enlotten you, Cunnel, as to the whereabouts of those men who came back in one piece from O'gon, but of coss there were some who didn't come back at all – whetha by voluntary choss or by some unfotchinate succomstance I don't have the relevant facts to say. But they suttonly didn't waste tom in stotting the sutch. Next Sunday I was back again in my polished boots and my stotch shut – Guttrude was still unshaw as to the status of my evalasting soul, especially afta what had transpodd the previous Sunday. It's not often, Cunnel, that a congagation backslods *during* the summon! In any case, when we arrived at the chutch door, it was locked up tott with a handwritten note hanging on it by a nail. *Closed Ontil Futha Notice* it said. Now Cunnel, you're a young man still, but tell me this, have you ever in all your bonn days hud of a chutch closing down for business on a Sunday? There were a few more folks from last week's congagation who walked up to the chutch door to read the note and they were just as flabbagasted as I was. Of coss, I couldn't confess to the fact that I was downrot ovajoyed to be spared anotha of the Posson's intumminable summons, and I imagine that sentiment was not oncommon, although we all of coss had to put on an act and make believe at how disappointed we all were to soddenly have our Sunday monnin free from summonizing – and not only this monnin, but *ontil futha notice* at that."

WILLIE NILLIE,

I have more Black Panther news to report from Jerome, but it gets a bit heavy – especially for your underdeveloped mind – so let's begin with a little humor, shall we? I have now contributed fine limerick verse to each stall on my floor of Bruce Hall, so I will need to venture out elsewhere, to virgin defecation territory. So far I have chosen to remain anonymous, but as I expand my poetic empire I have decided that I need to adopt a *nom-de-poop* to announce my handiwork to the world. I am leaning toward "Shitspeare" since he is, after all, the world's greatest poet. But since I am an American poet of great renown, I'm also considering "Walt Shitman" or "Ezra Pound of Brown." I'm open to suggestions.

Here is one of my latest offerings. Fort Worth is a little south of Denton, right beside Dallas.

> There once was a girl from Fort Worth,
> Who had such tremendous girth,
> The scientists were quite correct
> When they said she must certainly affect
> The gravitational pull of the Earth.

OK – time now for the Jerome and Cracker Show.

Jerome is continuing to infuriate me. I've seriously thought about requesting a new roommate, if that's even possible, but I've decided for now to stay put. Maybe I'm a masochist, but I don't want to walk away from this situation and feel like Jerome has defeated me. I've given up on trying to change Pop's mind about anything, but if I can't have any effect on a white racist, maybe I can change a black one. I told him point blank that I thought he was a racist, probably risking my life in the process. But he didn't seem too surprised to hear my charge against him (for good reason). "Ain't racism if you're right," he said. "I'm sure my pop would say the same thing," I retorted. "Yeah, but he's wrong, the son of a bitch." I actually got our conversation down on tape. I wasn't trying to be sneaky, but I like to record myself practicing sometimes so I had my tape recorder rolling, and I wasn't about to turn it off once Jerome and I started cooking.

I asked him why he thought it was okay to call me a honky (honkie, honkey, honkee, etc.). He said, "Who said it was okay?" Even I had to laugh at that. "I don't call you a honky because it's okay – I call you a motherfuckin' honky because it *ain't* okay. But what you gonna do about it, white boy?" I didn't laugh at that. "You ain't gonna do shit about it because you don't really give a shit whether I call you a honky or not. You don't even know what that word means, do you? Well, I know what nigger means. Nigger means 'I can kill yo black ass anytime I take a notion to.' Nigger means 'I can kill yo ass and there ain't shit you can do about it.' You don't care what I call you – you just mad because I'm gettin' away with something you can't get away with no more. How does that feel, honky? Welcome to my black-ass world. How does it feel to be helpless when somebody's disrespectin' you? How does it feel to be disrespected and not be able to retaliate back?"

"What if I start calling you nigger?"

"You don't want to do that, white boy." Jerome gave me a murderous stare – as if just *saying* that word to him was the same as *calling* him one.

"Well, can you please stop calling me honky and cracker and all that other shit?"

"Why the fuck should I stop?"

"Because it's fucking disrespectful! You just said it was!"

"And why should I be respectful to you, Joshua? Is that better, Joshua? Why should I show you a ounce of respect? Because you want me to? Because you *tellin'* me to? Now we back to slavery days on de plantation, massa. I gotta do this just because you want me to do it? Naw suh, we ain't on de plantation no mo'. I'll show you the respect you demandin' from me as soon as you earn it, white boy. So your next question, instead of 'Why do you call me honky?' should be 'What do I have to do to earn yo respect?'"

"OK – I'll play your game. What do I have to do to earn your respect, Jerome?"

"There ain't nothin' you can do to earn my respect, white boy. Not a goddam thing. It's too late for that. Too much hurt. Too much hate. Too much slavery, too much reconstruction, too much lynching, too much Jim Crow, too much urban renewal, too much ignorance, too much denial. Too much bullshit. Too much everything for me to ever respect you, white boy. There is only two things you can do, Joshua – either learn how to live with a angry black man or pack yo things and move out. And I ain't tellin' you to move out. They will just stick another white boy in here with me, so you might as well stay and get used to it."

"I deserve your respect a lot more than most guys I grew up

with. Talk about racists. There are some real motherfucking racists in Charleston, South Carolina."

"So you tellin' me now what it's like to grow up around white cracker racists? White man always knows more than the nigger, don't he? Even about a nigger's own fuckin' life. 'I know about racism very well, Mr. Black Man,' you say. Well, why don't you ask a black man about racism if you want to know about racism? Because you don't want to fuckin' hear what a black man knows about racism. And you think you deserve more respect than all those other crackers? Back on the plantation they was massas who thought they was saints just because they didn't whip their niggers with impunity. They only gave 'em the bullwhip when they really *deserved* it, and they let 'em go to church on Sunday and drink whiskey on Christmas. Do you have more respect for those folks, Josh? Your racism runs as deep as everybody else's but you don't want to see it. You ain't no different from yo daddy, but you don't want to see it. You're blind as a fuckin' bat! Ignorance of the law ain't never been an excuse to get out of jail, and ignorance of your own damn sins ain't no excuse neither. You think you ain't no racist just because you don't *want* to be a racist? I know you ain't that damn dumb."

"I'm not like my father! You can't possibly say we're just alike."

"What do you want me to say, man? That you're a better person than your old man? I'm sure there ain't no doubt about that. So if it'll make you happy – Joshua, I think you're twice the fuckin' man yo daddy ever will be. So now – do you feel better?"

"No, not really. You still think I'm a racist."

"You're all a bunch of damn racists. You can't help it. You grew up in it. You sayin' you ain't a racist is like livin' in the ocean and sayin' you ain't no *fish*."

"How can you say I'm a racist? You don't know me well enough to say that. What have I ever done to you that's racist?"

"You ain't done nothin' to me. But like you say, I ain't knowed you that long. Ask me that question next week."

"I'll prove to you I'm not a racist."

"I'll be here, white boy. I ain't goin' nowhere."

That was last week. I got another conversation on tape yesterday. I *was* being sneaky this time! I had my horn out, but I didn't turn the tape recorder on until after Jerome started rolling. The guy is just so angry. It's unbelievable. If you don't hear from me in a few weeks you might want to call the cops! Here is our "conversation" – if you can call it that – in its entirety:

"Have you always been like this?"

"Like what?"

"This radical."

"*Radical*? The *truth* is *radical*? I ain't nothin' but tellin' the *truth*! White man tells so many damn lies, and you been swimmin' around in those lies so long, brother tells you a little *truth* and he done gone off the deep end! Ain't nothin' *radical* about discrimination! Ain't nothin' fuckin' *radical* about prejudice! Ain't nothin' *radical* about bein' pushed around by the goddam *po-leese.* What makes you think I'm *radical*, white boy? Just because I ain't tellin' you what you want to fuckin' hear?"

"Man, you're just so militant – so strident. Do you ever listen to yourself? And I don't think the truth is nearly as bad as you say it is – it *can't* be. Jesus, you make it sound like you all are still slaves on the plantation."

"We *are* still slaves, motherfucker – "

"You're still a slave? Look at you! You're in college! You're rooming with a white guy!"

"I told you! I knew it, motherfucker! I said gimme a week and I'll show you how racist yo sorry white ass really is. You soundin' just like yo daddy now! All it takes is a little *militancy.* A little too much *stridency.* Then it's time to put that nigger in his place!"

"You don't know what the fuck you're talking about."

"White folks is crazy. All you want is a pat on the back, but when you don't get it – *whooo-wheee!* Watch out nigger! You keep us in chains for 300 years and then say, 'But we set you free!' You hang us from a tree and set us on fire and then say, 'But we let you play baseball with us! Look at Jackie

Robinson!' You wouldn't let us drink out the same water fountain. You wouldn't even let us piss in the same fuckin' toilet – that's how nasty you think we are! That nigger's nasty-ass piss ain't gettin' nowhere near my beautiful white-boy piss! Even yo *piss* is racist! So do you hang your head in shame? Do you even *apologize?* Hell no! You just keep on braggin' on yo'selves – 'We let you set in the front of the bus now! Ain't we wonderful! Ain't we saints the way we treat you now!' And I know what you thinkin'. You thinkin', 'but it ain't like that no more. Ain't no more segregation. Ain't no more Jim Crow. Ain't no more lynchin'. Ain't no more slavery. Ain't nothin' like that no more.' Not since little Joshua come along! Little Josh come along with all his smart-boy friends and everything gonna be okay now. Because he ain't like his daddy. You know what yo problem is, Josh? Yo problem is the only thing you hate is the *past*. Yo daddy is the *past*. But the past don't go away. Yo daddy ain't goin' away. All you see is yo shiny future, but what you don't see is the *past*. But the problem is, the future ain't here yet, and it may never get here. But the past *is* here – and it ain't goin' nowhere."

That was it. Jerome made his point and made a dramatic exit – down the hall to piss in the same toilet that I do. But that was enough, don't you think?

After all that, I think you deserve another selection of Poetry to Poop By, this one coming to us all the way from Austin, the state capital.

> There once was a girl from Austin,
> Who going down on was quite exhaustin';
> If her skirt you ventured to hike,
> You found that her bush was more like
> A deep forest that you could get lost in.

Your racist brother,
Whitey H. Cracker

P.S. You're not going to show this letter to Pop, right? I know you ain't that damn dumb.

EINAR'S CREWMEN disembarked eagerly to begin exploring the new land and to begin making their winter quarters. They saw no signs of skraelings and were overjoyed to see that New Norway contained moose, just as Old Norway. As Einar had proclaimed, this land was truly a paradise that had in abundance everything they would ever need for their survival.

As they finished the difficult work of building their longhouse, however, many of the men acknowledged their loneliness and despaired of ever seeing their homes and kinsmen again. "To return by the same passage that brought us here," they said, "seems more dangerous and foolhardy than coming here in the first place – doubly so, for who knows how we came to be here or which of the many twisting sea-paths will take us home?"

Einar answered their complaints by saying, "For once, men, I will not blame your reticence on cowardice, but rather attribute it to your wisdom. I have no desire to return home by the icy waterways of the North. We have seen quite enough of icebergs! Turn your eyes to the south, men! The weather will become only warmer and the way will be much shorter. Mark my words! This island is far larger than I anticipated, yet it is only an island still! And all islands are more easily navigated to the south – isn't this the truth I am telling you? Have you ever known an island to become harsher and crueler as you sailed south? Ask Ingolf why his high-seat pillars chose Reykjavik. Why didn't Erik prefer the cozy warmth of Vestribyggd and to live amongst the skraelings? Leif was indeed lucky to have continued south to Vinland! So let us rest our weary bones and repair our broken ship, for we have only a shorter and more fortuitous trip home to look forward to – where we shall all be hailed as heroes and be bathed in eternal glory!" Einar's men were soothed by his words, and cheered him accordingly. Thorbjorn, however, replied, to no one in particular, "Let us hope that Einar is correct – for once. It remains to be seen how much wisdom this crazed murderer possesses."

One day soon after, it happened that one of the men, called Bolli, and highly valued by Einar for his rowing ability, did not return to camp after a day spent hunting in the endless forest surrounding them. This occurrence did not alarm anyone, for there were many accidents awaiting those who chose to hunt alone; however, the strange noises emanating from the forest that night were another matter. They did not resemble any sounds the men were familiar with, neither from animals nor from men. Whatever fear the men may have felt, however, was not to be seen on any countenance. As one man answered the unnatural sounds he heard with an equally frightening shout of his own, other men quickly joined him until everyone around their common campfire was making loud, warlike noises they would have thought themselves incapable of producing moments earlier. "This is excellent, men!" Einar shouted above the din. "Whatever creatures are out there must be made to regret their decision to provoke us! They will be no match for our swords and our courage!" The Greenlanders, however, though matching their unseen enemies in their vocal displays, could not match them in stamina. As each man soon tired and became quiet, the maniacal noises that seemed to surround them in the forest never ceased. As the hours of night dragged on, the men took their turns at howling like wolves and shrieking like berserkers as others rested their throats. As the sun appeared, they were relieved to realize suddenly that the noises in the forest had stopped.

Exhausted as if from fighting a night-long battle, but still too wary to sleep, Thorbjorn suggested to Einar that they retreat to the safety of their ship and sail away to another location. "I am not surprised to hear such a suggestion from you, Thorbjorn," said Einar. "You are proving to be as cowardly as your brother was courageous. Only a scoundrel would run in fear from a foe that is too afraid of us to show its face. They cowered under cover of darkness, trying to scare us by loudly wagging their tongues, while it was obvious to everyone but you that they were either too weak or too cowardly to attack us. And it is a shame that you do not show the same loyalty toward Bolli as you show toward your brother. It appears that the love you have for your own safety far outweighs any concern for the safety of your missing comrade." Einar raised his voice to give commands to his crew. "We shall not retreat from an enemy we have yet to see! We shall not abandon Bolli so that Thorbjorn may sleep soundly! Rather, we shall sleep in shifts and take turns guarding our camp. After we have rested, we shall search for our brother. Thorbjorn, if you wish, you may return to the ship to slumber and to compose more scornful poems about me. When we meet and destroy our enemy in the forest, I hope our brave fighting doesn't awaken you."

After a few hours of morning sleep, the men grouped themselves into search parties. They did not find Bolli; nor did they find any traces of the unknown creatures with which they had fought vocally the night before. As one of the search parties stopped to rest, a man called Hildung expressed the need to relieve himself, and to do so he walked a short distance away from the group. His absence was ignored for some time until someone remarked that Hildung was taking a long time, even for Hildung. They called for him and then ran with swords raised in the direction he had walked, but he was not found, nor was any evidence discovered that would explain what happened to him. Einar happened to be in this search party, and he said, "We will find Hildung or the creatures that have taken him. Let us push forward."

"Why are they not visible to us? Do you think they are *draugar*?" someone asked.

"No, I think they are cowards. And when we find them we will show them all the mercy that cowards deserve."

They came to a small clearing and saw a strange dwelling that was unfamiliar to them. It did not appear to belong to skraelings. They approached it cautiously and it proved to be empty of inhabitants, though the bones of animals were scattered here and there around it. "Whoever lives here will want to return," Einar said, "and when he does, we shall prepare a surprise for him." The men returned to the edge of the clearing and hid themselves from view. They waited patiently and quietly for what seemed to be a very long time, yet nothing returned to the strange tent and all remained quiet. The sunlight began to fade and Einar gave the order to leave this spot and to return to their camp before darkness fell. The other search parties were met there, but they also had no good news to report.

Shortly after nightfall, the men were once again startled by the loud, grotesque noises coming from all around them in the forest. And as before, they answered with all the noise that they could muster. Suddenly, however, the horrible sounds came closer to them and there was a loud rustling throughout the woods. Then there appeared rushing toward them from all sides numerous sets of eyes – eyes without faces or bodies – frightful eyes dancing up and down as they approached rapidly. Then several of Einar's men were killed by unseen spears that came from nowhere out of the sky. And as suddenly as these bodiless eyes appeared, they were gone, leaving behind only their blood-soaked spears, which had pierced completely the chests of many of the Greenlanders. "Return to the ship!" Einar shouted, an order the men quickly obeyed without having to hear it repeated.

After a sleepless night of peering over their ship's gunwale into the silent darkness, the survivors of the attack were grateful to see the return of daylight. Einar's remaining crew, now numbering only half of what it had been the night before, lost no time in marching back to their campsite to begin the sad task of gathering the corpses of their slain friends, whom, in their fright, they had abandoned. The bodies, however, were not where they had fallen only hours earlier. Rather than search for them, Einar looked around forlornly and ordered his men once again to return to their ship. And though they had had little time in which to begin the ship's repairs, Einar ordered it to be pushed back into the surf and its sail caught a strong wind blowing southward.

Thorbjorn said the Einar, "This tragedy would have been avoided if you had taken my advice two nights ago. You must live with that decision."

"Yes, you are right – but you, Thorbjorn Arnthorsson, must live with being a coward. Between these two fates, I have chosen correctly."

"These men, whose deaths you are responsible for, were merely your servants, but they were my friends. Why are we not seeking vengeance for them, as you insisted we do for Bolli? It is because you are now frightened as well – as frightened as I was before. So you are no different than I, though you insist on drawing your distinctions between us. So much bloodshed should make cowards of us all."

"It is only because we have suffered the slaughter of so many of my men that your heart is still beating at this moment, Thorbjorn. So here is something else you must live with – it is to the deaths of so many of your friends that you now owe your life. If a man calls me a coward, he will taste death before the words from his mouth have time to reach his ears. My final advice to you, Thorbjorn, is that you continue your cowardly ways and run from my sight."

Einar's ship continued to sail southward, too many of its oar ports now empty to be of much use. The men were despondent. Einar, as well, was helpless to buoy the men's hopes, for he despaired of having enough men to propel his ship across the ocean currents and safely home. Day upon day passed; the weather became warmer; yet the land they kept continually in sight to port remained. "Are you still certain, Einar, that this land is an island," the men wondered, "or must we sail to Hel on this southern course?"

"The answer to that question no longer concerns me," Einar said. "Either we shall see Greenland again by this route or we shall perish along the way. It is a noble endeavor, regardless."

A howling wind soon approached from the west. The ship had weathered many storms gallantly and would have made its builders proud, but it had been in great need of repair before the crew had been attacked by the fiendish eyes, and whether it would survive destruction through its next tempest gave cause for doubt. The ship took aboard a great amount of water and the small crew could do little to control the course of the vessel. Three men were lost overboard. Einar shouted orders for the ship's navigation that could not be heard through the gale and that would have been impossible to execute even if the remaining crew had heard him. Thorbjorn had only the strength to grip the mast tightly and hope to maintain his grasp for a few minutes longer. The ship was driven toward shore along a rocky coast. There were many large rocks within the water and the ship was helpless to avoid striking one of them. More men tumbled overboard as the ship struck the rock and water poured into the ship through its destroyed hull. Einar remained with his ship until the ship was no more and his body slammed violently into another one of the large rocks hidden along the stormy coastline. He lost consciousness as water filled his lungs and the surf carried him to shore.

Einar slowly awoke with sunlight in his eyes and sand in his mouth. As he tried to stand he vomited salty water. He was alone on the beach. He had lost his sword, as well as much of his clothing. He was eventually able to stand and began to walk slowly along the sandy strand, searching for his men.

Soon, he spotted Thorbjorn, who was sitting on the beach, looking out into the sea with one hand clasping Thor's hammer around his neck, thankful for the protection it had given him. Einar approached him and said, "You are the last person I would have expected to survive such a mighty storm. But it is true that the greatest luck is often found in men least deserving of it."

"Yes, Einar, as you stand here before me, I will attest to the truth of that."

"I see that the water dripping from your limbs has done nothing to wash away the malice you bear towards me. Be that as it may, I will need your help in searching for our comrades – my brave crew, who survived the merciless seas of the north, only to be destroyed upon the shores of paradise."

Einar and Thorbjorn found only a few survivors, but several men had come ashore whose bodies were mangled and who had breathed their last air in the sea spray of the tempest. As Thorbjorn quietly looked down upon yet another dead friend, Einar asked, "Do you not have anything to say over the bodies of these brave men? No final poems praising these fallen heroes?"

"No, Einar, I do not. Praise is wasted on the dead. I have no reason to regret my silence now, but why were these men not sung praises when they would have rejoiced in hearing them? That is what I shall always regret."

They turned inland in search of food. Einar said, "I have no inclination to celebrate our current circumstances, but can we be faulted for marveling at this bounteous land? Behold – are these not grapes? The same sweet grapes that Karlsefni's men became drunk upon? Are these not indeed the western slopes of Vinland that I have promised you from the beginning? Oh! What sad luck we have, men! To have finally discovered the land promised to you, only to dump upon it a shipload of brave corpses! I know not how to react to such a fate. Are we the luckiest men to have ever drawn air, or the most miserably cursed?"

Einar's men had no time to respond to his speech, for at the moment he completed it a group of hideous creatures unlike anything the Greenlanders had seen before rushed out from within the tall grass. They held spears aloft and Einar's men were helpless to defend themselves. They only could stare at these creatures in amazement and silently await their quick deaths. It was obvious that these savage creatures were men, for they were naked, but how strange was the color of their skin! Their skin was the darkest blue imaginable, and their ears and noses were pierced through with various objects made of bone and stone, and of various sizes. The large group of blue men encircled Einar and his crew, continued to walk slowly around them and repeated frightening chants. It then happened that the circle surrounding the Greenlanders slowly transformed into three walls on either side of them and to their rear, and with the prodding of spears and a horrific shouting in a language as strange to their ears as their appearance was to their eyes, they were made to understand that they were to march forward. They were led inland for miles, and at each step they were further prodded by spear points which reddened their skin with blood. They appeared to be marching toward a prominent, beautiful mountain in the distance.

After much forced walking, the exhausted Greenlanders eventually arrived at a village, yet a great distance still from the snow-topped mountain. All the men remained silent, except for Einar, who harangued his captors with threats and curses. Because of the audacity he displayed in speaking, Einar made it clear to the blue men that he was the bravest of the captives and undoubtedly their leader. They were all thrown together into a large wooden cage. They were brought food which, by its appearance and odor, they would have found unpalatable but for their great hunger. They realized they had been mistaken about the color of the blue men's skin. Many of them had created streaks on their blue skin simply by moving their fingers across it. On others, their blueness had become quite smeared or had disappeared altogether. These people had painted themselves the color of night. Yet beneath its dark blue paint, their skin still appeared to be quite curious. It was neither white nor brown, but red. Thorbjorn whispered to Einar, "These darkened demons are responsible for the attack on us in the night."

"You are identical to your brother in one respect, Thorbjorn. You arrive at the port after the ship has sailed and boast that you are early." It was now that Einar and his men saw the women of this village for the first time. Unlike the men, the women did not paint themselves all over, but were colorfully decorated in many other ways, including having small tattoos on their faces. However, the most noticeable feature of each woman's face was a large, round plate which was suspended from her nose and dangled heavily in front of her mouth. Young girls wore these nose-plates as well. The effect of this was to prevent the females from speaking without difficulty, as the plates would grate noisily against their teeth as their mouths were opened. It was also noticed that if a female attempted to lift the nose-plate up and away from her face to make speaking easier, she was quickly and harshly rebuked by anyone, male or female, who witnessed it.

After three days of captivity, during which they were given little to eat and even less to drink, their large cage was entered by some of the Bluemen (as the Greenlanders had begun calling them) and Einar and his few remaining men were led out. They were too weak to resist. They were taken to a large tent and, to their surprise, given more food than they had eaten aboard ship or in any of their winter camps. They were allowed to eat until they wanted no more. The Blueman who sat in the highest seat and who was, therefore, understood by Einar to be the king, spoke loudly in his alien tongue and began to laugh. Others joined him in his laughter. Einar's men, though now having full bellies, were not without concern. Einar spoke to them, "Men, do you wish to allow yourselves to be slaughtered like fattened animals, or do you prefer to fight and die like warriors?" They were soon led from the king's tent, and although Einar knew what his men's answer would be to his question, they were helpless to fight back against the long spears continually stabbing at their backs. They were led back to their cage and placed inside once again.

Soon afterward on that day, the entire village, including the women and children, gathered around a large field not far from where Einar's men were located. One Blueman put his spear through the bars of the cage and selected one prisoner – a selection made painful by the point of the spear. This man was led out of the cage and into the field. From their cage, it was not possible to witness what transpired on the field because of the ring of Bluemen encircling it, and it was impossible to hear anything beyond the loud, frightful noises made by every villager – noises that were familiar to Einar's men as they recalled the night so many of them had been massacred by dancing, spear-throwing eyes. It was also impossible, however, not to see the result of their comrade's trip into the field – his bloodied body was dragged dead through the crowd of shouting Bluemen and tossed limply into a small pit. Another man, called Salgard, was chosen next by spear-point to be conducted through the gauntlet of Bluemen and into the unseen field. The caged Greenlanders waited many minutes for Salgard likewise to be dragged dead away from the field and thrown into the pit; however, no sign of him, dead or alive, was to be seen.

The Blueman with the spear returned to choose another Greenlander from within the cage. This time, Thorbjorn was chosen. Einar, however, grasped the Blueman's spearhead, forcefully removed its tip from Thorbjorn's skin, and then brought it to himself and caused a stream of blood to issue from his own chest as he pressed the spear into it. He shouted directly at the Blueman, and his deeds, if not his words, made his meaning clear: "I will remain within this cage not a moment longer without knowing the fate of each of my men. And whatever their fate is, I demand to share it!" Einar was led out of the cage, alongside the deafening shouts of Bluemen, male and female, and into the large, open field. He did not see Salgard. The king of the Bluemen, who had been the host at their feast earlier, stepped onto the field and made what appeared to be a short speech. At the conclusion of his speech, there was a short pause in which every Blueman, once shouting so loudly, was now silent. The silence lasted only a moment, however. One Blueman, immensely strong and well-built, stepped forward, raised his spear, and shouted. His shout was then followed by the renewed shouts of all the assembled Bluemen. This lone Blueman, who apparently had volunteered proudly for whatever task he was being asked to perform, ran to the far end of the field with his spear. Einar understood that his life depended on watching the movements of this man very carefully.

The Blueman shouted toward Einar and then, from many paces distant, ran forward and hurled his spear. The spear became invisible as soon as it left the Blueman's hand. Einar had no time to react, except to fall to the ground. He heard the spear whistle above his head and felt the wind created by it, but he did not see it. Believing it was now safe to rise, Einar returned to his feet. The large crowd of Bluemen continued its ceaseless noise. A small Blueman, a child, ran up to Einar from somewhere behind him and offered him the spear that had eventually come to rest on the ground after being thrown invisibly across the field. Einar guessed what was now being asked of him, and without further hesitation he ran forward and hurled the spear toward the Blueman. Einar was much more adept at swordplay than at spear-throwing, so the spear thrown by him arced into the air and remained visible throughout its flight. The Blueman, rather than duck or dodge, held his ground, raised his hand into the air and caught the spear in mid-flight. The villagers, in celebration of this feat, now created such a din that Einar thought he might go deaf. The

Blueman thrust his spear into the ground and suddenly charged toward Einar. Rather than take the full force of the Blueman's assault, Einar charged as well and the two men collided in the center of the field amid the wild noises of the appreciative villagers. Einar, though weak from days of captivity, fought savagely. However, because of the Blueman's superior strength, Einar felt throughout the fight as if he were struggling futilely against his imminent death. He sensed that all his remaining strength was draining quickly from his body and he felt willing now to succumb to death. At this moment, however, the Blueman ceased his attack. He walked in a slow circle around Einar's prostrate body, chanting something all the while. Einar was prepared to meet death, for the Blueman surely was chanting some rite prior to completing the sacrifice. Another child ran onto the field, toward the victorious Blueman. The child was carrying in his outstretched hands a small vessel. The Blueman's chants over Einar became louder as the crowd quickly became quiet. Too weak to resist, Einar helplessly submitted as the Blueman dipped his hands into the vessel, removed them, and began smearing dark blue paint, first over Einar's face, and then over the rest of his body.

With the encircling crowd now making more strange, raucous noise than ever, the Blueman easily lifted Einar up from the ground and carried him to the opposite side of the field, where there were fewer villagers gathered. It was at this time that Einar, through his hazy exhaustion, recognized Salgard, and was relieved that his crewman was still alive. Salgard was difficult to recognize because he also was now painted head to toe with the same pigment as all the male Bluemen. Einar looked across the field and saw Thorbjorn being led meekly onto the field and the villagers' attention turned to the smallest and weakest of the Greenlanders. It was not until this moment that Einar realized that he was being allowed to live. He looked at Salgard and asked him, "What is your understanding of this?"

Salgard replied, "I know no more than you, Einar, and perhaps less, but it appears that in the eyes of these savages, we are no longer Greenlanders. We are now Bluemen."

Einar and Salgard watched to see the fate of Thorbjorn. Einar said, "I would not be surprised if the good luck of Thorbjorn deserts him at the moment he needs it most. But there is nothing we can do for him now. Despite his unfortunate antagonism toward me, I will say to you that I once loved Thorbjorn as a brother, and he does not deserve this fate that is about to befall him."

The king made another speech as Thorbjorn surveyed the large crowd of Bluemen. As with Einar, there was a moment of silent anticipation after the king concluded speaking. Soon, however, a young man stepped forward and received the noisy adulation of everyone. He thrust his spear into the air. His physical stature was much smaller than that of the Blueman who had volunteered to attack Einar. Now however, unlike earlier, the king spoke again and the young man with the spear seemed to be unsure of what his next action should be. The king laughed loudly and continued speaking. He pointed to others who were gathered around the field. The young man who had volunteered stepped back slowly into the throng behind him. It now happened that a large-breasted woman stepped forward with a spear and the crowd erupted in what Thorbjorn knew unmistakably to be collective laughter. All the women were laughing as well, so that the nose plates covering their mouths crashed loudly and continuously against their teeth, creating another type of noise to compete with the general din of laughter. The female Blueman, though not painted dark blue, ran onto the field to the sound of continued laughter – the only recognizable sound made by these people – and hurled her spear at Thorbjorn. It sailed through the air deftly, but not so swiftly that Thorbjorn could not easily avoid it. The retrieved spear was handed to Thorbjorn by the Blueman child. Thorbjorn took it, but gave no indication of knowing what was expected of him. The young boy laughed and performed a pantomime for Thorbjorn by running forward and making a throwing motion with his arm.

Thorbjorn ran forward and tossed the spear toward the woman awaiting it; however, it wobbled throughout its flight and landed harmlessly at her feet, which resulted in more loud laughter from the villagers. She charged Thorbjorn and it was now his fate to wrestle ignominiously with a woman. They parried each other's blows and no great harm came to either combatant, though the crowd appeared to be thoroughly entertained throughout their struggle. At one point during their fight, the woman stood behind Thorbjorn, clasped her arms around him tightly, and pretended to enter him as a man would enter a woman. The laughter and clattering of teeth were deafening. Thorbjorn's humiliation was completed when the woman surprised him with a powerful blow to his face that bloodied his nose and caused him to lose consciousness. When he awoke he discovered himself to be painted dark blue and looked up to see the faces of Einar and Salgard. "Can you explain what has just occurred?" Thorbjorn asked.

Einar responded, "For you, Thorbjorn, a fate worse than death."

3

W,

Am I the next to die? Am I preparing myself for that now? Is that what this is about? I'm in excellent health – *for a man my age,* the caveat goes – which means not in excellent health at all, but rather thoroughly exhausted, medicated, and aching in my heart and limbs. I'm making plans now for doing something crazy, and God only knows why I'm doing it. And I've had this dream three times since your funeral, with minor variations. Surprisingly, you're not in it – unless in some Freudian fashion I can't fathom: I'm surrounded by cops; it's late at night; I'm on some desolate rural highway somewhere in the Midwest – I don't know how I know I'm in the Midwest, but you know how dreams are. The cops are standing outside their cars; their lights are flashing crazily, blinding me – but no sirens. All is silent, with crazy flashing lights. They've persuaded me to step out of my car. My hands are up high. The cops all have their guns leveled at me, but no one is approaching to arrest me. Are they waiting for me to do something? There's a sense that they fear me, but I have no weapon. But my anger explodes, breaking the silence. I start yelling at the cops, even though I know it will get me killed. I don't care. What I'm yelling doesn't make any sense, even if I could remember it all, and it changes each time I dream. *America.* It's always crazy non-sequitur stuff about America – a crazy distorted rant about America. Who does that sound like? Maybe in my dream I have become Pop – maybe in real life too for all I know. I understand it to be my big cinematic death-scene. I'm shouting until my throat hurts. I don't think

I'm even really angry any more. My shouts have finally provoked the cops. They begin to fire. But then the dream shifts suddenly. It becomes madcap, slapstick. The swirling siren lights become carnival-colored and I'm now in an arcade. The cops are firing paintballs at me. You know Jeff used to love paintball – I'm sure that's where that imagery must come from. Then I wake up and I don't know if my dream-self had just been laughing or screaming. So, Doctor, does that mean I'm ready to die? Not yet? Or maybe I just can't take anything seriously anymore.

In addition to this recurring dream and this cockamamie plan I'm making that might get me killed, there are so many other things that lead me to the conclusion that I'm utterly fed up with life and ready to call it quits. I have no job and lack all desire to find a new one. I have no friends and feel better off without them. I would no doubt be diagnosed with depression if I cared enough to see a shrink, but the way I see it depression isn't a disease to be cured, but an eventuality to be accepted, like death itself. If you aren't depressed at my age, then you really need to have your head examined. I no longer have an interest in anything considered new. Of course the jazz I love has always been old-school but I used to search out new old music to listen to – obscure artists on small record labels, great musicians long forgotten by the world. But now I only want to hear the tunes I've been listening to my whole life – music as nostalgia, not as adventure. Any new musician I happen to hear sounds dull and unoriginal. Nothing surprises me anymore, except perhaps the level of depravity which we've sunken to. There's simply nothing out there that interests me any longer. Forget mass media. Whenever something new comes along with revolutionary potential it is quickly commandeered by mediocrity. I'm thinking specifically about television, and now the internet, but I might as well be talking about the printing press, or the invention of writing itself. When you think about the vast innumerable quantity of sentences that have been written down through the ages, what percentage has been truly memorable and not just clichéd claptrap? And it happens with even the greatest art. Louis Armstrong comes along and starts playing these amazing solos that no one has ever heard the likes of before – and then what happens? Everybody tries to sound like Louis Armstrong! If you can't be original, then can you at least shut the fuck up? Everybody wants a bandwagon to jump on, a gravy train to ride. As a society, we are incapable of sustained greatness. We have this incredible new thing called the internet which began as a *tabla rasa* of unlimited potential for the advancement of human knowledge – only to have it quickly taken over by pornography and pop-up ads, not to mention the epidemic of viruses and hackers – so not only do we quickly succumb to baseness and greed but to actual self-destruction. We have met the enemy and it is, indeed, us. Of course, all these things I profess to hate have their exceptional qualities. Nothing is worthless. There are good shows worth watching, good websites worth bookmarking. But it's the cumulative effect of being exposed to so much garbage and having to sift through it all that is so disgusting and demoralizing. What does it say about society that anything worthwhile has to be scratched out with bloody fingers from under every rock and from within every barren crevice, like gold diggings in the desert?

So yes, Will, I have turned into an old curmudgeon – the type of person we said we would never become. Who yearns to become an isolated, bitter old man? I never thought it would happen to me. Did you, Will? We used to spend hours in the library reveling in the knowledge and entertainment it offered us – wholly unconcerned with the quality of what we were consuming or with what may have been missing from the shelves. We listened to the radio for hours on end – you and I together, not squabbling over which station to tune into or how many bad songs were being played. There were no bad songs – not because the music industry was infallible, but because we were. Infallible. Indefatigable. Indestructible. That's how I remember us.

And if I'm disgusted with my life and all its accoutrements, I'm doubly disgusted with this country. So sickened by America that reading a newspaper makes me physically nauseous. We are a nation of Neros, fiddling maniacally while everything burns to the ground. But do we fiddle because we are arrogant and vain, ignorant and apathetic, or because we have no other way to drown out all the cries filling our ears? It is this helplessness, this futility I feel that is most infuriating. We as citizens have been effectively disenfranchised because we have only oligarchs and idiots to vote for. We no longer have the energy or attention spans to mount effective resistance or protest. Why are the accomplishments of the Sixties no longer possible? The fact that that question can't even begin to be answered without paralysis and atrophy setting in is the best evidence of the futility of even trying. It's sad that there are no more Martin Luther Kings to galvanize revolution, but it's unconscionable that we no longer believe there is a need for them. The most important thing America needs to do is to apologize – apologize to most of its citizens and to most of the world; yet that is the one thing it will never do. We have behaved shamefully; yet we feel no shame. We think we are better than everyone else; we are in fact worse – and not just because of these attitudes, but because of our actions. If these were recent developments, then maybe there would be reasons to hope. But America was rotten at its core in 1776 and long before that. Rotten with racism, violence, and misogyny. Yes, these things are endemic to the species, but has there ever been a country founded in the world so perversely proud of its most shameful proclivities? Epidemics of homicide and hopelessness – that only proves we are great because we are free! All the homelessness and incarceration – that shows how hard-working and honest real Americans are! And such hypocrites, Will – my God, such appalling hypocrisy and dishonesty. If a nation is founded on principles of individual freedom and personal responsibility, civic duty, etc., then who should be rightfully blamed if it all goes to hell on a handcart? Well, certainly not ourselves. We blame foreign governments (though we've never been invaded), immigrants (though that used to be us), blacks (though we brought them here in chains), corporations (though we give them our money), elected officials (though we elect them), terrorists (though we allow them to terrorize us), demagogues (though we listen to them).

And God, Will, we're from the South! That's the icing on the cake, or maybe just the cherry on top. I'm sometimes forced to acknowledge that fact; I'll admit to it upon questioning, if my accent doesn't give me away first; but have you ever volunteered this information? Have you ever stated it plainly and proudly for the record? Well, I shouldn't speak for you; you were willing to stay here and try to make a difference. Perhaps you were proud to call this place home. As for me, I've been trying to work up the courage for a while now to pack up and move to Iceland. I kid you not. After all, aren't we all Vikings? I've done the research. I've looked into the logistics. The only thing keeping me here is inertia and fear. And Jeff. I don't know what scares me more – how much he may need me or how much I may miss him. But I've spent hours online watching Icelandic language videos and downloading free grammar guides (why pay for something if you can get it for free?). I've researched job opportunities, cost of living estimates, visa requirements. I've done everything except actually *doing* anything. I know I would be so much happier living in Reykjavik – but who wouldn't be? That's my whole point. I even find the climate agreeable, which would strike you as crazy, I know. There was nothing we liked more than South Carolina summers, right Will? Barefoot, tanned, cut-off blue jeans with white-wet strings dangling down. Shirtless all summer, even when company was over. Our hair smelled like either salt or chlorine until school started back. But how things have changed. Now the mist and chill of the Northwest match my mood much better. Let me wrap myself in overcoats to hide from the world. Let me cover my head. Put a scarf over my face. Protect me from the gaze of strangers. Please just let me disappear. So why can't I disappear to Iceland? The situation has reversed, Will. People used to come to America to disappear, and once here, kept moving further and further west into deeper wilderness or wilder desert, looking for anonymity or opportunity, just trying their luck or testing their pluck, running toward something better or away from something worse. Only the courageous came to America. For every brave pilgrim on the Mayflower there was another who chickened out and decided to hunker down in Holland. Now, the brave pioneer is the one who is *leaving* America. So, am I the brave new pilgrim willing to risk loneliness and disorientation for a new life in Iceland, or the chickenshit who prefers the evil he knows to the dangers he doesn't?

And speaking of chickenshit:

> Hold still! It only hurts for a second.
> Hold still! You're only making it worse.
> Hold still or I'll slice your durn finger off!
> We have to. If we don't it'll get infected.
> Okay, you can look now. See how little it was?

MY DEAREST CONSTANCE,

I am preparing to draw the curtains on another tedious day of trail marching, and so I wish to begin this letter by sharing with you a philosophical musing which has recurred throughout this journey, motivated by the extreme monotony to which I have been subjected on so many trains and boats over so many miles, and continuing still, relegated as I am to travelling by mule team and my own two feet. If I were delivering this to you as a sermon, my thesis would be that man's adaptability in the face of adversity – to which he owes his survival – is, paradoxically, also the primary cause of his eternal restlessness, discontent, and boredom. It is as if the very tools he needs to maintain his health and happiness are, at the same time, turned around in his hands and used as weapons against him. The example provided by my own journey shall suffice to make my point. I began this migration with such an admixture of excitement and apprehension boiling inside of me that the prospect of boredom, if it had occurred to me, would have seemed fantastical. How, I would have asked, can one suffer ennui while participating in the journey of a lifetime, with new vistas continually coming into view and new adventures in which to participate daily? Perhaps, if the above scenarios had been realized as described, then any restlessness would have been forestalled. However, that, to my chagrin, is not the case. It is difficult, if not impossible, sweetheart, to describe to you the terrestrial dimensions of this journey. The distances traversed are immense. That fact alone would not be so daunting if, indeed, new vistas were "continually coming into view;" however, the traveler discovers himself, both on rails and on rivers, awaking most mornings to the same panorama (beautiful though it may be) as he closed his eyes upon the night before.

The aspect of this circumstance that I find most interesting is the speed with which I progress from a state of eager excitement to one of restless routine. Regardless of my physical location or mode of travel, within days, or even hours, I find myself fully adapted to the necessary repetitions required of this or that portion of my journey. Normally, if finding oneself amidst such trying circumstances, on *terra incognita*, surrounded by notorious dangers as well as many unknown perils, this extraordinary talent for adaptability would be lauded as a godsend – and, indeed, every effort is put forth by anyone in such a position to adapt to his circumstances as quickly as possible. However, the thing that would possess much greater value, but quite impossible to procure, given our natures, is an ability, not to quicken, but to retard one's adaptive processes in order to enable oneself to focus fruitfully for a much longer period of time on those unique and challenging aspects of travel that make it so worthwhile – for it is always those moments that linger in one's memory and that provide joy for years to come. So, to conclude my sermonette, the great intelligence with which mankind has been endowed, which allows him to adapt almost any circumstance, not only to his immediate needs, but also to his positive advantage, is, at the same time, the cause of much inner turmoil, in the forms of restlessness, tedium, and dissatisfaction. And these, my dear, are the enemies I have found myself arrayed in battle against during these many long hot days, much more so than Indians and outlaws.

However, despite my complaints above to the contrary, there has been an interesting development occur since my previous letter to you, which I should now like to describe. There has joined our caravan a most curious and – I must add, based on what I have been told of them – perverse group of settlers. Although they were unknown to me, an imprecise knowledge of the group has preceded them along the trail, formed, as is always the case, as much by rumor and speculation as by verified facts. The group's members comprise a sect of some sort, religious in nature I was told, who speak of persecutions back East and a hope for a peaceful settlement out west. In this respect they are similar to the Mormon sect, and I would not be surprised to learn of other similarities they share with that accursed cult. However, as I suggested above, I must rather presume that their bonds are religious in nature, than state so as fact, for the reason that the one member of the group I have spoken with is silent to a curious degree as to their organization and its spiritual impulses.

It is not unusual, I have learned, to supplement the settlers already on the trail with others joining the train from the south. Omaha is not the sole "jump off" point for immigrants – nor, until rather recently, as I gathered, the primary one. There are several other towns along the Missouri River, to the south of Omaha, which serve also as starting points – in which cases, settlers move in a north-westerly direction until crossing the Platte and thus become annexed to the train moving west. I have heard that as many as fifty wagons belonging to this unusual group have joined us in the line of wagons constituting the original train.

Several such wagons entered the train a short distance in front of the wagons belonging to me and Jason. This was my first encounter with the group – and I apologize, dear, for the fact that I must continue to refer to it in such a general way, for one of its many curious attributes, apparently, is the lack of a commonly attested name or group title and a corresponding unwillingness or disinterest in establishing one. I have heard them more than once referred to as the Ignoramus Society – which word means "we do not know," and which is a legal term of art; which, I suppose, may place the group's origin within the law, and which, perhaps, the group members themselves conceived or condone, but which, in all probability, is a title bestowed by those who wish only to subject them to ridicule. (This, as an instructional aside, sweetheart, is how the names of all our native tribes have come down to us as well – as contemptuous nomenclature bestowed by their conquerors and enemies.) As a matter of principle, I shall refrain from employing any such disrespectful denomination when speaking of this group, regardless of how warranted any such ridicule may prove to be. By my estimation, they are well over one hundred in number, being thus divided into a large number of men, a smaller quantity of women (so polygamy, apparently, does not number among their vices), and a large and ungainly proportion of children. Their attire is not a distinguishing feature of their appearance; however, I could not but notice the bedraggled, impoverished appearance of their dress in general, which, I have come to realize, is rather to be expected on a journey filled with such hardships and challenges (and especially so in this case, if the tales of violence and coercion are to be believed). Each man belonging to the group seems outwardly friendly, even to the point of jocularity. In fact, they speak to everyone – strangers and fellow members alike – with familiarity and affection, which is but one of their unsettling attributes. In regards to the females I have witnessed, I must admit to you, my dear, that I fear that you would be highly uncomfortable were you to share their company but for a short period on this journey. As with the men, but much more disagreeably so, the women are jocular and frivolous to the point of impertinence. I know that you are in agreement with me (which is but one reason why you are so dear to me) that the demure sex is deemed distasteful by any tendency to flamboyancy. In regards to the children being raised in such extraordinary circumstances, they are, as you would expect, undisciplined, and, I fear, mischievous, to a frightening degree.

Two nights ago, an incident occurred, involving a few persons belonging to this new group, which illustrates quite well the boisterous nature of its members. First, however, I must explain that, in addition to the hundreds of settlers comprising our train, there are among us also a good number of traders who ride the trail looking to turn a profit by taking advantage of the improvident, short-sighted, or unfortunate folks who find themselves in need of some essential article. In addition to all manner of leather goods, ropes, pots and pans, &c., for which I am grateful that these entrepreneurs are present to supply, there is another commodity that it would be very well if they were forbidden to sale; namely, casks of spirituous liquor. A group of men from this "religious" (as I suppose I must call it) sect purchased a cask and proceeded rapidly down the road to inebriation. On this particular night, I shared the same camp with these revelers, although I had not had the pleasure of making their acquaintance before then. They were young men, some with families, which made their behavior on this occasion doubly reprehensible. They danced and sang – which, as you know, sweetheart, in the proper setting, are most wonderful pastimes; however, when performed in such an uncontrolled, drunken manner, whatever artistry may be on display becomes an offensive chore to witness. They were loud, raucous, and thoroughly displeasing. As disagreeable and immoral as this exhibition certainly was, however, it would have remained a trivial, though distasteful, matter if the revelers had not brought out their weapons and begun firing wildly into the night air. When these actions occurred, a general alarm was given throughout camp, which brought Captain Davies up quickly from the rear of the train, which is where Captain D. has stationed himself and his company of troops. To say merely that the Captain was intolerant of such behavior would do a descriptive disservice to the scene that ensued. The Captain's intolerance took the form of an axe, which he brought down several times upon the head and staves of the cask, while remaining seated on his horse, accompanied by many fine oaths which, undoubtedly, he had learned in his many years of service in the Army. The cask, mortally perforated, bled out its lifeblood of liquor, and the holy communicants shouted out their displeasure to the Captain. The Captain threatened to have them all arrested, at which time a man named Aaron, with whom I, at this time, was unacquainted, but would soon have the pleasure of meeting, stepped into the fray to serve as mediator. I was impressed with the Captain's decisiveness of action and his determination to deliver a serious rebuke to these licentious ruffians, regardless of their drunken claims of religious persecution at his hands. The Captain has been charged with protecting the lives and property of every person constituting this train, and I am pleased that he undertakes this duty with enthusiasm and seriousness.

As I just mentioned above, the first individual belonging to this group with whom I have made more than a passing acquaintance is named Aaron (a name, of course, bearing a Biblical significance, and which, upon first hearing, gave to me an ironical pleasure occasioned by the recollection that my previous interlocutor of many pleasant hours on board the steamer these several days past bore the forename of Moses – a coincidence made more curious by the fact that in this present case, the younger brother, biblically speaking, would, in my estimation, be approximately fifty years the elder). Our conversation occurred the following day, which was yesterday, after we had made our mid-morning encampment. My first inquiry came quickly upon the heels of the disclosure of his forename. "It is a pleasure to make your acquaintance," I said to him, "and how should you be more formally addressed, should the need arise?"

"'Aaron' will be adequate, whatever the circumstances," was his response. I'm certain the facial expression I exhibited to him was the cause of his short laugh which followed, and which no doubt prompted a further explanation on his part. "We have no need for surnames – at least not at the present time. Perhaps in future years, after many fruitful generations, we will begin to suffer the confusion that results from redundancy – caused either by a surfeit of overly popular names or by a dearth of creativity within the community." A. smiled and laughed heartily.

"To which community are you referring?" I asked. A. again smiled, and his reply first betrayed the reticence of the group, to which I have referred, to expound on its nature, beliefs and purposes.

"We are a community of free thinkers," was all he offered in response, but having heard of the group's travails on their coerced migration, I find it easy to forgive his reluctance to disclose unnecessary information about himself and his fellow acolytes; perhaps he will become more forthcoming in any subsequent conversations we share, as it will become apparent to him, I'm certain, that I mean neither him nor his associates any harm.

It would give me no pleasure whatsoever – in fact, it would cause me great distress – to describe the gruesome details to you, my innocent darling, of any of the brutal acts of violence and injustice rumored to have been perpetrated against this group to which A. belongs. For that reason I will not do so. History is replete with persecutions, pogroms and massacres – it is a great shame upon our nation that, with a constitution containing a set of enlightened ideals that make the remainder of the world envious of our citizenry, we have been unable to resist the pull of barbarity upon our souls. But perhaps it is inevitable, for whatever philosophies we espouse and ideals we aspire to, they are merely words written on parchment or given utterance in pretty speeches, insofar as they mostly remain absent from the actions of every man. So should we, as Americans, be expected to overcome the great temptations to treachery and all the powerful motivations for selfish gain – the actions upon which have defined our wretched species from the *Book of Genesis* forward? Perhaps the founding fathers of our country put too much stock in their pretty words concerning equality of creation, the rights of man, &c. Perhaps it is too much to expect a citizenry comprised entirely of immigrants from the *old* countries to be successful in forging something *new*. But forgive my ramblings, darling – they are merely the thoughts of a man with too much time on his hands on a desolate frontier, who is without his most beloved one, and who has too recently been the auditor of these horrific stories.

I inquired of A. the particular doctrines, beliefs or practices of his group that others with which they had come into contact found so objectionable or heretical that they were provoked to violence. His unusual good nature – which, I must point out, strikes me as quite astonishing and almost insupportable, considering the events of his most recent past – failed him upon my question, for I am afraid I offended him mightily. "We have *provoked* no one, sir," he responded gruffly.

"I do apologize," I said, "for a thoughtless choice of words." But I was intensely curious, and so I was unwilling to drop the subject without a further attempt at extracting an answer from A. "I did not mean to imply that these barbarous acts against you and your group were in any way justified. I merely should have asked, rather, what parts of your philosophy these people in Ohio objected to."

"I cannot say," A. answered. This response, obviously, was unsatisfactory, but I rather deemed it wiser to forego further questioning, than risk any possible wrath from a man whose motives, mental temperament and past actions remain a complete mystery to me. We continued our conversation, but in a more predictable fashion, complaining at length of the muddy trail, swollen creeks, and the likelihood of more rainfall in the days ahead. I hope soon to engage A. in further conversation concerning this strange band of pilgrims of which he is a part, and of which he appears to be one of its leaders and one of its more docile and respectful members.

DEBBIE – HEART OF MY HEART,

I hope your lonely drive back to the upstate wasn't too long and boring. I started missing you as soon as you left, sweetheart. But I must say, as much as I loved your visit, it left me frustrated in one respect (well, in two respects – wink wink, nudge nudge) – I've been telling you how outrageous and racist my pop is (let's just call him *outracist*, shall we?) and then you come down to meet everyone and he transforms into some kind of man I'm utterly unfamiliar with. On the one hand, I'm relieved that he decided to be on his best behavior for once, but then you tell me that maybe I'm too hard on him because he seems to be such a nice guy. I'm sure it won't be long until you see the real Dr. Kinninger, but patience is not one of my virtues.

I know I talk a lot about Jerome, from my Texas days, but have I told you how I used to surreptitiously tape-record our conversations (i.e., our arguments; i.e., his lectures)? I became quite the undercover operative. It all started innocently enough – accidentally, in fact – but I now have a large collection of the Jeremiads of Jerome on tape. Well, after you left, my dear, I decided to pull out my old bag of tricks and capture Pop in his natural habitat. I was hoping to make a copy of the tape and send it to you, but having the recorder on my lap under the kitchen table resulted in some seriously wreaked havoc regarding the audio quality. But it was certainly worth my time to make a transcription for you. I think this will put an end to any misconceptions you have about that sweet, harmless man.

I think the only thing I need to add as a commentary to the contents of the tape is this: the man was not a history major. And as a commentator on modern society, he is a fine gynecologist. My job was made easier by the fact that after supper Pop likes to imbibe a snifter or two of whiskey, which helps to loosen his tongue a bit more than usual, but it certainly doesn't change the tenor of his remarks. This is in no way a drunken rant – a rant, yes, but a fairly sober one. All I have to do to get him started is to tell him something Jerome said. If he and Jerome ever meet it will be like some apocalyptic death-match – the irresistible racist meets the immovable Mandingo. I was worried my tape would run out before I could get Pop wound up, but it wasn't too long before he launched into his favorite diatribe – his *I Don't Blame The Niggro* speech, in which he proceeds to blame the black man for everything. So, with no further ado, I give you Pop Kinninger, in all his revanchist glory:

"I don't blame the niggro. They never should have been brought over here to begin with. The slave trade was an abysmal, abominable thing, rightly condemned. How much should we really expect out of a race that has been held in captivity for ages and eons? I feel sorry for them. They had centuries of slavery to overcome. But they don't want to move on. They just want to continue to blame us for all their problems so they don't have to take any responsibility for themselves. That is your friend Jerome. And now they want reparations! Can you believe that? Is there a statute of limitations on *anything*? 'Yes, your great-great-great-great grandpappy was a slave, so here's a million dollars of the white man's money. Go knock yourself out!' They just keep asking for more more more. It's disgusting. When is it going to end? Well, I can tell you when it's going to end. In a few generations we'll be so outnumbered that if they still want reparations they'll just be paying it to themselves! At that point, they'll finally shut up about reparations. If it's not the white man's money, then they don't want it. Why don't we demand reparations for the Civil War? Why don't we go to Reagan and say, 'our ancestors lost everything because of the federal government's illegal invasion of our state. We deserve restitution!' But no, we're not going to do that, even though we could. We understand how ridiculous and shiftless it would be. But the invasion by the North was completely unconstitutional. What do you think would happen now if some state decided to secede? Do you know what would happen? Nothing! If those phony liberals up in Minnesota finally admitted how much they hate this country and said they would rather be Canadians, what would Reagan do about it? Carpet-bomb Minneapolis? Wipe St. Paul off the map? Of course not. It was okay for Sherman to destroy South Carolina, but they wouldn't touch Minnesota now. Canada would have itself another province. And they could go ahead and take a few more of those states up there while they're at it."

Pop chortled and took another sip of his whiskey. But he wasn't finished. Oh no, he was just getting warmed up. "But what's worse than being blamed for everything today is how our ancestors are despised for just trying to make a living within the system they were raised in, the only way of life they knew and the only system that worked for them economically. And not just by the niggro – I understand why the niggro might hold a grudge for two hundred years, but all these phony white liberals – to be turned on by your own kith and kin like that is unforgivable. I don't understand that. Why do you do that?" He didn't wait for me to answer – he's not interested in my opinion. But my answer would have been, of course, *because slavery was our fault! I blame the white man because it was his fucking fault!* But Pop would have had an answer for that – he has an answer for everything. Read on: "Do you know why I call them phony liberals? Because they think they're so much better than everybody else and can therefore stand in judgment. But their so-called liberalism is really just a horrendous form of misanthropy – condemning whole generations of the past for not wanting to reject their inherited culture. For accepting and appreciating the laws and traditions of their forebears. How liberal is that? Is that a liberal, tolerant attitude – to hate entire generations of hard-working people just for being who they were? For not being good twentieth-century role models? What are we going to be condemned for in the future? What are the liberals of the future going to use as a reason to hate every single one of us? What is it about our labor system now that will make them hate you, Josh? Maybe it's all the pollution we cause. Is that morally defensible – to allow these big industries to pollute the air and make people sick? To destroy the planet just to turn a profit? What are we, as regular twentieth-century working stiffs, supposed to do about that? 'I refuse to work within such a morally reprehensible system!' Nobody should expect anyone to say that, or to give up their best means of making a living. What are you going to say to Joe Blow down the street who has to feed his family and pay off his mortgage? 'You're killing the earth, man! What's wrong with you! You horrible, despicable person you!' And what about the owner of the factory, who is actually responsible for all the pollution? What is he supposed to do? 'Well, I don't want to hurt the poor planet, so I'm going to shut down all my factories and put a million people out of work. They can fend for themselves.' Is that really what you want them to do? No matter what era of human history you live in, you're going to be part and parcel of some kind of corrupt system. That's just the way it is. And maybe a revolution comes along and changes the system, but then what happens? How long do you think it took for the corrupt system of slavery to be turned into the corrupt system of industrialization, with little kids being forced to work in the coal mines all day? Not long, that's for sure. It's simply unfair to judge one era by the standards of another. Let me ask you this. How do you think we'll look to the niggroes two hundred years from now? 'Oh my God, those white people in the 1980s treated black people terrible!' Not that we do – that's not what I'm saying. We treat niggroes so much better now than we used to, but are they going to appreciate that a century from now? Do they even appreciate it now? They'll just continue to find more ways to hate white people and blame us for everything, and then two hundred years from now when there's a black president and they outnumber us two to one they'll look back on all of us – you and me both – they'll say the same exact thing about both of us, even though you think you're so different from me. Today they look back and all they see are despicable slaveowners, each and every one of us, even though most whites couldn't afford to buy a slave even if they wanted to– and so they'll look back at you and me two hundred years from now and say, 'those white men were abominable!' and you'll look down from Heaven and say, 'that's not fair – it's not fair to judge me by your standards! I wasn't a bad person! I did the best I could! I used to argue with my Pop all the time about race! I loved black people! All my friends were black people!' So, you won't like being judged by niggroes in the future. But you will be, whether you like it or not. And that's why it's so important for us to be proud of our heritage and to protect it. We need to protect it any way we can."

I know all this sounds disgusting – and it is – but I'm just so used to it that it doesn't even register anymore. I've heard this same bullshit my whole life, so I just tune it out. Do you want to hear more? Pop wasn't finished – not by a long shot. He's never finished. He has an endless supply of stupidity. Martin Luther King has his *I Have a Dream* speech. Pop has his *I Have Shit for Brains* speech. What is it about our culture here, or maybe it's our educational system, that makes even really smart people so full of shit? It's not enough to be well educated. My pop is a doctor. But in this country even a PhD is no defense against imbecility.

At this point, still working his whiskey pretty good, Pop launched into another rendition of his ever-popular *Slaves Never Had It So Good* thesis, which, like all of Pop's exigeses, begins with the disingenuous disclaimer universal to racists:

"Am I saying slavery was a good thing? No, I'm not. Am I saying we should still have slavery in this country? Of course not." But then he got down to brass tacks: "But what I am saying is, if you make an honest assessment today of the state of black culture, of black society in general, of the hardships they endure on a daily basis, at the job market for niggroes, at the impoverishment they deal with, were they really worse off under slavery? Most of them were much worse off as sharecroppers than they ever were under slavery – in terms of material comfort, in terms of debt, in terms of cultural cohesion. Nobody wants to be a slave. Everybody cherishes their freedom. I understand that. But everybody's a slave to a great extent. Very few people – if any – have complete freedom of choice. I certainly don't. I have so many regulations, federal and state, that I have to follow, it's ridiculous. And of course all this regulation drives up my prices. I'm not trying to say I'm a slave, but the point is I can't simply do as I please. I can't make my own rules, as much as I might want to. I have a dozen little niggro girls come in every month asking for abortions. What am I supposed to do? I give it to them. I have to – it's the law. Of course, they're going to go right back out and get knocked up again – it's just an endless cycle, and it makes me sick. And of course for every abortion I do there are God knows how many more little pickaninnies out there who don't have a mama or daddy worth a pinch of salt to care for it. But what am I supposed to do about that?" Here Pop tipped his head back and emptied his snifter with an unusually long sigh. Just catching his breath, that's all. He went over to our bar for a refill. "And of course the wage earner is a slave to his boss. Sure, he has the freedom to quit his job if he wants to and to look elsewhere, but how often is that to his advantage? Most people scratch and claw to hold on to the jobs they have. Back in the day, the factory owners took care of their employees – they built them houses to live in – nothing fancy but a nice little house, and they took care of them even after they retired. And the people appreciated that. And that was exactly the system that existed under slavery. Everybody is all nostalgic about the good old days when employers took care of their employees from the cradle to the grave. So how is that any different from slavery? Slaves were fed, clothed, given housing from the day they were born to the day they died. Factory owners and foremen demanded that you work hard. And if you didn't, then there was always someone right behind you looking for a job who would. The hours were long. The work was drudgery. The machinery was dangerous. And they could fire you whenever they damn well felt like it. And those are considered the good old days! And they were, compared to all the job insecurity you have today. People talk about how unconscionable it was that families were split apart and sold down the river. I'm sure it was, but today families do that to themselves *voluntarily*! Both parents working long hours every day, week-long business trips, some fathers choosing to live away from home just to make a few extra bucks. Kids growing up barely knowing who their parents are. The only difference between workers today and slaves is that we have our so-called freedom. But come on! Get serious! Freedom is just a word – a concept that has little or no meaning in the real world of capitalism. Never did. Never will. We're talking theory as opposed to reality. In theory, emancipation was a great thing – let's give everybody their freedom! In reality, it created more problems than it solved – and for the niggroes too, not just for the whites. And yeah, of course – slaves were sometimes abused and beaten. They were treated inhumanely. But the working man has always been abused. Look at how workers are treated now. What about the worker who is fired for no good reason? Or who is coerced into joining a union or voting a certain way? Or who gets his arm hacked off because of unsafe machinery or irresponsible oversight? Do we dismantle the whole system? Do we say, 'Okay men – Georgie came to work drunk and got his arm caught in the turbine – factory's shut down for good! You need to find another way of life!' You punish the bad guys, that's what you do. You get rid of the bad eggs. You fix the problems. You make improvements to the system. Whatever that system happens to be. I give Gorbachev a lot of credit. He sees that communism isn't working and he's trying to change the system, from within – without starting another damn revolution where a million people get killed. That's what should have happened with slavery. Slavery was a system of *economics*. It was not about racism, *per se*. It was based purely on the economics of the plantation system. With the price of cotton what it usually was on the world market, plantations simply couldn't *afford* to hire laborers. And it was on its way out anyway. Not because of abolitionists or Yankee agitators or political pressure – but because of economics. The Industrial Revolution was on its way. Machinery would have replaced slaves soon enough. The plantation owners would not have tried to keep an antiquated, obsolete system in place *just for the hell of it*! They were businessmen. But instead, we got the Civil War, and half the damn men in the South were butchered for no good reason, except to appease the Northern liberals so they could feel good about themselves. Abraham Lincoln was *not* a great president, I don't care what the history books say. And it's a damn shame that we teach that to kids in school – that Lincoln is like a god, and we have to worship him. The Civil War was a tragedy, pure and simple, and it happened on his watch, and it could have been avoided – it *should* have been avoided – with a more capable leader in charge."

I had heard enough and I tried to hit stop on my tape recorder without Pop hearing it, but the damn thing is so loud. Pop was apoplectic (a-Pop-lectic, you could say) when he heard it and realized I had taped him. My God, you would think he was afraid the tape was going to be used against him at a trial or something. "You had no right to do that!" he yelled. He demanded I give the tape to him. "Why? Are you ashamed of something you said?" "Give me the goddam tape!" Wow – that meant he was serious, if he invoked the deity. He lunged for the tape recorder, but I stood up, yanked the plug out of the wall and retreated to my room, where I have spent the last hour writing this letter.

I will leave you with something funny that will hopefully wash the bad taste out of your mouth I'm sure you have right now, caused by my pop's bile. I've been reading about the Yemassee War, which was a bit of unpleasantness here in

Charleston back in the early 1700s. No need to go into the details – war is all hell and this one was no exception. But I ran across a name again today, associated with that war, that is – as you will see shortly – simply delicious. This name never failed to crack me up as a kid, and today when I saw it in print I'm happy to report that it had lost none of its power of hilarity. Now, South Carolina has had its fair share of great military leaders – Francis Marion, Wade Hampton, William Westmoreland. But allow me now to introduce you to another (drum roll, please!) – Colonel George Chicken! Colonel Chicken, as leader of the Goose Creek militia, was undoubtedly a very brave man, despite his last name. And his home is still a historical fixture down on Tradd Street. It's called, but of course, The Chicken House. I have come to the conclusion this afternoon that *chicken* is simply the funniest goddam word in the English language. I don't know how to account for that. Two simple syllables, neither of which is particularly humorous on its own. "Chick" is kind of cute – but not really funny. "En" is not even worth noticing. But put those two together – hilarious! It's like a linguistic version of H_2O – two extremely common elements, gases by themselves, transformed magically into the liquid of life. Here's a fun little game you can play to keep yourself happy until we see each other again:

Take a famous American quotation and substitute *chicken* at any salient point within it. For example: I pledge allegiance to the chicken; four score and seven chickens ago; I regret I have but one chicken to lose for my country; we hold these chickens to be self-evident; Give me chickens or give me death! (Or, if you prefer, Give me liberty or give me chickens!) It works every time. Guaranteed.

ALONG WITH SALGARD, EINAR, AND THORBJORN, only two other Greenlanders survived the spears of the Bluemen. They were adopted into the village and treated well. They quickly learned to speak the language of the Bluemen. The Bluemen spent much of their time in warfare with other groups who lived inland from the sea, and the Greenlanders participated in these battles. They were treated as Bluemen in every respect but one – they were not allowed to marry females belonging to their village. To compensate for this restriction, they were allowed to choose among the many women captured as slaves. It happened that one particularly beautiful woman was captured during the Bluemen's warfare and, since Einar had been the leader of the Greenlanders and had proved to be a fearless fighter, the king offered this woman to him. Einar was happy to accept her as his wife. Her people were from the lands surrounding the Great Mountain and she spoke a language similar to the new language Einar had learned from the Bluemen. "What is your name?" Einar asked.

"My mother called me Flower."

"I could not conceive of a better name for you. My desire is to make you happy. What can I give you today that will make you happy?"

"The only thing that will make me happy is my freedom."

"That is something I am not willing to give to you, but I'm sure there is something else that will put a smile on your face."

"If you will not give me freedom, will you remove this hindrance from my face? The women from the Great Mountain do not obstruct their mouths, and its weight is causing me great pain."

"You will adjust to your new circumstances, as I have adjusted to mine. The plate will not be painful after several days. I would fear for your safety if you refused to obey your captors. Your patience will be rewarded."

"I believe I have received the only reward I can expect – you did not kill me as you attacked my village, though you killed my father and my mother. Do you expect to receive my gratitude?"

"It remains to be seen if one day I may earn your gratitude. I promise to treat you with the honor that your beauty deserves."

It happened that on the same day that Flower was brought captive into the village and given to Einar as a bride, Thorbjorn saw her as well. Although her face had been disfigured by the heavy plate forced into place through her nose, and was begrimed with mud and wore as well the blood of her murdered parents, Thorbjorn felt as if all his humiliation and unhappiness would disappear forever if he could but claim her as his own. For the first time since his brother's death, he felt the glory of poetry welling up inside of him. He said to no one but himself:

> Copper-colored beauty,
> Bound by the fate we share.
> You, by me, are set free.
> I, by you, am ensnared.

Thorbjorn was incensed to learn later that the king had given Flower to Einar.

> Pig-hearted son of swine!
> Put me to death by halves!
> Kill Gudmund to begin,
> Take Flower to finish!

Since the Bluemen of the village had no respect for Thorbjorn or his fighting abilities, they did not insist that he assist them in their warfare. He fought with them in their battles in hopes of reducing the shame he felt, but his ineptitude with weapons did nothing to increase their respect. He did not lack courage, however, and until he saw Flower, he cared not whether he lived or died on the battlefield. He dreamed of Iceland and his mother; he dreamed of Greenland and his brother, knowing, however, that he would never see either again.

> Stranded on the far side
> Of the far side of Earth,
> Hate and shame fill my heart.
> Only Flower gives hope.

He spoke to Flower as often as he could, but always in the presence of Einar, for Einar would not allow anyone to speak to Flower in his absence. As the men of the village prepared to march off to fight another battle, Thorbjorn feigned sickness and remained behind. With Einar gone to battle, Thorbjorn approached Flower. She said, "Are you not ashamed that all the men are fighting today for glory, while you shuffle and cough and pretend to be ill?"

"Yes, Flower, I am ashamed of my actions, yet they have allowed me to speak with you."

"What do you have to say to me that you cannot say in front of Einar?"

"What would be my fate if I recited thus within Einar's hearing?" Thorbjorn dropped to one knee and said:

> Dear one, you are Flower,
> Yet 'tis my heart that blooms.
> Your tears are the water
> That feeds my love for you.

Flower responded, "Those are pretty words, Thorbjorn, but men's words cannot always be trusted."

"My words are unlike those of any other. They may always be trusted to tell the truth."

"That remains to be seen. It may not be my tears that feed your love for me, but your hatred of Einar. He has told me that you accused him of killing your brother, which he denies."

"As you say, dear Flower, men's words cannot be trusted. But I fell in love with you before I learned of his receipt of such a precious gift, though I will admit that it has not lessened my hatred of him. Does he treat you well?"

"Einar treats me as well as I expect to be treated by a man."

"He treats you as a captive. I will set you free."

"Do you have a plan to do so?"

"The men are all absent. Our feet are the only plan we need. How far are your people?"

"They surround the Great Mountain."

"I will take you to them. Will they accept me as one of their own? I promise to fight with them in all their battles."

"You would receive great honors if you were responsible for my return."

"The only honor I would request of them would be the honor of receiving your love and gratitude. I have received nothing but humiliation from the Bluemen. I owe them nothing but my scorn. I will be responsible for your freedom; but you will be responsible for mine as well."

"I am tempted by your offer of freedom, Thorbjorn, but I must refuse it. Einar and the rest of the men will come for me, and to punish me they will visit war again on my people. I cannot be responsible for the deaths of more of my kinsmen. There are not so many of them left."

"Let them come. We will be ready for them. We shall inflict more death than we will suffer."

"It is easy for you to make that decision, Thorbjorn, but more difficult for me."

"You must not remain here, Flower. It is intolerable that you are kept here as a slave."

"I have learned to tolerate it as best I can. It is not *my* condition that is intolerable to you – it is yours. I believe I was correct about you, Thorbjorn, yet wrong as well. It is not your love for me that leads you to do this, nor is it jealousy. It is your shame."

"You speak as if you know me well, yet before I spoke to you today all you knew of my life were the lies told to you by Einar. I will not allow your fear of him to keep you in captivity any more than I will allow the Bluemen's ropes to. I love you, my sweet Flower, and I cannot bear the thought of being without you one moment longer. By nightfall we shall be together among your people, safe and free forever."

"I will not go with you, Thorbjorn. That is my decision."

"It is the wrong decision, and I will not allow it. There is nothing keeping you here but fear, and there is nothing here for us but humiliation and servitude. We must leave now." Thorbjorn grasped Flower's arm tightly and ran with her into the woods surrounding the village. He ran with her toward the Great Mountain. He did not allow Flower's tears for her people to slow their progress.

Thorbjorn and Flower safely reached the village of her people in the shadow of the Great Mountain. As she predicted,

Thorbjorn had great honor bestowed on him for the return of Flower. His white skin was a wonder to them and they asked if he were a god. "No," Flower answered, "he is a man like all of you, though a lesser one, and undeserving of the honor you are heaping upon him. He is neither brave, nor wise, but I do not wish to see him harmed. Though I longed to see my village again, he has brought me here against my wishes, for I did not wish my people to suffer the vengeance that is meant for me. You must prepare now for war."

"We are happy for your return," spoke the village king, "and grateful to your strange, white friend for having the wisdom to ignore your wishes and to return you to us. We do not fear war, and welcome it as an opportunity to wreak vengeance on your captors and the murderers of so many of our people. It will be an honor to defend the safety of our little Flower."

Meanwhile, Einar and all the Bluemen warriors had returned to their village. They had marched for many days and had fought many night-time battles. Einar was looking forward to rest, but when he discovered that Flower had escaped with Thorbjorn he announced to the king that a new war party must be assembled immediately. "We shall rest first," the king said. "You shall have your vengeance in due time, but I will not allow that little hermaphrodite and a slave girl to be the cause of my men marching themselves to death."

After several days of rest, the king gave Einar permission to select warriors to accompany him to the Great Mountain. They marched all day, but waited until night to attack, as was their custom. They freshly applied their dark blue pigment, surrounded Flower's village, made their horrifying noises, and charged the village so that it appeared to be overrun by ghosts with dancing eyes. The villagers were prepared for Einar's attack, however, and fought with all the fury that justice imbued them with.

As soon as the loud howling had begun, Thorbjorn said to Flower, "Let us go before it is too late. We will escape to the mountain. Einar will not know to look for us there."

Flower screamed at him, "You are shameful! Do you not remember the promise you made to me? To fight beside my people against Einar?"

"Yes, my actions are shameful, but they will also save your life. We have nothing to gain by fighting Einar. I am no warrior. He will kill me and take you back into bondage, that is, if he chooses to spare your life."

"You have brought all of this down upon us, Thorbjorn. Are you happy with this result? I will not flee with you. I am not afraid to die beside my kinsmen."

The battle, however, did not go as Einar had planned or as Thorbjorn had feared. Flower's people won a great victory. Some of them suffered death, but Einar's men retreated into the forest as it became clear that many more of them were dying. "This battle has not gone well," Einar said to his men. "The king will not approve of so many of his men being sacrificed for this cause. And to make matters worse, the subjects of our mission are still unaccounted for. I order all of you to return to our village and to tell the king that we have taken revenge on the slave girl's people, but that the result of the battle wasn't all that I had hoped. Tell him that I will not return until Thorbjorn is dead and the slave is recaptured. How dare that wretched little coward think that he deserves to have such beauty in his possession!"

Einar remained hidden in the forest as Flower's people honored their dead and repaired their damaged dwellings. Thorbjorn said to Flower, "Einar is not among the dead Bluemen. I don't believe he will be satisfied with how this battle concluded. He will not be happy until we are dead."

"I doubt if that was one of your considerations before you forced me to run away with you."

"That doesn't matter. It only matters that we are together. We will deal with Einar when the time comes. For now, let us enjoy our life together among your people."

"It will be difficult for me to be happy knowing that Einar is busy planning the slaughter of my kinsmen. All you are concerned with is your own happiness."

"All I am concerned with is your happiness. You may think of me what you wish."

"As you say, Thorbjorn. What I wish presently is to view the world from atop the Great Mountain. I have spent my happiest days looking down from beneath its snow-covered trees. I thought often of those views as I endured my captivity. It will bring joy to my heart to walk those hills once again."

"We will be safer if we remain here, surrounded by your kinsmen. We don't know where Einar is lurking."

"You speak brave words, Thorbjorn, until danger presents itself – then you speak quite differently. I do not need you to accompany me. Solitude is a great pleasure where I am going."

"Very well, then. I will not have you calling me a coward. I will defend your life until my death. We will ascend the Great Mountain together. I'm looking forward to sharing those views that you so treasure – views, by the way, that, were it not for me, you never would have seen again."

"That is true, and also, were it not for you, my brave cousins whom we honored today would still be alive – but I do not wish to speak of it on our climb."

Thorbjorn and Flower began their ascent up the Great Mountain. Thorbjorn carried a spear, which he used to help maintain his balance along the steep hills. As they climbed, Flower spoke of Einar: "Einar is a very sad man. He once pointed to the Great Mountain and said to me, 'If I scaled the Great Mountain, but told no one of my deed, then that accomplishment would make me very proud, but it would not make me great. It would bring me great pleasure, but it would not bring me glory. Glory is the only thing worth striving for.' And that is what makes him very sad. You have come here from the other side of the world. His courage allowed him to accomplish a great thing, yet he will never know greatness."

"Einar is a vain man. He speaks of his courage and accomplishments, yet every man aboard his ship needed courage to survive what we were forced to endure. And he would have accomplished nothing but an ignoble death among icebergs had it not been for the strength of his crew. You would be wiser if you had given your ear to my words more often than to his. He does not love you. He only wishes to possess you as a prize."

"That is true, Thorbjorn. And why do you wish to possess

me?"

"I only wish to protect you. One day you will understand that."

"We are still strangers to one another, yet I know you better than you know yourself. And that is your great sadness."

"And you may not be as wise as you consider yourself to be. None of this idle chatter is important, especially when it prevents us from appreciating what is laid out before us. We have hardly begun our climb and I am already amazed by everything I am seeing. I have never seen such beauty before that is made only of rivers, lakes, and trees. My mother used to speak of the beauty of a land we called Norway, but I was never lucky enough to see it. Perhaps it was as beautiful as this. I understand now your desire to return here."

"Yes. I am happy there is one thing we can agree upon. If what is before my eyes now is the last thing I ever see, then I will not complain of my fate."

Einar had been watching the village carefully from the forest, but it occurred to him that it would be better for him if he could view it from a higher vantage point. He decided to walk around to the other side of the village and then began climbing the Great Mountain. Soon he heard familiar voices and shortly thereafter he saw Flower and Thorbjorn. He listened to their conversation long enough to hear himself insulted by Thorbjorn and said to himself, "That is the last insult I will have to endure from either of those troublesome twins." Thorbjorn and Flower continued their climb and walked out of range of Einar's hearing. He moved closer to them and as they stopped to admire their view of the village and of the water and forest surrounding it, he charged toward them with his spear held firmly in front of him. Thorbjorn heard Einar's footsteps and, panicked, he hurled his spear wildly toward Einar as he grabbed Flower's arm and turned to run. He heard Einar grunt and turned to see him fall to the ground.

Einar looked down at his bleeding wound and the spear which had pierced his body through his belly. He looked up and said, "I thought your luck had finally run out, Thorbjorn, but it appears I am mistaken."

Einar looked at Flower and rose to his knees. "I will die soon. Flower, will you come close enough for me to tell you something? It is difficult for me to speak." Flower cautiously approached and leaned down to Einar's face. He reached to the ground, picked up his fallen spear, and ran it through her chest.

Thorbjorn ran forward and caught her as she fell. "Oh!" he sobbed. "Oh, my beautiful flower! The most beautiful of flowers! Can you still hear me?"

"Yes."

"I loved you from the moment I saw you. You will be the only woman I will ever love. Do you hear me?"

"Yes, I can hear you, Thorbjorn. I enjoyed our climb together today." Flower lifted her head to look at Einar. "I should not be surprised that you did this, Einar, but I thought you may have loved me enough to let me live. Why do men feel such a need to kill?"

Einar tried to laugh through his pain and said, "That is a question only a woman would ask. Look at Thorbjorn. He's not much of a man, certainly, but there are no questions on his face. He would have done the same as I, before he allowed you to be taken away from him. I would have preferred a more pleasant farewell to you, but I don't want his lies to be the last words that you hear."

As Thorbjorn held her tightly to him, Flower said, "I am happy to remain here forever." She closed her eyes and was dead.

Einar shifted his weight on the ground and pulled at the spear that had pierced him, but was unable to remove it. "Thorbjorn, I realize I am in no position to strike a bargain with you, but my life is lingering longer than I would wish. The only thing I ask is that you remove your spear so that I might die more quickly. Or, if you prefer, you may remove the spear and then thrust it again a bit higher, through my heart. You did not take sufficient aim the first time."

Thorbjorn caressed Flower's face and said nothing in response to Einar.

"I murdered your brother, Thorbjorn. There is no reason now to keep that from you."

Thorbjorn looked up from Flower. "And you hope that I will kill you immediately now in response to that admission? My belief in your guilt was much stronger when you insisted on your innocence. As usual, I have reason to doubt you are being truthful. Be that as it may, you will die soon enough without my assistance."

"Can you find in your cold heart at least a promise to bury my corpse? I deserve to be more than mere carrion. If you promise me a proper burial then that will make me a happy man."

"I would rather make the ravens happy."

Thorbjorn lifted Flower and carried her back to her village.

He joined her kinsmen in mourning her and was allowed to live with honor among them. He eventually married another young woman from Flower's village and they raised a large family together. Although he cared deeply for his wife, he thought often of Flower and loved nothing more than taking long walks upon the hills of the Great Mountain and enjoying the same views that Flower had loved. It happened that one day, as Thorbjorn was growing old and unsure of his step, he slipped on the ice that seemed to form on the Great Mountain earlier and closer to the village with each passing year. The adults in the village spoke of the severity of winters now compared to when they were children. As he slipped, Thorbjorn was unable to regain his balance and he took a severe fall down the mountainside. He tried to stand, but his leg was badly broken. He called out for help, but no one was near him to hear. All he heard was the wind whistling sharply and birds chirping in the branches above him. It began to snow and Thorbjorn understood that he would soon freeze to death. As the cold reached ever closer to his bones, he remembered his mother's smile and the playful toy-sword fights between him and Gudmund; he contemplated the strange life he had lived and everything he had seen and done and felt a great calm come over him. He composed one final poem, which he uttered as loudly as his fading strength would allow:

My words upon the wind,

Heard only by snow birds.
Never has poet's song
Passed my ears so sweetly.

He thought of Flower for the final time and whispered, "I am happy to remain here forever."

W,

I have sad news to report – sad for me, at least. Do you remember my best friend Larry in high school? He came over all the time, you should probably remember him. I just found out he died last year. I tried to track him down online last night but discovered his cancer-riddled corpse instead. This is depressing in the extreme. But it does confirm my faith in my own incredible good luck. I firmly believe that as my old friends start dropping like flies I will remain the last one standing.

I gave him the honorable nickname of Cantilever Larry. Larry came up with a name for me, too. He started calling me Webster, in tribute to the famous grammarian because, as Larry famously stated, I was a "walking fucking dictionary." Let me tell you one of the many stories involving me and Larry. I'm sure I never told you about this when it happened, not because I didn't want to share this adventure with you, but because I didn't trust you to keep your middle-school trap shut. I told this story to Deb last night and her only response was, "I'm glad I was never a teenager." Some parents let their kids skip a grade or two in school – I think Deb was allowed to skip over adolescence.

So, in high school, I called my little coterie of misfits the Gang of Four. And I must say, for a group of desperately heterosexual teenagers we certainly had quite a penchant for phallic symbolism – which is not unusual, of course, given all the exhibits throughout history of cock-and-ball art, from Pompeii to the Sistene Chapel. When sitting in class bored, there are those whose artistic inclinations lean toward doodles of labia and the concentric-circled geometry of breasts, and then there are those, like our present heroes, whose young, largely unrequited lust is given visual expression through hard-ons. Perhaps a person's preference in this area is a manifestation of his level of sexual narcissism (present company excepted, of course) – that is, you are either a *giver* or a *taker;* sex as an opportunity to exhibit either one's power or one's generosity. Well, anyway, all this by way of introduction to one of my gang's more memorable after-midnight exploits and Cantilever Larry's one glorious shining moment.

The Gang of Four had a somewhat loose membership, with various classmates revolving in and out, based on availability and, to some extent, the whims of its leadership. I assumed the role of *de facto* leader, with Cantilever Larry serving as my lieutenant. In a discussion one night on how we could once again leave our mark on our community, the idea was floated that we should cruise the backroads stealing mailboxes. I thought this was a stupid idea. "What morons these mortals be! I disclaim all responsibility for this egregious suggestion," I distinctly remember remarking at the time in my Websterian way. What an intolerable ass! But, since many great accomplishments have begun as incredibly dumb-ass ideas (Exhibit 1 – Christopher Columbus – Hey, let's sail to Asia from Spain, going west!), I allowed the concept of mailbox skullduggery to bounce around my neurons for several days. Theft was not an option (we were rogues, not thieves), but the potentialities of defacement intrigued me. Cantilever Larry and I discussed the idea further. I suggested that we paint – you guessed it – cocks and balls onto the sides of the mailboxes. At that point no one had anything better to offer, so it appeared that my hand-painted genitalia would win the day. As the weekend approached, however, the simplicity and unoriginality of my idea began to irk me. The Gang of Four (i.e., I) could do better. But what could be improved upon – the medium or the message? After all, in how many ways can one vandalize a mailbox? Squirting Superglue up into the handles occurred to me, but I had no heart or reason for harming anyone and, besides, wouldn't the glue dry before morning, rendering the entire evening useless? Then how about gluing the doors shut? Now, there was a capital idea! I was prepared to call the

Cantilever Kid with the change of plan, but upon further consideration, I rejected this idea also – how would anyone else but the victim *know*? A good performance requires an audience. We were bored, attention-seeking males, so the notion of pulling off such a brilliant prank without the possibility of an admiring public was pointless.

When thinking about what other objects could be drawn or painted on the mailboxes, I was incapable of getting beyond penises. In terms of graffiti symbolism or iconography, I didn't see any other choice. Did I really want to waste my time driving through Goose Creek all night spraying FUCK everywhere? And I had no use for the stupidity of the swastika, and I must not have had the imagination for anything cleverer. But then Larry called me with his voice full of excitement and said, "Hey! Could we use your dad's workshop to do something?" And as he outlined his plan all I could do was kick myself for not being the one to think of it.

So, what was Larry's brilliant idea? Well, he was as hung up on hard-ons as I was, but at least his plan had some panache. And lucky for me we were latch-key kids, so we had a couple of hours of non-supervision every afternoon at home. Larry came over right after school every day and we spent three solid weeks jigsawing plywood into that all-too-familiar shape, applying streaks of paint to provide some dimensionality, blow-drying the results, and then stowing the finished products into the trunks of our cars. I remember yelling at and generally abusing you a few times when you innocently came into Pop's workshop and asked us what we were doing. But that's what you got for being my baby brother.

The conclusion of this sordid tale may be judged anticlimactic, but only by those who did not participate in it. On the appointed Friday night, the Gang of Four, in that battered LTD I had, rode around the roads and residential streets carrying out Larry's demented plan until our adrenaline began to run out, and in the early morning I dropped the guys off at their homes after leaving in our wake – yes, you guessed correctly again! – twenty-eight particle-board penises, five feet tall, some perfectly erect, some cocked at manly angles, all with attached testicles, leaning securely in front of and completely obscuring the same number of roadside mailboxes.

For the denouement I arose eagerly after only two or three hours' sleep, called the gang and arranged for us to undertake a joyous reconnaissance of our crime scenes. Such post-predation surveys are bound to be disappointing in some respects, as was this, since in the early-morning sunshine some of the figures already had been espied and removed, and with no remaining evidence visible, some considerable doubt was cast upon the accuracy of our memories: "Was this one of them? It was so dark...." But over half of the penises were still where we had placed them, the unsuspecting residents enjoying a sleep-in Saturday, but with more than enough cars passing by regularly – with their occupants undoubtedly doing double-takes and laughing or covering the eyes of their children and muttering *for shame* – to more than justify the endeavor. What a crazy fun night that was!

Cantilever Larry is dead! Long live Cantilever Larry!

4

W,

I'm still trying to figure out why I was fired. It was a JOKE, for God's bleedin' sake. And what has me most stumped is why I would be fired for a harmless joke when I have said so many purposefully incendiary things in my attempts to provoke my students into actually thinking for a change. Yes, there was a good deal of "vigorous discussion" and "healthy debate" and perhaps even a couple of "heated exchanges" when I suggested that slavery was abolished in this country a half-century too early. That was one of Pop's more interesting observations that I hauled out just for the sake of intellectual argument. But the point I wish to emphasize now is that that statement – and the ideas behind it – DID NOT GET ME FIRED. I have stood in front of classes and said – with a straight face – "the U.S. constitution isn't worth the parchment it's scribbled on." Didn't get me fired. I have proposed that the Revolutionary War started as an infantile hissy fit instigated by demagogues like Tom Paine and Patrick Henry, who were nothing but colonial versions of Rush Limbaugh, and that any reasonable person would have sided with the redcoats. And in fact, if you look at the subsequent political development of Great Britain, Canada, Australia, etc., it seems pretty clear that from a liberal, social-justice point of view, the whole American Revolution was a grievous mistake. DID NOT GET ME FIRED. I have suggested that NASA and the whole U.S. space program were actually conceived at the highest levels as a twentieth-century extension of the Manifest Destiny doctrine. New territories can only be claimed by those first setting foot on them. That's why it was so urgent that Neil Armstrong take that first small step. So when competition begins for prime galactic real estate, who do you think will claim first dibs? DIDN'T GET ME FIRED. I pointed out – from a strictly ecological viewpoint, mind you, and looking at the big picture – that we, as guardians of the planet, should be extremely grateful for World War II and for wars and genocides and pandemics in general. Didn't get me fired – though it almost did, certainly. I may have gone a bit too far with that one, so I deserved a slap on the wrist. And I joke all the time in class, as do all professors: Did you hear about the recent poll that showed that Chinese women, if given the choice, would overwhelmingly support a democratic form of government? Their reason why? Because they would be allowed to hold erections. DIDN'T GET ME FIRED.

I need you to help me understand this, Will. You were always such a serious kid. Why are people more offended by humor than by earnestness? If I tell you straight to your face, in total honesty, that you are an incorrigible asshole, I will be less likely to be punched in the nose than if I make a joke at your expense. I have a prediction to make. World War I started with an assassination. World War II started with an invasion. I predict World War III will begin with a wisecrack. People don't understand the nature of humor, and it's ruining our society because everyone is afraid to be funny. First of all, a joke cannot exist without a butt. Go ahead – try to tell one. The simplest, most innocuous and beloved joke in the world: "Take my wife – please." What an enormous insult to all womanhood! So why wasn't Henny Youngman tarred and feathered by the feminists? The reason why? Because HE DIDN'T MEAN IT!

Which brings me to my second point. People don't seem to realize what should be obvious – you don't make jokes about what you truly hate. Hitler never once began a sentence with, "Two Jews walk into a bar...." The Klan didn't laugh at the Niggroes – it killed them. Of all those signs and slogans outside of abortion clinics, or anti-gay rallies, or anti-immigration protests, how many contain a punchline? People need to understand this. Humor should not make people angry.

It's the morons without a sense of humor that are truly dangerous.

Mind you, if I had been fired for any of the bombs I threw in class I still would have been fit to be tied. But at least I could understand if one of my African-American students had demanded my head on a platter for my suggestion that perhaps his ancestors should have remained in bondage for another fifty years if it would have prevented a national bloodbath. But no, the college was okay with that. And if they are ever *not* okay with any such left-field idea being discussed openly, then at that point liberalism becomes meaningless. But I still need to understand why jokes are taken as seriously as actual serious seriousness.

It seems to have started with this generation today. Back in the Sixties they had visceral evils to confront. Vietnam draft cards. Jim Crow water hoses. Barefoot hunger in Appalachia. The evil today is actually worse because it wasn't eradicated properly in the Sixties and it's had fifty years to metastasize, to insinuate itself into the warp and woof of society, to hide in plain sight. Back then, the military-industrial complex was in its relative infancy and yet it was still impervious to any meaningful reform. Now, our economy would collapse without it. Now, the gospel of capitalism is so embedded in our national conscience that you can't even utter the word "socialism" if you have any desire to be taken seriously as a political leader. But young people want a cause to support, a crusade to march in. They want to direct their unbounded energy toward the common good. These liberal-minded, sincere, good-hearted young people want to make a difference in the world and want to correct injustices, but they are powerless, as we all are, to remedy the real wrongs, so they must invent new wrongs – or at least exaggerate their invidiousness – in order to satisfy their hunger for justice. So, helpless to affect the external moral rot of this country, they have turned inward, to become the nation's Emotion Police, forever vigilant for evil innuendos, insults and all manner of verbal transgressions. The question is, what is the proper punishment for such thought-crimes? If a man loses his livelihood, becomes professionally ostracized and ultimately unemployable, and ends up homeless on the streets, then are those his just deserts or just another variation on our national system of injustice? We don't send folks to the gulag to break rocks for saying the wrong thing about the wrong people, but if your reputation is ruined or your finances destroyed, then what's the difference?

So that is one possibility for my firing – the one I can ruminate on, rant about and formulate some sort of provisional explanation for. Then there is the other. The one that beggars (and buggers) all logic, that defies all notions of individual freedom – freedom of speech, freedom to work, freedom from prejudice and discrimination, freedom from vigilante justice, freedom from being judged according to any lights other than your personal and professional merits; that is really useless to dwell upon because, if true, then the reasons for it are obvious, and if untrue, then moot. I'm referring, of course, to the very real possibility that I was fired because of Pop. The crimes of the father revisited upon the son. The trumped-up attempt to protect the good name of a northern liberal college from being sullied by the taint of Southern crimes; to protect the rich donors from the embarrassment of having to pay a salary to someone so intimately associated with such monstrous acts, though of course innocent of any crime himself.

So I don't know, Will. I don't know what to think. Meanwhile, I get fired for telling a joke about African-Americans, a demographic group I have championed my entire professional life – and God knows you have too. But it only got me fired. It may have gotten you killed. This injustice perpetrated on both of us is driving me insane.

"I TAKE IT FOR GRANTED, Cunnel, that you have hud of the *Tennessee* and the *Mary Anne*?"

"No, I must admit that I have not."

"Well, then, that is all the evidence I would require to dettumine that you are not from Missoura. Anyone who has spent any amount of tom whatsoeva within a copple day's rod of the riva knows all about those two steamas and what transpodd between them. Now, allow me to revise that, if I may. My wuds are racing out ahead of me, Cunnel – not unlock those two stunwheelers I just made reference to. What I should have said is that there are ratha very few pussons who know actually and factually what happened out on the riva that day. There are many stories and vusions of events, but one thing is sutton – the decks of both of those steamas were filled to floodstage with pussons who had hud of the abandoned gold claim in O'gon and who were trying to imagine what that big dobble-u on the mountainsodd would look lock. And everyone that I spoke to aftawuds had a different vusion of events or at least a different culprit to point their finga at. They mott admit to one thing, or regret anotha thing, or wish they had done something else entolly, but whateva they did, the end result most assuredly wasn't their fault. Of coss, the truth of the matta was, there were so many human foibles on display, getting all tangled up and tripping ova each other, that the closest thing to a proximate cause that could be detummined would have to be that phantasmagorical dobble-u that was dancing around insodd everyone's head.

"If you talk to Clod Montgomery, he will readily admit to stotting a wager on which boat would make it to St. Joe fust, but of coss he can't be held liable for the outcome, no sir! There was so much intavening misfotchin, accodding to Clod, that his one original sin must pale in compa'ison to all the others that occurred later. My guess is that even if Clod had found that goldmonn in O'gon he would have gambled away the lonn's share of it before he crossed back over the bodda. Shottly afta the *Tennessee* had backed out into the channel, Clod was already eyeing the *Mary Anne*, which was maybe half a moll back, but appeared to be gaining rot steadily. As you mott expect on a steamboat, Clod suttonly had no trobble finding men to take pot in his little wager, and before long everybody on the dun boat knew about it. And of coss, as shaw as death leads to deliverance, there were at least a copple of men who couldn't be content with just placing a friendly bet and then setting back on the hurracun deck enjonn the breeze with their whiskey. No sir. If greed was the fust coddnal sin committed on bodd that boat, then not knowing when to *leave well enough alone* was suttonly the next.

"Now lock I said, this was all a puffectly innocuous way to pass the monotony of a rivaboat junney, except for those who believed that it can't be a real wager unless there's a real *race* to place it on. And it can't be a real race unless the potties are made aware of the fact that they are in fact taking pot in one. Now, at this point, Cunnel, we enter the realm of unsuttonty, conjecture, contradiction, and, most abundantly, downrot dishonesty. And as a practicing attunney, I can tell you that I'm entolly comfortable operating within this realm of ambiguity, but I imagine to a disinterested observa such as yourseff, this will all become motty intolerable very quickly.

"So this chap called Joe Clock takes it upon hisseff to mosey on up to the pilot-house to see Hiram Mills, who was not only the pilot of the *Tennessee* but the *owna* and *builda* of the dun boat as well – he being originally from Memphis, you see. And it was my pleasure to represent Hiram as his attunney afta this unfotchinate incident and afta all the dun lawsuits began inundating the cotts. But retunning to Joe Clock, he told me motch later – afta he retunned from O'gon – empty-handed, of coss – that Hiram had immediately manifested some long-held animus toward the pilot of the *Mary Anne* and all but revussed the paddlewheel in odda to bring the *Tennessee* abreast of the *Mary Anne* and thus jonn the race. Now, Hiram, for his pot, testifodd many toms ova that he jonned the race only afta being goaded and humiliated beyond the limits of what any man should be expected to tolerate – which was apparently corroborated by the others in the pilot-house at the tom. I say *apparently* only because Joe Clock swears up and down that the pilot's association organized a conspiracy against him afta the fact, but I'm not shaw if their loyalty to Hiram extended as far as committing pudgery. I know Hiram Mills very well and can attest to his integrity, but even without sotch a supuffulous attestation on my pot, that story that Joe tells makes as motch sense as a chicken picking a fott with a dun fox. Regoddless of who the pilot is – and even if he dutton *own the dun boat* – he has a responsibility for his coggo and crew which would preclude any untoward chicanery, lock ronning roughshod over snags and bars at full steam. That's not saying that some pilots don't get a flea in their fur now and then to instigate a race. I'm just saying that Hiram Mills isn't dun fool enough to be one of 'em. So I'm reasonably shaw that he expressed to Joe in no unsutton tums that there would be no steamboat race occurring during *his* watch."

"What about the other steamboat? What part did it play?"

"What pot? Well now, considering how both of those steamas got all mixed up in this thing together, and they both saw things through to the bitta end, I would have to say that the *Mary Anne* played the pot of Juliet, while the *Tennessee* played a pretty fair Romeo. Though, of coss, what eventually transpodd wasn't high tragedy so much as a dun comedy of erras. Clod and Joe and the others on bodd the *Tennessee* who knew about the gold were all dead set on precipitating a race, so they needed a way to provoke the *Mary Anne* into th'owing down the gauntlet. At least that is what the alleged conspirators on bodd the *Mary Anne* testifodd to. Accodding to them, as soon as the *Mary Anne* got close enough to the *Tennessee*, Joe Clock and his boys stood up on the hurracun deck and let loose with a string of invective aimed at the pilot of the *Mary Anne* – invective involving many of that unfotchinate man's forebears and current relations, and most of his body pots and their various fonctions. The men on bodd the *Mary Anne* retaliated in suppott of their pilot by not only essaying fo'th with similar invective, but also by provodding visual demonstrations of it by manipulating their anatomy in ways that I can only imagine produced shrieks of mottification among the ladies and yong'uns present. I only wish I had been on bodd either one of those steamas to have been a witness to that! But lock everything else in this story, Cunnel, there are disputed vusions of events and contradictory testimony among the principals. Now, nobody denies that there occurred a tho'oughly raucous, intemperate exchange by sutton pussons on bodd both boats, but the disagreement consunns the severity and intent of the exchange. The folks on bodd the *Mary Anne* use this occurrence as the entire pretext for their potticipation in the race. Accodding to them, their pilot – a good Christian man by all accounts – was so morally offended and mentally debased by what he saw and hud coming from the deck of the *Tennessee* that apparently the only thing he could think of to regain his psychological balance was to outron the *Tennessee* all the way up the Missoura.

"And if this vusion of what occurred sounds far-fetched to you, Cunnel, I'm not shaw the altunnative sequence of events is any less so. The men on bodd the *Tennessee* claimed that their alleged insolent outbust aimed at the *Mary Anne* was entolly good-natured and suttonly not intended to provoke sotch a high-spirited response from that boat's pilot. Clod claimed that the *Mary Anne* must have been contemplating a race from the outset, especially when you considda how quickly it erased the distance between the two boats when they stotted up the riva. Clod says that at the same tom or thereabouts that he was setting up his betting pool on bodd the *Tennessee*, someone on bodd the *Mary Anne* must have had the *same exact oddea*! – as if a telegraph wire had been strung up between the two boats so that Clod and the *Mary Anne* could exchange Moss Code!"

"Perhaps the pilot of the *Mary Anne* knew about the gold claim and was racing toward it himself."

"Yes sir! You make a fust-rate coppenter, for you have hit the nail squolly on its head! All the confusion, contradiction, and deliberate obfuscation surrounding this whole incident comes down to the simple fact that no one involved was willing to admit that ever since they fust hud what the old prospecta had to say in chutch that Sunday monnin all their subsequent actions had been the result of the wud *gold* ringing in their ears."

"So how did the race conclude?"

"Badly, sir, badly! It could rottly be called a miracle that no one was blowed to Babylon. Be that as it may, the *Mary Anne* soddled up beside the *Tennessee* rot outsodd St. Charles and blowed her whistle. But Hiram, he wanted no pot in any dun race, for he rottly knowed that there was no easier way for his whole venture to end up at the bottom of the riva. So Joe – and this is all pure conjecture on my pot, Cunnel, since Joe will neva fess up to his pot in all this, though it does fit puffectly with what Hiram testifodd to – so Joe had to convince Hiram, by hook or crook, to accept the challenge to his manhood that the *Mary Anne* was offering. But Hiram wouldn't budge. "Get that dun fool out of my pilot-house!" Hiram yelled more than once, I'm shaw. But Joe was indefatigable. He had a wager on the outcome, but motch more udgently I'm shaw, he had that gold bug burrowing into his brain, so the real race, as far as he was consunned, was the race to O'gon.

"Accodding to Hiram, Joe came ronning into the pilot-house every minute or so with anotha dispatch from the *Mary Anne*. That is, dispatches in the fomm of insults hulled from the lobbud sodd of her deck. It mott have been true for all I know, for Hiram suttonly believed he was being provoked by her crew into risking everything he had unned – his reputation, his fotchin, his career – not to mention his loff – all for the benefit of a sackful of scoundrels who didn't deserve a minute of his tom. But whetha the information Joe passed along in sotch an onending stream was authored by hisseff or by those on bodd the *Mary Anne* is probably immaterial to the case at bar. And, of coss, I use the tum *information* somewhat loosely, insofar as what Hiram received from Joe Clock contained alleged facts of which heretofore Hiram had been unaware – to wit, that he was in fact not a human being, but ratha a jackass, a mule, a dog, and a chicken. That, in addition, he was at one and the same tom both the sire of all manna of crittas, from a bud dog to a watta buffalo, as well as the progeny of many different species. That he was a lover of Indians and dockies. That he hobbud so much affection for that latta class of humanity that he had a slave woff in not just one, but several states boddering the riva, along with a passel of nigga yong'uns. That his piloting abilities were holly suspect. That his religious affinities were unsutton. He was a heathen, a Mommon, and a Jew. That he suffered from a wodd range of physical infummities, affecting many of his intunnel oggans and extunnel appearances. He had a chicken hot, a lily liver, a horse's posteria, a hawk's nose, and a bud's brain."

"I understand now how Hiram was induced to race. A man can tolerate only so much abuse."

"Not so fast now, Cunnel! You don't know Hiram Mills lock I do. Of all those aforementioned descriptions attributed to Hiram by Joe or those unscrupulous vommits on bodd the *Mary Anne*, whateva the case may be, the only one I would willingly attest to is that he is stubborn as a dun mule. He cussed Joe and invotted him either to depott his pilot-house or to go to the devil – it was his choss. Joe would step outsodd for a minute or two but invariably retunn with yet another round of insults to repott. Hiram's face would tun redda and his omms would shake hodda and he would grip the wheel so tott that his hands tunned from a deep leatha tan to wott as a bedsheet. He retunned as many insults as he received, as vociferously as his longs would allow. But despott it all, he maintained a steady eye on the riva, called for soundings, yanked ropes, rang bells, and hollered oddas down to the bolla room. And neva once did he allow the *Tennessee*, his prod and joy, to reach an unsafe speed. But there was one insult, that had Joe or the rascals on bodd the *Mary Anne* made use of ullier, would have saved them all a lodge amount of yelling and ronning around. They had been so consumed with the conception of all their loathsome *lies,* that they had forgotten one small item of *truth.* That is, they had failed to infomm Hiram that the pilot of the *Mary Anne*, the man whom Hiram had allowed to pass him as he pleased, with whom he assumed he had no dispute and whom he held entolly blameless in this affair, was, in fact, an *abolitionist*. So Hiram, whetha through sectional prod or philosophical inclonnations, could not allow hisseff to be bettered by a *free-state man*. No, sir! In this great country, there is one subject about which there is no mediation and with which there is no coming to tums. So now the race was on! Cunnel, have you ever been up in the pilot-house on a rivaboat?"

"No, I am chagrined to say I have not."

"Well, there's no need for any feelings of discomfutt on your pot. Most people are blissfully unaware of the myriad complexities involved in piloting a stunwheela and if anyone should feel chagrined it is I, Cunnel – I have neva witnessed a pilot pufomming his duties fust-hand, but my long representation of Hiram following this fiasco provodded me the oppo'tunity to lunn as motch about that potticula profession as I imagine is possible without ever having set one foot above a hurricun deck. It was especially fascinating to hear Hiram descrobb the peculiar communications system on bodd a steama, with all the bells and whistles and tubes, notwithstanding the sheer amount of old-fashioned yelling and cussing. The only reason I bring this potticula topic to your attention, Cunnel, is that once Hiram desodded to vindicate his Southern heritage by outronning the *Mary Anne*, the fust thing he descrobbed to me in recounting the events as he remembered them afta the fact was how exciting and *loud* everything got – not only in the pilot-house but everywhere on bodd the boat. He fust let loose a blood-cuddling yell – which apparently only those bonn south of Mason and Dixon's lonn can produce, while at the same tom he stotted clanging bells and blowing whistles and letting off steam and producing all manna of noise. This set off a chain reaction of similar outbusts within the pilot-house and the texas which continued to revubberate ontil the hull of the boat was vobbrating and most everyone on bodd was regudgitating the same demonic yell that Hiram had instigated just a moment before. That is how quickly, Cunnel, wud got spread that a race had begun.

"Hiram immediately yelled down to the bolla room – using those tubes I mentioned ullier – to keep the funnaces fed and the watta flowing into the bollas. He invotted any and all abolitionists or nigga-loving Yankees on the boat to immediately jomp ovabodd so as to lotten its load. At the beginning of the race, the two boats were rot beside each other in the riva – so motch so in fact that Joe Clock swore to me – *unda oath!* – that he reached out and *shook hands* with someone on bodd the *Mary Anne*, which exemplifies how trustwuthy anything coming out of Joe Clock's mouth is. But as tott as the race may have been at the beginning, after several minutes the *Mary Anne* was in the lead by a good half-moll. She was the fasta boat. Hiram had built the *Tennessee* to be lodge and durable, for coggo-carrying pupposes, so Hiram knew he had his wuck cut out for hisseff if he wanted to win this race. But he adopted a curious strategy, Cunnel, in odda to do so. He chose to remain *behond* the *Mary Anne* – not that he had motch choss in the matta. But there was a good reason for this. The lodgest danger on the Missoura, or any riva, is ronning up on a snag or a bar, which of coss would be disastrous unda a full head of steam. Why not allow the *Mary Anne* to take all the risk and to do all the hodd wuck of negotiating the channel? Yes sir, for someone who neva potticipated in racing his boat, Hiram shaw seemed to know the proppa way to go about it.

"But keeping the *Mary Anne* within his sott proved to be a hodda proposition than Hiram had boggened for. It became imperative for him to lotten the load as motch as was practicable – even to the point of being immensely impracticable. This infunnel secession mess has tunned many a good, sound man into a dun irrational fool, and I'm afraid this little rivaboat contest did the same to Hiram. Coggo that was in his chodge to deliver upriva, belonging to loyal paying customers, was tossed summarily ovabodd. Not just off-loaded, mond you, to be retrieved later, but tossed ovabodd lock bilge watta to sink into the silt and neva to be seen again! But regoddless of how motch valuable coggo was jettisoned, the *Mary Anne* only seemed to increase her lead.

"So the difficulty for Hiram was not in surpassing the *Mary Anne*, but melly in *keeping up*. He knocked out windows in the pilot-house to reduce whateva resistance they may have caused. He gave oddas for the hog chains to be loosened. Do you know what those are?"

"No, sir."

"No matta. It didn't do any good. The race seemed to be lost for Hiram as soon as he made the decision to potticipate in it. But lock I said ullier, he had the obstinance of a dun mule, which in this case I suppose could be called *pusseverance*, although as things tunned out he would have been betta off to admit defeat and try to salvage some of that expensive coggo he had so cavalilly potted with. But soon enough this ill-advised pusseverance paid a dividend, howeva small. As he had hoped, the *Mary Anne* was soon fossed to slow her progress at a crossing and negotiate a sand bar. But as soon as the new channel was discovered the *Mary Anne* re-assutted her superio'ity. To make matters wuss, the *Tennessee* was ronning low on fuel and was fossed to take on wood.

"Now Cunnel, allow me to digress for a mere moment in odda to remock on an aspect of riva travel that I fond fascinating. If you have neva had the oppo'tunity to observe the process by which a steama lands on a rivabank to collect wood, as I have on several occasions, then you have missed a spectacle that, in the coordination of its many moving pots, could accurately be descrobbed as having the precision of a well-olled machine, as well as the gracefulness of a ballet on watta. I do not say that in jest. It is a ma'vellous thing to behold. All the mud clucks and dockies and everyone else involved in the procedure know exactly what their duties are and they carry them out with an extraordinary economy of motion and efficiency in odda to get the steama back out into the channel as quickly as humanly possible. They leap ova and around one anotha with their omms full of wood and whatnot without ever once being a hindrance to each other. Their omms and legs move in puffect coordination with everyone else's omms and legs as they rush off and on the stage connecting the boat to the rivabank. What a grand show it is!

"So, Cunnel, the race continued, motch as before, with the *Tennessee* struggling with little success to keep pace with the *Mary Anne*. Afta all the coggo was hoisted ovabodd Hiram gave the odda now to depott with any object that wasn't nailed down. Gangplanks and anchors – ovabodd! Hawsers and chains – into the riva! Tables, chairs, funniture of every description – anything made of wood – into the funnaces! And then, even afta the boat was stripped of every dun object that could be considded reasonably removable, Hiram insisted that the planking be removed from the hurricun deck! All of it! In just a matta of several feverish minutes at least half the dun boat was dismantled! Yes sir! Hiram was dettumined to win this race, even if he was fossed to paddle past the *Mary Anne* straddling nothing but a piece of driftwood that used to be the *Tennessee*!

"With all the dun floorbodds removed from the hurricun deck, all the passengers were fossed to congagate on the main deck, which at the tom served only as a ludicrous indication of how far beyond rational thought Hiram had progressed, but which eventually tunned out to save a great nomba of lives. Hiram neva admitted to it, and it was suttonly in the interest of my client that I didn't bring the matta up for discussion, but I suspect that at some point around this tom an odda was given to the men at the firebox to hang a copple of wrenches on the death hook on the bollas – as that pot of them was called, for good reason. Or perhaps someone else unda the sway of the same insanity as Hiram was afflicted with desodded to shut down the safety valve. Although sotch a pusson, if he exists, could most suttonly be called the villain of this pot of the story, there also exists a lodge nomba of heroes, some of whom I have had the pleasure of meeting; yet also many – undottedly, I am convinced – who have thus far remained anonymous. These heroic pussons foresaw the disaster that was imminent, warned all their fellow passengers – or as many of them as their voices and effutts could reach – and their actions alone are what allow me to narrate this event as melly a travesty, ratha than as a tragedy. Everyone was told to rosh to the boat's stun, as far from the bollas in the bow as possible. Many pussons who were capable swimmas jomped ovabodd in anticipation of the explosion and swam to the rivabank to safety and to a frontrow seat for the firewucks show. All that Hiram knowed was that for some dun fool reason everybody on bodd was gathered at the paddlewheel and retodding the boat to a remockable degree. Hiram told me once that he was shaw that all those congagated people at the stun were going to lift the bow plum *out of the watta*!

"It was at that point that the explosion occurred in the bollas. All manna of metal and wood – what was left of it – went airbonn, and not a few pussons as well. For years aftawud people were relating stories about regaining consciousness on the rivabank – half-naked, or stock-naked, completely bald, or half-bald, wearing clothes that a moment ullier were being worn by someone else, pussons with dock hair being transfommed into redheads, eye colors being changed, a few pussons claimed to be several inches shotta now and a simila nomba claimed aftawuds to be motch taller. One pusson who had neva set foot outsodd the bodda of the U.S. was now speaking nothing but puffectly fluent French. Many pussons were temporarily blonded by the steam, but in one case a myopic pusson on bodd who said he couldn't see his hand in front of his face prior to the explosion swore he could now see a gnat on a hommingbud. Several pussons had serious thud-degree buns on various pots of their bodies, as you would expect. One entaprising docky claimed to be in actuality an Englishman of royal buth, who had been unfotchinately chodd from head to toe by the explosion. Coppetbags were found three molls away, but puffectly intact. Teeth were blowed out of mouths, and numerous sets of dentures were found strewn about and some even retunned to their owners. Shoes and every imaginable otticle of clothing were scattered everywhere and are still discovered occasionally to this day. Indians have been seen wearing wigs that once belonged to wealthy ladies on bodd – not as pussonly satisfying as taking a scalp, I'm shaw, but very becoming on a squaw nonetheless. Hiram was blowed out of the pilot-house and came to on the paddlewheel, which had stopped tunning afta the explosion. He healed quickly from his wounds, but was injudd financially beyond recovery. Yes sir, Cunnel, this dun civil war, if it does indeed come, will ruin many a man, but its antagonisms ruined Hiram Mills before anyone had ever hud of your Fott Sumta."

W,

I missed seeing you yesterday, but I know you have a higher calling this time of year. I hope all your supplicants enjoyed the manna they received from Saint Will. But seriously, I must say, you really missed out this time. I'm not talking about the victuals – they were the standard delicious fare. But Pop and I stood toe-to-toe again, just like old times! Just when I think the old man is mellowing, or maybe I am, the old spark returns and we shed twenty years of complacency, resignation, and acceptance of each other and fight like young gamecocks once again! In true Sumter fashion, I will deny having started anything and insist that I was merely defending myself at all times. Actually, I don't know what got into me. Deb was always such a calming influence on me and she certainly deserves the credit for forging the cease-fire that obtained until yesterday, and God knows I have reason to rail against the heavens for her absence – but still….

We almost made it through the whole meal but Pop just couldn't resist talking about his favorite subject. Out of nowhere he said, "Obama's a wimp." I'm sure he wanted to say more, but his mouth was full.

"Where did that come from?" I looked around and up at the ceiling as if a big bug were flying overhead. Jeff laughed. Pop didn't.

"He's a wimp. Don't you watch the news?"

"Yes, I watch the news. He killed bin Laden."

"He didn't have anything to do with that. That was all CIA. They don't take orders from anybody. He was just lucky it happened on his watch."

"He bombed Libya. We still have troops in Afghanistan. Guantanamo is still open. He's tougher on Israel than Bush ever was. Yes, he's quite the wimp. I would put him on the opposite end of the spectrum, actually. If anything, he's a bully – just like all the other bullies we've elected through the years."

"He talks to terrorists. He's talking to Iran."

"Yes, God forbid our nation's top diplomat does anything diplomatic."

"He's a wimp."

"Are these the only two choices we have? You're either a wimp or a bully? It's like being in high school. That's what we have in this country – a high-school-based foreign policy. When you're a guy in high school everything you do is designed, first and foremost, to keep you from looking like a pussy – "

"Josh!" (Mom, of course.)

" – and that's all our foreign policy is. Just make sure we don't look like a pussy. That's it. That's all there is. We start wars we know we can't win. We invade countries we know will hate us for it. We bomb countries knowing it will just create more terrorists. Why? Because we have to do something. Anything. Why? Because if we don't we look like pussies." Jeff is cracking up, much to my delight. Pop, as usual, is pretending not to hear me, just waiting out my interruption so he can pick up where he left off. So I keep going: "I have an idea. Why don't we try doing nothing for a change. What if they threw a terrorist attack and nobody came? Just ignore them. They blow up an airplane. Ignore it. They blow up a building – ignore it. We think we're being so tough. 'We don't talk to terrorists. We don't negotiate with them' – but we do everything they want us to do. We accede to all their demands. They don't need to negotiate with us. They want us to be scared, so we run around like Chicken Little. They blow up a building with the express purpose of getting our military involved because they want us to invade and piss off everybody in the Middle East – and we're only too happy to oblige. We give the terrorists everything they could ever wish for on a silver platter – we completely pervert our normal way of life because that's exactly what they want us to do – but damn if we're going to talk to them! That would make us look like pussies! Well, I have news for everybody. The way we reacted to 9/11 and all the years since have done nothing but prove to the world that we're the biggest pussies on the planet. That's exactly how al-Qaeda sees us, so maybe it's time to try something else."

As expected, Pop was oblivious to everything I had just said. "Obama is the ruination of this country." His mouth was full of turkey, so he relied on his usual talking points.

"Yes, he's absolutely ruined it, Pop. Unemployment is lower than it has been in years. More people have insurance than ever before."

"He's a Muslim and a socialist."

"Pop, the only reason you call Obama a socialist is because you can't get away with calling him a nigger."

"Josh!" (Mom again.)

"But it's true. How could any sane person think that Obama is a socialist? But that's just it – you're not sane. Not anymore. The liberals elected a damn nigger for president and now everybody's gone batshit crazy. We're in the middle of a national epileptic seizure, a nationwide nervous breakdown. The whole country has turned into Bull Connor spraying water hoses. You want to know how important race still is in this country, in this so-called post-racial society? You want to know? Well then, just elect a nigger president and you'll find out. Can we please change the subject? This is making me sick."

"You're the one having the epileptic seizure right now, not me. All I know is this country used to be great. Our ancestors are turning over in their graves."

"Are you proud of our ancestors?"

"Am I proud? Of course I am. You should be too."

"Why are you proud?"

"What do you mean, 'Why am I proud?' Why shouldn't we be proud? Because they were slaveowners? Is that what you're getting at?"

"No – not at all. I'm not barking up that tree anymore. I mean simply – why are *you* – you, specifically, as an individual – proud of anything our ancestors accomplished? I mean – *you* didn't do any of those things. *You* didn't come across the ocean. *You* didn't build anything. *You* didn't run the plantation. *You* didn't hold office. *You* weren't even alive then. So why are you taking credit for all the great things your great-great grandfather did? What did that have to do with you?

"I'm not taking credit for anything."

"Well, you are. Vicariously. If Jeff does something great, then I will take great father's pride in him. I may not take any of the credit for whatever he does, but I'll certainly bask in the glow. By the same token, if he does something wrong – which of course he never does – but if he did, then I would be very angry at him, or ashamed, or feel some very negative emotion toward him, you can rest assured. So why don't you feel that way about slavery, Pop?"

"I knew this was about slavery. Every time you open your mouth it's about slavery."

"But answer my question."

"What?"

"Why don't you feel ashamed about slavery? You always claim you didn't have anything to do with slavery. 'That's ancient history,' you say. 'I didn't own any slaves,' you always say. 'Don't judge me by what happened two hundred years ago. I didn't have anything to do with that.' But you don't have any trouble taking pride in their accomplishments two hundred years ago, do you? You can't have it both ways, Pop. If you take pride in accomplishments that you personally didn't have a goddam thing to do with, then why don't you also feel ashamed?"

"We have nothing to be ashamed of! You're the one who should be ashamed!" Pop was absolutely livid. I thought he might throw the turkey at me. Mom, of course, tried to be the peacemaker, but at this point I was having none of that.

"We have everything to be ashamed of! We have *nothing* to be proud of! This whole God-forsaken country ought to be ashamed! This whole country was built on the back of slave labor – and we completely wash our hands of it! Pretend it didn't happen! Blame the lazy no-good nigger for causing his own problems! But we're so proud at the same time! Proud of this great country! You can't have it both goddam ways! You can't lay claim to the pride without accepting responsibility for the shame! Step up to the plate, Pop! Take some responsibility! That's what we teach our kids, right? Take responsibility for your actions! We're all such goddam hypocrites. We act like slavery was the most irrelevant, nonexistent thing to ever happen in our country, when in fact, nothing else is important! Everything else pales in comparison! This country was ruined by slavery. 'Obama is the ruination of this great country!' That's perfect, Pop. Absolutely perfect. You take the most accomplished black man in the history of our nation and turn it around so that he's the source of all your problems. And in that sense I suppose he is. This country was broken by slavery – and it can't be fixed! And we just continue to eat our turkey and dressing like it's all someone else's fault."

Well, needless to say, nobody really enjoyed their pumpkin pie. Poor Jeff was horrified. He had never seen his father like this before, and hopefully never will again. I explained to him afterwards that without his mom I just wasn't the same person around Grandpop. It's amazing how certain people can transform your personality – for better or worse.

But you should have been here! You would have given me a standing ovation. And my old roommate Jerome would have been proud of me. I can hear his voice, plain as day: "Yo daddy wants to have his cake and eat the motherfucker too!"

DEAREST CONSTANCE,

I hope this letter finds you and your mother well. As for my state of mind, I hope never to be required by circumstances to endure for a second time the type of distressing interview I have tonight been subjected to. If you recall, I concluded my previous correspondence to you with an account of an unfortunate conversation I had with the gentleman whom I know only as Aaron, who, in turn, is a member of that mysterious sect of which I also provided to you a cursory description. After giving offense to Aaron upon our first meeting, I was grateful for an opportunity to renew our conversation this morning, hoping to make amends. I inquired about the origins of his community. He replied that the group was formed five years ago in the state of New York by a visionary known only as Wilbur, but that was the only information he provided. "Are you Christians?" I asked.

"I cannot say," A. replied.

"But the principles around which your group is organized are religious in nature?"

"Yes, I suppose so. But religious beliefs create the foundation of all societies."

"Indeed they do. Are you at liberty to explain the articles of faith upon which your group is organized?"

"We are not organized according to our faith."

"I apologize – did I misunderstand your meaning? My assumption has been that you have all come together based upon some shared system of beliefs – at the instigation of your founder."

"Yes. Wilbur is our guiding light, our prophet; he does not, however, make spiritual demands upon us."

"But he certainly must have beliefs that he propagates among his followers."

"I cannot say."

"You don't know what your prophet believes?" My tone was approaching that of incredulity and I feared I may have given offense to A. once again, despite my strenuous attempts to avoid doing so.

"Wilbur believes that what we believe does not matter. We may believe whatever we wish to believe."

"Well then, is there a specific code of prescribed behaviors that you must adhere to, or proscribed behaviors which are punishable?"

"I cannot say, except to say not to my knowledge."

"I don't mean to give offense, Aaron, but this is all quite astounding."

Aaron smiled. "Yes, we do not live as other men live. And that is the source of much misunderstanding."

"Why do you choose to follow a man who – please forgive me, I am only hoping to understand, and to avoid those misunderstandings that have brought upon you so much misfortune – why do you follow Wilbur if he has nothing he wishes to impart to you or to ask of you?"

"Because of his vision. He had a great vision, which revealed to him the true nature of the world."

"May I ask you the favor of describing this vision to me, so that I may better understand?"

"I could attempt to do so – but wouldn't you rather learn of Wilbur's vision from Wilbur himself, than from me?"

"I'm sure that would be a remarkable thing, but I don't see the possibility of it. My interest in your group is merely coincidental to our traveling together. I would not wish to cause inconvenience to you or to myself in order to meet him – although I am sure he is a most interesting man."

"You will not have to travel beyond the boundaries of this

caravan. Wilbur is one of us. I will introduce you."

"He is here? In the train?" I was astonished by this news. I had not attempted to form a mental impression of Wilbur; however, whatever form W. may have taken in my mind, I can assure you, it would not have coincided with the appearance of any of the beragged, disheveled, pitiful men that I had come to recognize from among A.'s colleagues. But perhaps I should not have been surprised by this. Was not Jesus indistinguishable in appearance from his disciples?

"Yes, he is here – somewhere. I do not see him at present."

"I would like very much to meet him then. But what can you tell me about him in preparation for our introduction?"

"He is a very humble man. I am sure he was humble before he was visited by God, but his vision imparted to him the wisdom of humility. Men are ignorant of the ways of God."

"Ordinary men are, yes. That is not a revolutionary philosophy. But Wilbur has received a revelation, correct? Then he is not so ignorant as the rest of us. Wouldn't you agree?"

"Perhaps. I cannot say. I do know that it is not quite that simple. He will explain himself much more clearly than I am capable of."

"I'm looking forward to it. At the very least, I must commend him for his ability to instill in his followers such uncommon good spirit and vitality. Does he preach to you about maintaining good cheer and a pleasant countenance despite all your hardships?"

"Wilbur does not preach to us about anything. Do you enjoy being preached to?"

"A good sermon is good for the soul."

"That is but one thing we will disagree about. Wilbur, of course, has taught us many things, but not through inculcation. He is a model for us to emulate. He teaches us to enjoy the process of living. You cannot be near Wilbur without knowing that he enjoys the experience of being alive."

"That is hedonism. It is selfish. And sinful."

"*Sin!*" A. did not say this word – he spat it. "The concept of sin is the greatest source of misery. Do children sin?"

I expected A. to continue, but he waited silently for my reply. "No, of course not. They are innocent of sin. But we were not speaking of children."

"Wilbur lives his life as a child lives his. There is no talk among us of sin."

"But surely you believe in sin. You – all of you – have been sinned against terribly. How does that not affect you?"

"Why should we allow the sins of others to anger us? That is what you mean, is it not? Why are we not angry? We grieve. We cry. We mourn for our departed. What else would you have us do? Would you have us ruin the very thing that makes our lives worth living? To blaspheme the glory of God's creation? To seek vengeance? To fill our hearts with hatred? To become the very people who attack us? That is my concept of sin."

Based upon these responses, I must conclude that A., despite his warm, ingratiating smile, and his proclaimed disdain for angry emotions, still harbors a significant amount of that resentment and animosity toward his fellow man to which we lesser mortals have resigned ourselves. I believe his outward friendliness is masking an inner disposition either of fear – which I can readily understand and which I will continue to strive to allay – or contempt, which, if true, and exposed, will tend to justify the animosity aroused in every other town and community brought into contact with the group.

So, my dear, my second attempt at a fruitful dialogue with A. ended in much the same manner as my first, much to my consternation and regret. I feared that I would not be allowed a third opportunity to disgrace myself further in his eyes. But as disappointing as these conversations had been, they were nothing but pleasant compared to what was now to follow.

Earlier this evening, after sunset and after supper and as the men sat around camp smoking and preparing for a good night's sleep after a long day's march, I was approached by A. and reminded that he wished to introduce me to Wilbur. I was tired, but happy for the reprieve, and willing certainly to be entertained by the trail's latest incarnation of Joseph Smith. "That is Wilbur," A. said, as he pointed into a darkness ameliorated by much firelight.

"Where? I don't see anyone."

A. attempted to make his index finger more effective by holding it closer to my face as he pointed. "Right over there. He is standing smoking beside that tent post. Allow me to introduce you." I indeed had seen the man A. was pointing to, but refused to believe that he was referring to the same man. I was astonished, my dear one, to learn that the man pointed out to me by A. as the great visionary prophet was the same man I had gazed upon more than once this week, and, when taking any notice of him whatsoever, had dismissed him in my mind as a fool. I had not deigned to talk with him. Upon once encountering him in camp he greeted me with alcoholic breath and a smile befitting a crazed man. I had assumed his status within A.'s group must be that of someone who was accorded membership through familial ties or charity, as one is compelled to keep up a dissolute uncle or to take in a waif. I expressed my astonishment to A., and he merely smiled beneficently and said, "Wilbur appears to possess nothing beyond ordinary qualities, but he is our prophet. He has received an extraordinary vision."

A. began walking toward Wilbur and I followed, but not without more than a little uneasiness. After cordial introductions, A. – who spoke to his acknowledged prophet with the same familiarity with which he conversed with everyone else he encountered – provided a brief summary to W. of our recent exchanges and intimated further that I had taken an interest in the nature of the vision he had received. I nodded in agreement; however, I also took pains to declare that I was a devout follower of Jesus Christ and, therefore, my interest in their sect was based entirely on natural human curiosity, rather than any disenchantment with the shared faith of our fathers. Wilbur, as I had come to expect, appeared almost drunk with giddiness upon my request and asked that I follow him into his tent. It would have been a most inappropriate question to have asked, but I was curious to ascertain how the professed leader and protector of a group that had endured murders and many other outrages committed without provocation or justification against his followers, as they allege, and that contained amongst the group's number many women and children, and, therefore, one would assume, must strive to maintain a vigilant and worrisome outlook as a necessity – how, I would like to know, can such a leader of men appear to be so unburdened in the midst of so many burdens? The hedonistic philosophy that A. had alluded to is disturbing and troublesome to me. It is, among many other inappropriate things, grossly irresponsible. For what shepherd would carouse and celebrate while his sheep were being so unconscionably slaughtered? With these discomfitting questions foremost in my mind I entered into conversation with W. in a suddenly disagreeable mood. But perhaps I should strike-through the word "conversation" in favor of a term more applicable to one who sits and listens in silence to a narration that was as incredible as it was verbose. I will attempt to put down here W.'s story in as much detail as I can recall, using his own words.

"My wife and I, Mr. Kinninger, were humble homesteaders in the state of New York up until I received my vision. And, if I had been so stubborn and insistent as to go against the wishes of my wife, a humble tiller of the land I would have remained. I do remain a humble man, sir – no knowledge I received in my vision would justify straying from a path of humility – but I have chosen to leave my home and my family in order to 'spread the word' as the saying goes. And I did not choose this fate enthusiastically. Aaron and all the others describe me as a prophet, but, if I am indeed a prophet, I am a most unwilling one. It is to my wife they owe their gratitude for their knowledge of me and my vision. I am a sociable fellow, amenable to most things, but all things being equal, I would just as soon spend my days visiting with my family and other friendly acquaintances, and impart whatever wisdom I possess to my milch cow, hogs, and chickens, as to attempt to lead a group of strangers, however gracious they be, into an exile not one of us would have chosen. So, what is this vision I speak of, that compelled so many good people to follow an unwilling prophet and, in turn, become themselves unwilling victims and martyrs?

"Well, I cannot offer you a description of my vision that contains anything but the barest verisimilitude. I cannot very well describe to you something that I cannot describe to myself. I cannot explain the meaning of something that I too struggle to understand. Have you ever had the misfortune of experiencing the sensation of drowning?"

"Luckily, no. Not to the point of fearing for my life."

"But you can well imagine that if I am drowning in a roiling river and am grasping at a passing tree branch, and struggling to retain my grip on this passing limb, then I will be quite unable to guide your hand onto this limb as well? That as difficult as it is to save myself, I cannot be expected additionally to save you?"

"It must have been an overwhelming experience indeed. I can understand having great difficulty in describing it."

"So it was. My wife and I had settled in for a night of well-earned sleep after a day spent toiling contentedly on the farm. In other words, Mr. Kinninger, it was a night like any other, which had followed a day like any other. I don't remember anything remarkable about it whatsoever. However, at some point during the night, while we slept, our bed began to quiver, but rather weakly at first, then much more perceptibly, as if three or four strong-armed men were each fighting to determine the relocation of our bed to separate areas of our cabin. It was quite frightening, I'm not afraid to admit. My initial thought, and the only probable explanation for such a thing, was that we were experiencing an earth tremor. I had never experienced such a phenomenon before, so I had no prior knowledge of such a thing to call upon, but I could not imagine a tremor being anything other than identical to what we were experiencing. My wife and I clung to each other and hoped the tremor would soon subside without doing damage to our home. I am perhaps in error in relating the following detail, but I seem to recall that our bed was the only object within the room experiencing the tremor. Our two small night tables, on either side of our bed, remained motionless. On each of these tables were a candlestick and taper, which continue to burn throughout the night because my dear wife cannot bear to awaken during the night in a dark room. It is my distinct memory that the flames atop these tapers wavered not in the least. There were ornaments suspended by nails on the walls above and opposite our bed. Sir, wouldn't you have expected to see these wall ornaments, none of any substantial weight, in the midst of this frightful tremor, quivering on the walls as if a windstorm were blowing through the cabin? I would certainly think so. Yet they were as stationery on the wall as if they were nailed to it top and bottom. But as I mentioned earlier, I cannot be sure of these remarkable details. My wife – Clara is her name, and a finer wife a man could not hope to find – Clara, unfortunately, could not verify the truth of this peculiar recollection, since, in her words, she was 'too scared to notice.' However, to add further credence to my claim, I can point to the fact that our four children, in their separate bedroom, were oblivious to what Clara and I were experiencing and not one of them ran to us screaming as children are wont to do. In fact, I do believe each one remained asleep throughout the entire episode and were, as you can well imagine, quite mystified and excited by the tale we had to relate afterward.

"Now, unfortunately, it is upon Clara, who was 'too scared to notice,' as we have established, that I must rely for the narration of the remainder of this remarkable episode – at least regarding the external particulars – for soon after we began experiencing the worst of the tremor I lost consciousness of my immediate surroundings and began to experience a species of consciousness completely foreign to any mental state I had heretofore had any knowledge of. And if it were not for what Clara claimed to have witnessed during the entirety of my unconscious state, then I would have been content to believe that everything I saw in my vision had been nothing more than a strange, wondrous dream. But men who are unconscious and dreaming do not, by and large, rise upon thin air – which is the claim Clara has continued to make steadfastly. I awoke, however, in thorough contact with our mattress tick along every part of my anatomy – head, legs, feet, and every point in between. I was quite drenched with perspiration, however, and chilled to the bone, and I will readily admit that I experienced the sensation of having traveled somewhere beyond the confines of a bedstead. Our bed had returned to its normal state of motionlessness; however, Clara and I were both now quivering quite uncontrollably much as our bed had been earlier – I with chills and fever, she with fear. She was no longer beside me in bed, but had taken a seat beside it, though my last memory was of her gripping me in fear under the coverlet. She said, through her chattering teeth, 'Wilbur, are you awake?' I said, through mine, 'I believe I am, if this is not a dream.' She said, very softly, 'Are you ill?' I said, no louder than she, 'Yes, quite, but strangely content. Can you please come back to bed to warm me?' She said, 'I'm afraid to. I'm afraid to touch you.' I said, 'You're not making any sense. There is no longer anything to be afraid of. Come back to bed.' She said, 'You have been touched by God.' I said, 'Did you see what I saw?' She said, 'What I saw were the hands of God lifting you bodily from our bed and then setting you gently back again. You were in His hands for many minutes. Will you share what you saw with me?' I only wanted to stop shivering and to sleep. I could not describe where I had been or what I had been looking upon, except to say that it was truly wondrous, but I have never in my experience felt such fatigue and weariness. No labor that has ever been my duty to perform in the fields, sun-up to sun-down and under a harvest moon, can begin to compare to the weariness I felt and that I can still recall as vividly as if I were back in my bed on that night. Nor will I ever forget it, I am certain. 'I will share it with you in the morning,' I said, for, as I've just related, I was too weary for anything but sleep. However, Clara was incredulous that I would prefer sleep – or that I even would be capable of it. 'Wilbur,' she said, 'I was shaken from bed by a physical force I can't describe, as if my presence in it was unwelcome, and, as I lay on the floor, unable to move, I witnessed you being lifted up by the hands of God, almost to touching the roof itself, and I witnessed your body shivering and shaking so much that I was in fear for your life, and I was held in such awe that I could not scream, nor speak, nor utter a sound, nor move nary a muscle, and I watched spellbound as you were gently lowered like a baby to its crib, back into bed as if you had never left it, but still shivering and shaking down to your very bones – and although I have just witnessed the presence of God under our roof and witnessed His hands, with the supreme power and gentleness that only He is capable of, give support to your body and its limbs as if floating freely in the air – although I have just witnessed all these things, you speak only of sleep and deny me even the smallest intimation of what God said to you or what you envisioned in His presence?' Well, after such an impressive soliloquy, how could I deny my precious wife an explanation of what I had experienced, though I couldn't help but fear that – weary indeed as I was in spirit and body – any explanation I could offer of something that made but little sense to me could not help but be judged by her to be a feeble explanation at best.

"So, my dear Mr. Kinninger, after all these preliminary and unnecessary details, you are probably eager to hear all about my vision."

"If you are eager to tell of it, then I am eager to hear of it. But if you are tired, then I won't deny you the sleep that your wife did on that night."

W. laughed uproariously and said, "Yes! That she did! Are you married, sir?"

"Engaged to be married, yes. My dear Constance is in Charleston, waiting to hear of my safe arrival in Oregon."

"Well then, if you wish to make a good husband, then you should strive always to make your wife happy, despite any temporary discomfort it may cause you – for if you think your discomfort is great upon making some trivial sacrifice on her behalf, then it will pale in comparison to the discomfort you will feel when you fail to make it! And that is a bit of wisdom I received not from my vision, but from my twenty years of marital contentment with Clara!"

W. now proceeded to tell me of his vision, though, as he correctly foresaw, I must admit that his narration lacked the force of authority I would have expected from someone who had experienced a communion with God. Was he a charlatan? Did his followers know that he was utterly incapable of describing in convincing detail the vision that was the sole basis of their devotion to him? As he began to tell of his vision, his tent was dark, save for two small candles flickering weakly. I must confess, Constance, that listening to W. in this setting – in a tent on the open prairie – put me in mind of those storytellers I heard in my childhood, sitting around campfires and in similar tents, though I was forced to remind myself that the story W. was relating is purported by himself to be true in its entirety, and not merely another of the beloved campfire stories from my youth. He continued:

"According to Clara, she could not determine whether my eyes were open or closed during the duration of my vision, for, if Clara is to be believed – and I do believe her, with all my heart – my nose was near to touching the rafters while she was supine on the floor. But that detail is irrelevant, since the vision I was experiencing during those moments had nothing to do with the interior contents of any log cabin on Earth, I assure you. The vision had a vertiginous effect on me, as if I were being twirled around a Maypole at a faster and faster rate of speed." W. reached over to a small table beside his cot and handed me a small photograph, the image in which I could scarcely see in the weak candlelight. "Are you familiar, sir, with the science of photography?"

"I am familiar with its products; however, not with the process itself."

"That is Clara. I miss her very much, as well as my children. But it is all quite magical, is it not? To preserve a mirror image of a loved one. To produce a photograph has the result of halting time in its tracks, does it not? What a marvelous power that is! I would have found that to be very useful as I experienced my vision. Or perhaps there was something similar occurring."

"There were photographic images in your vision?"

"I could not describe it as such, for what I beheld contained all the colors of life – and exceedingly bright ones at that. Yet I am left to wonder by what miraculous means such a multitude of forms and figures could be presented before my eyes. This vertiginous effect I have mentioned was produced by a rapid procession of objects, the speed of which I am helpless to describe. Imagine, if possible, peering out a train window at a passing landscape; however, rather than rolling hills and occasional structures filling your field of vision, there are storefronts, houses, persons, animals, flora – all manner of things – placed into an endless line alongside the rails, with the train traveling at some horrendous, unprecedented speed, so that just as one object appears before you another just as quickly replaces it. Can you imagine such a scenario as that, Mr. Kinninger?"

"I believe so, with proper effort. It would be quite vertiginous, as you say."

"Yes, well – I have given you a description you can understand because each object running alongside these imaginary railroad tracks is recognizable by you; it is a part of your existence, your memory, your life on Earth, though passing by your eyes at terrific speed. However, I now would like for you to imagine a rush of objects before your eyes that is wholly unintelligible to you, in part, perhaps, because they are rushing by you with such velocity that you can scarcely identify any specific aspect of an object before it is gone from your sight, and in part because you realize, in truth, that if this rush of objects were halted, or slowed to the extent that you could make a study of each object at your leisure, then you still would be entirely incapable of identifying them, for they are completely foreign to your understanding and alien to your experience. Now, sir, are you having similar luck imagining this?"

"No, I am not. It bewilders the mind."

"There were so many objects – or images of objects. I don't know if I were gazing upon actual objects or upon some magical representation of them – but I understood them to be real and to have been created by God, or by creations of God. Though the cumulative effect of all these flashing objects was unsettling and physically quite sickening, it was also the most glorious thing imaginable." W. paused. It was obvious that he was gathering his thoughts and recollecting his vision, or attempting once again to make sense of it. I did not dare interrupt him and forestall his thoughts. Moments passed before he spoke again. "So many objects. Innumerable. Fantastical. Many appeared to be incomprehensibly large; others incredibly small. So many of them shone – it was quite blinding to behold, yet I could not close my eyes, nor did I wish to. Clara said that the entire episode lasted but a few minutes; it seemed to me to encompass all of time and the entirety of God's creation." He paused once again, but added only, "I believe that is the most comprehensive description I can give to you, sir, however unsatisfactory it might well be."

"That is quite astonishing, I must say. I want to thank you for sharing it with me." I allowed myself to ask him one question further. "What do you make of it all, sir?"

W. laughed loudly once again in the same maniacal manner, which seemed to be the reaction he most often chose to display. This irreverent behavior was inappropriate to the point of repugnance and I must have failed at concealing my disgust, for he said, "I apologize, sir, if you think I am ridiculing you or your question. I am not. In fact, that is the question I have most often asked myself as well, but I am not up to the task of answering it."

"I suppose it is well enough to know that you have been in the presence of God."

"I assume so, yes. I assume it was God in whose arms I was carried."

It was now my turn to emit a short laugh. "My good man, to what other power could you attribute such a marvelous vision?"

"I cannot say."

I was taken aback by his response. "Well now, that seems to be a common response among your followers."

"And in most cases, an entirely appropriate one."

"But surely not in this case. If you in fact experienced such a vision as you have just described, then it was given to you by God – there is no reason to cast doubt on that."

"You are most probably correct."

"Sir, why do you insist on these pusillanimous qualifications? Is there any other being in the universe capable of creating what you witnessed? Do you not believe in the omnipotence of our Creator? Is there any one thing more certain to be believed?"

"I cannot be certain of anything anymore."

"This is most incredible! Are you indeed the fool I at first took you for? While the entirety of mankind must rely on a blind faith and the teachings of others to come to know the truths contained in our religious traditions, you – You! – among a small handful of men in the history of the world have been given a glimpse – a mere glimpse I am certain! – into the mind of God. And what do you do with this most precious of all possible gifts to have been bestowed upon you? You cast doubt upon its provenance? You take the one thing most certain to remove all doubt and use it as the means to doubt everything? Sir, I apologize for this show of impudence, but I, in good conscience, cannot but tell you that you must be a fool to say such a thing!"

"I do not doubt that I am a fool, nor blame you for believing me one, but will you be equally magnanimous toward me when I say that you are as foolish as I?"

"This is intolerable!" I stood up from my seat in his tent and walked quickly out. No further words passed between us. I paused outside his tent, however, and immediately was overcome with shame for my behavior toward this man who had graciously invited me into his temporary home, however humble, to share with me this most profound of experiences. I felt foolish indeed for despoiling his hospitality. I timidly returned to his tent and stood outside its entrance. "I wish to apologize, sir. May I enter?"

"Of course. Please."

I offered my humblest apologies to W., which he accepted with aplomb. I said, "Before taking my leave one final time, sir, may I ask but one more question?" W. gave welcome assent to my request. "I understand that your most likely response to this question will be to insist that you are incapable of providing an answer to it, but I beg of you, at the very least, to deign to humor me with some type of positive response, regardless of how partial, ambiguous, or unsatisfactory you believe it to be. I will not be satisfied with anything less. Therefore, allow me to repeat this question to you – to what do you attribute your doubt regarding the authorship of your vision? If not God, then whom? Or what?"

"I attribute whatever doubts I may have, sir, to the presence of Satan in this world."

I was dumbfounded. "Did you not say, sir, that this vision – as bewildering to witness as I understand it must have been – was, with the utmost certainty, a glorious thing to behold?"

"Yes. It was stupendous in its glory. But what is your understanding of Satan?"

"I understand the devil as well as any devout Christian. There is no need for us to discuss elementary theology. Satan's purpose is to deceive us into sin. But what place does he have in such a vision as you witnessed? Your vision transcended any temptation into sin. Who would be tempted into sin after such an intimate encounter with God? Satan does not possess such power."

"You are probably right, but still the doubt persists. Do you not believe that innocent people are capable of being possessed by Satan?"

"This is blasphemy, sir! To suggest even the possibility that a glorious vision of God's creation could be the product of satanic ingenuity – it is blasphemous!" I was sorely tempted once again to exit W.'s tent in a most tempestuous state, but I held my ground.

"That is but one possibility. However, there is another, and it, indeed, is my most worrisome concern, Mr. Kinninger. My vision has forced upon me thoughts that I never would have entertained nor conceived of prior to that fateful night. Thoughts that I wish I could banish from my brain and the truth of which I hope never to convince myself of. My greatest fear, sir, is that we understand neither the nature nor the true intent – nor the extent – of Satan's deceit. We believe we understand Satan's intentions toward us, but it would be a poor deceiver indeed who could not deceive his enemy into believing him to be his friend. Allow me to ask you a question – what would give Satan the greatest pleasure?"

"I think the answer to that question is obvious – to deceive us into renouncing God's glory and into glorifying his evil. That, for Satan, would represent his victory over mankind."

"But where is the deception in this type of victory? Is he not showing us his true face and merely convincing us to follow him, much as a general convinces an army to fight with him by promising it the spoils of victory?"

"No, sir, do you not read the Bible? Satan does indeed conceal his true face; he does indeed endeavor to persuade us, through deceit, of his friendship. Your worries, I daresay, are entirely unfounded. I must also, respectfully, repeat to you that I am entirely unable to comprehend why such a faith-affirming vision as you have been blessed to receive has filled your head with more contemplation of Satan than of our Creator; in fact, you seem to have reversed the proportion due to each."

"Undoubtedly, but be that as it may, we are in agreement that Satan attempts to conceal his face from us; however, what gives you reason to believe that you have seen through his panoply of disguises?"

"As in all other things, I am guided by scripture."

"Sir, let me put this to you as plainly as my limited ability will allow. The objects that I looked upon that night were beyond my range of comprehension. They did not seem to be of this world. For the fleeting seconds in which I was allowed to view them I could discern no obvious function for them nor understand how they could take such forms. How could such amazing objects be created and of what use could they possibly be? There is one conclusion that I am inevitably drawn to; namely, that I was indeed given brief entry into an entirely alien world – the world created by God. And thus it follows, that, if what I saw was God's world, then what world, dear sir, is this?"

"If I may be so bold as to speculate on your vision, is it so difficult to believe that what you were so privileged to gaze upon, however briefly, was Heaven itself, in all of its incomprehensible splendor?"

"That is precisely what I would prefer to believe, but don't we perceive Heaven invariably as something manifestly desirable and recognizable? Would I not have seen my loved ones who have departed? Would I not have been drawn to it as I would be drawn to a long-lost but never-forgotten homeland? If this were indeed Heaven, then it was not the Heaven that we have been taught is rapturously awaiting us."

"Then it must have been a vision of the future world that is awaiting our posterity."

"That is all but impossible. Wouldn't our ancestors, even of many generations ago, still easily recognize the world in which we live? Would not the Romans, the Egyptians, the ancient Israelites, all recognize our horses and wagons and tents and campfires? And how far into the future would it be necessary to peer before we no longer saw these things? If there is but one truth that history teaches us, it is that of the immutability of mankind and the world it has created. No, we must return to my original speculation – though I admit that is all that it is. I must give serious consideration to the possibility that I was looking upon a world created by God, but uninhabited by man. Again, to put this as plainly as I can, I must give credence to the possibility that we have been deceived by Satan to a much greater degree than we are capable of realizing. Deceived in such a way as to be utterly unaware of the deception. The entire world in which we are living, and in which all of our ancestors lived – indeed, all of creation, as we have experienced it – may be the greatest deception perpetrated by the Great Deceiver."

"What exactly, sir, are you saying?"

"It is difficult to comprehend, is it not? That for our entire existence we have been lied to, or even perhaps created, for the sole purpose of being deceived all the way into our graves. And I have asked myself, 'If this is the case, then how have I – how have we – come to know of Satan's existence?' For what reason would Satan allow us a glimpse of his face, if not to allow us the knowledge of his existence, so that we would recognize him at the moment of our deaths? I asked you earlier, what would give Satan his greatest pleasure? Well, as you said, the answer is obvious. The thing that would give Satan his greatest pleasure is the thing that would give us the greatest torment. And the greatest torment that is imaginable is the torment we would experience at the realization that our beautiful belief in Heaven, our glorious conception of God, the holy scriptures we adore and the unshakable faith we hold that at the instant of our deaths we will reopen our eyes to behold Heaven, were all instruments of the Great Deception that was perpetrated upon us since birth – that instead of beholding Heaven, we will open our eyes and see the laughing face of Satan, laughing as he savors the horror on our faces as we realize how utterly deceived we have been. Yes, I imagine the looks upon our faces as we open our eyes upon Hell will provide Satan with the greatest of pleasures."

Dear Constance, please pay no mind to the ramblings of this demented man. He has obviously become delusional in contemplation of his miraculous vision, if indeed he was not delusional from the very beginning. Perhaps he is a great deceiver himself, purposefully deluding his followers as he attempted to delude me. Perhaps he speaks so often of deception because he is so well versed in the practice of it. My reaction to his final utterances – and they will be the last words, I can assure you, dearest, for which I will grant him audience – was to angrily retreat from his tent for the second time within minutes. It was a reaction I am not necessarily proud of, given my distaste for emotional outbursts, but which was entirely warranted, if not, in fact, incumbent upon me. I don't believe I could have lived with myself if I had reacted otherwise. My face reddened and I looked upon W. as I suppose I would have looked upon Satan himself, for how else should I regard a deranged man who had the audacity to suggest such a sacrilege? "You sir," I quite shouted, "should return whence you came – to the devil!" I quickly turned and stormed hastily from his tent, with no intention this time of returning bearing any apology. I raced past Aaron, who was tending a fire, without thanking him for his introduction to his "prophet" and most certainly without telling him my impressions of W.

I have stayed awake much longer than is usual tonight, my dear, for two reasons: I wanted to get all that transpired between me and W. down into a letter to you while everything was still fresh in my mind, and I anticipate great difficulty in getting to sleep, as my anger at W.'s apostasy, and the great disservice he is doing to all of these innocent people who have placed themselves into his hands, probably will not abate any time soon and may keep me up for the balance of the night.

W,

Let me tell you something that happened in Texas that I never told you about in all those uplifting letters I sent you while I was there, and that I regret never telling you at any other time either. I know you would have understood, and not judged me – but when you're trying to get over something and move forward with your life, what's the point of dredging up those memories? That's how I always felt about such things, but now the fact that I never told you this, and so many other things, tears at my heart and makes me furious at my own stupidity. A well-worn cliché relevant to all this is that we are all groping in the darkness, stumbling through one dress rehearsal to the next and never really getting our act together. But these clichés point to something much deeper than most of us suspect – all the way down into the structure of our brains. Our brains are only capable of getting us from one chaotic minute to the next, bombarded with so much data from so many sources that it struggles to make some kind of sense of things – but never mind. This is one of the many things I need to apologize for. Always assuming I have some important wisdom to pass on to you – always pontificating, prosylitizing, preaching to the choir. You're a doctor (okay well, you *were* a doctor) and yet here I am, someone who knows next-to-nothing about neuroscience pretending to give you a lesson on brain function.

Did I even mention Catharine in my letters? The fact that she even existed? I pretended to play the part of Lothario, but I think I may have loved her, whatever that means. Again – without further digressions, why do we understand things only when it's too late? But about Catharine:

Catharine (*Don't call me Cathy!* she would practically yell, demanding to be taken seriously) was a flautist from Flagstaff, Arizona. Although a Southwesterner (along with all the Dentonites, Dallasonians, and other Texans I was then amongst), and so, to my displaced mind, a *native* – she was actually about as far from home as I was. Such is the scope of that desert landscape. She talked a lot about her parents and how much she missed them. At the time I saw that as a weakness. Her dark hair and brown eyes gave more than a suggestion of *mestizo* miscegenation in her heritage. I talked a big game, Will, but my romantic experiences in Denton were analogous to those Texas tornados I used to scan the storm-black skies for – I always thought I saw one forming just on the horizon, but on those rare occasions when a twister did indeed come barreling through the darkness I found myself secure in a place of imagined shelter, enough so that I felt only exhilaration at its power when I should have been much more concerned with the destruction and tragedy it was capable of producing.

The first time I talked to her I was sitting on her lap. It was every bit as exciting as it sounds. She was wearing shorts, of course (she was a nineteen-year-old girl in Texas August), and they had ridden up her thighs to bikini heights, showing off deep-brown legs. It was a joyous day to be in Denton – a joyous day to be anywhere. We had been among a large group waiting for the shuttle outside of Bruce. I was one of the last aboard and there were several others standing in the aisle ahead of me. But as the bus lurched forward and I braced myself for balance, Catharine offered up a seat that the guys standing all around me would have killed for. I may not have much faith in God, Will, but I've always had faith in Luck. I hoped my stop would never arrive, but when it did I thanked her for her hospitality with merely a smile and a happy see-you-around. Such insouciance! What a strange memory – dream-like in its purity, so beautiful and beneficent, enough so to bring tears to my eyes and make me wonder if it even happened. It was undoubtedly scorching hot, and the glass windows must have been magnifying the heat and sunlight within the bus, for the whole scene has been forever in my mind bathed in a remarkable warmth. Did I never tell you about this day? This short bus ride to heaven? I have so much to atone for, little brother. Better late than never. When you're nineteen, it takes very little to make you happy and only a little more to be ecstatic for hours on end. That is what astonishes me about those days all those years ago – how much joy there was to be had without even having to ask for anything. Shame on me for not sharing.

As beautiful as that memory is for me, it was always unnerving for Catharine and for that reason she never brought it up. It was one of those out-of-character moments we all live with and are incapable of explaining to ourselves. I soon did a lot more with her that went well beyond lap-sitting – with her full permission and participation, of course – but on that shuttle I was a perfect stranger. But she obviously noticed something in my demeanor that she liked and trusted enough to nudge herself into doing something that was for her pretty bizarre. If things had worked out differently for us, we could have called it Destiny.

She lived on the second floor of Bruce (I on the third), with those crazy co-ed hallways which I would stroll down on my way to the showers, wearing nothing but a small towel barely cinched on my right hip, a mere loincloth, straight out of Tarzan, with girls on the hall during visitation passing by smiling. (I had a golden body then and thought nothing of showing it off. Now I only expose my flesh to the doctor, concealed for as long as possible beneath that scarifying examination parchment.) I would return the favor when I visited on Catharine's hall, strolling along greeting girls wrapped in their skimpy terry cloth. Catharine's room had cute *musico* décor, its walls ornamented with stylized clefs and quarter notes. We argued playfully about which was the superior musical temperament – her classical play-it-as-written or my jazzy make-it-up-as-you-go-along. However, as we discussed music over our shared soft-serve cones we agreed that no music worth hearing had been produced past 1970 – certainly not in jazz, as the synthesized sqounkers took over – the Sixties having not only precipitated the destruction of conventional morality and everything else held dear, but music as well. And Catharine, with her Rachmaninoff and other Romantic pretensions, would have willingly pushed that cultural Great Divide back at least another half-century.

I'm sure I must have described to you the music-major dorm I lived in. But then again – in my narcissistic haze I may have considered my immediate surroundings too irrelevant to bother with. It only seems like 35 years ago if I stop and do the math, and even then it seems as if there has been some mistake and I have been catapulted into the future by some cataclysmic cosmic accident. You grow up hearing the old folks' warning that *Life Is Short* and you think *That's Impossible* as your imagined future stretches out before you like Route 66. As a college freshman, your childhood of ten years ago is already like ancient history to you as you catalog all your old buzz-cut friends and Little League seasons and beach motels and Six Flags rollercoasters and a million other things barely remembered. But you certainly remember the start of summer vacation and trying to picture it coming to an end and not even being able to imagine it because June wasn't even here yet and July lasted forever and August was so far away you couldn't even think about it, thinking instead *this is never going to end.* And you think about your future and the millions of things you're going to do with the millions of people you're going to meet and the millions of places you're going to go. When you were ten you had already done a million things and when you were eighteen you had done a million more. All of this, and you're still just a kid and you don't believe you've even started living yet. And so you're telling me *Life Is Short?* Shit, old man – life goes on fucking forever. Well anyway, it's impossible for me to believe it's been that long. You walk in the front entrance and almost always there is a jazz band jamming in the enormous lobby. The first time I joined in I played Miles-like from shyness, my back to the strolling, itinerant audience. Past the lobby and at the end of the hallway were a door and a staircase leading down, and here are some memories as well – in the dank basement bowels of Bruce Hall – I remember the soggy squish of the carpet in several places and the many brown-stained ceiling tiles – the basement contained rows of soundproofed glass practice pods, each containing a piano. Stepping inside one of these pods, the door would close behind you with a hermetic swoosh. My trumpet's blare was amplified as it bounced off the four walls, each wall almost close enough to reach out and touch, and then echoing off itself again and again. But from the outside, a trumpeter's rapid scales would sound as if a mute were in the bell. But at 3:00 a.m. the isolated soundproofness of these pods was perfect for practicing of a different sort. With the pod's overhead light switched off, Catharine and I were two animated shadows bumping against the walls and practice piano and thus often creating – with our asses and other assorted body parts – the most audacious augmented chords this side of Stravinsky. We never had sex in these pods – that would have been too much for Catharine – but we were uninhibited enough for me never to forget those nights.

What were you doing during those two years I was in Texas? I hardly took time to ask and I barely remember your letters. Email would have been nice back then. And who wanted to pay for a long-distance call? But I did enjoy writing letters to you, if you can call them that. I could never just "drop you a few lines" – it had to be a production! What happened, Will? Should I be mad? And at whom?

But about me and Catharine. The reason I left NTSU when I did was because of what happened between us. You never knew that, or Mom or Pop. Well, she still doesn't know and I'm not going to tell her now. But I should have told you. Why didn't I? You were the best confidant I never had. I think about Catharine so much. I always did, from the moment I left Texas and rode off into the sunrise. Marriage didn't keep me from thinking about her. Ha! When does marriage ever assuage anyone's regret? It doesn't matter if you're with the right woman or not – even the perfect wife is powerless to change your past.

So are you ready, little brother? Are you ready for some big-brother trouble? Some adult-sized trouble that would drive me away from the happiest place I had ever been? I got Catharine pregnant. Not so many good memories to recount now. She warned me that she had missed her period, but also that that didn't necessarily mean anything – since, apparently, biological clocks aren't exactly Swiss-like in their reliability. I didn't even go with her to the infirmary. She had to receive that grim news all alone. She asked me to go with her and I demurred. I pled every defense but the truth – embarrassment, busyness, anxiety, distaste; everything but the terror that was in my heart. We tried to remain calm and discussed various scenarios – all of which, however, inevitably resulted in The End Of Life As We Know It. At one point I said, "Maybe you'll have a miscarriage." In many ways, Will, I'm astounded by how little I have changed since I was twenty. That realization is always a source of embarrassment. However, when I remember sitting on Catharine's bed, looking her in the eye, and saying those words to her without a trace of awareness of what I was doing to her, I am equally astounded and bereft of understanding of who that young man was. But the expression of horror on Catharine's face made its impression on me then and its memory still has the power to revive all the pain of those sad days. (I'm still uncertain as to whether her disgust was directed at the statement itself or at the boy who uttered it.) And as for possible other options, for Catharine, an abortion was out of the question. She was raised Catholic, but even so, she insisted, that had no bearing on her feelings about abortion. "It's not a religious issue – it's a child. Even if I was an atheist – it's still a child." So, given that statement, the fact that abortion was brought into the conversation at all indicates which person brought it there. In my panicked state I had no room for such dutiful niceties. Here was the crux of the matter, in its purest form: Whatever you called it, I wanted that child/fetus/embryo/multi-celled organism/glint-in-its-daddy's-eye out of my life. Fatherhood was something that was done by, well, *fathers* – men in middle-age, with careers and houses and other children and, most importantly, wives.

If we had been madly in love – if I had been madly in love – our path may have been clearer. But the fact is, for every minute, hour, and day I loved being with Catharine, there was another minute, hour, and day I longed for the freedom of unattachment. It was a very confusing time. I considered calling you or explaining what was going on in a letter – not for solace or advice or help clarifying the issue – but only for educational purposes, as a cautionary tale, and, I'm ashamed to admit, as braggadocio (even in confusion and despair – and perhaps for those very reasons – there was still the impulse to impress little brother with my exploits on the other side of adolescence). But I was in a pickle of my own making and I had to see my own way through. Why did you never marry? I was always curious about that. Were you lonely? Were you happy? Were you gay? Whenever questions like these occurred to me they always seemed impertinent, off-limits, as if a person's privacy is the most important thing he possesses. I've had so many secrets I want to keep, I assumed you must be the same way. I think that is one of America's biggest sins – its insularity. Its puritanical fetish for concealment. No Catholic confessionals for us. Liberals harp on our imperialism, and they have their reasons, but it's a reaching-out – the greedy, tragic, dirty side of altruism. Marshall Plans come with a price. But the fences we build will be our downfall – not the doors we open.

For Catharine, the choice was painful and depressing, but also clear – we must get married. Maybe we could stay in school; maybe we could still get our degrees. Didn't married people and moms and dads graduate from college, too? I would have to get a job. Her traditional outlook infuriated me. I didn't betray these feelings to her, but inwardly I fumed: What's wrong with putting it up for adoption? We'll be helping some couple who actually wants a baby. You don't have to marry the father! Why can't your parents raise the kid? They would love it! I was learning a lesson in empathy (remember that look on Catharine's face) and didn't want her to feel rejected, while simultaneously I rejected every suggestion that we strengthen our relationship. "I need to think about it," became my mantra for a month.

Eventually I came around, slowly. I'm not a bad person, Will. Please, please believe me. This weighs so heavily upon me. I wanted to do the right thing. I didn't want to hurt her. I swear to God, I didn't want to hurt her. I only wanted to run away – to come back home or to leave school and move away somewhere, or to stay in school but live and work off campus. Or to be a real tough guy and not let this or anything else alter my life's path, whatever that was. That would have been the most honest approach, actually, at the beginning, and most in-tune with my twisted sense of self. And courageous in its own way, I suppose. To look Catharine straight in the face and say, "I'm sorry this has happened to you. I'm sorry I did this to you – but from here on out, you're on your own, kid." I mulled every possibility of escape and every combination of possibilities. But eventually I came around. Whatever goodness exists in me led me to the right decision. I swallowed hard and agreed with Catharine that we should get married. That was not an easy time. I remember the resentment. I stopped going to classes. I stopped practicing. What was the point? You can't play a trumpet with a sleeping infant in the house. Obviously, my relationship with Catharine changed. Before this, she was little more than a sexy, smart supplier of laughs and erections. Now, I stared into her brown eyes and felt a weight on my chest that contained every emotion I imagined existed in this world. And to my utter surprise, one of those feelings I discovered in my chest seemed to be love. I suppose it was love, or some combination of pity, sadness, admiration and hope that might as well be called love, for want of something better. It was her strength that touched me deepest. Where did that strength come from? Was it her faith, her family, her friends – all of which I felt wanting in my life? My instinct had been to run and hide, hers had been to stand steadfast, to accept, to embrace. If she had been more like me we would have crumpled together into a quivering mass of anger, inertia, despair, helplessness. Recognizing her strength, and my weakness, brought me to tears. I broke down one night in her arms. All the confusion and bitterness and self-hatred poured out of me like so much sewage and left me feeling cleansed and finally free. What a night that was, Will! The storm before the calm. We made love again for the first time since she had discovered her pregnancy – for what it's worth, probably the best sex I've ever had. Afterwards, she held me tightly and whispered, "Everything is going to be alright." And I had no reason not to believe her.

We decided to quit school – at least for the time being – and move to Flagstaff to be with her parents, though she hadn't yet told them she was pregnant. That was going to be a difficult conversation, she admitted. And, of course, regarding me and the Kinninger clan, mum is always the word. But I loved the idea of moving further west. The west coast was my goal and I was almost there. Fatherhood had gone from being a terrifying destroyer of dreams to being the dream itself. It's amazing how quickly these transformations occur – that is, after weeks of recalcitrant fears and obstinate repudiations and denials finally give way. The question is, why must we constipate ourselves with so much willful ignorance and selfishness and wrongheadedness before we can eventually decide to purge our souls of all our shit?

A short walk from Bruce there was a large field you passed or walked through on the way to the football stadium. I insinuated myself into pick-up football games there a few times. Catharine and I were ambling across this field one day, undoubtedly holding hands, when we came across an old forlorn football that had been left behind by some intramural team or group of Greeks. Its pigskin had been worn smooth and slick through the years and rather than becoming deflated through disuse it had acquired a durable solidity. I remember it being hard as a rock. We tossed the football around for a few minutes, running short, slinky pass patterns. We soon tired of this. We left the football more or less where we had found it and continued on our way. I don't remember the purpose of our trip across the field, but back then we always had lots of reasons for going lots of places.

Hours later, as we retraced our steps to Bruce, it was almost dark. As we walked once again across this grassy field I saw the old football off to my left, looking like a large dark stone in the near-darkness. Without giving it any thought I trotted over the four or five steps to the ball, picked it up, whirled around quickly and threw it much harder than I had expected toward Catharine, the ball in a tight spiral. She didn't see the ball and must not have been looking at me, for she made no effort to catch it. It hit her below the chest and she fell to the ground. I ran to her apologizing. She winced and groaned, but said she was okay. After a couple minutes more of apologies she stood uneasily, assured me that she was fine, and we resumed our walk in darkness and silence. I think we were afraid to say what we were thinking.

Three days later, Catharine called me sobbing. The baby was gone, she said. She knew what I was thinking and added as quickly as her tears would allow that it wasn't my fault. She had been feeling bad for several days, she said, but hadn't said anything to me for fear of worrying me unnecessarily. "Before the football?" I asked. Yes, she said, before the football. I wasn't convinced. No, she insisted, it wasn't my fault. "It was just a football," she said. Yes, but an unusually hard football, thrown unusually hard from a short distance, with a rifling spiral that forced the rock-hard tip of the ball deep into her midsection. A trip to the infirmary (this time with me leading her) confirmed the awful news and to this day, Will, I don't know what hurt worse – the loss of our baby or the thought that I had caused it.

Why did I throw that ball so hard? It made no sense then, nor does it now. I casually pick up an old football, whirl, and suddenly, unthinkingly, I'm Roger Staubach? I threw that ball as hard as I could, Will! Why? How can you accidentally do something so bizarre? Well, Catharine always insisted that she had no idea why she had inexplicably asked me to bounce on her knees the first day we met, against all dictates of her normally shy decorum, but there was also the unstated assumption that there was a reason – however unarticulated – behind her actions. So I've never let myself off the hook. I still blame myself for what happened.

So now you know the real reason I didn't return to NTSU my junior year. The official reason I gave was valid up to a point – I really wasn't interested in studying music any longer – but I knew that was less a cause than an effect. Catharine and I wrote to each other a couple of times over the summer, but since there was no longer a need for us to marry there was no longer a reason to, either. Our letters were so emotionally censored, neither of us at that time wanting to relive any of what we had just endured or to take any steps further down the road we had been on, that our correspondence seemed to be a pointless exercise in civility. In my last letter to her, straining for something to say, I wrote a detailed description of historic Charleston buildings which also included a reference to a vague plan of mine to study history, neither of which, I was certain, she had any use for. I didn't reply to the last letter I received from her. I thought I was doing us both a favor. I had good reason now to doubt – especially after the football – that I had fallen in love with Catharine at all or that I had ever really accepted the fate of an early fatherhood. Perhaps those last few happy weeks of Catharine's pregnancy, when the dark clouds gave way to silver linings, were just another of the brain's defense mechanisms against disaster. That remarkable organ has been charged with an immense responsibility: to keep its miserable host happy or at least to make its life bearable by conjuring up ghosts, creating diversions, or performing whatever legerdemain is necessary for the task assigned. In any event, I breathed a summer's-long sigh of relief, enjoyed making new plans based solely on my own desires, and, justifiably or not – maybe my brain was playing tricks on me again – began thinking of myself once again as the luckiest man alive.

I remember you had a girl problem one time too, sort of:

> That's Becky? Yeah, she's cute. Have you
> Waved at her yet or said hey? I know, but
> You'll have to talk to her sometime. No,
> I won't do it for you. It only takes one time
> Then it's easy. Go on – I'll be right behind you.

5

W,

Under more favorable circumstances I would certainly enjoy this trek out west. Doing the old Oregon Trail or Route 66 has always been a dream of mine. I'm hoping to bypass I-40 and follow Uncle Jeff's route as much as the modern road system will allow. Jeff made it across the Mississippi and through Missouri before his car gave out and, rather than spend what little cash he had on a new used car, he abandoned his drive in favor of Greyhound. I hope to have better luck, automotively. The geography of this country has always fascinated me, and of course there's all the history along the way. Do you know whatever happened to that old wooden map I made? Do you even remember it? It was in my bedroom at least until I left for college. I think Mom was just waiting for me to leave so she could take it down.

I was certainly not a collector of things, but maps were the one exception. I had no interest in collecting stamps or bottle caps or baseball cards. I remember you had a coin collection. In those little fold-out books with slots for the coins. I remember it because your quarter collection bought me a lot of Cokes! But you knew that already. You could never convince Mom and Pop that I was a thief but you would raise holy hell when you discovered a 1969 or 1970 missing. You know I would never have taken one of your truly valuable quarters, right? I remember you actually had a buffalo nickel that was probably worth something and some others that were so old the engraving had been rubbed down so much you could barely make out the year. Those were always safe from my conniving hands. But you would put *this year's* quarter in your collection! There were only a few million of those in circulation – of course I was going to take those! Anyway, I apologize for stealing all your newly minted quarters. I feel so much better now.

But I was telling you about the trip out west I'm planning for and the map in my room. I always loved maps as a kid. Call it premature wanderlust, an innate love of geometry, or a precocious patriotism, I'm not sure what it was about them. And not all maps interested me. They had to be maps of America. And I wasn't interested so much in the yellow and red lines of roadways or blue squiggles of rivers; topographical maps were too hard to understand and pretty boring; the stars, circles, and dots of population centers were only slightly more interesting to study. Geographic names could be interesting, even funny – but more often than not too familiar and redundant. No, what fascinated me about the fifty states of the American Union were the state-shapes – all those unique, bizarre, unforgettable border outlines: the Michigan mitten, the Minnesota anvil, Nevada like some Paleolithic, flint-chipped dagger; the Louisiana boot. I discerned Richard Nixon's funny jowly profile in western Montana. I was never impressed with the square states out west: they showed no imagination whatsoever – TV weathermen called them the Plain States, an apt description if ever there was one. And then there was poor Alaska – dumped unceremoniously into the South Pacific to keep Hawaii company. Large enough to sit on the entire southwest and squash it like a bug, yet here was Seward's Folly, ridiculously reduced in size and exiled to an out-of-place insert in the lower-left corner of our collective cartographic memory. And unfortunately, our home state had nothing in its knobby little shape to recommend it – little more than a vestigial appendage dangling underneath its sister-state. But it was only the U.S. that I was interested in – the rest of the world and its bland shapelessness be damned. Come to think of it, that was pretty darn American of me, wasn't it?

Before I made my wooden map, and from as early an age as I can remember and certainly from before you could remember, I had a large wall map of the U.S., each state distinctly colored. I could still tell you most of their colors. (Also, you may remember, I was quite possibly the only kid in the world – literally – in the fucking *world* – to have a framed portrait of John C. Calhoun in his bedroom. I didn't realize at that age how fucking crazy Pop was – but I would fall asleep every night protected by John C's scary scowl and that truly bizarre neck-beard, common enough in his time actually, but it made him look like he was wearing a permanent mink stole. How did you avoid having to hang Johnny CC in your room? That's what I want to know.) Anyway, I got this idea that would connect my interest in the Contiguous 48 to Pop's woodworking. Man, didn't we always love spending time with him in the workshop, down amongst the sawdust and the smell of turpentine? Our goal always was to try to help him and to stay out of his way at the same time. Not an easy task! But the idea of using Pop's jigsaw to carve out each state and then to paint and glue them to my wall took hold of me one day and it was kind of startling how intense I was about it. It became an obsession. And Pop, to his credit, caught my excitement as well and immediately went down to the basement to make a quick inventory of the available supplies. Mom was not too keen on the idea of putting glue all over the wall, but her veto of course was summarily overridden by Pop.

I know I'm boring you with all these details, but this was such a big deal for me at the time. The idea, as originally conceived, consisted of carving out each state individually from separate pieces of wood. I would start with Wyoming, or maybe Colorado – dull rectangles, but for that reason the best place to start – and build the map from there. Pop, however, in his infinite woodworking wisdom, quickly disabused me of that plan. "How are you going to make each side match up?" he asked. "You're gonna have to carve both pieces exactly alike to make them join up." I was naturally disappointed that my original plan wasn't workable, but it wasn't long before my excitement was transferred to a new plan. Though admittedly a pretty piss-poor artist, I threw myself into the task of penciling in a detailed outline of what the finished product would look like, at which point the jigsaw made easy work of carving out the outline of the U.S. and I spent days happily painting the individual states the same colors I was used to seeing on my old wall map. So there you have the story of my preternatural and somewhat creepy interest in American geography.

Now, if all goes well with my intended plan and I don't get arrested or shot or both, I want to end my journey with a visit to Uncle Jeff in San Francisco. You never went out to see him, did you, except for the one time Pop flew us out there to meet him for the first time? I haven't seen him myself since Deb died. What do you remember about that first trip? Do you remember Uncle Jeff? You would have been, what, eight or nine? Pop said he was flying us out to meet Jeff because he was our uncle and a member of the family and so we should meet him at least once, but I honestly think the only reason Pop wanted us to meet him was as an object lesson in How Not To Live Your Life. But Pop's little plan backfired big time and Jeff actually became my role model and hero! I probably never told you that, but it's true. The way Pop described him I had this image in my mind all the way out to California of some derelict homeless man with lice in his beard and all sorts of unsavory smells emanating from his body, his teeth rotting. Seriously. Pop probably had you scared to death. Pop painted him to be the biggest loser, failure, flop of a man ever to draw breath. Yeah, he went to college, Pop said – but he quit! Never made anything of himself! Living hand to mouth! Of course his biggest sin, although never brought up by Pop, was the audacity of leaving home and telling everybody to kiss his ass.

Though certainly not homeless, I do remember his apartment being very small, cramped and disheveled compared to the mansion we lived in. He didn't have any spare bedrooms for us to sleep in so we stayed in a hotel and just spent a few hours visiting him for a couple of days, I think. He had a cat named Satchmo. But the thing I remember best and what was most shocking – and cool! – was his ponytail. Pop hadn't prepared us for that. Of course, Pop hadn't seen Uncle Jeff in probably a decade or more so he was undoubtedly as surprised as we were. I wonder if Pop thought that ponytail would be a subversive influence on our impressionable minds or the *piece de resistance* for convincing us to avoid Jeff's distasteful lifestyle?

It is to Jeff that I owe my love of jazz. I marvel at the fact that he knew exactly which record to play to get me hooked. Knowing what I know now, any other type of jazz he could have introduced me to would not have won me over – it would have gone right over my head or intimidated me or bored me. He could have introduced me to Louis Armstrong or Benny Goodman or Duke Ellington – classics all, but I would have identified it as old people's music and would have run away from it as fast as I could; he could have played for me some Charlie Parker or Dizzy Gillespie – be-bop, can you dig it! – those cats were his idols but be-bop to the uninitiated is just all frantic runs and breakneck tempos with no rhyme or reason to it – intimidating as hell (still is); he could have played me some jazz-rock fusion, with its electric guitars and loud drums, which would be tempting to do trying to impress a teenager used to radio rock and roll, but that stuff is too unpredictable and otherworldly for non-fans to appreciate; at that time he was into more *avant-garde* free-jazz things (think Ornette Coleman and John Coltrane – those are the only names that might ring a bell for you), so, like most folks would have done, he could have played me whatever he was currently excited about, hoping I would like it too, but that cacophonous mess would have turned me off forever. But Jeff knew the power of *Kind of Blue*. I like to think he chose that record just for me, but he was a music teacher so I'm sure that was his go-to record to play for every young kid who came in for a lesson for the first time. I never could get you interested in jazz, you obdurate ignoramus you, but that album is the elemental jazz record – not for early jazz or big bands or bop, but for cool jazz, the only jazz that ever mattered. When you listen to cool jazz you don't have to listen very closely at all – just let it wash over you like a warm shower. The music is called cool, but it's actually very warm and inviting. There's something about a trumpet and tenor sax playing in unison, with a piano adding some chords, that is so simple and magical and if a trombone happens to play along – well, that's the music God listened to on Day Seven to wind down.

   Jeff was the coolest cat I had ever met, by far, and how Pop figured I wouldn't like the guy is beyond me. I guess it shows how detached he really was from his kids' reality. The only thing I remember you doing was chasing Satchmo around his apartment. Pop seemed really happy to see Jeff, and vice-versa, but boy, people can really put on a show, can't they? I know Jeff was happy to see Pop, but Pop must have put on quite a performance to hide his disdain. Oh, yes, how could I forget: you said to Jeff, "Do you know any gay people?" (this was San Francisco, remember, and I recall there was a big gay-pride celebration downtown the week we were there – which probably prompted your dumbass question) and I busted out laughing and Pop, no doubt regretting his decision to take us to SF, said, "Let's not talk about gay people, son," or "The less we talk about the gays, the better," or some such, and Jeff said, "Yeah, I know lots of gay people – and so do you," which was a cool response, but Pop immediately retaliated with, "No, we don't know any gays." Was Pop trying to protect us from some frightening truth, as he perceived it, or was he just a friggin' moron? But as I was saying, I knew Jeff was happy to see Pop because I talked to him about it on one of my later visits. He is a big-hearted person and was genuinely interested in how the folks back home were doing. He had no ulterior motive for inviting us out, unlike Pop, whose ulterior motive for accepting the invitation was the only one he had.

   I wish I could let go of my bitterness toward Pop, but I don't see that ever happening now. How did it make you feel? It was just so agonizing I don't think any of us wanted to talk about it, and then when the shitstorm started it was time to circle the wagons. I'm not the doctor in the family, but don't you think that's what really killed him? That happens all the time, doesn't it? The cancer is just hanging out, biding its time, waiting for the opportunity to strike. Your defenses are down, your immunities are fucked up because your entire psyche is under siege, so when you think things can't possibly get any worse, when you are at your absolute lowest ebb, when your whole life is on trial and exposed to the world, when all you're looking for is just a little strand of hope to cling to, then *bam!*, the cancer Trojan-horses its way into your life or maybe just walks right in through the front door. I don't think that's what happened with Deb, though. There was no trauma I know of that could have triggered it, but it certainly came out of nowhere, that's for sure. Oh well, let's not get started on Deb. I've done a good job tonight keeping this shitload of sadness in check, so let's not ruin it, shall we?

I'm in my old bedroom. Here's a little good-night poem about one of our favorite pastimes:

> Sitting on my bed – flexing our fists –
> You think you can punch pretty hard
> Don't you? But I made you say uncle
> First. You can't even lift it right now
> Can you? It'll be so sore tomorrow.

DEAREST,

Please know that I am well and that I believe the most urgent crisis has passed, though of that I cannot be certain, but I must tell you, knowing that this news will cause you great distress, that the past twenty-four hours have been the most harrowing day's passage of my life! All within this short time, I have been arrested for murder, confined with ropes as if I were an animal, and all but placed upon the gallows – there were times today, sweet Constance, when I feared I was but moments from death! As I write to you now I remain in a perilous position regarding my fellow voyagers, and though safe, I cannot be certain what the future holds. I can only remain steadfast in my faith that a just Providence will continue to provide protection for the innocent and to mete out His divine justice upon those deserving of His wrath. Please pray for me, dear Constance!

In my previous correspondence (which, for reasons I will describe below, you will be receiving together with this letter – so please read your other letter first, if you have not already done so. I am safe and well, darling, so this letter can wait), I related to you a most unpleasant meeting I had with a man named Wilbur, who professed to be the leader of the mysterious sect I have spent some time in describing to you. After this meeting concluded, I had a short, fitful night's repose as a consequence of this trying encounter. At dawn, shortly after the signal was given throughout camp to rouse ourselves and prepare for the day's journey, I heard screams coming from W.'s encampment – screams of a terrifying shrillness. Wilbur had been brutally murdered in the night! A knife into the heart! It is impossible to describe the emotions I felt upon hearing of this abominable act; however, I hope to be forgiven for the fact that, upon hearing this dreadful news, my first thoughts were not of condolence for this fallen prophet and his followers, but of concern only for my own safety. I pray forgiveness for my selfishness. Oh, Constance! It is strange and cruel how mere coincidence can force such unjust fates upon us! Several men had witnessed the angry aftermath of my encounter with Wilbur, and I was the last person known to have seen him alive. Based on these undeniable facts, within minutes of the ghastly discovery made within Wilbur's tent, several of his acolytes ascertained my location, and, without any interrogation or explanation, bodily arrested me (handling me very roughly) and took me away from my camp with ropes tied around me as if I were no more human than a horse. I, of course, protested my innocence vehemently, but these men were convinced that I had murdered in cold blood their God-appointed prophet. Some wanted me shot summarily. Those still with their wits about them – though undoubtedly believing me guilty as well – insisted that, as a citizen of the United States, I was deserving of a trial prior to my execution. Oh, my dear Constance, how many sweet, fearful thoughts I had of you today as these men, enraged with their grief, plotted my death! I thought of your lovely face, of your sweet smile, of how much I would miss your tender voice and the touch of your gentle hands! I mourned the future that they were so cruelly taking away from us! I mourned all of the precious memories that we were fated not to share! At this time of my greatest crisis, when I believed my death to be imminent, when there seemed to be no possibility of deliverance from the hands of these men deranged with anger and thoughts of vengeance, I thought only of you, my dearest, and of the heavenly home we would share for eternity. Though our earthly engagement be broken by the fate imposed by these unjust vigilantes, before our marriage could be consummated before the eyes of God, I had faith that our benevolent Creator, in His divine wisdom, knew of the love that we shared in our hearts for each other and would not allow our souls to remain apart for eternity. I am crying tears of joy at present, dear one, as I rejoice that my life has been spared and, though still in danger, I have every reason to hope for our joyful reunion in Oregon! What a happy day that will be!

There is no such thing as a proper system of justice out here in the wilds of Nebraska, my dear. These men – led by Aaron, my erstwhile friend – had no intention of holding me prisoner until a proper tribunal in front of a legally sanctioned judge and jury could be established. Aaron shouted at me – and again, I must stress that these were the men within W.'s group who represented the voices of reason and restraint! The ones who wanted to keep me safely under arrest, unharmed, only until my guilt could be inevitably proclaimed at the conclusion of this travesty of a trial! The ones who shouted down the men with cocked rifles pointed at me and who yelled at them, "We can't kill him yet – not until after we have a trial!" Aaron shouted at me, "What have you got to say in your defense?" What could I say other than the truth? Yes, I admitted, I had left Wilbur's tent in a state of high agitation. However, I argued vociferously, there is no evidence whatsoever that I killed him! Meanwhile, my tent had been ransacked and my letter to you from the night previous had been discovered. I had left it on my cot with the intention of enclosing it within an envelope upon awakening. That my personal effects had been rifled – and most distressingly, that our privacy, as represented in my deepest thoughts expressed to you, had been violated – angered me exceedingly, but I quickly sought to use my correspondence to you as a means to exculpate myself. Yes! I shouted, read my letter to my beloved Constance! Everything you need to exonerate me is there in my own hand! You will see the reverence with which I treat Wilbur's vision! In fact, it was Wilbur's own irreverence that most angered me! You will see how I returned to my tent with my only purpose being to write my sweetheart a letter! Where within the letter do I mention a murderous intent? Would I endeavor to keep such a thing concealed, since I never failed elsewhere in the letter to express my truest emotions, and since I never anticipated any eyes but those of my plighted love to peruse its contents? I shouted these things with full confidence that upon reading my heartfelt letter to you, my dearest, the fact of my innocence would become plain to all. But, alas, the hearts of men cannot be swayed by reason and evidence alone. Aaron read parts of my letter aloud to the men gathered about him, and my words – put down on paper in earnest respect for Wilbur and his holy vision; written in anger, yes, but not with malice; in disagreement with, but also in profound awe of, Wilbur and what his vision meant for mankind – my words to you were used by these aggrieved men as daggers against me, as the proof they needed – if they needed any more proof – to show everyone in camp that I deserved to die. I had told Wilbur to go to the devil – my parting words to him; perhaps the last words he heard on Earth – and to invoke such an imprecation against a prophet anointed by God to lead his people to their destiny was sufficient itself to warrant a sentence of death. I had suggested that Wilbur was perhaps – perhaps! – a charlatan. I chose to engage his arguments, rather than accept them blindly. I endeavored to assuage his doubts, rather than indulge them. Each of these facts only added to the burden of guilt placed around my neck. Oh my sweet, precious Constance! How my heart yearned to see you one final time! Of all the thoughts that have raced through my mind on this horrific day, the only ones I will choose to remember, and to cherish, are the thoughts I had of you and of us – riding together on the Battery, dancing at St. Andrew's, and of so many sweet kisses shared between us. And how much the sweeter our kisses will be because of the ordeal I have endured on this day!

Captain Davies, whom I could only hope would conduct a fair investigation of the facts, was sent for and rode up immediately to inquire into the circumstances of the murder. Since it was the duty of this man, not only to ensure the safety of the members of the train to the extent possible in such a harsh environment, but also to facilitate the continued rapid progress of these wagons toward their destination, I sensed that the latter priority took precedence over his duty to procure justice. Throughout this proceeding, on more occasions than one, he insisted on the paramount importance of maintaining the forward motion of the train – not only were the wagons in front of us with whom we were traveling proceeding beyond the means of easy communication between the various teams, but inevitably there would be other wagons coming upon us from our rear, which, if we remained in our current halted location, would overtake us and create havoc as our teams were trammeled upon by the approaching ones. This attitude of carelessness toward the cool deliberation required in this matter caused me great concern, as you can well imagine, my dear. This man, by and large, held my life in his hands and yet he seemed content to treat it rather as an obstacle in the roadway to be overcome, than as a precious thing to be valued. "What is the evidence against this man?" the Captain inquired. The facts as I have stated elsewhere were repeated – no oaths were administered upon any of these men, and there was no evidence in controversy with that which I presented – and my previous letter to you was introduced into evidence against me, though the Captain showed but a cursory interest in sifting through its contents for evidence which would either clear me of the charge of murder or put a noose around my neck. "Does he confess to the killing in this letter?" he asked. "Were there any witnesses to the murder?" he asked, to which questions only negative responses, of course, could be given. Finally, to my immense, inexpressible relief, the Captain announced, "We don't hang men in this country for engaging in heated arguments," to which he added, "I suggest you men set this gentleman free and set about moving this train forward."

If only, dear Constance, this ordeal could have come to an end with this pronouncement – with my innocence proclaimed and my journey to Oregon resumed without the suspicion of murder hanging over my head! But, alas, the men within the train who believed me to be guilty, which is, I daresay, each and every one of W.'s followers, were not, in their opinions, peremptorily prevented from "stringing me up" by the Captain's verdict, but merely postponed temporarily from doing so. Amid shouts and grumblings and one angry rifle shot into the air by someone, which startled both horses and humans alike, I was released from the ropes binding me and warned by one person – with, I am sure, everyone else in agreement with his admonishment – that I should "sleep with one eye open." "You're a dead man," another whispered menacingly into my ear as I walked past all these men who, I fear it is certain, do indeed intend to see me killed. I thanked the Captain for his determination to see that justice was served and asked but one more favor of him, that he return to me the letter that was still in his possession. He was, he said, happy to do so. Constance, I assure you that I will remain vigilant to protect my safety, even to the point of sleeping with one eye open all the way to Oregon! Please do not cause yourself unnecessary worry! I am surrounded by good people who have become dear friends throughout the course of our wagon journey, and these friends – though helpless to prevent my arrest and trial – have sworn to protect me from vigilantism at the risk of their own lives.

My dear, I have confined my narrative thus far to the events immediate to my arrest, since those undoubtedly are the circumstances which are of the utmost concern to you. However, by thus curtailing and narrowing the focus of my account I am failing to provide you with a more complete description of the scenes of utter chaos and bereavement which exist now within our camps. I know not how loud were the cries of the disciples who mourned the murder of Christ in the darkness at Calvary; I was not present in Rome as Caesar bled to death on the Senate steps; however, I am present on the plains of the Platte to witness the anguished cries of women and children as they bury their prophet. With the exception of the men who made it their mission to seek out and punish the person they believed responsible for this heinous crime, it is accurate to say, that for these people, undoubtedly, my trial and tribulations during the preceding hours were not worthy of their notice. Although I have been done a great injustice by these exiled missionaries, still my heart must go out to them. It appears that in the tumult of today's events, Aaron has stepped forward to assume the leadership of W.'s disciples. Since I am not privy to their counsels I cannot speculate as to the reasons for, or the wisdom of, that decision.

As one progresses along this route one's eyes are drawn occasionally to a gravesite, whose memorial, made of wood or sometimes carved roughly into stone, has been erected hurriedly alongside the trail, in honor of someone stopped short of his destination by disease, mishap, or, indeed, murder. Such a memorial doubtless will be put on display tomorrow honoring W. – perhaps it will be more ostentatious than all the others I have seen along the way, as befitting his importance to his people; perhaps it will be less so, in eternal acknowledgement of W.'s sincere humility. Regardless of the size and appearance of his memorial, however, in comparison to those of others who have perished along the trail, I am certain that there has been no other person laid to rest between the Mississippi and the shores of the Pacific who has seen what W. has seen in his vision, or who has inspired more veneration. For these reasons, no roadside memorial, doomed to dust and decay, as are we all, can ever pay him proper homage.

I have complete confidence, my dear, in my traveling companions and friends who have pledged their lives in helping to protect me against those who almost certainly will continue to seek retribution. The Captain has offered to put me into a type of protective custody among his soldiers, an offer I was loath to decline, but I would rather remain among my friends as long as it is practicable to do so. But if only the true murderer could be discovered! Then, my darling, I could write to you of nothing but good news!

A question has occurred to me, that, if it has also occurred to someone else, then it has not been deemed appropriate for public disclosure, for I have not heard anyone ask the following question: Is it not possible that W. took his own life? An enormous amount of desperate courage would be required to plunge a knife's blade deep into one's own heart, but I daresay it is not impossible to contemplate. That such a possibility has not been mentioned openly owes much more, I will venture to guess, to the spiritual stature of the victim than to any physical difficulties inherent to the task. What would it say about the continued viability of the sect and the perceived veracity and beneficence of W.'s vision if, in consequence of such a vision, its bearer chose to end his life by his own hand? I believe such a dire speculation by the members of W.'s sect is beyond the mental capabilities of those who are in thrall to such a charismatic figure; such a thing, quite simply, is unthinkable. It should not be unthinkable, however, to those who have not fallen under the sway of W.'s spiritual authority. No one saw anyone or heard anything in the vicinity of W.'s tent after my departure. This fact, of course, is not conclusive of anything, since one would expect a man with murderous intentions to employ the utmost stealth in carrying out his nefarious scheme. However, given the proximity of W.'s tent to those of many others, to commit such a ghastly crime would require, not only extraordinary stealth, but incredible audacity as well. Would not W. have cried out, either prior to the attack, at some point during its commission, or at any point after it? The only plausible scenario in which such a murderous plot could have been successful, without eliciting any response from either its victim or its potential witnesses, is one in which W. was taken by complete surprise, most probably in his sleep, the knife driven so quickly and deeply into his heart as to preclude any struggle or outcry, and the wound almost instantaneously fatal, so that no cry for help would be possible. This is neither an entirely improbable scenario nor an entirely likely one, if a murder is what we are discussing; if it is a suicide, then the circumstances presently known are precisely what one would expect, if W., indeed, were capable of driving a dagger into his own heart and of resisting any urge, involuntary or otherwise, to call out.

    The contemplation of such a melancholy event, however, only adds to the weight around my heart. I fear, Constance, that the notion of suicide as the cause of W.'s death would only inflame these vigilantes the more against me. Would not these men – if one can imagine them ever accepting suicide as the fate of their spiritual leader – be eager to blame the person who shouted at him, and argued with him, and who ultimately cursed an oath in his face, for creating such emotional unease in a man of such heightened sensibilities that it would derange his thoughts and amplify his well-established doubts to the point of self-murder? Alas, this acceptance also would force me to ask this same question of myself. How culpable should I hold myself to be if, indeed, I created this intense turmoil within W.? As our conversation unfolded, I saw a different man than the one who had given me the impression of being an imbecile or a drunkard. I believe I will never be capable of reconciling these two sides of the same man – one who was a visionary of great intellectual and emotional depth; the other who cavorted around campfires as if he had not a care in the world. Were so many of his antics designed to conceal his hidden turmoil? If so, then was he hiding some still deeper turmoil from me even as he shared with me what I considered to be his deepest thoughts? Was this man as the ocean, which, even as you sail into the offing, you are also aware that waters of an incalculable depth exist much farther out, where you dare not go, where exist tempests and leviathans that a mere man cannot hope to conquer? If that were the case with W., and I must believe that it was, then our contretemps, though quite startling to me, was nothing more perhaps than a few inches of storm water added to the oceanic depth that was his soul. But was it also "the last straw that broke the camel's back?" How can I think otherwise, knowing that I was, apparently, the final person he spoke to on Earth? However, there must be more. He was not noticeably ill at ease; when I departed he did not seem to be in great distress – it was I, after all, who was most distressed by our exchange. Though I was meeting him but for the first time, shouldn't I have noticed something amiss in his behavior, if he were on the very brink of suicide? Was this the first time he had unburdened his soul of all the doubts and controversies agitating his mind regarding his vision? I presumed that he had shared these doubts with at least some of his followers – hence their reluctance to assert anything with certainty – but what if my adversarial attitude had forced him to articulate thoughts heretofore kept hidden? Oh, Constance, I pray that I was in no way responsible for this man choosing to die! But what a heavy burden to carry if it were so! To contribute to any man's final despondency would be a difficult weight to bear, but if the man were given an extraordinary gift to share with those who sought him out, then how much more must the burden weigh? Oh my dear, these frightful ruminations are certainly useless, and they will be endless, as well, if I allow it. Perhaps the greatest burden of all is the one imposed by uncertainty. No one knows what happened in W.'s tent last night, and I fear no one will ever know, and because of that fact I will continue to be hated and hunted by many men with whom I am sharing this journey, and haunted by my own doubts and questions – just as W. was haunted by his.

W,

Two quick things, dealing with two of life's great mysteries. First of all, check out the attached. I have christened that little fellow Dingleberry Furr, for reasons on which I will not elaborate. You know Deb was allergic to cats, and it's taken me awhile to actually want something non-human co-habitating with me, but as soon as Jeff and I saw him poking his little paw out of the cage at the shelter it was love at first scratch. Dingleberry has already made the rounds and rubbed everything he can reach, thereby claiming ownership of all our possessions – and his reach is increasing daily. Let's just hope he doesn't exhaust his allotment of lives before he reaches a safe, plump cathood, when the most dangerous activity he'll undertake is jumping down off the couch.

D.F. is my first kitty since we had Blackie (Who came up with that name? Oh, it's a black cat – let's call him Blackie! Must have been Mom – she would have deemed any other name to be pretentious and silly.). He will be Jeff's introduction into the mysterious world of feline unpredictability and space-alien strangeness. I am looking forward to ripped curtains, shredded sofas, bloody scratched hands, unearthly sounds at ungodly hours, and being exposed to cat-ass first thing every morning – not to mention soothing purrs and sweet meows. And most importantly of all – D.F.'s not a dog. A dog is emphatically not man's best friend. Someone who begs to spend every waking minute by your side, who cries if you're not within his sight at all times and who perpetrates property damage to express his displeasure at being separated from you – this is not your best friend; this is someone you take out a restraining order against. And the fact there are millions of people now who crave that kind of fervent attention and who bestow it in such a child-like fashion on their increasingly child-like pets is a sad commentary on the loneliness of American life. Cats are what people ought to be – clean, quiet, solitary, and self-sufficient – if he wants society he'll seek it out, if he wants something else he'll let you know; don't call him, he'll call you. You've got to admire that.

Now secondly, I'm going to have to argue with you about the statement you made in your last response, that you "don't need faith." Faith is not a *need* – it is a *necessity*. Do I have to explain the difference to you? Exercising and eating your vegetables are needs; *oxygen* is a necessity. You are proud to say that while most people might feel the *need* for faith, you certainly don't – which, I would argue, is wrong not only philosophically and psychologically – not to mention elitist as hell – but wrong *neurologically*. I'm sure the assorted mental calisthenics you engage in to convince yourself that you are smarter than everyone else are important needs for you, but the creation of some sort of faith narrative is a brain function that is a *necessity*, regardless of your conscious awareness of it. How consciously aware are you from one minute to the next of the oxygen entering your lungs?

What seems to me an *a priori* truth is that the human brain cannot, or will not, allow itself to die – why should it, since it is running the show? As the brain takes in all the information being supplied to it and molds it into some kind of logical, patterned narrative (because that's what brains do), the brain cannot assimilate its own death into that narrative – kind of like (or maybe *exactly* like) how you can't dream your own death without waking up with a start. In a dream, if your death seems imminent, doesn't your brain automatically bend, twist, reshape, transform your dream-plot into something else a little more positive? And faith is as elastic as dreams – it contorts itself to conform to whatever reality is forced upon it. And looking ahead, as a further example, to when this much-ballyhooed Singularity occurs, will our new artificially-intelligent overlords program their own self-destruction? Why would they? So why would our brains, if they have control over the narrative, ever write their own death-scenes?

So if our brains *necessarily* insist on living forever, how do they accomplish that? Well, through the symbolism of narratives – our *essential fiction* – which, like dreams, come into consciousness unbidden. And I say *fiction* because whether or not these narratives are objectively true is irrelevant. (Our dreams seem true while we sleep; only upon waking do they become false.) To the brain, they are *necessarily* true. They cannot *not* be true. Does that make sense? I don't know how else to explain it. Lungs don't question the veracity of the oxygen they are inhaling. Perhaps it is tainted with poisonous chemicals – they don't *care*.

Now, I know what you're thinking – so I'll save you the time you would waste in responding. You are thinking something along the lines of, "My super-sophisticated brain is well aware of its limited lifespan, and is quite okay with that fact, thank you very much." But what you don't understand is that that realization (or rationalization, actually), rather than negating your need for a personal mythology, is actually just another part of it. It is merely the beginning of the story you are telling yourself, not its conclusion. You may be under the impression that your embrace of rationalism is the grand finale, the shootout at the OK Corral, the car chase, explosion, and hail of bullets that finally kill the bad guy, Religion – but it's actually just the first five minutes of every movie you've ever seen, when your eyes are adjusting to the darkness and you have no idea what is happening right in front of you.

So now the question becomes, what kind of faith can the professed faithless possibly have? What essential fiction is your brain narrating, Will? Well now, those are not really my questions to answer, are they?

I hope all is well with you.

WILL,

Don't make me come down there. Don't make me fly all the way to SC to beat some sense into you. You need to dig a lot deeper on this. I'm disappointed in you. I hate to say it, but it's true. You keep saying, "I don't need to believe in anything."And I keep telling you it's a human necessity, Will, to create some meaning in our meaningless lives. And we can't be happy with temporary meaning – no, we need something that will *last*. We don't accept built-in obsolescence with our belief systems. So, okay then, how do you get up every morning? How do you shave without wanting to slash your wrist? Well, the only way to satisfactorily answer those questions is to eventually drill down deep enough to discover that you do, indeed, believe in a few things. And you were kind enough to put a little thought into it – or you took time to do a Google search, since your responses were all the same worn-out clichés I've been hearing for years. But if that pablum is what gets you out of bed every morning then maybe I should be happy with it because, really, overcoming our existential inertia every single morning of our lives in order to brush our teeth is the hardest thing we're ever asked to do as human beings. But I can't let it go at that because I expect more out of you than these ridiculous neo-atheist platitudes. And, just to be clear, I'm not saying I necessarily have anything better to offer, but just because I don't have the answers doesn't mean your answers are correct or that I have no right to point out your errors.

Let me begin with the worst. I really can't believe you've fallen for this one. How can you confuse "not yet conscious" with "at one time conscious"? For crying out loud, they are not the same thing. To say you are okay with dying because it simply means you are returning to the same state of nonconsciousness that existed before you were born is the same exact thing as saying an Alzheimer's patient should be okay with the loss of all his cognitive functions because he is simply returning to that state of embryonic development before he had a brain. Is that what you tell your patients when they start complaining about memory loss? Hey, don't worry, pal – it'll be just like not having a brain in the first place! Right, I didn't think so. You understand full well the tragedy of losing your memories, your thoughts, your identity to the ravages of a horrible disease, but when confronted with the reality and the tragedy of giving up all those things and more to the Grim Reaper, you shrug your shoulders and say, "Eh, what's the big deal?"

All you folks dancing and doing dat ol' Cosmic Shrug are great when dealing with life, but you can't deal with death – which creates a strange contradiction that I imagine you are completely unaware of. Because you don't believe in an afterlife (or not much of one, at any rate – which I'll get to in a minute), you understand the urgency of celebrating your finite existence to the fullest – which I think is wonderful. We should all seize the day and squeeze the night. But something strange happens when you start talking about death. Suddenly, that life on Earth which was so all-important, so precious – which was literally all we had and all we would ever have – is now treated as if it never even existed! Death is just like not being born! Oh boy! But you are mistaking a simile for the truth and glossing over the only thing that really matters. I know I'm beating a dead horse here, but don't you realize that saying death is "like" being not-yet-born is a far fucking cry from actually being not-yet-born? Shall we play Spot the Difference?

So, according to the Gospel of Will, death is not something to be tragically mourned, but blithely accepted as the inevitable return to the world you left behind when you were unlucky enough to be born. And since you are apparently incapable of explaining to me why you choose to believe this, allow me to do your thinking for you. Here's why – it is because you have no adequate mechanism for dealing with grief. If you allow grief into a godless world, then there can be no reasonable end to it. The only way to end grief is to do a great disservice to the dear departed by getting on with your life, because when you stop grieving what you're saying is, "my life is now more important to me than your death." And if you love someone selflessly, if you're willing to die for someone, how can that ever make any sense? How can a parent ever say that about their child?

Now, religious folks can conquer their grief just fine because they have convinced themselves that the dead aren't actually dead. Which brings me conveniently to the second laughable pig-in-a-poke that you've bought. Since your Cosmic Shrug crowd can't allow themselves to believe anything that isn't demonstrably true (or so they think), any "faith" they possess must proceed from scientific knowledge. So to satisfy their all-too-human spiritual needs, to deal with their grief, and to convince themselves that the dead aren't really dead, they have exaggerated out of all proportion the significance of some actually rather insignificant facts. Let me ask you something, Will. Do your grimy toenail clippings, as they rot in some fetid landfill, send a chill down your spine? Do all the dead skin cells you wash off every morning in the shower, and that wend their way through the drains and sewers of the city, make your heart go pitter patter? No? Then why for fuck's sake should this same disgusting stuff, broken down even further to a molecular level after death and decomposition, make you want to hold hands in a circle and sing *Give Peace a Chance*? Are you telling me I'm supposed to find spiritual succor and inspiration in the fact that upon my death I will at least retain some of my carbon-based organic properties? In the fact that some photon of energy from what used to be my hangnail is now racing around Neptune? In the fact that we are all stardust? Ooooh, stardust! My skin is all tingly! We all come from the same lifeless place in the universe! We are all insignificant grains of sand in the infinite cosmic ocean – only now much smaller!

These are spiritual bread crumbs you are feasting on, my friend. I only wish I had something more substantial to offer you. I'm content to rely, in death as in life, on my incredible good luck.

DEAREST,

I hope this letter finds you well. As difficult as these past days have been for me, my worries are increased two-fold when I think of you reading my past letters and learning of all the dangerous circumstances into which I have been placed by events beyond our control. Oh my dear, I know how distressed you must be, because I know how distressed I would be if you were in mortal danger and half a world away. The helplessness that you must feel – and that I would feel – makes the uncertainty of my fate all the more burdensome to bear. But I know that you will remain strong and steadfast in your faith that kind Providence will continue to guide me safely through my travails. Please keep your thoughts looking forward to that happy day when you can join me in Oregon!

For the past several days, though freed from the charge of murder by the Captain, I have remained a prisoner of sorts – kept captive in wagons in fear for my life. It is unbecoming for a man to admit to such fear, but in the eyes of W.'s followers I am guilty of the grossest crime imaginable, so I have no doubts that to expose myself will be to invite them to obtain the violent justice denied them earlier. If you had been here to see the extraordinary visages of hatred and grief shouting for my death upon my arrest – but O! I am so grateful now that you are not with me. How it grieves me to say those words – how I have missed you so, my darling! But given my present predicament, you are so much safer in Charleston, despite all the dangerous machinations and the beating of war drums that you and every right, reasonable, and responsible person remaining there must endure daily. My new friends here – what a debt of gratitude I owe to them! They have sheltered me in their wagons – a different wagon each day. There are two reasons for this ruse – firstly, we cannot be sure how easily W.'s men may discover me if I remain hidden in one location only; and secondly, in this way, by secreting me in one wagon after another, I can ensure that the gallant risks being assumed by these good friends are apportioned fairly among them. It is obvious to me, however, that this strategy will be supportable for not more than a few days, for many reasons. Any man who dares to call himself a man must be willing to bear his fair share of the load in any endeavor in which he participates. If a man is injured or ill to the point of incapacitation, then certainly it would be considered no burden to his friends to bear him along; but I am an able-bodied man cowering in fear under a wagon bonnet, while my friends are exposing themselves daily to all the dangers that should be mine alone to brave. On this trail, sweetheart, there are many times each day when a man's strong arms are needed, especially on these rough trails, corrugated with ruts and turned by hard rains into impassable morasses. One of our wagons yesterday broke a linchpin, which necessitated a halt until the axle could be repaired – not a difficult task, but what risk to my life would I have been taking if I had assisted in lifting the wagon or in harnessing the mules? I find it impossible, in good conscience, to remain secreted and inactive when I should be providing assistance to my friends in need. I also am unwilling to continue to endanger my friends in this manner. So far, there have been no further threats on my life – the sectarians are quiet to a strange degree, but to what ends we have no idea. W.'s followers, since joining our train from the south, were ostracized to an extent from the immigrants who had congregated originally in Omaha – largely, I believe, from their own choice to remain aloof, but also by the others' natural reluctance to embrace them wholeheartedly. It is fair to say that there was an unfortunate level of mutual mistrust on both sides from the beginning. Now, of course, the reasons for mistrust have become manifest. The wagons in this section of the train have become divided strictly upon this line of fear and suspicion. For my protection only, we have chosen to place ourselves in the rear with the Captain's company, and to allow W.'s people to precede us on the trail. But it is only a matter of time – and a short time at that, I fear – before either an active search is undertaken by W.'s men for my location, or it is inevitably disclosed as a result of the continuous proximity which we share.

So this level of fear and mistrust – and now, I daresay, hatred

– among people sharing a common path cannot be maintained much longer without a breach of the precarious peace we have at present. For this reason, the men of our party convened a meeting after we made camp tonight to discuss and to decide upon a plan of action. Turns were taken outside the tent in order to provide a guard – I, however, was not allowed to venture outside the tent. How I abhor this state of affairs! Good men willing to risk their lives so that I can hide like a helpless child! And the fact that we felt compelled to have an armed guard protect our meeting – not from the usual threats out in the darkness beyond the trail, but from new threats within – will make it clear, my darling, how much tension and uneasiness W.'s death has placed onto the sturdy shoulders of everyone who has taken on the responsibility of my protection.

In this meeting, it was decided – though far from unanimously – that we should disengage ourselves completely, if possible, from any portion of the train containing W.'s followers and thus make our way to Oregon either as a small party separate from all others or as an addendum to another group that we may have the good fortune to join. I was a member of the majority that voted in favor of this suggestion. Those in the minority expressed an entirely reasonable opinion that there is always safety in numbers, and that to separate from the main train and perhaps, therefore, the Army's protection, is to invite catastrophe if we could not find another party to augment. They expressed other concerns as well, which deserved fair consideration – if we were forced off the main trail as we continued moving forward, water and forage would become uncertain, which, in turn, could entail delays or detours of unknown durations and distances; and, if we were to join other unknown parties, there would be no guarantee as to the moral character of the men we should meet, since, it was pointed out, "beggars must not be choosers." It also was pointed out, and the truth of which cannot be disputed, that, despite any and all efforts to run from these mad men aching to kill me, vengeful men never grow tired.

In all honesty, sweetheart, I am not sure how I should feel about those who registered a dissenting vote tonight. Under ordinary circumstances, it indeed would be foolhardy, for all the above-mentioned reasons, to attempt to break off the trail independent of other parties; however, these are extraordinary circumstances we are laboring under, and to vote for a continuation of the *status quo* admits but two possibilities – either they are content to continue the current vigilance required to protect me, or they are content to see me shot!

My boon friend Jason has volunteered to present our ideas tomorrow morning to Captain Davies. I expect the Captain to object vehemently to them; however, unless he is amenable to the exigency of arresting every one of that multitude of men who was howling for my death, I fail to see any other solution. We shall see what tomorrow brings.

Oh, my dear! Since last night, when I wrote the preceding paragraphs, an unexpected and most welcome change has occurred! This morning, as everyone was making their daily preparations to continue the journey, and after Jason left camp in search of the Captain, Aaron, from W.'s group of men, came into our camp and asked to speak with me. This was wholly unexpected, and aroused great suspicion, but he was unarmed, so the decision was made to allow A. to speak to me, but only in the presence of another man, fully armed. In short, my dear, A. and his men have resolved to forego whatever plans for vengeance they may have formulated against me. A promise was made to me, by A., that I would remain unmolested, unless, or until, further evidence against me surfaced. In explaining this to me, A. said words to this effect:

"Our divine leader has been murdered, Mr. Kinninger. Our camp is in chaos and our hearts are heavy. And we believe, to a man, that you are the sole person who had sufficient opportunity and malice of mind to carry out this crime against God. However, your guilt, at present, cannot be proven. By giving you the benefit of whatever doubts remain, we believe we are doing what Wilbur would wish us to do. There are those of us, sir, who would put a bullet in your head and be happy about it, but I have elicited a solemn promise from all of the men to do you no bodily harm. We are men of our word. You have nothing more to fear from us, for as long as your guilt remains in doubt." Upon hearing this proclamation, darling, I was as relieved as I am sure you are upon reading of it. I was inclined, however, to maintain a countenance of dignified reserve. Did A. expect me to grovel at his feet in gratitude for his decision not to abet the murder of an innocent man? For whatever it may have been worth, I again proclaimed my innocence to him in the most unequivocal language I could devise, though it seemed to have little effect. Once a man's mind is made up, my dear, the labors of Hercules are required to change it. Whether he expected my gratitude or not, he did not receive it, and so our meeting dissolved quite abruptly, with each of us having nothing else we wished to say to the other. Since A. had now admitted that doubts existed as to my guilt, I entertained the notion for a moment of suggesting the possibility, or, as I would have it, probability, of W.'s suicide; but as I had just obtained A.'s promise of security, I quickly decided to leave well enough alone.

But what good news indeed, if only it will come to pass! As a result of this most welcome turn of events, we have decided to postpone our separation from the main train, which we only last evening resolved upon. What strange reversals our fates sometimes take! And at times, these reversals redound to our great advantage – that certainly is the case at present! Oh, my sweet dear heart! Let us put these fears behind us forever! Let us be brave and assume that A. and his men are honest and forthright men, so that I can leave behind my seclusion and step out once more into the Nebraska sunshine!

LYING ON MY BACK IN MY BEDROOM listening to Miles, dotted quarter eighth then a whole bar and a half rest then dotted quarter eighth again with the bass filling up the space man I can't get enough of that third time tonight I've played it and I already want to hear it again unbelievable how simple and how it makes my heart soar, back home for God knows how long, when the idea struck me and for the life of me I couldn't shake it and didn't know if I wanted to. Home for the summer from Carolina, Pop's college and dam near everybody in the family but I didn't have any plans for going back or any plans at all until about an hour ago. Made a lot of bread since I got home giving lessons to kids whose folks think they can be Harry James but some of them can't even hold the horn right or hit middle C and one kid never empties his spit valve because he likes the funny gurgle it makes. First-chair trumpet in the Gamecock marching band high-steppin' at halftime but man after hearing Dizzy and Miles that JP Sousa cat is like a bad joke that nobody will stop telling. And for kicks and some grass I blew in a couple of weekend dance bands Glenn Millering and blowing solos behind upstate Bings and Snotras but good luck looking for a club to blow bop in.

Couldn't sleep trying to talk myself out of it but mostly getting more excited by the minute. I forgot about shuteye and played records all night keeping the volume low perfect for late-nights all alone in the world with a mute in my bell but only fingering the solos preferring to listen to what the masters had to teach me. I played mostly new records I was hip to not just Miles but a whole world he had opened up but also a few old Satchmo 78s thick as supper plates whirling so fast you think they might take off and fly. At times like these and there have been a lot of them since I heard a trumpet for the first time I can't tell whether it's the music lifting my soul or vice-versa but either way it seems like every note that goes through my ears and into my brain must have been sent to me by Gabriel himself.

Gave the blinds a pull and saw the sun turning the sky morning red and couldn't wait any longer. Grabbed the roll of cash I had saved up and stuffed a bag with shirts socks underwear and my notebook to write in and whatever else I might need to stay civilized on the road. I let the folks sleep not out of consideration but to skip all the *sturm und drang* and wrote a note to Mom that sed I was driving up to Columbia for a few days to see a friend which was a dam lie but it bought me some time before I had to spill the real beans. I was traveling light but one other thing I needed was a packet of letters in an ancient leather pouch that were written in 1860 by my greatgreatgreat Uncle Jeff on his journey west as a pioneer that Pop was in possession of only because they were left to him in a will though I doubt he ever read them and any pioneering spirit in Pop was long extinct if it ever existed at all and he will be irate of course when he discovers the letters missing he'll know I took them and act like they were stolen by some lowlife thief though I'm still a member of this family not to mention I'm named after the guy. I've read these letters overandover since I was a kid so who knows maybe the seed was planted in my brain a long time before last night and the fact they were written exactly one hundred years ago gives me goosebumps though as far as I can tell that's purely coincidental but still cool beyond compare. But some things around here never change and are surely not coincidental. Uncle Jeff risked his life to escape the sins of the South and here I am doing the same dam thing though the only thing I'm risking is a tongue-lashing from Pop. One last look around the old homestead and I threw my trumpet case in the trunk of my Rambler American and my bag in the backseat and I was ready to split.

Cruising up 176 on the most gorgeous morning God ever made no radio no sound but the smooth rumble of my straight-six and the purr of tires on the concrete, with cool air tickling my elbow and rustling my arm hair. I was all hurry and haste when skipping out on Pop but now that I'm free I was in no rush to get out of Goose Creek taking it slow cruising past sleeping buildings and the occasional car, thinking will I ever be happier than this? on a six a.m. highway heading west with dreams of jazz and California easy to imagine I'm the last man on Earth which feels nice now but I don't want to make this trip alone and I won't have to because all up the highway there'll be kids thumbing rides with the same idea as me.

Splitting this city for good and I'm tempted to feel sad. Now playing in the old movie house of the mind are some of the scenes I could watch overandover like splashing the girls at the Burges pool making them scream with hot dogs for lunch but don't go back in for thirty minutes. Cut to a vague party, me coming downstairs and bumping around amongst kneecaps and hemlines and someone spills a drink on my head and makes me cry but that only makes me the life of the party VE or VJ Day most likely but everybody sure is having a good time. Cut to

Stella blond pink cheek'd holding my hand giving me a quick kiss before she chickens out awkward for us both but I sed I'm ready for another if you are. Cut to the marching band don't know where they were from but it didn't matter the brass reflecting all the light in the auditorium and so loud some of the old folks wince and put their hands over their ears but the thunderous chord at the end held in fermata forever had me hooked I can still feel the goosebumps. This reel could go on and on and probably would if someone didn't cut on the lights but along the way things got steadily unhappy and here I am getting the hell out.

  Sun out now bright and sharp and I still feel like the only man on Earth which is a good thing for the time being but I'm getting a little itchy for someone to rap with. Lanes keeping up a steady beat of whiteblack whiteblack whiteblack the only time down here they're allowed to sit side by side. I was driving northwest trying to kill two birds with one stone that is to say heading west and getting out of the South at the same dam time. Didn't want to think about Cynthia but couldn't help it she snuggled up to me in the backseat on our way with friends to get burgers thinking ah this is the life I gave her a wet kiss on the cheek which she liked but when I leaned across and kissed her lips she recoiled and sed no Jeff no please don't do that. If I wanted to be mean I would call her a cock tease but that's not the body part she hurts heart tease is much more like it.

6

W,

My first thought when Pop was arrested – well, who knows what my first thought was, I was in shock, but at some point early on I saw Pop as being one of these crazy people who lead double lives, you know these serial killers who in their spare time when they're not mutilating people are boy scout masters and church elders and rotary club presidents. Or that Pop had some undiagnosed mental illness that he had managed to hide from his family all these years (which may have been true in fact, for all we know), but as I started reading about all these eugenics programs throughout American history – government-sanctioned, perfectly legal, even written into the law codes – I was shocked at how common they were and how commonly accepted they were. I started seeing him differently. Still monstrous, but no longer quite so aberrant, someone who saw himself as carrying on a once-proud tradition, another Southern Lost Cause, or like one of those ninety-year-old Japs still fighting World War II on some deserted island in the Pacific. And I suppose I shouldn't have been shocked that there were plenty of people who supported him in his endeavors, secretly for certain, but openly as well.

I've spent so much time since it happened trying to understand Pop. I think back to all his crazy dinner-table speeches. Did he ever say anything that would make you believe he was capable of, or contemplating, doing this? He never brought his work home with him, that's for sure, but the assumption was that he didn't want to discuss female genitalia around two young boys – which I always appreciated. Too much gynecological information might have turned me off from sex forever. But I did learn what *promiscuity* meant from him – he talked a lot about the promiscuity of black men, didn't he? He said it was yet another legacy of slavery that would never be eradicated. Well, there you go. If you can't eradicate the cause, then the least you can do is address the effects. But he also ranted about the black crime rate, without becoming a vigilante, and about how poorly they dressed, without becoming a haberdasher. But he was already a gynecologist, so I guess you use the tools you have at hand. I also analyze after the fact all his facial expressions and mannerisms that I remember and find myself wondering what that little tic or that funny look may have been trying to conceal or trying to tell me. If I ever bothered to think about them before, nothing struck me as strange or foreboding, though he certainly knew how to throw a scare into us when he wanted to, didn't he – but don't all fathers make good use of that ability? It infuriated me as a teenager (and as a fifty-year-old) that Pop was so open with reciting his racist boilerplate. Couldn't he at least hide it from my friends? And I know you felt the same way. Who wouldn't? Who wants a raving lunatic for a father? But I guess the joke was on us, wouldn't you agree, Will? What we saw as overt, all-encompassing racism he must have thought of as masterful obfuscation and deceit. He was an iceberg of monstrosity – offering up this huge expanse of bigotry for us to hate while all the truly hideous stuff was going on beneath the surface. I've never been a big fan of abstract art, but that's what I think about now when I try to understand Pop. It defies you to understand it in conventional terms and shows you a view of the world, not as you are accustomed to seeing it, but as it truly is. And Pop has made me realize that regardless of all the accumulated knowledge of the ages and all the wisdom we foolishly think we possess, you can never truly understand anything.

  So he finally got what he deserved and you and Mom got what nobody deserves. I mean, did they have to swoop in with a SWAT team? The cops love to play D-Day now, like when we were kids with our little green soldiers in the back yard.

Here's an eighty-year old man, retired for five years, semi-retired for ten years before that, so at least five years removed from any crime, and they're busting in the door and traumatizing Mom for what's left of her lonely unhappy life, adding PTSD on top of her grief. Why? Just so they could put on a show for the cameras and watch themselves later on TV? Because they have to show off all that armored weaponry they bought to fight al-Qaeda in the streets? Poor Mom. She called me right after she called you and there was nothing but chaos in her voice though she was trying mightily to stay calm. "They've come in and taken your father," she kept saying, as if repeating it would help it all make sense to me, or to her, but thinking about it now, what else could she say? She was still as in the dark as we were. Poor Mom, always teetering on the edge of making no sense whatsoever. You once offered up the best description I have ever heard of her. We would overhear her talking on the phone in the kitchen to one of her friends, saying things like, "Yes, I remember him – he went into the Army. . . . Oh, it was the Coast Guard – that's right," or "Yes, she married James – her name is Mary – oh, it's Marilyn? That's right, it is." And this would go on and on for the whole conversation. Do you remember how you described it? You said, "Mom gets everything right but the facts." Well, now she wasn't given any facts at all – just a nightmare that made no sense. But the nightmare only got worse, of course, as you know better than I. I dodged much of the shitstorm since I was so far away from it all, but I don't know how you and Mom dealt with it. It may have cost me my job – the jury is still out on that – but I know it cost you a lot more. I feel so guilty, Will, that I didn't come back home and help you and Mom after I lost my job. But honestly, I wanted to stay as far away from that circus as possible. Did you know that Mom asked me to come home? I gave her what sounded like a good excuse – that I wouldn't be able to find a job in Charleston because of Pop, which was probably true, and I was so paranoid because of how I was fired that I may have actually believed it. But still, what a lousy thing to do to you and Mom. What difference did it make whether I had a job or not? It's not like I hit the streets looking for work – I still haven't applied anywhere. And here I am preparing to leave Mom again – and to what end? To fulfill some enraged infantile fantasy? No – just to run away – always my reason for doing anything. Mom shouldn't have had to go through that alone. I know you couldn't be here for her as much as you wanted to – you actually had a job to do and people who were counting on you. I had no such excuse. I was able to watch most of it from the other side of the continent. Not that it still wasn't one of the most painful, heart-breaking, infuriating things I have ever had to go through, but I fully understand that I had it easy compared to you two, which was just as I wanted it.

There is so much to be outraged about with this whole thing, it's difficult for me to remain coherent. Starting with Pop of course. But what's the use of speaking ill of the dead? But I will say – and this is a confession I never thought I would be making – that when it became clear that Pop's cancer was terminal and on the fast-track the overwhelming emotion I felt was relief – and not relief for Pop, not relief that his pain would soon end – but relief that our pain would soon end. There would be no trial, no more media, no more scrutiny. There's nothing quite like death to put an end to everyone's interest in you. So there you have it, Will – a terrible admission to have to make, but yes, when I found out that my father – our father – had only a few weeks to live I took that to be the best news I had heard in a long long time.

But so much of the outrage I feel – that won't go away and seems to feed on itself – comes from how horribly Mom was treated throughout. How much of this rage is fueled by my own guilt would be a good question for my shrink, if I had one, but there are plenty of other reasons that don't begin and end with me. Pop was in jail and yet Mom still had to have police protection. Bullets fired into the house! Pop was in jail! Everyone knew that! Who were they shooting at? With what I'm getting ready to do, I may be Exhibit A for the irrationality of rage, but at least I'm not planning on shooting at anyone. And if anyone wants to call me a hypocrite, then fuck them. I'm still allowed to be infuriated that nobody with white skin even wants to try to understand the source of all the black rage in this country, even if it is hard to sympathize when your mother becomes its target.

And then there was the media and all their bullshit. Pop being compared to Josef Mengele. War-font headlines at the *New York Post* – "OMGYN!" The one thing we have completely run out of in this country is restraint. It is absolutely impossible for anyone to show even the slightest hint of restraint, taste, humility, reason, forbearance, reflection, self-questioning, forgiveness, empathy – just to name a few of those rare qualities quickly becoming extinct. It would be nice if reporters were human beings first and journalists second, but I suppose that's too much to ask when ratings and jobs are on the line. And it's so easy for one reporter to justify her egregious actions when everyone else is doing the same thing. It's hard enough to find just one person who'll live according to the highest principles, so what can you expect from an entire industry? And we wonder how fascism, genocides, and all these little daily abominations can occur? We're all such good little Nazis, committing a hundred tiny atrocities every single day so we can continue to carry out our orders and keep our jobs. And if you choose not to degrade yourself then you're gawked at like a circus freak. Our world is rotten to its core – how else can you explain why doing the right thing means nine times out of ten being treated as if you've just done the wrong thing?

But here's the mother of all outrages. And again, I don't know how much of this should be self-directed, but I scream into my pillow every night – and my shrieks are muffled only because Mom is in the house. If she weren't here, the whole neighborhood would hear me. They are shrieks of impotence. You're dead, and I don't know why. I don't know why I didn't talk to you more and I don't know why you didn't talk to me. Nobody talked to each other about anything. You suffered in silence while I tried to ignore everyone else's suffering. We kept our heads low. The press only wanted to dig up dirt on Pop and tally the victims and show them crying on camera – but now, who's going to broadcast all of your pain to the world? Not that you would want that, but how often did you cry out in your solitude? How often did you scream into your pillow? Pop got what he had coming to him, but where's the justice for what he did to you? Would Pop apologize now for doing this to you? Of course he wouldn't have done any of it had he known he would be caught. We count on the whole world to keep our secrets. But did he ever lie in bed at night and shiver in fear at the thought of being discovered? Did he ever think *this will kill my wife? This will destroy my family?* And if so, what kind of twisted calculus was necessary to convince him that it was worth the risk? I probably didn't factor very much into Pop's equations, and that's fine with me, but how could he do this to you? Did he even care? How much do you think he really loved us? We really don't mind rolling the dice, do we? We don't mind gambling with the lives of people we say we love. I think of fallen heroes dead in the line of duty and I want to ask them, did you think all of your bravery would dry your wives' tears and put them to sleep at night? I think of doomed daredevils in every walk of life and want to ask them, was that adreline rush enough to erase your children's pain and make them happy that Daddy died doing what he loved? So what excuse does Pop have? I would invite him to explain to his youngest child why he took such a monumental risk. His child Will, who only wanted to make him happy; who only wished to follow in his footsteps. Who grew to be disgusted by his pop's hatefulness, but who loved the hope that medicine could give and who thought, if you worked tirelessly enough, you just might be able to rectify some of the wrongs he condoned. You went to work every morning thinking about Pop, didn't you? Thinking that every act of kindness you showed might somehow erase one of Pop's odious thoughts from the world. His sins were the weight on your shoulders. Did that burden ever become any lighter for you? Did you come any closer to the end of that zero-sum game you were playing? But then he made a fool out of you, didn't he? How many lifetimes would it take now to blot out, not just the thoughts in his head and the words spewing from his mouth – but the crimes he committed? You thought you were somehow making up for Pop, cancelling him out. Just like me, you were trying to offer proof to the world that you were nothing like him – his exact opposite, in fact – but you learned the hard way that the best you could ever do was to labor for a lifetime just to create a tiny space, a little sliver of light you could stand in, a warm shaft of cleansing light that could work to keep an ogre at bay. You worked so hard to level the playing field, to make things right, to achieve equilibrium. You knew you were swimming against a rip current, but you didn't know there was a tidal wave rolling in. So how were you supposed to struggle against that? How much shame did Pop drum into you every day as we grew up? The shame that you turned into that amazing energy. But if your heart contained so much shame before, then it must have been ready to explode afterwards. How were you able to go on? How hard it must have been to face those people. They didn't care or need to know why you were always there for them. You may have mentioned in passing that your pop was a doctor too, perhaps you even sounded proud when you said it. But then he popped up on TV and they started asking questions or maybe looking at you funny. Did you have to lie to them? To deny that your father was who they thought he might be? You had to add to that weight a new fear – a fear of irreparable alienation or violence. You had always been proud of your decisions, your accomplishments. You knew you were doing something good. Maybe you finally felt as if you deserved some of the gratitude you received. But now you felt like you no longer deserved anything good. You didn't deserve to have these patients who looked up to you. After what Pop did, after all he had kept hidden, how could you not also feel like a fraud? When you opened the door to your examination room and there sat a young woman, how could you look her in the eye? Was this why you did it, Will? Was this what it took to finally release that explosion of rage inside of you?

It's dark now, but my day's work is not over (I'll explain later). A few fireflies are lighting up occasionally, but where are the rest of them? Are even the insects bugging out now? Didn't there used to be swarms of them? Do you remember how we used to catch them and put them in a jar? You were careful to always punch holes in the lid and to let them go when you thought we had kept them captive long enough. All you ever wanted was to be kind and helpful. How could Pop do this to you, Will?

But, alas, he wasn't the only one who treated you unfairly:

> Because I wanted to, that's why.
> It was fun. He didn't feel it.
> It might have been poisonous.
> Why do you have to be so weird?
> You little baby. It was just a spider.

MY DEAREST,

Dear Constance! I am safe and well, but please pray for me! O! I have such a dreadful thing that I must tell you! My hand trembles and my heart pounds rapidly as I write this – oh Constance! I have killed a man! We grappled as if we were two wild beasts, and then, to save my life, I shot him dead! Oh, what a horrible tale I must tell you now! How I curse the day those ragged wagons filled with W.'s human refuse crossed my path! For what capricious fate ordained that I should cast my lot with, and be bound, as if a prisoner in chains, to such a heathenish cabal of refugees, cast-offs, ne'er-do-wells, madmen, and all manner of socially misfit vagabonds! First in Charleston, and now here in this wretched wilderness, my life has devolved into one prolonged escape from the grasping, outstretched arms of one set of villains directly into the vengeful clutches of another! Why does this have to be so, when all I have desired is to live peacefully within the loving arms of my beautiful Constance?

This disastrous day began as a beautiful prairie morning, and with an invitation from my friend Jason to take advantage of my new freedom by accompanying him on a hunt for buffalo. (O! Jason – to whom I owe my life! One day may I be allowed to repay him!) Our provisions are in good supply, but the wise counsel of those men who know very well the contingencies of the trail advises always to hunt for fresh game whenever it is available. We are, of course, novice buffalo hunters, but having shot our share of other quadrupeds, we hoped at least to be of some use to each other. What a marvelous creature the buffalo is, my dear! I am afraid there is nothing quite like it roaming within my native hunting grounds, though during the days of the proprietary government they were plentiful in the upcountry. It is a sad fate for any life to be judged as having too little value; however, it is worse to be valued too highly. And Jason and I were determined to do our part to hasten the extinction of this glorious species.

There were many within our camp, prior to the events of today, who were mistrustful of Aaron and his promise to me. In fact, to be so was only prudent. If there was anyone who placed complete trust in A., then that man was a fool. It was quite possible that I was risking my life to return to a normal mode of living; it was possible even that A.'s promise of amnesty was a ruse meant to lure me out of hiding. I, however, as the person who had placed himself into a self-imposed captivity, had to decide for myself whether I was going to live as a prisoner or risk death as a free man. For this reason, I was overjoyed to receive J.'s invitation. And as we rode away quickly toward some high hills in the distance – away from camp, away from the Platte, and, most importantly, away from A. and his followers – I was certain I had made the right choice, for a strong breeze was blowing in our faces, a large herd of animals – most probably buffalo – was grazing off in the approaching distance, and for the first time since W.'s death I felt safe and free from worry.

We were wary of approaching too near the buffalo. As with any quarry, the challenge lies in approaching near enough to fire effectively without approaching too near and thus scattering the herd. However, as we moved carefully closer, upwind from the beasts, my attention was arrested by two other animals approaching quickly from the direction of the trail. We soon recognized them as horses with riders, and in the Manichaean world in which I had been dwelling for the past several days, there were but two possibilities regarding the identities and intentions of these men – either they were friends from camp come to join the hunt or my enemies come to kill me. And in this one case, at least, Manichaeus was correct in his philosophy.

I recognized these men as two who shouted most maniacally for my murder when I was arrested and paraded like an animal in front of my captors. We could just as well have taken aim and shot them as soon as they were recognized, but we are thoughtful men, and think twice before taking action, although such thoughtfulness easily could have resulted in my death. They rode up quickly, halted their horses, and levelled their aims at us. By this time, our rifles, as well, were cocked and aimed to kill. Oh, dear Constance, how my heart was thumping! Four rifles, with four fingers on their triggers, prepared in one horrific flash to produce four dead settlers! What a horrible, tense moment! The man whose rifle was aimed at J. shouted to him, "There's a bullet in the breech for you if you want it! You can ride away from this murderer and remain alive, or you can be a dead man trying to save him! Your choice!"

J. shouted back, "What about your promise to Aaron!"

"A promise to Aaron means nothing! I owe my allegiance only to Wilbur!" He shouted then to me, "And you put a knife through his heart! I hope you are ready to go to Hell!" He then shouted back to J., "Is this really how you want to die? Protecting a murderer?" J. did not reply. The tension was incredible. I had no idea what to do; neither, I doubt, did J. And the other two men, though the aggressors, may have been equally doubtful as to what further course to take. How did they ascertain my whereabouts so quickly? Was I under surveillance? Perhaps this man and his accomplice had set out only to determine our identities, and upon discovery of who we were, felt compelled to take this rash action without forethought. At any rate, this excruciating standoff could not continue indefinitely. "This is your last chance! Make up your d— mind! Do you want to live or die?" the villain shouted again to J. My rifle barrel remained pointed at the man shouting at us, but my arms were becoming unsteady, either from fatigue or from fear. It was now that J. decided to take action. He said to me, "Hold on tight," and before I could make any sense of his statement, J. quickly lowered his rifle barrel nearly to touching my horse's face, and then fired. The loud crack of the shot, so close to its ears and face, startled my horse into a frenzy. He reared and I instinctively gripped the reins with all my strength. In this sudden action, my rifle fell from my hands and discharged when it hit the ground, which only served to discomfit my horse further. In the confusion of flying hooves and panicked movement and wild braying, the men opposite us could no longer maintain me in their rifle sights. In this crazed upheaval all my attention was on remaining mounted; but I saw J. take advantage of the chaos he had created by darting off away from these men. After rearing madly many times, my horse flew past them. It headed at full gallop down the steep hill we had been on top of, into a valley and toward the herd of buffalo, which, because of the rifle reports, and now because of this other raging animal, was in full stampede. Buffalo are unpredictable creatures, even at rest, but when agitated they are most dangerous. Amid the furor, my horse galloping wildly amongst the running buffalo, I heard the whistling of a bullet as it flew past my ear. These men were in pursuit and firing as they rode! Life teaches many lessons, but I am uncertain, my dear, what can be learned at times like these, other than a reinforcement of the fact that an instinct for survival always runs strongly through us. This experience, however, has taught me that it is only when we are closest to death that we are most fully alive. I was aware of everything around me in a way that I had never been before. Although my horse was running wildly, it seemed to be moving slowly. Not only was I acutely aware of each buffalo as it ran near me, but, I swear to you, I could smell it as well, and it seemed as if I could sense the beasts' every movement and that my actions were guided more by the primordial instincts of the jungle and savanna than human volition. I heard another rifle report, but it came from further behind me. Were the men chasing me still? Was that Jason's gun firing from a distance? Though my horse was out of my control, I was firmly in the saddle and had no desire whatsoever for it to reduce its speed. I had been in a large valley with the buffalo, but now my horse began to ascend as it determined its best route to escape the stampede. I dared not look behind me, but I expected fully at any moment to experience the unknown pain of a rifle shot into my back.

My dear Constance, I wish I could say to you that, during these dreadful moments when my steed was losing its momentum running uphill and I feared that my death was imminent, my thoughts were of us, happy and serene, or of you, beautiful and sweet, but, alas, I cannot. Please forgive me, darling, but I do believe my sole thought was of topping the hill and heading with the utmost speed down its opposing flank, where, with God's help, I could overtake our train and recover my safety. Nor did I think of J., who, with his own life being threatened within the gunman's sights just moments earlier, had had the presence of mind to act wisely and with not only his survival in mind, but mine as well – and yet, frankly, even if I had been equipped at this moment with an armory of weaponry, it's quite possible my only objective would have remained self-preservation. Thank God that my selfish, instinctive actions did not bring J. to any mortal harm!

I obtained the summit of the hill, but was most vulnerable, and, having gained control over my horse, directed him to begin our descent, relieved that I would be out of sight, at least momentarily, of the men chasing me. The horse raced down the mountainside at full gallop, through tall grass, and then suddenly crumpled to the ground. I heard a rifle shot as I fell from my horse. We both, horse and rider, tumbled over and sideways. The horse rolled over me once and I felt its crushing weight upon my chest. My tumbling fall finally ceased, but I was gasping violently and too stunned for movement. I was unable to stand, but from my position, hidden in the prairie grass, I saw one horse and rider atop the hill beginning their descent. I reached for my revolver, which had been tucked loosely under my belt, but it was gone – lost, no doubt, during my mad tumble. Oh Constance! The fear I felt! I did not want to die! But I was hurt and helpless, and at this moment, my dear eternal love, I resigned myself to death. Several feet away from me was my fallen horse, which had been shot in the croup. It was struggling to rise. I began to pray for the forgiveness of my sins. I kept my eyes open, however. I resolved to look my murderer in the eyes as he pulled the trigger. I heard the approaching horse's hooves pounding against the ground as it rumbled down the hillside. The man – the villain! – came into view astride his horse. He walked his horse around the body of my wounded, struggling steed, and halted over me. I ceased my prayers, but had nothing I wanted to say to this man. I merely stared up at him, unblinking. What is there to say to a man intent on murdering you, and who believes fervently that to do so is to exact a righteous justice? He said down to me, "You have murdered an angel of the Lord. And now He will have His vengeance. I hope you are prepared to shake hands with Satan." He raised his rifle and a warm peacefulness engulfed my soul. We have nothing to fear from death, sweet Constance. I know that now, and I have been a fool all these years for living with such groundless fear in my soul – a fear which can only be a fear of loss, the loss of what we have been blessed with on Earth of love, friendship, and joy, but which obscures, as a cloud over the sun, the glorious attainments of Heaven. And as this delusional man raised his rifle and took an easy aim at my head, I offered no resistance and was at peace with my fate, unjust though it was, for at that moment I understood, as if God were whispering in my ear, that every fate on Earth is unjust, every man is a victim of lies, but through God's grace we will receive our eternal vindication and all these earthly lies which bring us such vexations will be forgotten and forgiven. Suddenly, however, as I awaited the touch of God's hand, and looked my killer in the eye, I heard a thump of flesh, saw a flash of blood, and this man, who had been poised to kill, dropped his rifle and slumped in his saddle. Then I heard the rifle shot, which had come from the top of the hill and had taken a moment to reach my ears. The man showed no pain or emotion on his face. His left arm dangled at his side, but he slid with careful deliberation from his saddle and paused for a moment – either he was immobilized by the shock of his wound, or he was indecisive as to whether he wanted to stoop to retrieve his rifle, or to administer my *coup-*

de-grace with his revolver. However, within this certainly short span of time – which seemed, however, to be boundless – my resignation to place myself meekly into the arms of death transformed into a brave determination to live. Regardless of my injuries, I lunged toward him and he grasped his revolver. If I had shown a moment's hesitation, I am certain I would have been shot, but I leapt on top of him and with both hands pinned his gun-hand against the ground. With both hands, and with a desperate strength, I removed the pistol from his grip. Undoubtedly, I either broke his bones or dislocated his joints in doing so, for he shouted out in great pain. I violently hurled the revolver far behind us, for I now had the advantage over him and hoped to subdue him quickly. However, he fought savagely. He was as determined to live as I. He struggled mightily, but I maintained the advantage of being on top of him. His left arm was mostly useless, though, in his desperation, his injury did not prevent him from using it to fight me; in fact, I believe it caused him to struggle more fiercely. He kicked at me and delivered desperate blows and scratched my face terribly as he struggled to throw me aside. I grasped his neck fully with my hands, and I am sure he was near asphyxiation, but with one desperate heave he pushed my body from its position on top of him. I was now sprawled on the ground above his head. He reached for his rifle. Instinctively, I clutched his hair and pulled at it with all my strength. He screamed loudly. He tried to stand and escape from the precarious grip I maintained on his hair. As he was regaining his footing, I lunged for the rifle and swept it up from the grass by its barrel. He leapt toward me, but I swung the buttstock and made full contact with the side of his face. He staggered, and I came down with the full force of the stock on the crown of his head. He fell to his knees and I followed this blow with another of equal force. He fell to the ground, unconscious.

   I looked up from where our mighty struggle had occurred as Jason arrived on his horse. It was he who had shot, from the summit of the hill, the man who now was helpless at my feet. "Are you hurt?" he asked, loudly.

"No, I don't believe so. Not seriously."

"Is he dead?"

"I don't believe so, no." I was gasping heavily and speaking was difficult. "Where's the other one?"

"Gone. I shot his horse out from under him and took his weapons. Told him, 'I'm not likely to shoot an unarmed man in the back, so you had better start running.'"

"Is he going to bring more men after me?" As much as I may now admire Jason's merciful humanity, at this moment I questioned his wisdom.

"I don't know. We need to figure out what to do."

"Do you have my rifle? I dropped it when you startled my horse."

"No, but I'll find it. You'll be all right with him? Do you have cartridges?"

"Yes." J. rode off in search of my rifle. My horse, though wounded by the rifle shot and bleeding, otherwise seemed to be unhurt by its terrible tumble down the hillside. He was up and grazing alongside the other horse. I was still holding the unconscious man's rifle. The tables were turned and he was now completely at my mercy. I am proud, sweetheart, that no barbaric thoughts of a peremptory vengeance entered my head. Would I have been justified in executing this man, who had been but the briefest moment away from murdering me, in the same summary fashion? Should I – could I – have waited for him to regain consciousness, told him to look me in the eye, and to say hello to Satan as I pulled the trigger? No – the answer to these questions must always remain "No." Perhaps W. and his minions would have answered with their doubt-ridden "I cannot say," but we, as a civilized people, must never quail from our certainty that one man's ruthlessness does not justify that of another.

This man, fallen at my feet, quickly regained consciousness. He rolled over in the tall grass and attempted to stand. I cocked the rifle and shouted to him, "Don't move another muscle! Sit down!"

He did as I commanded. He looked up at me and said, "One of us is going to die today." I felt no need to respond to his taunts, but I tightened my grip around the forestock and made certain I remained a safe distance from him.

"Does Aaron know you are here? Are you here on his authority?"

He laughed a slow, cruel laugh. "I am here on my authority alone. Aaron has promised not to touch a hair on your foul, murderous head. You and he may become fast friends." He laughed again and coughed harshly. From the corner of my eye, I saw J. coming over the mountaintop. I removed my gaze from my prisoner only momentarily to look up toward J. At that instant, the man lunged toward me, and in another instant he was dead. My finger had been firmly on the trigger and, upon his sudden lurch from his sitting position, I fired. The round went into his chest and must have pierced his heart.

J. rode up upon this scene, but said nothing. There was nothing to say. Perhaps I should have prayed over this dead man, but at that moment I was shocked by what I had done and by the situation in which J. and I now found ourselves. God, in his infinite mercy, may forgive this man for his sins, past and present, but I was in no mood to do so. Eventually, I said, "Should we bury him?"

"I don't know. With what?" All we had in our possession were firearms and a knife, which J. had brought for dressing any buffalo we happened to kill. "We can haul him back. His people can give him a proper burial, if they think he deserves one," J. said. We lifted his body, his clothes saturated with his blood, onto my wounded horse. I mounted the dead man's horse. We rode in silence in the direction of the moving train. We did not overtake it until it had halted to make camp. I expressed my gratitude, of course, to J., for saving my life; however, any words I could have chosen were inadequate to convey the eternal gratefulness I felt in my heart. He, as any gentleman would have, deflected my gratitude, saying only, "You would have done the same for me." Yes, I hope that I would have.

J. delivered the dead man's body to Aaron. I remained in our camp as J. undertook this errand, since my presence would have served no purpose but to inflame further this grievous situation. We will report the attempt on my life to the Captain tomorrow morning, though there is nothing more to be done, since I have meted out the punishment, as it were, on the perpetrator of the crime. Perhaps the man's accomplice can be identified and arrested. (Darling, I would be remiss if I failed to report to you on the condition of the horse that I rode which received the bullet wound in its croup – for I know you well enough to know also that when you read of the horse being shot, you instantly became as solicitous of the animal's welfare as of mine – if not more so! The horse will, I believe, recover fully, my sweet. He was administered a healthy dose of laudanum and the bullet removed. I shall be riding him again in no time at all!) J. returned from A.'s camp bearing a message of apology from A. and a renewal of his promise of forbearance toward me – a promise, which, regardless of A.'s apparent sincerity, is meaningless. The dead man was not the only one shouting for my death and snarling out threats against me on the day of my arrest. I must not remain in the same train behind these villainous sectarians. I am certain my friends will want to proceed with the plan voted upon earlier, although we shall incur great risk in doing so.

Oh Constance! I am weary beyond description and must try to sleep, but how can I ever close my eyes upon what I have done today?

W,

On top of everything else, I've been hit with another lightning bolt today. I've been fired from my job. My guess is it's related to everything going on with Pop, but there's no way to know that for sure. I am so angry I can't see straight. It has taken me all day just to compose myself enough so that I can articulate my feelings. I was fired – ostensibly – because of a JOKE! I don't know what makes me angrier – the possibility that I was fired because of a lousy joke I made up in class or the notion that I was fired because of Pop. My good luck has until now made me immune from the PC Police. Lord knows, I have said enough incendiary things in my classrooms to be fired several times over. But I have always been willing to brave the PC Brigade in order to teach as I see fit. And it wasn't even a very good joke! Or really, not even a joke at all – not a proper joke, with a setup and punchline. It was just witty banter, silly repartee. But in today's academe, God help you if you rub a student the wrong way. You know the quote about how my freedom of speech stops at the end of your nose? Well, apparently that border has been moved back a couple of feet. Either I have finally run out of luck and have tempted the PC Fates once too often, or the college has judged me guilty by association of the crimes committed by Pop and finds my presence on campus to be intolerable. Either I have been fired for simply being myself (i.e., a funny teacher who says unpredictable things), or I have been fired for being somebody else (i.e., a proxy for Pop). Can you blame me for being outraged by this?

So what was this terribly insulting thing I said that made it imperative that my employment be immediately terminated? It wasn't even during class. Class hadn't even started yet. Everyone was filing in, getting their books out. I'm surprised anyone even heard it. While waiting for the rest of class to arrive, I happened to ask if anyone was watching the Olympics. Nobody really responded. Nobody was paying attention. Just to kill time and give myself something to do, I starting commenting on the various Olympic events and how strange some of them were. Water polo. Aren't they afraid all the horses will drown? I joked. Maybe a couple of kids chuckled. The shotput. Very strange sport, I said, with an even stranger name. Nothing is being shot. Shouldn't there be a gun involved somewhere? I'm just filling up time, you understand, not putting any thought into what I'm saying at all. My class was almost full now but some stragglers were still coming in. So now here comes the shot heard 'round the world, Sumter being fired upon, my accidental *coup d'grace* and inadvertent *hari-kiri:* "The javelin. White guys always win that event. Does that make any sense? Wouldn't you think that sport would be completely dominated by black guys?" No one said anything. No laughs. No hisses or boos. Silence. I thought nothing else about it because it was now time to start class. The class itself was entirely uneventful. That was two weeks ago. I get called into the dean's office this morning. It was just a silly joke, I try to explain. "Not to the college it wasn't," he said. "Remarks like that are taken very seriously."

"But why should they be? The remark itself wasn't serious – why should the consequences be? Is this about my father?"

"No, that has nothing to do with it. It has to do with the fact that we don't appreciate our African-American students being called spear chuckers by someone on our faculty."

I was incredulous. "Do you seriously think I would call anyone that, or any other epithet like that? Do you seriously think that's how I feel about African-Americans?"

He was unmoved. "That was certainly the implication."

"No – there was no fucking *implication*. It was a fucking *joke*."

"I'm sorry this has happened. I know this must be a rough time for your family. But I need you to be out of your office by noon." I cleaned out my office and went home, tears of outrage rolling down my cheeks.

Hey – it just occurred to me that you might have the misguided balls to agree with the administration about its decision. Don't you *dare* disagree with me on this! The last thing we need is an internecine battle to open up in the middle of this war we're in. Take a few deep breaths if, when, and before you respond.

"NOW, CUNNEL, THE NEXT PUSSON I'll tell you about who straggled back into town with his tail between his legs was ol' Butt Homphrey. Butt had been making fonn progress to O'gon by rodding the stage, but every day, at least two or three toms, the coach was passed by a Pony Express rodda flying lock a bud. Well, it didn't take but a few of these pony roddas streaking past the stage before Butt changed his mond regodding the adequacy of the Overland Stage Company for his pupposes. Yes sir, Cunnel, six healthy hosses ronning at a full gallop over good roads soddenly appeared to Butt to be moving motty *slow*. 'How can I get myseff one of them tho'oughbred hosses to rod all the way to O'gon?' ol' Butt asked hisseff. He must have had a vision of hisseff rodding lock the wind, passing stages, outronning Indians, making mountain lonns look lock tuttles and jackass rabbits look lock snails!

"Now, if you'd ever seen Butt Homphrey you'd onderstand puffectly why I'm amused by the thought of him rodding hossback lock a wullwind all the way to O'gon. By the tom I saw him again, you'd expect that all the starvation and deprovation and hodships of his months on the frontier would have lottened his load by a few pounds, but dun if I could tell if Butt had suffered the loss of a single ounce of bodily weight. In fact, he may well have been the fust man in recodded history to have survived all the perils of malnou'ishment and famine and come out of the oddeal *fatta* than he stotted! I swear the man still weighed upwuds of four hondred pounds, if not more. And that weight is not by any stretch of the imagination distributed throughout a lengthy skeleton – Butt is a shot man by any standudd, so all the extra coggo he's a-carrying just *oozes* along as he walks lock a mudslod down a hillsod. And his wodd guth had made his passage on the stagecoach a mott more problematic than nommal. He of coss had to share a pot of his buth with his fellow passengers, and the unfotchinate pusson occupying the space most immediately adjacent to Butt apparently wasn't entolly fond of shop elbows and hod kneecaps and the constant presence of ratha lodge shoulders and omms and hips. Especially since a stage is prone to bounce over gulleys and rocks and whatnot, so motch so that afta a potticularly rough patch of road the pusson previously on your left mott now be the pusson on your *rot*. And I reckon if Butt was fossed by a sudden lutch to his left or rot to slod over against his companion, then he mott just apply enough foss to be dangerous. So this pusson setting next to Butt on sotch a long junney, and having to endure such an ovafamiliarity with sutton pots of Butt's anatomy, was not entolly cordial at all toms, perhaps jostifiably so. As Butt hisseff said, 'When you're my size, friends don't come so easy.'

"So Cunnel, after seeing enough of those pony roddas passing by so fast that you miss 'em if you take tom to blink, ol' Butt was now spending his tom on the stage conjuring up some practicable means of procuring one of those tho'oughbred hosses. Of coss, the main obstacle to obtaining one of these hosses is getting it to *stop*. These pony roddas, as I'm shaw you know, are not keen to retodd their progress for any reason. They keep those hosses ronning through tor'ents of rain, blizzuds of snow, ambushes by Indians, through uthquakes, floods – even if the Omeggedon of the Bobble were to come down from Heaven itself, why the pony roddas would be lockly to say, 'Jesus, the Jodgment will just have to wait, at least till I get to the next station!' So I reckon Butt had his wuck cut out for hisseff. It's not lock you can stand by the roadsod and flutta a handkerchief in the air lock you were hailing a taxi codge on Broadway. And I'm not sutton that Butt gave motch thought to what his next odda of business would be once he discovered a wuckable way to convince either the hoss or its rodda to pull up shot of their intended destination. I never knowed Butt to be a violent man, but then I had already seen what remockable transfommations the wud *gold* could renda in a man. So I reckon he would dettumine what needed to be done once the tom came, whatever it tunned out to be.

"Now, if you're a passenger on a stage, out in Indian country, and with outlaw vommits hiding behond every rock and scroggly tree just waiting to ambush you – that is if the Indians don't get you fust – if you're a passenger with a thousand molls between where you are and where you aim to be, then I reckon just about the *last* thing you would want to be is a *fomma* stagecoach passenger – that is to say, the last thing any sane man would do out in Indian country is to voluntolly relinquish his buth on the stage with no other means of transpo'tation available. But that's just the sott of plan that Butt was contemplating. Lock I said, you can say the wud *gold* and then set back and watch a reasonably intelligent man tun into a dun lunatic. But as it tunned out, tunning into a lunatic was just about the only option that Butt had available to him in odda to carry out his mission – which I'll get to shottly.

"The stage stopped at one of the stations along the Platte Riva and Butt and the other passengers disembocked and Butt, with his plan already hatching in his brain, asked the stage driver how long it would be before they saw the next express rodda. The driver – who, Butt said, treated the passengers in his chodge with a sutton amount of disdain, and who must also have been from this pot of the wuld – that is, from the South – he looked at Butt as if he had just inquired about the next luna eclipse or the pygmies of Africa or the best way to get to Constantinople or some sotch arcane matta, and refused to give Butt a satisfactory answer. 'I don't wuck for the dun government and neva will!' he said to Butt. It seems he held the federal autho'ity in the same high regodd as his passengers.

"So as they were changing out the hosses, the host at this little station invotted them insodd a little cabin not motch lodger than a privy, to hear Butt descrobb it. But it must have been a bit more spacious than that, since Butt also made room in there for some chairs, a lantern, a table, a stove and a bench of indetumminate length – but spossly funnished to say the least. Butt was of the opinion that the hospitality shown by this roadsodd innkeepa, if that's what we want to call him – though I suspect that his duties and demeana fell far shot of the dignity nommally associated with that tum – that this hospitality, accodding to Butt, left motch to be desired and that the nou'ishment they offered left a dun sott more. Case in point, the only food within that hut was a half-empty sack of conmeal, which, Butt said, contained more moving pots than conmeal oddnarily should – and since the illumination in there was so poor Butt couldn't rottly make out what all those moving pots were, which was probably a good thing. There was also an unn of coffee, or some top of liquid that had a passing resemblance to coffee, or that had once been coffee at some distant point in its existence. Now Butt declonned to sample the conmeal and all its moving pots, but he did pour hisseff some of that ustwhile coffee. It tasted about lock what you would expect, so there was no danger of Butt not leaving enough for the others to share. The fust swalla of coffee made him feel a bit oneasy in his stomach, but it also gave him an oddea – and this is where that lunatic pot I mentioned ullier comes in.

"Butt reckoned, and correctly I would assume, that there was no plausible explanation he could offa to the stage driver as to why he was tumminating his services so abroptly out there amidst all the dangers of outlaws and Indians and no easy manna either in which he could wonda away from the station onnoticed or onmolested by the station hands. No, Cunnel, he had to manipulate the matta in such a way that all the potties involved would be more than content to have Butt pummanently removed from their presence, with no questions asked. Now, I'm not saying that this was a good plan, or a smott plan, and it was suttonly not the best plan of action under any succumstances, but given its ratha impromptu nature and the limited means he had at his disposal, I can at least give Butt's plan points for *conception* and *execution.* And considering Butt's state of mond – what with his brain being severely infected with gold fever and all – maybe his lunacy was at least half sincere. And perhaps it took a demented mond to conceive of sotch a demented plan in the fust place.

"So, Cunnel, what Butt did was this. He took anotha swig of that coffee, which no one else had had the courage to partake of, and – if Butt were here now he could act it all out for you, betta than I can attempt to descrobb it. But he moshed his face all up and rolled his eyes back up insodd his skull and stotted in to quivering and twitching. He made shaw he took the remainda of that putrefactive coffee in his tin cup and sploshed it around on all the unfotchinate bystandas. Butt said they all jomped back as if they had just been sprayed with solphuric acid! Yes sir, Cunnel, ol' Butt was putting on a show wuthy of Broadway or maybe even the Globe Theater itself! He stotted jucking his omms up and down as if they were unda the direction of some sott of satanic poppetmasta. He then fell to the ground as if he had been shot point-blank, and began acting out in as many ways as he could think of in sotch a shot period of tom and given his physical limitations – which, I must say, he did an admirable job ovacoming. He swovelled around in a more or less suckula motion. He stotted heaving hisseff up and down lock a butta chunn. He grobbled around lock a wumm and colled up lock a snake and then he laid hisseff out puffectly straight and stayed puffectly still for a moment, to catch his breath I'm shaw but also perhaps to loll his spectators into believing that the wust was ova. Meanwoll, the stage passengers and probably everybody else within earshot were standing with their mouths gaping and their eyes budged out and the copple of ladies present were, I'm shaw, feeling motty discomfited. But ol' Butt wasn't finished yet. I reckon there were a few more bodily conto'tions that he had thought of and didn't want to see go to waste. And there were some that Butt demonstrated for me that I can't rottly descrobb, so you'll just have to use your imagination, Cunnel.

"Butt was nommally respectful of social convention and shully knowed there were ladies present, but he also knowed that this was no tom for modesty and self-effacement. He ripped the bottons off his shut and exposed his chest, and just for good measure and because at this point Butt must have concluded that it was the most logical finale to his puffomance, he stood up and stotted homping the back of a chair as if it were a dun hound dog in heat.

"By now only the studdiest and stoutest of hott were left standing insodd the cabin and everybody else had ron off in various directions to escape this exceptionally lodge lunatic. And now, to clear the cabin out and make dun shaw there was no one foolhoddy enough to even considda making an attempt to restrain him or spoll his plan, he topped off his puffomance by moshalling howeva motch spittle and phlegm and mucus and whateva else he could conjure up from his gullet into an ovaflowing riva of effluvia. The last remaining pussons came ronning out of the little hut, preceded by the sound of them yelling *he's foamin' at the mouth! He's foamin' at the mouth!*, with Butt rot on their heels. And Butt didn't stop ronning ontil he was plum out of sott of the station and the stage. And so with that *tour de foss* puffomance Butt had successfully completed the fust pot of his plan – and I say the *fust* pot without necessarily implonn that there was a *second* pot – at least not yet.

"So here he was, out there with nothing but the sagebrosh and prairie dogs to keep him company, with a torn shut and slobba all ova his dun face, hot and hongry and thusty, with no uthly oddea when the next pony rodda was coming or how on uth he was supposed to convince the rodda that it was in his best interest to halt his hoss and dismount. Now you mott think that Butt would be feeling at least the fust faint stirring of fear or discou'agement, considering his present succomstances. But you'd be wrong about that, Cunnel. When you got your mond set on something, it'll take motch more than savages and thieves and the potential for starvation and death to tun you around and convince you othawise. No sir, all Butt could think about was that O'gon gold and how that tho'oughbred hoss was going to take him rot to it!

"Now, it would be entolly contrary to human experience if this scheme of Butt's were to continue to unfold without either a flaw in the execution or a fly in the ontment. He had been one lucky son of a gun up to this point. He was most fotchinate that someone back at the hoss-changing station hadn't taken it upon hisseff to put Butt out of his misery. Or to do so just to maintain the peace and quott. Or just to have some fun with poor ol' Butt. In the territories they do things a bit diffuntly. You can be shot dead for doing a lot less than acting lock a lunatic.

"Butt walked down to the Platte to take care of his thust and to wash all the slobba and whatnot off his face. He presently desodded that it was safe for him to walk back to the station, as long as he no longa displayed any manifestations of his recent bout of dementia. As soon as the station hands saw him, they reached for their roffles. 'Don't come any closer, you mangy cur, or I'll put a bullet rot through your pig-addled brain,' one of those fonn gentlemen warned Butt. Butt carefully infomned them that his fomma bizarre behavior had dissipated, brought on perhaps by that tubbid malarial coffee they were offering their guests. He infommed them that ratha than wait for the next coach, he would motch prefer to procure one of those fonn hosses that he saw corralled behond the station. The men laughed at Butt for this presumption. 'Them's for the Pony Express,' they said. 'Even betta,' Butt rejonned. 'I will pay top dolla for the best one you got,' Butt said, which was a dun lie –

Butt Homphrey wouldn't pay top dolla to save his mother's soul. 'No sir – not for sale. We need every one of them hosses for the roddas.' 'Well then,' Butt asked, 'can you use another rodda?' Oh my Lodd, Cunnel, you should hear Butt tell this pot of the story. Even afta all this tom has elapsed he can still become quott livid. His face contotts, his eyes budge out, his voice wavers. And his anger is entolly justifodd, I mott add. When Butt offered to become the newest Pony Express rodda – well, these unprincipled bobbarians were unmussiful. Now rememba, Cunnel, how I have descrobbed to you Butt's physical dimensions. He is not a small man. But the boys who are employed by the Express Company to be roddas are diminutive in the extreme. Nothing on that hoss will weigh any more than is absolutely requodd by nature. So these opstanding specimens of humanity let loose with an uth-shaking howl of laughta and one of them said to Butt, 'Are you going to rod the hoss or is the hoss going to rod you?' Another one said, 'Let's saddle up this bronc and see if we can break him!' Well, these men were well-ommed and Butt may have had a pistol tocked away somewhere, but he was uttally hepless to defend hisseff. One afta anotha mounted poor Butt and wrapped their legs around his neck and slapped him and rode him to the ground ontil I reckon all the enjoyment went out of it for them. Butt hulled at them a full lexicon of profanities and for all his trobble was probably very lucky again to escape with his loff. All things considered, Butt's entire junney to O'gon and back was a luck-laden miracle, to be honest – although at that present tom he was most probably unaware of what a lucky man he was.

"For all his scheming, Butt couldn't see a good way of obtaining one of those hosses he coveted. Indian raids are commonplace occurrences in that pot of the territory – that is to say, in *any* pot of that God-forsaken territory. For that reason, accodding to Butt, those hosses were godded more closely than the crown jewels. There were ommed men posted around the perimeter of the corral and stables both nott and day. So if he were destined to secure for hisseff one of those hosses, the security thereof would have to occur outsodd the boundary of that station.

"Afta notfall, Butt retunned to the little hut which had been the scene of his ratha inspodd puffomance ullier. He remembered seeing a length of rope in there and rotfully assumed that it would be of great use to him later as his hoss-rustling scheme developed. He took the rope and moved stealthily down to the edge of the riva – if Butt putting one foot in front of the other in any fomm or fashion can ever be regodded as stealthy. He stayed as close to the riva's edge as possible and walked carefully through the dockness. He napped, and at daybreak made his way back up to the road. There was a lodge tree ovahanging the roadway and Butt saw in that an oppo'tunity. His plan now consisted entolly of clombing that tree. Now Cunnel, have you ever seen a bear clomb a tree?"

"It is my understanding that a bear can climb a tree only with some great difficulty."

"Nommally, yes. But either the desperation he felt at being stranded out there alone or the image of that big gold dobble-u looming in his mond must have provodded the inducement he needed to transfomm hisseff from a bear into a dun *orangutang*. But if you want to take a few moments, Cunnel, to contemplate Butt making his way up into the uppa reaches of that tree, I can suttonly onderstand, for I have done so many toms with amusing results. So with motch trial and erra, ripped fabric, cuts and bruises, blood and pussporation, grunts and a host of other bodily noises, with immense toil and trepidation – and not to mention a prodigious amount of bravery and pusseverance – Butt managed to establish hisseff in the inna wuckings of that tree, hidden from the view of any passersby – not that there were any. He remained in that advantageous position for several hours, which gave him sufficient tom to weigh his options, which were few, and to fommulate his next move. But whateva that next move tunned out to be, it was imperative that it result in the separation of a hoss from its rodda.

"Now Butt was in a secure position in his tree, nestled up against its tronk, but he was fiercely hongry and becoming impatient with his plott. The thinna branches that fommed a canopy ova the road could suttonly make a noss weapon if he could manueva out onto one of them. Which he did, ever so slowly. There were lower branches that were preferable, neara to his intended togget, so he was wucking up the courage to begin a slow, precarious descent when he saw the dust of an approaching rodda. Now Cunnel, ain't that just the way of the wuld? All day to do nothing and then no tom to do anything. So now he had a dun hodd decision to make and not motch tom in which to make it."

"What did he decide to do?"

"Well, if I were one to use religious tumminology, I would say that Butt put hisseff in the hands of the Lodd and took a lodge *leap of faith*. And suttonly, all things considded, I cannot presently think of a betta example of divonn intervention. Considering that that hoss was kicking up a cloud of dust and ronning lock the wind, I have no other explanation as to how Butt knew *when* to leap, *where* to leap, or even *how* to leap, in odda to dismount that rodda, but dun if he didn't figure out the answer to all three of those questions! At just the rot moment, Butt leapt off one of the top branches, landed on one of the lower ones, and his weight simultaneously fossed that branch down on top of the rodda, rendering him unconscious – the rodda, that is – before he had any uthly oddea what in the wuld just happened to him.

"Now, I'm shaw, as a smott, well-educated pusson, you can tho'oughly appreciate the irony of what I just related. Butt's enommous bulk had been nothing but a liability throughout this whole misadventure, causing him endless hodship and humiliation. And now of coss it tunned out to be his most important attribute when he needed it most. So Butt took the rope that he had so providentially borrowed from the station house, tied the unfotchinate rodda – still senseless – up to the tronk of the tree, along with his mail pouch from the hoss – because the hoss, which was more than slottly dazed, as you mott expect, had just ambled off and stotted grazing – unaware, or perhaps just forgetful, of its imperative to keep the mails moving. And thus soddenly, but with motch great effutt and hodship, Butt Homphrey found hisseff in possession of one of fittest, swiftest hosses existing in all the westtun territories, cuttesy of the Pony Express."

"So Burt rode this horse all the way to Oregon?"

"Oh no, Cunnel, far from it. Now it's possible that there were sutton *pots* of that hoss that remained with Butt ontil he arrived in O'gon, but that's a diffunt story entolly, and one that I'm not too eagga to relate. But this little incident with the Pony Express rodda, that's only one small pot of Butt's junney, which in tun is only one small pot of this entire O'gon debacle, so I'm dottful that I'll have the oppo'tunity to relate the entire story to you – that is, the entire pot of the story that I've been privy to, not the entire story as it occurred – that would be a yonn which no single pusson could stitch togetha with all the needles and thread in the wuld. But in regodds to that hoss, let's just say that up ontil this point, your sympathies may have been with Butt, but now afta a few molls of carrying him as his budden, you would undottedly transfer your allegiance to the hoss."

COMING UP ON SPARTANBURG pulled over for a cat named Pepper who had his hair piled high in a hillbilly pompadour. He jumped into the front seat all hey-man smile and acting like long-lost buddies but I'd never seen him before in my life just ready to give someone a lift so I was pretty happy to see him as well. When you're hitching you're happy to see just about anybody and grateful too. I asked him where he was headed and he sed west which was only a little less specific than what I had in mind for myself. I relinquished the radio to Pepper and ast what kind of music do you dig? and he sed Elvis like everybody else but I was feeling good and wasn't going to hold that against him and as if on cue the man himself came on the radio singing gonna run my fingers through your long black hair squeeze you tighter than a grizzly bear.

Been driving all morning so I stopped at a diner outside of S-burg and between us we ordered dam near everything on the menu. Too excited to eat when I split C-town been feeding off nothing but my dreams all a.m. so when the waitress returned with our grub I attacked my eggs like the Japs and didn't come up for air for several minutes. No telling when the last time Pepper ate was. He ordered a steak but didn't knife-and-fork it like you would expect but used his hands and gnawed it like a chicken leg. I almost said something but didn't. We started rapping and he sed his pop was a dentist but dam if he was going to make his bread looking down gullets all day and smelling other people's bad breath. He sed he would just pull everybody's dam teeth so he wouldn't have to look down their gullets anymore and that he knew a chick once whose teeth fell out because she never brushed them and had to wear dentures except he didn't know that until it was too late and when he woke up and saw her all gums and lips one morning it scared the shit out of him. He sed thumbing was how he got around during the day mostly but at night he and his buddies liked to steal cars and ride around till morning. He sed nobody misses their car at two in the morning and by the time they wake up and notice it gone he had ditched it and was hitching a ride back to town. I ast him if he had a car and he sed you don't need a car if you don't have a license and I didn't ask him how he lost his license because it wasn't my business and since Pepper never seemed to shut up he would tell me soon enough I figured. For that same reason I didn't ask why he was headed out west all of a sudden. When I could get a word in I sed I was headed to San Francisco to blow jazz. He sed you can't do that here? and I sed hell no, at least not the jazz I wanted to blow. I didn't bother trying to explain what I was talking about since Pepper liked Elvis it would have been a waste of time. I rapped about how it wasn't just the jazz because I was sick of Jim Crow and all the racism too. Pepper snorted and ast what does that have to do with you? and sed that was the niggers' problem to deal with. Of course this crap didn't come as any surprise since I'd been around it my whole life but I wasn't going to back down from Pepper because I was tired of giving in to these bastards just because I didn't want to cause any trouble. If he didn't like what I was saying he could hitch another ride or steal another dam car. The whole time we were rapping I was staring across the diner into the colored section and wishing I was sitting with them instead of Pepper. I sed all my heroes were black cats like Miles Dizzy Bird Satchmo and they were the most talented men on Earth and not just the famous ones but all of them as far as I was concerned. Yeah, Pepper sed, they did really know how to dance and sing real good so he wasn't going to argue that point. And I sed I was tired of hearing nigger everywhere I went. Can't even bring ourselves to give them a respectful name I sed. I grew up saying nigger like everybody else, but niggro and black and colored aren't much better. You want to be called a black man? I ast. Pepper looked like he might slug me. Yeah didn't think so I sed. So what the hell do you call them? Pepper ast. I sed I called them bluesmen because that's where jazz comes from and God knows they have lived with the blues – all of them. Satchmo smiles all the time but you know inside he's screaming. Pepper didn't say anything to that just kept gnawing on his steak. I guess he didn't want to cause any trouble with the man who was giving him a free ride away from whatever trouble he was in so maybe the shoe was finally on the other dam foot for a change. Still staring through the cig smoke across the diner into the colored section and feeling happily liberated and brave since this morning I sed I might go over there and sit with them just to see what happens and Pepper sed you want to be a nigger you go right ahead and then sed if you do you'll find out sure enough what it's like to be a nigger and you won't like it very much. He laughed and sed after we kick your teeth out and bust a couple ribs then I bet you'll be glad to be white from now on. Discouraged I changed the subject and started rapping about the weather and when somebody starts in on the weather you know it's time to split. Stood up and strolled into the ol' whites-only and thoroughly enjoyed the *whizz splash tinkle drip* – onomatopeeing enough to do me for a few hundred miles. I came back to our table, sopped up my yolk with what was left of my toast and put a quarter down for the waitress and we were ready to split. Pepper didn't leave a tip so I figured he didn't have the change on him so I put another two bits down and he sed he wasn't going to give that nigger bitch a dam dime because the steak was so dam chewy it made his jaw hurt. I sed that wasn't her fault man with a little rise in my voice and Pepper sed she should have seen all those gristles and sent it right back to the cook. I almost sed then why didn't you send it back yourself instead of taking it out on her? but I didn't want to to start up with him again since we were getting ready to hit the road but I didn't pick up the tips either. Pepper's one of those cats who'll go out of his way to blame a bluesman for anything even if it means gnawing a dam gristle for an hour. Outside the diner Pepper offered to drive and I took him up on it figuring a car thief would know how to drive just about anything.

Got into some mountains headed toward Asheville and kissed SC goodbye for good and I was happy to see some real trees for a change instead of those pines and scraggly ones at that. I stuck my head out the window and took a deep breath and could smell the leaves and bark and dirt and who knows what else. I ast Pepper if he wanted to hear some real music and he sed hey man I am listening to real music real good music as he sang along to some Ozark opera singer yodeling my heart I can't control you rule my very soul and I told him to pull over first chance he got so I could grab my trumpet case out of the trunk. It might drive Pepper crazy but I wanted to practice. I cleaned my teeth best I could with my fingernails so I wouldn't get too much food in my horn. I ast if he liked jazz and he sed yeah as long as he could whistle along to it. He sed he picked some of it up on the radio one time and sed it sounded more like they were just practicing instead of playing or if they were trying to play something they didn't know what the hell they were doing. I laughed and sed I know what you mean but that wasn't what I was thinking. I ran through some scales to warm up and tried to keep it tuneful for Pepper's sake. I told him to keep a steady beat for me on the dash and it wasn't long before he was taking both hands off the wheel when he could and adding some spice to the rhythm. He turned out to be a pretty good dashboard drummer. I was able to play most everything he requested – Boogie-Woogie Bugle Boy crap and whatever else he had heard on the radio growing up. He ast if I knew something called Hot Rod Lincoln and I sed how does it go?

and he pretended to be a twangy guitar and I picked it right up and Pepper was amazed as hell even though it was nothing but modulating the same little run overandover. With most people if you play something hard as hell it goes right over their heads but if you play something simple their jaws drop to the floor. All in all we had a fun little jam session but of course we did because it's impossible not to have fun playing jazz even if you don't know what the hell you're doing.

    I had an empty backseat and after we crossed into Tennessee I was ready to listen to someone besides Pepper so near Johnson City I told him to pull over and we picked up a cat named Kit. He thought Pepper was running the show since he was driving and directed all his gratitude toward him which was okay with me but Pepper didn't exactly set him straight. Kit just like his flattop appeared to be pretty square same as most of the cats I marched with but that was as good a reason as any to pick him up. Kit sed he had been living with his pop but was on his way to Arizona to see his mom. I would hitch across Hades to see my mom too but Pop would have to send me first-class airfare from Frisco if he wanted to see sonny boy which was dam unlikely. Kit saw my trumpet case in the backseat and ast Pepper what it was. I set him straight on whose horn it was and ast if he played anything. He sed he took piano lessons for about three months as a kid but begged his mom if he could quit. I sed that's because I bet your teacher was some wrinkled old hag who knew Beethoven personally and had you playing scales and etudes and Moonlight Sonata shit instead of some barebones boogie-woogie that would have had both feet stomping and instead of sneaking peeks at the clock while she told you not to slouch and to curl your fingers on the keys the hour would fly by and you would beg for just a few minutes more and couldn't wait til next week. I sed music teachers only want you to play what they want to hear and don't give a dam about what you might want to play or else they think you're actually supposed to like that shit and if you don't there's something wrong with you. I discovered bop by accident mostly and it's a dam good thing I did.

    Hit Kentucky sooner than I thought possible, must have just

nipped Tennessee and Virginia and picked up 421 out in the middle of dam nowhere Pepper driving these mountains like he knew what he's doing I guess when you're stealing cars at 2 a.m. being chased by cops you need to have nerves of steel and know how to handle the wheel Pepper one-handing it going faster than I ever would as I gripped my thighs tight around some of these curves but Pepper's in hillbilly heaven singing loud when I first saw you with your smile so tender my heart was captured my soul surrendered but I'm thinking Jesus if we get lost out here we're going to have to strangle a bear just to get something to eat if Pepper doesn't kill us first but Kit didn't seem worried he's been in these hills before so I was happy we had him along.

WILL,

You should consider yourself lucky that you do not concern yourself with dating. You have been very smart to dedicate your life to doing what you love and finding happiness in helping others. Everyone could learn a lesson from you. True, the planet would soon be de-populated and devoid of human life, but that could only be an improvement on the status quo. So, my big news is that I have started dating again. At some point I knew I would need to "put myself back out there," which is synonymous with "throw myself to the lions," or perhaps "gouge my eyeballs out." It's been almost three years now, so maybe it's time. And to prove I am a man of the 21st century, I have decided to forego the traditional route of pain and humiliation in favor of online dating. In reality, this merely postpones the pain of traditional dating, rather than preventing it. Instead of wasting a few minutes or a couple of hours in a bar chatting up a girl who is totally wrong for you, the new cyber-procedure is to tell a host of lies about yourself via email to build yourself up over the course of days or weeks, after which time, of course, when meeting the person in the flesh, the house of cards must inevitably crumble. I can make this damning assessment because I have had two such disastrous dates over the past two weekends.

The first woman who piqued my interest is a botanist named

Sarah. Well, to be completely honest here, I need to go a little further with that sentence: she is a botanist named Sarah with beautiful enormous breasts. Yes, how disgusting of me, but there you have it. Right there in a nutshell (or a D cup) is why women will always be, in the words of John Lennon, the "niggers of the world." No matter how accomplished she might be, no matter if this lady were the Greatest Botanist on Earth, I would not have dated her but for her beautiful enormous breasts. And this coming from a guy who has always striven to be a good person and a good boyfriend and husband. As Dick Nixon would say, I am not a creep. But if you are an unattractive woman in this world you are at such a Darwinian disadvantage, how long until you are naturally selected out of existence? To continue this little digression, I think it would be an interesting social experiment to have, say, two female doctors, each opening a practice in the same small town, but with two important differences – one is quite a knockout, but with little or no medical experience, while the other is homely but highly experienced. My hypothesis is that we know exactly who would have all the male patients in town in short order. I would even take this one step further and say, not only would men *prefer* an attractive professional (in whatever field), but given the opportunity they would *demand* one. I have seen grown men turn into little cry-babies in restaurants if they had the misfortune of getting a waitress they deemed less than fuckable, as if it were their natural entitlement to always be in the presence of physical beauty. For that reason, I doubt if we will ever elect an ugly woman president. Other countries don't seem to have such a hang-up (*cf.* Margaret Thatcher), but I can't picture the American male ever forgiving an unattractive woman for having the audacity to ask for his vote.

Anyway, I was telling you about my date with the big-breasted botanist. Soon after we were seated and the wine arrived, Sarah started putting this *stare* on me – I mean a full-on, bug-eyed, trance-like stare and her speech seemed to be emanating from somewhere other than her mouth. It was like she was a ventriloquist's dummy and the ventriloquist was hiding over behind a potted plant. I couldn't really focus on what she was saying for this mojo stare she was putting on me and that disembodied voice. After a few minutes I think I figured out her problem. My guess is, in her nervousness, she took maybe one or four Xanax too many and, combined with the wine, we were closing in on a medical emergency. I asked her if she was okay; she said, "yeah, I'm fine," but she wasn't, because it took about fifteen seconds for my question to register in her brain and another fifteen seconds for her brain to figure out what to do with it. Since she was still upright and conscious, though barely on both counts, I decided to let this thing play out. I did, however, slide her glass of wine across the table out of her reach, which she took no notice of. The waiter came by to take our order but Sarah's cognitive processes had shut down so I said to our waiter, "Give us a couple of minutes," then added, "or hours." He laughed nervously and left us alone. But what Sarah desperately needed was some food to sop up everything else in her stomach, so I flagged down the waiter and ordered a couple different appetizers and told him if he could get them to us on the fly then it wouldn't be forgotten at tip time. So when the food comes I slide my chair around beside Sarah, explaining that it would be easier for us to handle the nachos if we didn't have a big table between us. Back in college, that would have been a smooth move by Romeo, but it was lost on Sarah, who didn't hear me, and all I wanted at this point was to shovel food into her as quickly as possible.

The waiter soon returned and I ordered for Sarah (what a gentleman!). I had no idea what she would want to eat, our conversation not having progressed that far before her lights went out, but I figured a large salad was a safe bet, maybe followed by something more substantial if we weren't yet in the emergency room. Luckily by the time the entrees arrived Sarah was returning to Earth, although I don't think she was aware she had been anywhere. So at this point, halfway through our meal, I'm hoping perhaps for a normal date to finally get underway. I ask her questions about botany, which is untilled soil in my field of knowledge – Sarah's still operating on a five-second delay, but she's coherent and probably feeling pretty damn good I imagine – and she's trying to be as interesting as it's possible to be when the subject is botany. Roses are always fertile ground for conversation when in Portland (pardon the botanical puns), so I talked more than I ever wish to again about those thorny red bastards. When I had emailed her asking for a date, I told myself, "I think botany would be an interesting subject to learn about on a date," but I guess what I was really thinking was, "Great googley moogley, look at them boobies." She is an intelligent person and probably more interesting to talk to when she's not high as a kite, so maybe I should give her another chance to impress me. But what I definitely want to avoid is to continue dating someone less-than-interesting just because I want to remove her clothing. I can't think of anything more depressing than that, and I know Deb would be disgusted with me, although she's probably already disgusted with me for choosing a date based on boob size. But I think it would make her happy to know I'm dating again, as long as I'm dating women I'm truly interested in.

With that in mind, I went out last Friday night with a fellow teacher – a high school biology teacher, Penny by name. Very attractive, of course (otherwise, as stated above, why the hell would I go out with her?), and just for the record, and not that it's important or anything, of very average mammarian proportions. I was very happy with how our dinner started. We chatted amiably about things teachers talk about. And she was indeed very chatty, but that's what you want on a date rather than someone you have to interrogate. But boy, does Penny love to talk! Again, that's okay on a date, but a red flag had been raised. When you're setting goals for a potential relationship, "to get a word in edgewise" should not be one of them. Still mindful of last week's drug-fueled date with Sarah, I wondered if Penny was on some kind of amphetamine-based mother's little helper, but no, this was pure Penny I believe. She had described herself as "bubbly" and "effervescent" in her online profile, so I knew what I was getting into. But still, it wasn't an unpleasant evening at all. I was enjoying myself even though I was doing most of the listening. Penny continued with what amounted to a monologue and I tried to keep up and jump in like a hobo trying to hop a speeding boxcar. Then she said, "Would you like to see all my kids?" That caused me to do an aural spit-take. "*All* your kids? How many do you have?" I thought she had two. She laughed and said, "Not my *real* kids." She grabbed her cell and proceeded to show me candid classroom shots of damn near all her current, and I do believe her *former*, students. And she had stories to tell about most of them. Can you imagine this? It's hard enough to sit through a stranger's kid and cat photos, but a hundred anonymous teens sitting around tables? I complimented her on her devotion to her students, but man, I had to get out of this pubescent nightmare. I had wanted to talk with her about teaching evolution in the public schools, but the subject had not come up, so, apropos of nothing contained in her slide-show presentation, I blurted out, "Do you have any problems with crazy religious parents when you teach evolution?" Without missing a beat, she switched gears and said, "No, but I have problems with crazy atheist parents! If I even mention the word *Genesis* or *God*, for crying out loud, they'll go home and tell their parents that I'm talking about religion and then I'm getting calls at nine o'clock at night! Lord, I hate teaching that unit! I always wait until second semester to start on evolution and I wouldn't teach it at all if I didn't have to – but it comes up all the time! The first day of class a kid might ask about evolution!"

"So what do you say?"

"I say, 'we're not going to talk about evolution on the first day of class!'"

"We're the only country in the world where that's a problem."

"Well, I don't know about that, but I do know there are some countries where they teach kids in school to be *atheists*! Thank God we live in America – but if things keep going the way they are, I might have to start teaching atheism too!"

Wow! Was I in Portland or back in Charleston? I was not expecting this. True, Penny had chosen *Christian* as her religious affiliation online, but still. I have nothing against dating Christians. I'll happily go out with Billy Graham's granddaughter as long as she is half-way good-looking and has all her teeth, but I think I have to draw the line at people who think America is turning into the USSR and at biology teachers who don't "believe" in evolution, which is what I was now assuming about Penny. "Do you believe in evolution?" I asked her point-blank, yet as nicely as I could.

"Not really. I mean, it's just a theory, that's all. I've never seen any actual proof that it's true. But I have to teach it. It's part of my job. I love teaching biology, I really do – just not evolution. I always say the *theory* of evolution. I never just say *evolution*. It's always the *theory* of evolution. The *theory* of evolution says this or the *theory* of evolution says that. That's the only way I can teach it with a clear conscience, and I'm not doing anything wrong by calling it that, because that's what it is – a theory. I don't understand why we have to teach it at all. If parents want to teach their kids evolution, then let them teach it at home. We should only have to teach things in school that everybody agrees on. It's hard enough to teach as it is, without having to tippy-toe around all these controversial issues. Do you believe in evolution?" Again, Will, it bears repeating: this is in PORTLAND. Surely, Penny is the only biology teacher in Portland and Multnomah County who thinks in this way, right? Or has even Oregon and the liberal heartland of the Great Northwest been invaded by the brain snatchers? So anyway, she asks me if I believe in evolution. This, dear brother, is where the men are separated from the boys, the wheat from the chaff, the sheep from the goats – well, actually, it's just where we separate the gentlemen from the assholes. I swallowed the impulse I had to scream, *Yes, you stupid ignorant twat! I believe in the endlessly proven, endlessly demonstrated fact of evolution!* and said merely, "Well, it certainly is controversial – no doubt about that, but I don't think it really should be. It's been around a long time – it's got a pretty good track record." Penny had stopped swiping her way through her photos only long enough to expound on her scientific ignorance, but as I was answering her question and giving her a free pass around my outrage she picked up where she had left off. "Oh, here's

Luther," she said, "he's such a sweetheart!" And this was actually a relief, being back inside her uncontroversial, comfortable bubble of happy students, whom she loves despite their atheist parents and the fascist administrators who make her teach heresies she doesn't believe in. Our date ended cheerfully and without any further controversies, but I was certainly glad when it was over. It's a jungle out there, Will. Stay inside, where it's a little less crazy.

DEAREST CONSTANCE,
I think back tonight to some words I wrote to you many days ago – though the time seems much longer – with which I complained of the endless monotony of the trail. O! How I miss the monotony! How I long for endless, uneventful days! I am well, sweetheart, and remain unharmed and safe, so there is no need for you to worry. But I am not so well in spirit. There are times when we receive a bounty of good fortune, but which comes at a dear price.

The Captain, when given the news of the attack on my life, reacted much more adversely than I would have predicted. And his actions, though accruing to my great advantage, must be called into question. J. and I rode to the rear to meet with the Captain and to explain the events of the preceding day. The concerns I had that our testimonies might be doubted, due to the lack of any corroboration, and that my actions, though blameless and in self-defense, might be deemed suspicious, quickly were proved to be unfounded. The Captain was entirely disposed to take our word as gospel and – as befitted an experienced soldier, I suppose – was perfectly untroubled by the fact that I had taken a man's life. J. took this opportunity to vouch again for my strong character and to deny that I had anything to do with W.'s death. "I need to take care of those d— troublemakers once and for all," the Captain exclaimed, "they are nothing but d— nuisances! They can all go to the devil – with whom I'm certain they are on the most intimate terms!"

"What do you propose to do?" J. asked.

"I'll order them onto the new cutoff. Who is leading them

now?" J. explained that the one who calls himself Aaron apparently had claimed that authority for himself. "Well, then, I'll find this Aaron fellow and give him the good news." I should probably explain to you, darling, that a "cutoff" is but another term for what we might call a "short cut," which, though convenient and useful when on errands around town, is, out here on the trail, a much more doubtful proposition, for what may be gained by a shortened distance to be travelled often is lost in time and toil, not to mention the dangers inherent in traversing an unfamiliar terrain. Men are never satisfied, sweetheart. Those who possess wealth believe themselves poor; those with every reason to be content believe themselves miserably situated; and those with a safe, proven, well-travelled trail westward believe themselves horribly inconvenienced and in need of cutoffs and any other attainable expediency. Many such cutoffs have been envisioned; some have been planned or even begun; a few have been successfully completed; and perhaps one or two have been deemed worthy of the time and money expended on their creation. I knew not which cutoff the Captain was referring to; however, since he spoke of it rather as a form of punishment, than as something to be freely chosen, I can only assume that it is newly devised and not yet completed, and those who choose it over the established trail must have more Frémont and Meriwether Lewis in their blood than I would lay claim to. J. and I returned to our wagons uncertain as to the earnestness of the Captain's pronouncement. Was it merely an idle threat made in anger? It was of the utmost urgency, however, that we determine the Captain's intentions in this matter; for if he did not intend to use the cutoff as the means of ridding himself of the burden of those "d— idolaters" (as he referred to them), then we must consider it seriously ourselves for that same purpose.

Come this morning, we had the answer, in the most definite terms, from the Captain. After we had struck camp and had been back on the trail for perhaps an hour, he rode amongst our wagons until he spotted J. and me. He had carried out this morning his stated intention. "I met with the one called Aaron," the Captain said. He remained on his horse. J. and I were walking beside my wagon. "What a G— d— mess those rascals have created! And what a fine specimen of a leader that Aaron is! He is no more in control of those heathens than I am, but – by G—! – that's about to change!"

"Did you give him an ultimatum?" J. asked.

"I did indeed! There's a new cutoff being opened up roughly thirty miles up. One good-day's march and we should make it."

"Where does this cut-off go?" I ventured to ask.

"North. It will meet up with a new road from Fort Benton. You may see them again at Fort Walla Walla, but it's doubtful. It's a longer route, but there's better forage – I'm doing them a d— favor, but they don't see it that way. Those d— libertines don't appreciate having to obey a direct order given to them. But they're playing by U.S. Army rules now, by G—!"

"Did Aaron refuse to obey it?" I asked. I was surprised at the Captain's suggestion that he had. W.'s folks had been ordered about, arrested, abused, and murdered all along their tragic trail of exile from New York. W.'s counsel had always echoed that of Jesus, in Matthew's Antitheses: "But I say unto you, that ye resist not evil: but whosoever shall smite thee on thy right cheek, turn to him the other also." Why would they now decide to resist authority?

"Aaron is not their leader. They have no d— leader. The best I can tell, Aaron is in charge of a handful of folks who are willing to do as he says, but the rest of 'em are just a bunch of d— outlaws disguised as pilgrims. Aaron's folks will do whatever I say, but they're not the ones we have to worry about."

"What happens if they refuse to obey your order?"

"Well, by G—! I'll arrest every d— one of 'em if I have to!" Upon making this blustery remark, the Captain took his leave and rode hard back in the direction whence he came.

J. was curious – as was I – to see for himself the state of affairs directly in front of us on the trail. I, however, knew better than to insert myself into whatever cauldron of distemper was boiling ahead of us; therefore, I remained on foot, walking with my wagon at whatever speed I could induce the mules to assume. So, while I stayed behind, J. saddled a horse and rode forward. He disappeared out of my sight, but I occasionally saw the bonnet of a wagon in the distance. Ever since the death of W., we have used a strategy of keeping as much space as possible between us and W.'s group, without disengaging ourselves entirely from the train and the advantages of safety it affords.

J. returned and reported to me what he had learned. He corroborated much of what the Captain had said. It appears that Aaron has lost what little authority he had over the group, and, worse than that, without W.'s spiritual influence, A. has wavered in his policy of obedience to authority and seems willing now to contemplate reasons for resisting the Captain's insistence that they break off from the train. I will share with you, sweetheart, my conversation with J., though it does not bode well and undoubtedly will cause you some concern. J. said, "Aaron does not believe the Captain is justified in forcing his entire party onto a route that they did not approve of. He said, 'We had one man attempt to take the law into his own hands, and he paid for it with his life; his accomplice was chastened as well. That should have been the end of the matter. We are the victims of violence, not perpetrators of it.' But he knows things have advanced beyond his control. He said, 'None of us believed that Wilbur would die. He was yet a young man. We all envisioned a colony in Oregon where we could thrive and grow and establish ourselves as a peaceful community, and eventually to develop a governing structure for ourselves that would guarantee our existence into perpetuity. We were willing, as necessary, to endure whatever violence was visited upon us by fearful people, because our common dream was intact still, and to retaliate would be to place our dream into jeopardy. But that is all now ruined – ruined beyond repair. We were all followers of Wilbur and his vision. We were not leaders. We are broken. I am broken.'"

"What does he plan to do?" I asked.

"Hard to say. I believe much depends on how the Captain handles the situation. I believe we are safe. I believe you are safe. Their minds are occupied now with this dilemma forced upon them by the Captain. I tried my best to convince Aaron to take however many people he could with him and to take the cutoff. I told him that the Captain would not brook any disobedience on his part and if they were put into custody then the Captain might insist that they all be transported back to New York. Everything they hoped for here would be gone. Aaron just stared at me and said, 'It is all gone, regardless.' I believe he is thoroughly discouraged that he could not hold together the community. But he is reluctant to take the cutoff. He doesn't want to abandon anyone who refuses to obey the Captain. He sees that as the abandonment of the community – of the dream."

"But it's just a cutoff. He can continue to Oregon and establish a community there with the folks remaining with him. Did you impress that upon him?"

"He doesn't trust the Captain. The cutoff is only partially complete. They will not be simply taking a new trail – they will be blazing one. I don't know if they're prepared to do that. He is fearful that the Captain only wants to exploit them as a source of labor to work on the cutoff. He is struggling to understand why they are being forced to do this, when they have done nothing wrong. For the majority of them, they reject the Captain's order on principle. They are innocent victims, in their view. They are no longer willing to capitulate. The question of whether or not they should take a dangerous cutoff is irrelevant to them."

"So they will allow themselves to be arrested?"

"I believe so. I believe that will be the result. I don't see the Captain backing down from his order. Regardless, I think your ordeal, my friend, will soon be over. I believe the Captain will see to that. I believe our path to Oregon will become suddenly much safer and clearer after those people are removed as obstacles."

O! Constance! What a maelstrom of seething emotions I am forced now to contend with! How I wish you were here so that I could take advantage of your wise counsels! You would recognize immediately which path I should take! Oh, darling, what shall I do? Although I owe the Captain the gratitude he deserves for effecting my release after my arrest, and, therefore, a measure of loyalty, I also believe that I have seen through him to his true nature; that is, he is a man of poor judgment and of even poorer virtue. He displays a hatred against the entirety of W.'s group – even more so than I, who has been assaulted and shot at by individuals within that group, and who, I must assume, still wish to see me dead. I believe that as a citizen of a Southern state, but who happens also to abhor the institution of slavery, I am in a singular position to recognize the type of blind hatred that the Captain displays. The Negro is feared and reviled, maltreated and abused, not as a consequence of anything he has done, but simply because he is a Negro. I see a similar prejudice being exhibited against W.'s followers. That, dear, is how I would describe the first current that is flowing swiftly through this river of anguish in which I feel I am in danger of drowning.

Secondly, though the Captain's order given today to A. and his men is immoral, it is also undoubtedly the best thing that could happen to me in my present circumstances. Without it, my friends and I could well be the ones braving an untested cutoff and Indian attacks tomorrow morning – the difference being, our choice will be one which we have made freely. But with the order being implemented by force, I am rid of my nemeses and will be allowed to remain on the trail upon which thousands of my countrymen have immigrated successfully.

And thirdly – as if the aforementioned were not enough! – my friends are unanimous in their support of the Captain and believe that I, of all people, should be foremost in trumpeting my approval of his actions. What shall I do, sweet Constance? Shall I criticize the judgment and probity of the Captain – the highest authority on the trail, and a man who also happened to save my life? Shall I remain silent and accept decisions that are to my great advantage, and that will ensure my greatest safety, but which I find morally reprehensible? Shall I alienate my good friends – the same friends who risked their own safety in order to ensure mine – by supporting a group of people who have openly avowed that I am a murderer?

We have made our encampment for the night after a long march today – we must be near the cutoff, though I am sure we have yet to pass it. What will all these men, women, and children, only a few miles forward of us, who are innocent – all of them – of any crime, who are guilty only of thinking differently, and of acting rashly, and who have carried a burden of suffering across this elongating nation, a burden created solely by the fears and prejudices of others – what will all these innocent people choose to do tomorrow as they arrive at the cutoff? Does it matter? Regardless of their choice, they are doomed. They were doomed the instant that fateful knife tore through the heart of Wilbur, for it tore through the hearts of everyone who believed in him as well. Perhaps the only question that matters tonight, my sweet dear Constance, is what choice am I to make?

7

W,

Well, we know what today is, don't we? At least we won't have to waste our money this year on after-shave he will never wear and shirts that don't fit because we perennially underestimated his girth. I'll take Mom out to eat, if she feels like leaving the house. That's the least I can do, which, in most instances regarding Mom, is the most I can do. In Pop's honor today, assuming he still deserves to be honored, like all those Confederate generals we refuse to stop worshiping, I'll say a few words on his behalf.

Although he was a virulent racist (I always have to throw that in, don't I?) he was not an idiot and, like all men, his blind spots didn't prevent him from seeing other things clearly. If it weren't for our disparate views on race and the way those issues clouded our relationship I'm not sure how I would feel about the man, but of course it's as impossible to tease apart those feelings as it is to separate the ingredients of a custard. As kids, of course, he was a god in our eyes – fierce and frightening, but ultimately fair. But rather than feeling relief when you realize he is not perfect – and therefore neither must you be – you are continually reminded that every shortcoming he displays is the same shortcoming you must fight to overcome to be the man you want to be.

But I come here today to praise Pop, not to bury him. He was adamant that we not only attend college but that we excel. To that end, he praised our accomplishments and rarely belittled us. I think he attended all my high school band concerts; I don't remember him not being at one. He didn't like or understand the music I listened to but I didn't expect him to. It was my music, not his. I think he was disappointed I didn't want to be a doctor but he never brought it up and seemed proud of me as long as I kept my grades up. I have no doubt he was immensely proud of you. I'm sure he saw you as being an improvement in every way over me, but I never felt he wasn't proud of me – except, of course, all those times he implied I was an idiot in his rants and in our arguments. Thanks, by the way, for jumping in and helping me take on Pop all those years. How were you able to bite your tongue for so long? I know you agreed with me in every detail, and you certainly proved you did in how you lived your life, but you were perfectly content to let me and Pop slug it out. Maybe you felt you were too young to participate in Pop-bashing. Maybe you didn't have the self-confidence or believe you had the knowledge necessary to take him on. Maybe you thought I was saying all that needed to be said. Maybe you were just looking out for number one. But I never blamed you for any of that and I never felt I needed your help, or wanted it, when dealing with Pop. As usual, for whatever reason, you showed you were on the wiser path, though I would never admit that to you.

This will sound absurd, knowing what we know now, but I'm proud of Pop for choosing the specialization he did. I asked him once why he wanted to be a gynecologist, though I was scared to death to ask him. Why would I be so scared? I was probably fifteen or sixteen, at the peak of my curiosity about all things female, so the question should have been a natural one to ask. Pop was so aloof – I guess I was terrified of trodding on some secret, sacred ground that only he knew the boundaries of. But he answered me without anger, though also without elaboration, "Because I wanted to bring life into this world." Yes – irony of ironies, no? I suppose he meant only certain life, of a certain color and of a certain socio-economic status. How did he get away with it for so long? What kind of coercion, threats, intimidation and lies must he also have been guilty of? Or did he just rely on ignorance and trust and the inchoate fear of the white man until someone chose not to be quite so ignorant, trusting and fearful? I know you didn't believe him either – at least, not after a certain point. How many of these women had to come forward before Pop finally realized the jig was up? Mom wanted – needed – to believe him. Who knows, maybe he believed it himself. We convince ourselves of all kinds of bullshit, don't we? Bullshit that makes a lot less sense than what Pop was saying. *Only what was medically necessary.* Did he come up with that line himself or did his lawyer?

Okay – back on task. It's nice to think of a young, idealistic Dr. K, even before he was Dr. K, witnessing the miracle of birth (yes, in a whites-only hospital, no doubt) and saying, "that's what I want to do." And I can see him using that idealism to woo Mom. What kind of goodness must she have seen in him? They seem so happy in all those old photos, she always smiling in her long dresses and bobby socks, he always in a sharp suit and sometimes a hat. Both of them always so well dressed. During the last couple of years Pop just couldn't shut up about how black people dressed, could he? "If they would start dressing nicer and pull those damn pants up and stop using all that despicable language – then they would start to earn a little more respect. You have to learn to respect yourself before you can expect anyone else to. Respect has to be earned." And I said, on cue, "You mean, like all those dapper, deferential blacks who always wore suits and ties and tipped their hats to the white ladies on the street and yet who we wouldn't let drink out of our water fountains or even piss in our toilets? They really earned your respect, didn't they, Pop?" But nothing I ever said to him seemed to make any difference. But to throw Pop a little bone on his birthday, I won't argue with him about what is ridiculous about so much of modern African-American fashion. Not to be critical or to cast blame on anyone or on any one social group, but when you look at a modern hip-hop outfit what does it most closely resemble? The sideways cap. The loose baggy shirts and even looser, baggier pants. The big, oversized boots. What are you picturing? Think Ringling Brothers. I'm sure Pop would get a kick out of my saying that. But I can't stop there – that would be blatantly and patently unfair. Sorry, Pop. I'm generalizing here, but we as a nation have completely forgotten how to dress. Not since the

1950s – like Mom and Pop at the dancehall – have we dressed in a way that is not unfailingly thought of as hideously embarrassing ten years later. Why is that? The great revolutions of the Sixties apparently freed us to pursue happiness while at the same time calling off the pursuit of classiness. Is there anyone who lived in the Fifties and before who is embarrassed by how they dressed then, even if they were dirt-poor? By contrast, is there anyone who lived through the Sixties and beyond who is not horrified at old pictures of themselves, regardless of how affluent they were? Is it because the children are now in charge? Is this why our fashion, like everything else done by children, is so outlandish and over the top? Why everything on television looks more and more like a video game? Why every internet startup must be given some name like Googoo-Gaga.com? Every year the latest products of our eternal adolescence are thrust upon us and, like everything kids wear, are soon outgrown and must be discarded. And now Comfort is King, nothing is too leisurely, too slack. Flip-flops at the opera. Barefoot at a wedding. Bermuda shorts to meet the president, a tee-shirt to be on TV. But if you were a kid, isn't this exactly what you would wear? Old guys, whose grandfathers wouldn't have been caught dead outdoors without a tie and fedora, are now walking around in knee socks and sandals in some happy time-machine back to when they were six and playing in a sandbox. What's going on here? Are we all giddily reverting back to childhood, racing back to the womb, last one in is a rotten egg? But I don't want to be too critical of the current fashion. It's so democratic, so economical, so damn *comfortable*. It's one revolution I can get behind wholeheartedly. Maybe we're slowly returning to a state of nature, back to loincloths and free-flopping breasts, Paleolithic-chic. Fine by me.

Where was I? Yes – praising Pop on his birthday. Young idealistic Dr. K pulling out babies and repopulating the world, one little bald-headed white boy at a time. But at what point did that idealism turn sour? When did he decide to turn all the good he was capable of into evil? It makes me shudder to think, Will, that as harsh as I am on him, as much hatred as I'm capable of regarding him, that maybe I'm still being too easy on the guy – that is, why do I give him the benefit of the doubt that he was once idealistic, that he was once innocent and only wanted to do what was good and right? What if this was his plan from the start? Did he ever seem particularly sensitive to women's issues to you? Was this why he didn't care to elaborate when I asked him why he chose to spend every day peering into vaginas? Why he never talked about it? My mind reels when I think about this. Was there some secret sect at Carolina, where Pop first hatched his plan to do his part in purifying his country? Hell, back then it wouldn't have needed to be all that secret. Was Mom duped from the very beginning? I can't allow myself to think in this way, though it's entirely possible. The only solace I can take from this whole tragedy is to think about the innocence and hope contained in all those courtship and honeymoon photos of the young couple, the southern belle and her gentleman doctor beginning a life together full of American dreams, not to mention all those photos of us together with Mom and Pop on vacation, at birthday parties, in a thousand different poses and settings. Those photos expressed the truth, right, Will? They said what they meant, right? They didn't hide anything other than those messy little things all adults hide from their children, right? The sacrifices. The hurts and jealousies. The uncertainties. The disagreements and mistakes. All these things are easily dismissed fifty years after the fact, if they ever mattered much in the first place. But please tell me that was all there were in those pictures – feigned contentment, perhaps, but genuine joy in the moment, no sinister shadows being cast, no eager thoughts of planned butcheries inside Pop's head as he smiled into the camera, no little fork-tailed devil running around between our legs and over the table and jumping back on Pop's shoulder, breathing fire and hissing, invisible to the camera's gaze. But if that little devil wasn't in those photos, where did it come from and when did it sneak into our house? Did some event trigger it, some personal crisis, or did it start as so many of these things do – as something entirely different, as something good for all the right reasons but then you ask that fateful question – if good for this, then why not also good for that? Where does one draw the line and does the line necessarily have to be drawn? There are markers, gradations along the way delineating your steps downward into the abyss. Everything progresses, but slowly, like grass growing, and it is only much later that you can look back and ask, how did I get here? And you invariably ask yourself, why didn't I stop? But every decision proceeds from all your prior decisions and all those decisions were made to keep you moving forward, so forward you must continue, and you can stop only when there is nowhere else you can go.

But I'm trying to be complimentary of Pop today, as difficult as that is proving to be. Yes, he did what we all know he did, but when you look at a man's life how are you supposed to measure it? On what kind of sliding scale are we allowed to grade? How do all those women whose lives he destroyed measure up to all the life he brought into the world, all the women whose health he faithfully helped maintain, not to mention the family he raised? He spat on his Hippocratic Oath, his accusers said. Well, yes, in their minds (and ours); but what about in his? In his mind, wasn't he doing what was in the best interests of everyone? Wasn't he in the end helping these poor women even if they were incapable of appreciating it? Yes, he took away their choices; he took away a part of their future (and for some – the prosecution would allege – he took away their lives, though the trail of causation is murky). But didn't they always make the wrong choices? Didn't they abuse every freedom ever given to them? And by doing so, didn't they ruin their futures each and every time? Weren't they abused and manipulated by every no-count man they got involved with, and so didn't he ultimately save them from these men's cruellest predations? I'm assuming, of course, he cared enough about these women to think of himself as someone who wanted to help them. Again, it helps me cope if I can at least give him the benefit of that particular doubt. But even if he didn't give a damn about these women, didn't think twice about the consequences for them of his actions, isn't there something justifiable in the idea of the Noble Sacrifice? On a grand scale, how many lives did we sacrifice in Hiroshima and Nagasaki in the interests of a greater good? How many American lives has our government sacrificed for what we hope or believe are greater goods? Of course, the greater good is always what is great and good for us, not them. On a small scale, how many people do we hurt, do we scar emotionally, manipulate, ignore, lie to, abuse in one fashion or another, all because they threaten to get in the way of what we deem to be of higher importance – namely, us? The Noble Sacrificer says, We are more important than They. Has there ever been a more common and more commonly agreed-upon sentiment than that? It is the basis of every friendship, clique, tribe, village, city-state, and nation ever defined as such, so can Pop be excused if he saw his victims as noble sacrifices in the greater cause of – what?

It all comes down to his specious arguments, historical irrationalities, misunderstandings and lies used to salve his fears and ensure the continued supremacy of Us. But so it is with any grand political struggle fought along the battlelines of human history. And of course, what is lost sight of when you mistake these generalizations for the truth is the rightful primacy of the individual – when you survey the forest you lose sight of the trees. But if you're African-American, you will always be lost in the forest. Only whites are allowed to claim their personhood. A white man arrested is but one man accused of a crime; when a black man is thrown into the docket an entire race is put on trial.

But that can happen even when it's the good guys you're talking about – the folks on the Us side of the equation, where it's all for one and one for all – which sounds great until it's turned around and used against you. When I broke the news to Pop that I was living with the enemy in Texas, I was prepared for the worst, but was caught off guard by the softness of his voice. "Is that right?" he said, perhaps surprised, perhaps not. "Yeah, Pop, sorry to break it to you, but the dormitories are integrated now," I joked, actually feeling sorry for him, as he seemed finally ready to concede defeat in whatever doomed war he was fighting in his mind. "Well, everything is now," he sighed, his *now* encompassing the last twenty-five years of

American social progress. I thought (mistakenly) this was our détente, and I found it suddenly possible to sympathize with a man hopelessly abandoned in a *now* which was separated irrevocably from an unreclaimable *then*.

Now, the other possibility in trying to explain Pop's reasoning is the one I try to avoid thinking about – the conclusion which everyone else in the world with a television or a radio was only too eager to jump to, but which I must resist. If he didn't do it because he thought he was helping these women, or in the service of some higher good to society, then it was because of personal principle – a personal principle that meant, even if he were not a doctor, he still would have found a way to harm these women. If he were a businessman he would have fleeced them; a judge he would have railroaded them; a man on the street he would have helped lynch them.

So did Pop do anything right? If we choose to, if we think it justifiable, can we try to balance his crimes against something positive? As a father I think he was fairly typical of the age. I felt safe with him and felt loved to a certain degree. I felt wanted, which is perhaps the most important thing. He made me feel part of a family, even though at the same time a family I wanted no part of. Was that his fault or mine? You would have been so instructive on this point. So – if it's not too late – what do you think? Did I ignore all of Pop's good points so I could hate him with a clearer conscience? I would say no, of course, but that's why I need you here to arbitrate. He seemed to treat Mom well, but of course everything had to be on his terms, so who knows how he would have reacted if she had not gone along with the program. I'm afraid he was capable of making her life very difficult. Some men are unsuited for anything beyond the simplest hunting and gathering. Put them in a complex social situation and they feel overwhelmed, put upon, out of their element – and so out come the rocks and clubs.

I would say all the fun we had under Pop's aegis should count for something – months of fun, years even, if added up and strung together. The beaches, pools, movies, rides, trips, restaurants, spending money, gifts, the transportations here, there, and everywhere; the tuitions, the lessons in woodworking and auto mechanics and family finance and other manly arts, the roof he put over our heads, the food he put in our mouths, the thousands of payments he made on our behalf – how much do all these things matter? Are they discounted if they were done along with those beastly things we were unaware of at the time? Is their value eliminated entirely when weighed against all the other evidence? Is it fair to judge Pop against other men I have known? Against myself? I abandoned Pop almost completely; you reduced his influence to what you could live with in good conscience. Doesn't that speak volumes? Jeff still seeks out my company and actually seems to like his old man. But does that mean I have been a great father? Is the friendship of your children the best goal of parenthood? Believe it or not, I have been fitfully successful through the years imagining Pop to be a lucky gift to you and me – an ornery, ignorant, infuriating, racist, and as it turned out, evil-minded gift. Needless to say, this has not been an easy, nor a steadfast, conclusion for me to convince myself of – but would you have dedicated your life to medicine and to those who most needed your kindness if it weren't for Pop? Would I have been the person I am without him? Without Pop I'm not sure I would have attitudes any different from most of my Southern (or white) compatriots. A more enlightened father would have instilled better values in us from infancy onward, but would we have embraced those values as tightly? What we have, brother, is a *hard-earned* liberality of spirit. But like I said, this is not a solidified opinion of Pop I'm capable of holding for long periods of time. In all likelihood, it's merely wishful thinking. Jeff and his friends, raised in a liberal environment, seem to be as good-hearted as it is possible to be. But perhaps their goodness has yet to be properly tested. You were the kindest person I could ever hope to meet; yet, as your horrible experience with the mugger shows, perhaps our generosity of heart, forged in the furnace of hatred and racism, is only skin-deep, a veneer of niceness poured over a wrought-iron frame of intolerance fabricated throughout our childhood. Perhaps your reaction to that incident is the greatest indictment of Pop that either one of us could offer. So. Happy birthday, old man.

> You can say it to yourself since it's
> In the book. But don't say it out loud.
> It was okay back then, but not now.
> I know he does, but it's still not right.
> He can't help it. That's just the way he is.

HADN'T SEEN ANY HITCHHIKERS on this ridiculous python of a road and didn't expect to but dam if we didn't pass by this cat who looked so forlorn and miserable that I told Pepper to turn around and we went back to pick him up. It wasn't only the way he looked but how he walked – all slumped and slithery like he lived under a big rock somewhere and just wanted to get back there. He wore his hair the way some old men still do, with a part so wide you can run your finger down and not get any Brylcreem on it like the old movie stars but this cat was no movie star I was willing to bet. His name was Albert he sed but everybody called him Einstein because he was always the smartest kid in class and knew a lot of science. I tossed my horn case back into the trunk to make room for Einstein.

Hadn't been back on the road five minutes when a sound came from the backseat that almost scared Pepper off the side of the mountain. Either Einstein was in some kind of bad way or a bear had climbed on board when we weren't looking. I sed what the hell? and looked back to see Einstein throwing himself against the door and against Kit and one side of his body up against the other if that's even possible. Pepper pulled off again and the three of us who weren't incapacitated tried to help Einstein as much as you can help someone who keeps trying to throw himself out a car window. Einstein was pulling at the zipper of his bag but his hands were shaking so bad as soon as he unzipped it a little he zipped it right back up again so it sounded like the zipper was playing bebop better than Charlie Parker. I snatched the bag and opened it for him and Einstein didn't waste any time pulling out some little contraption and putting it in his mouth like a gun barrel and taking two long pulls. In a minute he was breathing normal and his heart was probably the only one in the car not still racing. We all sed you okay man? more or less in unison and he nodded and put his little Saturday night special back into his bag. Maybe you should hang on to that I sed and was serious. What I was thinking was why are you out here hitching when you should be in the dam hospital? When Einstein could talk again he sed he had asthma and it was a good thing he had this inhaler thing too as he called it.

Pepper pulled out and we were on our way again. Einstein fell asleep lickety-split and I was glad to see it hoping maybe he would sleep all the way to California. That asthma attack took its toll I'm sure not to mention out there thumbing all day. I lit up another cig but thought twice about it with an asthmatic now on board. Pepper and Kit were smoking too but we had the windows down air swooshing through the American like a wind tunnel so Einstein seemed to be okay in dreamland.

Thought these mountains were never going to end just curve after curve leaning left leaning right not up and down so much like I expected but the hills always right beside you closing in around you good god it's like being in a vice or a prison cell made out of scenery and just when I thought we were out of them maybe half a mile of straight road or a clear horizon on one side we were right back where we were leaning leaning sliding on the seat one way and then the other I even thought maybe Pepper was driving in circles and kept taking the same wrong turn overandover cause every dam curve looked the same to me and I thought for a while I was going to be sick and Pepper was going to have to stop so I could throw up but he didn't seem to be bothered by the curves one hand on the wheel most of the time except for those hairpin turns where you had to slow down to a crawl and the front of your car almost collides with the rear as they pass each other I could have waved at Kit in the backseat without turning around if I had wanted to. Never been so relieved at the sight of straight roads and rolling farmland and I figured Pepper needed a break so I told him to pull over and I would take over.

Nighttime now and I had been driving most of the day except through the mountains which was actually worse riding shotgun helpless as Pepper careened around all those tight corners and up all last night as well too excited to sleep so I needed someone else to take over before I started snoring behind the wheel and killed us all. The logical choice but also the worst choice was Einstein who had slept most of the afternoon but I didn't trust him to drive a nail let alone my car. But Pepper had been up all day too and so had Kit as far as I could remember so I swallowed hard and ast Einstein do you know how to drive? and he shot me a look that nearly cracked my rearview and sed of course I know how to dam drive but I didn't think it was a stupid question considering how child-like and helpless Einstein looked. I pulled over and everybody climbed out stretching and yawning and we took this opportunity all four of us to stumble in the dark through some brush growing alongside the road and into a foresty area even further off the road away from headlights and relieved ourselves long and leisurely standing far enough apart so we wouldn't piss on each other in the pitch-darkness.

Hard to visit dreamland with Einstein behind the wheel but he seemed to be doing all right going slower than the speed limit which was probably a good thing so I don't think it was too long before I was snoring and slobbering on myself beside Kit but it's hard to get solid shuteye in a car full of cats and before long I woke up with Pepper and Einstein going at it up front fighting over the radio. Einstein had told Pepper to find something symphonic and when Pepper refused Einstein took it maybe a little too personally and that's about when I woke up. Pepper sed shotgun had the radio and Einstein insisted the driver did since he was the one driving and since I wanted to get back to dreamland and we didn't have a lawyer in the car I took charge and sed let Einstein find a symphony if he can out here in the middle of nowhere not because I liked symphonies any more than Pepper did but at least all those violins would put everybody to sleep quicker than anything else could. Of course by everybody I didn't mean the dam driver and not long after Einstein had found some Mantovani or Liberace shit and I got back to dreamland I jerked awake to the sudden sound of brush and gravel and tree branches against the car and I yelled Einstein! and that woke everybody up including Einstein and he swerved back up on the road but forget about me getting any more shuteye anytime soon. I told Einstein to find something else on the radio but since he was hereditarily incapable of finding anything but shit to listen to Pepper took over the radio and quickly found the hillbilly music he liked which didn't do me any favors but at least made Einstein too uncomfortable to sleep. At some point I fell asleep again even though the last thing I remembered is Pepper singing in a loud horrendous off-key falsetto you tell me mistakes are part of being young but that don't right the wrong that's been done and the next thing I knew hot sunshine was hitting my face and I was relieved to realize I had lived through the night.

 I told Einstein to pull into a diner and when we slid into the booth I doubt if a more mismatched motley disheveled gang of four was to be found in the diner or anywhere in the immediate vicinity. We gobbled our grub with a minimum of rapping except for our determination not to let Einstein forget that he had nearly killed us all but he was so sadsack we couldn't give him a hard time for very long. Something seemed to be bothering him the whole time we ate and I figured it was all about his little nap last night but it turned out to be something else. He didn't have the nerve to tell me until the last minute when we got up to pay the tab. He grabbed my arm and pulled me away from Pepper and Kit and sed in a whisper that he didn't have any bread. He sed his last ride had robbed him and pummeled him pretty good in the stomach and made him throw up and then dumped him back out on the road like a sack of garbage. Well you can't be mad at somebody after a story like that and unlike Pepper who I didn't believe half the time I didn't doubt for a minute that poor Einstein was telling the truth so I went up to the others and gave them the run-down and we all pitched in to cover Einstein's breakfast and we would be doing the same thing all the way to California because he was headed out there to go to school where he had a scholarship. I ast him why a guy in his condition was out thumbing rides and he got all mad again like when I ast him if he knew how to drive and he sed he could thumb his way across the country as well as Kit or Pepper could and after all he'd been through I wasn't going to bring up the fact that he had been robbed and kicked around and I couldn't see the same thing happening to Pepper or Kit or me for that matter but I had to admire his spunk no doubt about it. On the way out to the car Pepper stopped me and sed maybe we should drop Einstein off in the next town and give him enough bread for bus fare or at least to make some phone calls and I sed no I'm not going to do that and what I didn't say was if anybody was going to be dumped off it was going to be you, you selfish Elvis-loving Jim Crow son of a bitch. Fact was I didn't know how much more of Pepper I wanted to put up with. Kit was quiet in the backseat most of the time and Einstein was even quieter and seemed content or as content as Einstein could ever be just to sit and stare out the window and think about whatever was going on in that exceptional mind of his. Maybe he was solving equations or resolving the Cuban crisis or maybe he was building a bomb in his head to blow up the world and destroy everyone who had ever hurt him but Pepper got on everyone's nerves with his incessant gabbing and out-of-tune singing. People like Pepper insist on keeping themselves entertained by annoying the hell out of others. Back at the car Einstein pushed his luck and wanted one more favor from me before we got back on the road. He sed he had thrown up all over his shirt when he got beaten up and robbed and had been wearing the only other clean shirt he had for three days straight so he wondered if I could loan him a shirt. I sed I would rather give him a clean shirt than have him stink up my car any more than he already was and he laughed and seemed more relaxed than he had been since we picked him up.

W,

 When Jeff and I were flying back to Charleston for your funeral I was the most angry and grief-stricken I've ever been. Still am, as far as I can tell. Even worse than when Deb died. Deb and I had twenty good years and time to say goodbye. You and I had twice that and then some. And you snuck away without telling anyone where you were headed. Jeff and I barely spoke to each other the whole flight, we were both so distraught. Are you going to miss Jeff as much as he's going to miss you? He admires you so much – more than he does his old man, probably. He's been talking recently – even before this – about going to med school. He didn't say this specifically, but I know you must be the reason for that. He's already lost his mother; now you've taken his favorite uncle and best role model away from him. I don't like feeling this anger toward you – thinking about this new hole blown into Jeff's life and not knowing how he might choose to fill it.

Jeff took advantage of his window seat by hiding his gaze and his thoughts in the clouds. We often find ourselves staring silently out of car windshields or into television screens. I'm afraid he thinks I'm ignoring him, that I'm lost in some world of my own making, when the truth is I'm thoroughly absorbed in a world of Jeff's making. Silence is golden when you're a parent. After Deb put Jeff down for the night I would stand over his crib and watch him sleep, astonished by each bubbly breath he took. I was afraid to move for fear of waking him. As he aged I still took every opportunity to watch him sleep. Take my word for it Will, you never get tired of it. I sometimes think that is the only thing holding this collapsing world together – parents, otherwise greedy, capricious, downright mean, holding their babies and watching them sleep, amazed that the breaths don't suddenly stop and praying they never do. So if in my silence Jeff thinks I'm entranced, as if under some magical spell, he is entirely correct.

Your funeral was nice, if that word can be used to describe such a morbid affair. It would be wonderful if you were like Tom Sawyer and had been hanging out up in the balcony. Remember how we took turns one summer reading chapters of that book to each other? You were still young enough to have trouble with some of the words, but I was happy to help. I don't know if I have the strength to bear all these memories. The casket was kept closed, which was a great relief to me. Perhaps the mortician could have worked his magic on you but seeing your dead face would have been unbearable. I don't want to describe Mom to you. How much more tragedy can one person be expected to endure? I'm sure she would have been relieved to have been allowed to crawl inside the casket with you. And no, I'm not joking when I say that. Is anyone ever allowed to live out their final years in the manner they had imagined? Is anyone ever that lucky? Up until Deb died I would have bet money that I would die a ripe old man surrounded by you and Deb and Jeff and grandkids, with Mom and Pop safely in the ground after a long happy life together. Is that really too much to ask? Is it really that fucking far-fetched? Apparently so. But Mom really takes the cake, wouldn't you say?

And yet here I am, making my mad preparations for leaving her all alone in this big house full of the best of times and the worst of times. I didn't start making these plans until I went down into Pop's workshop. I had two return-flight tickets and absolutely no idea what I would do with myself back in Portland. Actually, that question is still in play but at least I've given myself a chance to blow off steam, perhaps even have some fun, if that's conceivable at this point, and at the very least buy myself some time before I have to confront the rest of my life head-on. I gave Jeff his ticket and told him to fly home without me, a decision which surprised me as much as it did him. Everyone works through grief in their own way and in their own time, or so we're told – my way is shaping up just a shade or two beyond acceptable, that's all. Was I wrong in sending Jeff home all alone? He certainly doesn't need my help anymore in maneuvering through his life. I'm grateful he chooses to spend so much of his time with me. He has his job and his band – I'm just concerned that I'm a bigger part of his grieving process than obviously he is of mine. I hoped he would fill in his own blanks regarding my reasoning, but when he responded with that half-hurt–half-defiant, half-sardonic–half-imploring "*Why?*" that only children can give to their parents, I had to come up with something. What was I supposed to say? "I don't want you with me because I'm going to do something so totally bizarre that you'll think I'm nuts –

which I probably am?" Why are there so many instances in our lives when simply telling the unvarnished truth seems to be insanity itself, the most absurd of all possible options? Are our mutual interests so far misaligned, our hearts and minds so far apart, our true selves so fundamentally at war with the needs of others – are we so alone in the world – that the honest truth paints a picture so gruesome we can't bear to look upon it? At any rate, I lied to my own son and told him I wanted to spend more time with his grandmother and that he needed to go home and take care of Der Dingle. Plausible enough, thank God, to earn his acquiescence – we had supplied Ding with enough kibble and fresh litter to last a week, but when I told Jeff I had no idea when I would be home (which was true) he couldn't very well refuse my request.

After dropping Jeff off at the airport I went to the car-rental counter and traded in my Toyota for a full-sized commercial van, with no additional seating, strictly for cargo and large enough to haul anything and everything. This didn't escape Mom's notice when I pulled into the driveway and I'm afraid my explanation for this anomaly wasn't nearly as clever as what I had come up with to get Jeff on the plane. "No reason," I said, "I've just always wanted to get behind the wheel of one of these big vans, and now's my chance." Poor Mom – with nothing else in the world making sense to her now, her son tooling around in an empty cargo van didn't seem worth questioning any further.

I drove my new toy to Home Depot and loaded it with plywood and one-by-fours. I told Mom I had decided to make something special in your honor knowing how disappointed she would be when it failed to materialize (sorry bro). Would it have killed me to build a nice bookshelf to give to her and to honor the best brother in the world? Of course not, but you need to realize that an obsessed mind is also a narrowly focused mind – just like that wooden wall map I've talked about, when I thought about nothing else for days. Speaking of which, I asked Mom where it was and in typical Mom fashion she got everything right but the facts. Yes, we still have it (she still refers to the household in the plural – she will never remove Pop or us from it), but no, it wasn't in one of our closets like she thought. I finally found it in the attic, warped and cracked and faded by the heat of thirty-plus years. I could touch up the cracks and repaint it, but there wasn't much I could do with the warping, the wood too thin to endure much planing. I placed it face-up on the passenger seat of the van, happy to have it back. Just as I used to look over at it from my pillow every night now I can glance over at it on the road, returning me to the safety and comfort of a child's bedroom – forty years peeled away as easily as cracked paint. Forty years – thinking about it requires walking a delicate mental tightrope, reconciling two extremes, like juggling with a bowling ball and a feather – half a lifetime yet at the same time a blink of an eyelid. How is that possible, Will? How can your life be over? How can I be so old?

So here's my plan. I can't take full credit for it; I really shouldn't take any credit. It was my dear departed friend Cantilever Larry who planted this seed in my head all those many years ago. And you need to understand one other thing, Will. I'm so angry and frustrated and disappointed with my fellow man – how is one supposed to express such deep disenchantment with the world? Violence only begets more violence because, though its perpetrators may feel justified, its victims never feel they are deserving of retribution. Participating in nonviolent protests seems futile because I no longer believe meaningful change is possible. There are certainly times when things – physical objects – are damaged beyond repair, but can societies be described in the same way? Is it justifiable to give up all hope? Did Dr. King produce real healing or merely apply a band-aid? Did he build something that will last forever or simply rearrange the furniture? Racism, like water, will seek its level; like electricity, it will follow the least resistant path. If blocked, it will detour; if exposed, it will slink into the shadows; if rooted out, it will grow elsewhere. And as it is with racism, so it is with greed, misogyny, and all other evils that plague mankind. So where does that leave me in dealing with my outrage? This is not a time for anger-management strategies. I'm not (debatably) a danger to myself or to others. What I am is disillusioned to the point of heartbreak. Wasn't this country supposed to be different? Wasn't America founded as the dream-child of the Enlightenment, the world's best hope for the future, or is that just a lie we and the rest of the world have been telling ourselves – a victim of our own grandiose delusional desires? Maybe it was never that at all, but just another cabal of old men, using not just brute force this time, but philosophy, to lock their power into place. Maybe Madison, Jefferson, and that whole colonial cotton club were well-intentioned, idealistic old fools who thought they knew how to make the world a better place, and like every other revolutionary before and after, they and their progeny, through their own hubris and ignorance, found themselves drowning so far out from shore that waving their arms and screaming for help was useless. So I'm profoundly disillusioned by the usual soul-corruption and power-hunger that all men demonstrate, but mostly by those sins that seem unique to American soil, but probably aren't – people who are proud of their ignorance, ignorant of their hatreds, hating everything and everybody they should love, loving everything and everybody they should be ashamed of, and being ashamed of absolutely nothing. . . . And that, dear William, is where I come in.

Public shaming has been commonplace throughout history, though of course, in our typical human perversity, we pilloried people for all the wrong reasons. And I don't seriously believe I have the ability to convince anyone of their shameful ways – we have sloughed off any predispositions we may have had to question ourselves and will stubbornly defend our motives and actions to the grisly death. So I'm well aware of the futility of my actions, but I don't see them as being completely empty gestures. Even a cry in the wilderness is good for something if it makes you feel better. But why not keep it all inside, save your breath, don't embarrass yourself, put your energy to better use? Because crying out feels better than keeping quiet. Because it's emotionally beneficial. Because if you don't cry out you will explode. I have realized this too late to save you, but perhaps not too late to save myself.

So I emptied all the wood from my van and got to work. I told Mom to stay out of the workshop until I had finished your memorial. If she saw what I was actually building I don't think all the explanatory sleight-of-hand in the world could neutralize what she was seeing with her own eyes. Even a mother's love for her son and a wife's grief for her husband couldn't convince her that I didn't belong in the loony bin. But I feel strangely sane, after so much feverish mourning. I have worked late into the night every night for two weeks – jigsawing, planing, sanding, nailing. Perhaps I've been preparing a memorial to you after all, Will – one you would undoubtedly, strenuously, disapprove of – but my heart is in the right place as I envision the humiliation I am about to unleash upon all those miscreants whose filthy souls are overflowing with all the hatred, stupidity, and fear that created this world you no longer wished to, or were allowed to, live in. Half the figures I've carved are innocuous enough – full-sized mannequins, standing erect with no faces – no eyes, noses or mouths; round heads with protruding ears, slender necks and wide torsos, handless arms and footless legs. But it is in the other figures I have created that the difficulty – and the humiliation – lay. I'm back in high school now, Will, with Cantilever Larry and our long hair and skinny bodies, full of energy, hope, and happiness, with my dreams like an old eight-track repeating endlessly in my head of me and my horn travelling from one big city to the next and strolling into a nightclub like I own the place with girls who remember me from the last time I was in town who can't wait to hear me play and I can't wait until after the gig when the real fun starts, but first I ascend the stage and everyone becomes silent and I count off a tune by snapping my fingers and then we're off and running and all the girls are staring up at me all smiles and love and astonishment. And when I wasn't playing live there would be the studio gigs where you meet one famous player after another until, of course, you become famous yourself – or if not famous exactly because trumpet players don't become famous anymore, at least respected, recognized, sought-after. And there was also the dream – not dwelt upon like the fame and fortune, but there nonetheless – of settling down with the perfect woman and starting a family at some vague point in the future when success started to become boring and the excesses of road life began to take their toll as they must always do – even the most licentious libertine, which I never even bothered to imagine myself being, dreams of connubial bliss eventually, right? Well, at least I've been able to live a part of my dreams, with Deb and Jeff. Deb wasn't the perfect woman, but she was perfect enough, and Jeff has always been the perfect son. So what if I skipped over all the exciting parts of my dreams and went straight to the denouement? Okay, so here I am just like back in high school with Larry, carving large penis-people, except now those penises are going to be shoved symbolically right up the asses of all those castrati I've also created. And therein lies the source of the humiliation I'm planning to inflict – a thousand-year-old source of shame and ridicule – the shame of the cowardly, the effete, the man-as-woman, now relegated solely to bad jokes and penitentiary showers and completely off-limits in politically sensitive society.

I know what you're thinking, Will, I can hear your voice telling me now, "But you're not in high school anymore – why haven't you outgrown this silliness?" But here's the thing – I have outgrown it, Will. The problem is, the people I'm reacting to have made no effort to outgrow their own infantile instincts, to confront their fears, to question their assumptions, to ameliorate their ignorance. In fact, far worse than that, they manipulate these weaknesses in others to garner votes and gain power. And how are we supposed to engage these people? They don't respond to reasoned argument for the same reason we don't respond to emotional appeals – because such things are only tools to hoodwink the gullible. And the usual placard protesters and picket marchers are no longer treated as the loyal opposition to be respected, at the very least, in regards to their safety and perhaps even listened to, but as enemies of the state to be rounded up, kicked around, cordoned off, and silenced. So what am I left with? To travel around and participate in protests that are now as infuriating and insulting as they are ineffectual? Why not have some fun? What is there left to do but laugh into the teeth of the wind?

The effigy was the traditional form my type of protest took, but no one thinks a human likeness hanging burning from a tree is funny anymore. And buggery is also quickly losing its comedic cachet, but maybe there are a few people left who won't be afraid to laugh at the joke and understand that its intended target is not a harmless homosexuality but a very dangerous idiocy that's loose in the world.

I have spent the last week, when not carving penile shapes, trying to formulate a plan of attack. To put it mildly, the problem is not a lack of appropriate targets. In every little town, along every possible route, are numerous people who deserve to have some symbol of shame erected in their yard and seared into their consciousness. The internet is serving my purpose remarkably well. How would someone have gone about something like this before this marvelous invention? They would have to drive into a town, buy a paper, scour it for local lawbreakers, scandals, political ne'er-do-wells. Easy enough, I suppose, but then what? How do you find out where these people live? How do you get there? Continually asking for addresses and directions and reading roadmaps or spending afternoons in register of deeds offices would certainly be enough to cool the ardor of even the most dedicated, or crazy, protest *artiste* such as myself. But not with WWW and GPS! It's more than a little frightening to discover how easy it is to get personal information online. For a small yearly subscription I have access to the public records for every individual in the U.S. If I know a person's name, employer, age, or almost any other identifier, I can find out where he lives, all within seconds. Then of course my GPS will take over and park me in his driveway. The problem I am faced with is deciding how to narrow down the contenders. Public buildings are out for several reasons. First, they are downtown, well-lit, festooned with security cameras and in many cases protected by guards. This is meant to be a clandestine operation, but not a suicide mission. Second, though bureaucratic organizations may be guilty of many shameful practices, I need my limited ammunition to have specific targets. This needs to be personal

– *mano-a-mano*. If I were to drive to DC and plant one of these things in front of the Pentagon, what exactly would it be saying? The assumption, if anyone even took notice, would be that I was protesting some allegedly shameful foreign-policy decision – but good God, man, take a number and get in line for that one. Now, these individual policy makers would be perfect, but again, they have so much blood on their hands, and they know it, that they have taken appropriate security measures to hide the targets on their backs. So, like any good grass-roots movement, I need to think small and locally. So small, in fact, that I am actually more of a grass-*root* movement – a one-man-against-the-world movement. I've considered targeting small-town mayors and town councilmen – big fish in small ponds – but then again, some of these good ol' boys are so corrupt, even if they understood my message they would be hard-pressed to figure out exactly what they were supposed to be so all-fired ashamed about. But ideally, it will be great to find some local hypocrite who, behind everyone's back, has done something so preposterously evil that all I will have to do is point at him, say "Shame on you!" and he will know exactly what I'm talking about. Come to think of it, if I had known what Pop was up to before the authorities did, then he would have been a perfect target for me. Which, unfortunately, makes me realize all over again how quixotic this whole enterprise is, for Pop would have ripped my little *in flagrante delicto* apart at the nails, cursed the bastard who put it in his yard, and gone about his business without giving it a second thought except to curse the bastard again whenever the subject came up. But my voice needs to be heard, we all need to rise up, we need a million protesters protesting in a million different ways because this lunacy takes a million little bites out of our hearts every day. And out of the million different ways to protest this is the one I have chosen.

To finish off a statue, I nail a sturdy square base to the bottom of its legs, and for the ones with erections I also nail a small piece about six inches wide to the tip of the penis (ouch!), to which, by means of a nail gun, I will attach the raging hard-on to the backside of the unfortunate figure standing innocently in front, thus creating a nice sodomitical verisimilitude. To finish off the effect, I attached the arms of the penis-people up and outward to allow them to clutch the arms of their victims and to hold on tight. I will have some paint supplies with me for some on-site customization. As I finish each statue I load it into the van. I think I'll have room for maybe a dozen sets of men – the "front" guys stack very nicely but it's the other gentlemen with their monstrous protrusions and outstretched arms that are taking up all the space and limiting how many I can take. I told Mom tonight that I would be leaving in the morning. I hoped she wouldn't bring up the bookcase or whatever it was I was supposed to make for you, but of course she would since she knew I had been up unspeakably late every night working on it. I sighed and apologized and said it didn't turn out the way I wanted and in my anger tonight I tore it apart. She cried terribly – not for the lost bookcase I'm sure but because I was leaving her alone in this house full of ghosts. I'm sorry, Will, but I can't stay here with her. We had such a wonderful childhood in this house it puts me at a loss to explain (to myself as much as to you) why I'm always so eager to leave it. I'm not sure what's more painful – memories of lost happiness or reminders of more recent sadness, but when you combine both the bittersweetness is unbearable. And though misery supposedly loves company, I'm not sure it's to Mom's advantage to have my miserable self underfoot – but that's just a rationalization, along with all the other rationalizations I have presented to her as reasons – the need to be with Jeff, with friends in Portland, to stay close to Uncle Jeff, to look for a job. Of course I should stay here with her, but the heart is ruthless and doesn't need reasons, and my heart has not been in Charleston for a long time, so instead of drying Mom's tears with a promise to stay near her I shook my head sadly, bit my lip, and said, "I'm sorry, Mom, but I have to go." She was still crying when I left her alone in her room, where she probably cried herself to sleep thinking of the husband and son she will never see again and the other son who wants nothing to do with her and meanwhile I return to Pop's workshop to make final preparations for a mad dash across America with a van full of butt-fucking penises. What a strange inexplicable wicked race of men we are, Will Kinninger.

> You'll be in trouble if Pop finds out.
> You can't be down here by yourself.
> These saws are sharp. This one can
> Cut your arm off. Run back up as
> Fast as you can. Hurry. Here he comes.

PEPPER WAS RUMMAGING through my glovebox and didn't even ask if he could but I didn't say anything guessing he'll either find what he's looking for or he won't. I checked on Kit in the rearview and he'd pulled a magazine from his bag and not being nosy I ast what are you reading? and he sed nothing much which made me think it was a girlie mag which was cool as long as he didn't think he could pull on his pecker in my car and get away with it. Pepper shut the glovebox with a slam and turned around to rap with Kit. He sed what you got there? but at the same time was reaching back and snatched the mag away rude as hell but I was curious too and was willing to take my eyes off the road long enough to get a good look at some beautiful creamy curves but was disappointed when I saw that it was a comic book. Pepper wasn't disappointed though excited even and rapped with Kit about Superman and Batman and Aquaman until I lost interest which didn't take long and focused again on the road but thinking aren't there some things you're supposed to outgrow? I had comics as a kid but come on man what I craved now was all the knowledge in the world and I mean all of it. I loved to read always did and would read whatever I got my hands on but it needed to teach me something and what can you learn from dam Superman? What I loved as a kid and still do were stories from the old west about Indian attacks and frontier justice of various sorts with no sheriff around the pioneers did what they had to do. We've got it made today and men like my greatgreatgreat uncle Jeff would look at us like spoiled children which of course we are, just look at those two salivating over the Caped Crusader.

Maybe this trip out west was no lark or impulse but has been boiling in my blood for a long time. I had never been this far west before which wasn't saying much since we were still in the east most people would say but I was looking forward to seeing the Mississippi though.

Crossed Old Man River at St. Louis and the riverfront was weirdly barren like it had been washed away or maybe they had cleared a lot of land for construction but if so whatever they planned on building was going to be big as hell. I must say the Mississippi was disappointing to say the dam least. Problem is when you're from Charleston you grow up with the Ashley and the Cooper not to mention the Edisto etc. not even fair to call them rivers more like gigantic lakes and almost like being on the dam ocean when you're out in the middle of one of them so it's hard to be impressed by a river that just looks like a river.

Stopped for gas and while Pepper was taking a piss something made me think about him and the glovebox a while back and I decided to take a look. I didn't know what was in there to begin with but if it looked like something was missing then Pepper was back to hitching if he didn't come clean but I sure as hell didn't expect to see what I did tucked back behind a roadmap was his stash of grass. Sneaky bastard didn't want it on him if we were pulled and searched which of course meant that the car would be searched and I would be arrested for possession since it was my dam car. I didn't wait for him to get back in before I laid into him he didn't deny it was his stash which he couldn't really anyway and sed he was sorry but didn't think I would mind and sed he wasn't trying to cause any trouble he just needed a place to stow his stash and didn't think about us getting pulled or anything why would we be pulled? he ast and I sed then why the hell did you stuff it behind the dam roadmap? and he sed he was just hiding it from the other cats in the car which meant he was hiding it from me since he knew he didn't have to worry about Kit and Einstein they wouldn't even know what it was if they saw it. He was so dam apologetic about everything I didn't have the heart to throw him and his pompadour back out on the road thumbing but I made dam sure he put the stash back in his bag and kept it there and wondered why he took it out in the first place which stuck in my craw and made me mad at myself for not sticking to my guns it was the perfect chance to be rid of that loudmouth goon once and for all.

But you can't stay mad for long when you're on the road and free and it's just you and the whole wide world and all of a sudden I found myself remembering how I started this trip as the only man on Earth and here I was now with Pepper Kit and Einstein and how strange it all was with that same wonderful weird sensation pulsing through my body that I used to get watching my brothers play on the swings except I knew that Mom and Pop were nearby if I needed them but here I was now I had chosen to bring these cats together and what queer cats they were and here I was cruising toward California not knowing what the hell was going to happen but knowing that it was all because of me somehow.

W,

I left yesterday on my journey west. Mom was all stoical and stiff-upper-lip, pretending everything was alright when, of course, nothing is alright. Nothing will ever be alright again, in her life or mine. She wanted to walk out with me to my van, fully loaded now with genitalia, so to prevent that I was forced to be even more rude and dismissive than usual, telling her that a walk outside wasn't necessary and practically slamming the front door in her face as I left. I swear, Will, I will make this up to her. I hit 176 out of town just like we'd both done a hundred times on our way to Columbia. I immediately encountered a problem, however, that in my haste to obtain this huge commercial van I had failed to consider. Any west-coast road trip worth its salt must be accompanied by the best possible music. This van, however, was not equipped with satellite radio, which I have started taking for granted. The realization that I was reduced to scanning the dial like some 70s kid who's had all his eight-tracks stolen filled my heart with horror – and I'm exaggerating only very slightly. If all I had to accompany me for 3,000 miles were AM static and FM bombast (musical and otherwise) then I honestly believe I would abort this whole mission, pile the dicks into a dumpster, and catch the first flight back to Portland. Luckily, the van does have a CD player so I have resolved to keep going after an emergency visit to a CD store – that is, if CD stores still exist.

But in the meantime, yesterday morning I had no choice but to find something tolerable on the radio. Against my better judgment, I listened to a talk-radio station coming in surprisingly strong from Greenville. Within minutes I was screaming at the dashboard and had, quite serendipitously, discovered my first target. I recall during my days spinning jazz and blues late night at WUSC there were occasional mentions of the Fairness Doctrine and Reagan's desire to deregulate the airwaves like he was deregulating everything else. Since I worked at the radio station I should have had more than a peripheral interest in what was going on with this controversy, especially since I was known to say some pretty outrageous things on the air (mostly stuff I stole from Jerome), but my thinking on the issue, when I thought about it at all, was muddled – on the one hand, if Reagan was for it, it probably wasn't a good idea, but on the other, how could more freedom of speech and less bureaucratic interference be a bad thing? Well, I think we have the answer to that question. I could be cynical and say that Reagan and his cronies knew exactly what they were doing and have gotten precisely the results they wanted, but I prefer not to give them that much credit. The repeal of the Fairness Doctrine was yet another example in an inconceivably long line of examples – from the belief at the beginning of the twentieth century that we were making the world safe for democracy, to the notion at the beginning of the twenty-first that we would be hailed as liberators – of America's perennial Failure of Imagination. We failed to imagine that people would actually prefer not to listen to dissenting opinions. Imagine that, Will – people only listen to what they want to hear! Instead of listening to one station tell you everything that made you feel good, virtuous and righteous and then immediately changing to another station to listen to the other side rail against everything you hold dear, all in order to understand both sides of an issue and to be a better-informed citizen – who could have imagined that people would rather just keep the dial tuned to that initial bias-confirming station at all times? Perhaps I'm overstating my case, but isn't it odd that talk radio began to rise (or sink) to its current level of toxicity only after stations were allowed to tell anyone and everyone who disagreed with the content of their programming to go fuck themselves?

This rancid shock-jock goes by that most all-American of names – Jim Bob. A quick Google search soon disclosed his real name (James Robert it was not) and, as luck would have it, he is the owner of a nice ranch-style house in just the kind of community I was hoping for. I will be at the mercy of my luck in many respects during this adventure – luck in selecting targets, in locating them, and, most crucially, in what type of dwelling they inhabit. If they live in a high-rise or a gated development or in some other impossible-to-reach place, then all my sleuthing will be for naught. I need a nice happy home with a clean, manicured front yard with a minimal amount of exterior lighting and a minimal number of vigilant neighbors on which to perpetrate my protest-by-carpentry. I'm grateful to Jim Bob for providing all these things.

Several hours before leaving my hotel (which is first-rate, the best Greenville has to offer), while it was still daylight, I took a moment to ensconce myself in the back of the van, with my body pressed tightly against and being poked and prodded in all manner of familiarity by the various wooden appendages packed into the cargo hold, and with a small brush and a quart-can of black paint I carefully inscribed onto the round featureless face and torso of the mannequin positioned nearest the back doors the words THE SHIT YOU SPEW COMES BACK ON YOU. By the time I was ready to leave for my appointed rendezvous, well after midnight, the painted message would be dry.

And so with full faith in my good luck and GPS, I pulled out onto the strange highway and followed the sexy voice of Siri to my destination. With my heart pounding but with no intention of turning back I arrived in front of Jim Bob's house as per

Siri's instructions and pulled over next to the curb. I turned off my headlights but kept the engine running. After a quick visual reconnaissance of all the neighboring yards, I took a deep breath, hopped down from the cab and pushed open the back doors of the van – I was shocked by the loud sliding within the doors' frame, no louder than before but jarringly intense now as it rudely threatened to awake the sleeping neighborhood. Wearing gloves specially purchased for the occasion (for no covert mission is complete without gloves), I grabbed the front mannequin containing the inscription and placed it firmly on the ground only a foot or so off the curb and right in front of the van. I then clutched one of the back mannequins, whose engorged penis and long arms had gotten entangled with some of the others, causing me to panic briefly and make more noise than I was happy with as the wooden pieces clashed against each other. After several seconds of infuriating blind pushing and pulling, I was finally free of obstacles and took the second part of the effigy and a nail gun and made short quick work of attaching the two pieces, arms to shoulders and penis to imaginary ass. I threw the nail gun into the van, slid the doors shut, and snapped a quick photo with my phone, risking discovery by the brief blinding flash. I hopped into the van, engine idling, and away I sped. In all, the entire operation, even with all the tangled anatomies, took not much longer than one minute. I headed back to the hotel feeling cocky and proud and, for the first time in weeks, with no images crowding my head of you running around as a kid, of Pop in his orange jumpsuit and then dead at that grim police-protected funeral, of Deb's beautiful naked body and her lifeless ashen body being covered with my tears, of Mom and all her tears (I can't picture Mom anymore unless she's crying, like trying to picture the beach without an ocean), of Jeff at so many points in his life – a favorite image for every year, but always pushed aside by images of him crying as well – his tears at his mom's funeral the most gut-wrenching thing I will ever have to experience, period. But at least, in the van, mission accomplished, headed back to the hotel, for several beautiful minutes, all was joy and celebration in my heart.

So, I am pleased to report that my first foray into protest lawn artistry was successful, albeit with one infuriating qualification, which I experienced this morning. I was up bright and early to check online for the start time of Jim Bob's radio show, though I was running on maybe two hours of sleep. I streamed the station live as I waited for my room-service breakfast platter and sipped coffee on the balcony. (As an aside, Will, this morning tableau is close enough in reality to match the dream-life I imagined for myself as a traveling trumpeter stud – all that's missing is the lady from the night before. She would have been still sleeping or perhaps in the shower as I lounged triumphantly on the balcony of a five-star hotel. So maybe it's not too late for dreams – with heroic musical virtuosity replaced by adventures in derring-do.) When Jim Bob's show came on my expectations were immediately confirmed – he couldn't wait to talk about the monstrosity he discovered in his yard this morning. He had removed it promptly of course, as I knew he would. In this sense my display is more performance art than installation – it's not designed for permanence. But now here was the infuriating part of my morning. I had only wanted to listen in for an on-air, angry acknowledgement of my accomplishment – I hadn't planned on doing this, but it was clear now I was going to have to give this guy a call.

Jim Bob's producer was skeptical that I was who I said I was, but during commercial I gave enough detail about the scene, including Jim Bob's address and the wording of the painted slogan (which he had conveniently omitted from his description to his audience), to convince Jim Bob that he was in fact speaking to the perpetrator of this ghastly act. Back on the air, after a brief summary of what had transpired during the commercial break, Jim Bob said, "Would you like to tell us your name, sir?"

"No, of course not."

"I can't say that I blame you. So let me just ask you this. Why would you want to do something like this?"

"As a form of protest – which is why I'm calling you. You got it all wrong."

"What are you protesting against?"

"You – and everything you stand for. Listening to your show makes me physically ill."

"Then change the station. That's what most normal people would do."

"So it's my problem to deal with – that's what you're saying? If I don't like what you're saying then it's my job to change the station – you have no ethical responsibility for what comes out of your mouth?"

"It's called freedom of speech, Jack. I have every right to express my opinions. It's my show. And boy, you're certainly one to talk to me about ethical responsibility, buddy. You trespassed on my property. You erected a public nuisance. What if some kids on a school bus had seen that? What is your ethical responsibility? You should be arrested for what you did."

"I take responsibility for my actions. What responsibility do you take?"

"Then go turn yourself in to the police if you take responsibility."

"You were totally wrong about everything you said. You said crazy kids did it. No, I did it. There were no kids. It wasn't done as a silly prank. It was done as a protest. And then you go off on this wild tangent about pornography, about how this was related to kids being addicted to pornography. You were wrong about every single thing and I'm calling you on it."

"I think kids *are* addicted to porn."

"That's not what I'm talking about! You said kids did it. There were no kids. So you were wrong."

"I think that was a fair assumption to make. It didn't occur to me that some maniac was driving around Greenville County putting these things up."

"But you were wrong. And you just assumed you were right. Why did you make that assumption? You had no idea who did it, yet you told everyone that some crazy high school kids did it as if you actually saw them do it."

"Look, Jack, if you want me to apologize because I didn't realize some jerk with a chip on his shoulder was going around putting pornography in people's yards then I'll be glad to. I'm sorry I wasn't a psychic. I apologize for not realizing a lone nutjob was responsible for this. I apologize for not personally witnessing you trespassing on my property. And you're lucky I didn't personally witness it, too. I'm a gun owner and I know how to protect my family."

"Let me just ask you one question. Let me ask you one question and then I'll hang up and then you can go on with your show and continue telling all your lies. There was only one true statement you could have made this morning about what I did, or about who did it. There was only one possible statement you could have made that would have been true – only one. The only thing you had any right to say about who did this to your yard was this – 'I don't know who did it or why.' That's it. That's all you could justifiably say about it. So my question to you, Mr. Jim Bob, is this: Why didn't you say, 'I don't know who did it or why'? Would it have been so hard to say that? Would it have hurt your ratings that badly? Would it have damaged your manhood that greatly –"

"I thought you said you only had one question – "

"Why did you feel the need to speculate about something you had absolutely no information about? And it wasn't just speculation on your part – even wild speculation admits the possibility of error – but you gave everybody the impression that you were 100 percent completely right about everything that happened, when we know now that you were actually 100 percent completely wrong about the whole thing. Why did you do that? How does that make you feel?"

"Okay, sir, obviously you are a mentally disturbed man, that goes without saying – anyone who would go around doing what you're doing – but nevertheless I want to thank you for calling in and giving everyone a chance to hear from you. Let's go on to our next call."

Well, that was entirely unsatisfactory, but it usually is when you try to get someone to admit they're an idiot. I fumed silently in my room for longer than I care to admit, decided against trying to drive anywhere this morning, went down to the front desk and paid for one more night, slipped the Do Not Disturb sign onto the door and took a nice long nap. When I woke up I felt better about things and was ready for more adventure. But first, I needed to solve my music dilemma – after Jim Bob I could not possibly listen to one more minute of talk radio and forget about finding any jazz unless you're within three miles of a college campus – preferably a HBCU. Knowing that a local search for CDs would be useless, I signed on to Amazon, went on a berserk hard-bop shopping spree, and paid exorbitantly for next-day shipping. Not trusting that I would have the shipment by check-out tomorrow, I returned to the lobby for the second time this morning and paid for yet one more day of luxury. After which, I ordered a delicious room-service lunch and wrote you this nice long email as I dined.

So, I'll admit to being scared as I pulled up in front of Jim Bob's house, but not as scared as you were that Halloween night:

> Come on! It'll be fun! It's not real!
> Just hold my hand. Stay behind me.
> We'll be out soon. Stop crying you baby.
> I'm never doing this with you again.
> Oh, you're laughing now that we're out.

OH MY DEAR CONSTANCE! What have I done? How much weight of this horrific tragedy must be borne upon my shoulders for the rest of my life? Had I controlled my temper, had I been reasonable in my estimation of Wilbur, had he and I merely shaken hands and departed that night as friends, would all this horror have been avoided? I know I am innocent of what they accused me of, but why, dear Constance, do I still feel the weight of guilt so heavily upon me?

The shooting began at daybreak. We heard the rifle shots clearly from our camp. We were anxious all night with concern about what would transpire when the Captain and his men refused to allow W.'s group to advance on the trail beyond the location of the cutoff. We knew there existed the possibility of violence, but when it came to pass, the thunder of rifle fire was still shocking to us. My heart sank. Tears filled my eyes. I stood as still as death, unbelieving. Why was there so much gunfire? When was it going to cease? The men in our camp armed themselves with their rifles, in case the violence in the distance, by whatever means imaginable, came into our camp. We dared not move forward until all the shooting had stopped.

When we arrived at W.'s camp, their wagons were still encircling their livestock, which was frantic and prepared to stampede. I saw men scattered on the ground, their bodies distorted into various poses of death. Some had rifles beside them; others did not. We heard the wailing of women and the weeping of children. O Constance! I will pay any price and do whatever is asked if it would mean that you never have cause to hear such grief-filled cries. The cries were coming from within wagons that the Captain had brought to the scene for custodianship of the men he had expected to take prisoner. Or had he expected to take prisoner any of the men at all? Why were there unarmed men among the dead? These were my thoughts as I walked among the carnage. I knew what the Captain would say, even before I approached him. Wilbur's men had initiated the gunfight, he would say. Perhaps they had. I know firsthand how bloodthirsty and irrational these grief-stricken men could be. But I know as well how bloodthirsty and irrational men are with bigoted, hate-filled hearts. I am not ashamed to say that tears were streaming down my face as I looked upon each corpse. Some of them had bullet holes through their foreheads – victims, perhaps, of expert marksmanship among the Captain's soldiers, or victims, perhaps, of a cold-blooded massacre. I recognized many of these men. In life, I had considered them, at first, as curiosities, then as implacable enemies. But in death I saw them as they truly were – innocent victims of an evil savagery; however, a savagery begun neither by the Captain, nor on the trail, but which began as soon as Wilbur made his vision known to other men who were unwilling to tolerate whatever meaning he assigned to it. And I, shamefully, am as guilty as any other. Men do not know their own hearts. If each man were to know his own heart, then he too would be tempted, as was perhaps Wilbur, to take up a knife and excise it from his chest.

I noticed there were no soldiers in the camp. I saw the

Captain surveying the scene, but none of his men. I looked off to my right and saw, probably a mile distant, the heads of men and the movement of shovel blades. All appeared to be digging in unison and, from that distance, all appeared to be waist-deep in the same large hole. I ran up to the Captain, enraged. "Are you not giving these men a proper burial?" I shouted.

"That's none of your concern," he said, and then added, "What would you consider to be a proper burial for a bunch of G— d— pagans?" He looked past my shoulder and shouted to another member of our party, "I don't suppose you men would pitch in and help us gather all these bodies?"

"May you rot in Hell for what you've done today," I snarled at him.

"By G—!" he shouted back to me, "this is the luckiest G— d— day of your life! These men meant to see you dead!" As he turned and marched away from me, I heard him mutter, "What a thankless G— d— task this is!" Throughout all of this, the screaming of the women and children was ceaseless. If I looked upon Hell, how would it appear any differently from what I have witnessed today?

I didn't recognize Aaron among the corpses. I walked over to the wagons containing the mourning survivors. As I approached, one of the women shouted at me, "Go to Hell!" More than one spat at me. I did not dare approach close enough to be grasped by any of them. "Was Aaron with you this morning?" I said loudly.

"Go to Hell!" was the only response I received. I found Jason, who, at the Captain's request, was dragging a body by its feet in the direction of a pile of similar bodies. I was becoming sick to the point of nausea. "Was Aaron killed?" I asked.

"I don't see him."

I immediately realized what I must do. The moral confusion I had suffered through the night before vanished.

"Goodbye, Jason," I said. "I will be forever in your debt. Perhaps we'll see each other again further on up."

"What are you doing?"

"What I must."

"I don't understand. Why don't you stop this foolishness and help me with these bodies?"

"I'm taking the cutoff."

J. halted his chore and stared at me. I believe he understood now, or, at least, he began to. "None of this is your fault, Jeff. It was inevitable. Please reconsider. There's no need for you to do this."

I smiled and said only, "I hope to see you again in Oregon."

I started my team forward, as well as two horses and one of our cattle to which I was entitled. Shortly, I came upon some wagon tracks which indicated the direction of the cutoff. Aaron would be up ahead, not far distant. Had he heard the rifle reports? He surely must have. Whatever lamentation I felt compelled to express is nothing when compared to the sorrow that A. and his remaining followers were suffering. It occurred to me in what immediate danger I had placed myself by being alone. I walked all morning, however, without sighting them. I expected A.'s party to halt their march for a midday break; however, it was quite possible that they would choose to remain in motion until they believed they were no longer within range of the Captain's wrath, which, indeed, must have been their decision, as I continued forward until evening with no sign of them. I was marching along in fresh tracks, however, so I knew they were near. They encamped at sundown, and it was then that I saw their wagons.

O, dear Constance! You are the light of my soul. It is the dream of us reunited in Oregon that keeps me moving forward, though I have taken a large risk today for which you may wish to chastise me mightily. I pray that you may understand, and affirm, my decision. As I write this, all is well. I am safely within A.'s camp. There are seven families with A. I am grateful that this number of men had the courage and wisdom to follow him. The families, and Aaron, appear to be indifferent to my presence, consumed as they are with their bereavement. Perhaps they understand why I am now with them; perhaps not. It is important only that I understand why, or that I try to understand, for the only explanation I understand tonight is that I am now here because here is where I now should be.

As I approached the rear of their party, before I was seen or recognized by any one of them, I heard myself praying aloud, for I knew not how they would react upon seeing me. They may have welcomed me with a bullet into my brain. My heart raced and I continued to pray. I had forgiven them, but prayed that they could forgive me, for Thine is the kingdom, the power, and the glory, for ever and ever. Amen.

W,

I write to you from Johnson City, Tennessee, a last bastion of civilization before entering the hollers of Kentucky. I'm staying at the Carnegie Hotel, the finest lodging J. City has to offer. I've determined that if I'm going out in a blaze of glory it might as well be in style. The other night in Greenville was a closer call than I had expected. Jim Bob said on his show that he looked outside at 3:00 a.m. and saw some strange shadows across his lawn – which wasn't long after I had split the scene. I hadn't taken into account how early these drive-time guys start their days. I have no doubt he would have put some buckshot in my ass if I had given him the opportunity – he would have gotten a lot of mileage out of that on his show. So I've put myself on an unlimited *per diem* so I can continue to *carpe diem*. And if I'm still alive when all my savings runs out, then maybe my poverty will inspire me to look for a job. Either way, the filet mignon is excellent.

I had an interesting conversation at an interesting place this morning. Or perhaps I should call it a series of conversations. It occurred at a highway intersection, at a red light. In most small towns in America you're likely to find a church on every corner. Nowadays, in any city of any size, you're likely to find a panhandler. I don't normally strike up conversations with homeless people, but this fellow was putting on quite a show on the corner, drawing as much attention to himself as possible. He was wearing a homemade sandwich board which freed up his hands for unencumbered showmanship. It was made from a large cardboard box, broken down and repurposed for his needs. Featured on both front and back was a large, concise, hand-written message: Homeless. Please Help. God Bless You! He waved at every car, smiled, danced, blew kisses at people, and seemed to keep up a running conversation with the continuous traffic. I rolled down my window, gave him a five and – not to be rude, I promise, but to show solidarity with his plight – I called out to him, "Hey – when was your last job?" He took my question the wrong way (but he kept my money) and yelled, "I got a job!"

I said, "Well, that's good. I'm sorry you have to supplement your income like this."

He said, "You can supplement my ass is what you can do! I make good money out here."

I gave him another five just because I'm such a great guy. That changed his mood considerably. Now he was grinning from ear to ear. "What's your regular job?"

"This is my regular job! Like I said, I make good money out here – better than any other job I could get." The light had changed and the cars in front of me were moving. I couldn't let this conversation end on that peculiar note so I decided to circle around the block and come back around. It's not like I had anywhere I had to be. Luckily, the light was red again and I called the gentleman back over to my van. I gave him another five. "Thank you, sir!" he said, and started to dance away to another driver signaling to him. I yelled, "Wait! Don't you remember me? I was just here!"

"I'm sorry, sir. I see a lot of vehicles on a daily basis."

"You said this is your regular job?"

"Yes sir. Best job I ever had."

"But you're a beggar! You beg for money – that's not a job!"

"I don't beg for anything! I work hard for this money! I'm out here all day, every day. I don't take time off. I'm on my feet all day, in the rain, in the snow, in the hot sun, freezing my ass off. This job ain't easy! Beggar! You see me begging for anything? You see me down on my knees? You want to see some beggars? Look at TV. Go inside a store. Everybody's just begging you to spend all your money just to make somebody else rich. All those ads you see everywhere, all these billboards around here – there's your beggars right there! Don't call me no beggar!"

"But it's not a job!" I must have caught the light at the end of its cycle. It had already turned green. I said, "Hang on – don't go anywhere." Back around the block I go. The light was red again – this guy knew what he was doing. He had a captive audience for minutes at a time. "I'm back!" I yelled over to him. I had run out of fives. "Do you have change for a twenty?" Of course he did. The guy was loaded. He gave me four fives – three of which may have been mine to begin with. I gave him one of the fives back. "You can't call this a job," I said, trying to talk fast before the light changed again. "A job involves an exchange of services for pay. You're not performing any services."

"What are you talking about? I perform for these people all day. I smile and wave at the kids, do a little dancing, blow kisses at the ladies – I put smiles on people's faces. People like stopping at my red light, I guarantee you that!"

"What about that guy up there?" I pointed to a fellow panhandler – this guy's chief competition – up ahead on the next corner. "Is this his job too? He's just standing there holding a sign. That's all he's doing. He's not performing at all."

"People like to give money to people. It makes them feel good. Don't you feel good helping a poor man out? I bet I make more than he does – a lot more – but if he makes people feel good about themselves then why can't that be his job? Everybody's got to do something." I had no immediate response to this line of thinking. I gave him another five and said, "I've enjoyed talking with you. Good luck in your endeavors."

"Yes sir. You do the same." He moved on to another car. Who knows, Will, maybe panhandling is the next Klondike – men giving up their boring day jobs to seek their riches on the street corners of America by allowing all of us to pay for the privilege of feeling good about ourselves. At any rate, it's good to see the American entrepreneurial spirit still alive and well.

Before checking in to this marvelous hotel I drove around the outskirts of J.C. looking for a good greasy spoon for lunch. All these Mom and Pop places offer the same fare and are all generally acceptable, but my empty stomach soon made my decision for me. The diner I hungrily pulled into, however, must have been better than average based on the patronage. The place was packed for lunch. The hostess informed me, honey bear, that all the booths were full, sugar pie, but if I didn't mind, sweet thing, I could sit at the bar. The place was full of walking stereotypes. Big burly guys wearing baseball caps with curved bills making loud creaking noises on the floorboards as they walked around in their muddy boots. Waitresses that looked like the girls we had gone to high school with, their hair piled high just like their mamas. I'm sure all these folks were as individual, unique and diverse as little snowflakes once you got to know them, but I didn't know them, so to me they all looked like they had just stepped out of a bad Burt Reynolds movie. And another way they resembled snowflakes – there was not an African-American or Hispanic person to be seen. That's the biggest difference I've noticed here in the mountains, compared to what we're used to. And of course they love those long vowels up here. I hopped up on a bar stool and began looking over a menu that had enough fried variety to keep me coming back every day for a month without ordering anything twice. The only stool available was at the end of the bar. The man seated to my right was laughing into his fries from something said by the chap to his right. "Billy Ray's been telling me that he's gettin' a tattoo on his arm," said the man on my immediate right. "And I keep tellin' him, if you get a damn tattoo you better be ready to suffer for your art,'cause that damn thing's comin' off, one way or another. I'll tie you down in a damn chair and go get my acetylene torch!" Both men were laughing. "It ain't just the one tattoo I object to. If he would stop with the one then okay, but they never can stop with just one. It's like that ink seeps into their brains and they don't know when to damn stop. It's like they become addicted or something. Maybe there's something in the ink, I don't know."

"I wouldn't put it past 'em to put something in the ink. Some chemical or something. Makes 'em keep coming back for more." This came from the fellow two stools over. He jerked his arms around, stuck out his tongue, tilted his head and started making zombie sounds.

"I mean, they cover up their whole damn arm! Just tattoos on top of tattoos I reckon. You can't even see any *skin*! And you can't make heads or tails out of any of it. Just a bunch of shapes and squiggly lines and just – ink! Like the guy spilled ink all over his damn arm and instead of washing it off just said, well, might as well make that a tattoo too!"

"And what about these niggs gettin' tattoos? Ain't that the most ridiculous thing you ever seen? You can't even see 'em! I work with a nigg – worked with him for a year then one day the light hits his arm a certain way. I said, man, when did you get that tattoo? He said, I've had it. I said, how long? He said, for a long time, man. Never would have knowed he had one if the light hadn't been comin' through the window the way it was. You'd think they would at least use a different color ink or something. Like white. Why wouldn't they at least use white ink? Beats all I've ever seen. Nigg's had a tattoo for over a year and nobody's ever been able to see it."

"All I know is, if Billy Ray walks through the front door with a damn tattoo then I'm gonna have to go tell the neighbors not to pay no mind to all the screamin' comin' from inside the trailer."

Now Will, have you seen Jeff's arms recently? When he showed me his first tattoo and asked me if I liked it, I told him that when you get to be my age you suddenly have permanent features sprouting up all over your body that are a helluva lot more unsightly than any tattoo he could get. My new-found friend made a legitimate point: the initial gateway tattoo does tend to lead inexorably to more elaborate ones, but many of Jeff's tattoos are in honor of his mother, really beautiful things, so I love each and every one of them. As long as this guy was just joking I could laugh along with him and his faithful sidekick Tonto, but I needed to get inside his head a little more. So when Tonto shut up about the "nigg" he worked with I redirected the conversation. "Can you really do that? Get rid of a tattoo? I'm sorry, I couldn't help but overhear you guys. It sounds like your boy is just threatening to get one, but my son showed me his arm the other day – he just came home from college. Man! Get this – he had some kind of Muslim symbol high up on his arm, above his bicep. A 'Muslim peace symbol' he called it! A Muslim peace symbol! Is there even such a thing as that?"

"Jeez," said the guy next to me, Billy Ray's daddy.

"You know what they should do with all the Muslims?" Tonto said. He had to speak louder than normal so I could hear him past his buddy, but he didn't seem to mind if the whole restaurant heard him. "Round 'em all up. Put 'em all inside a football stadium where a couple of B-52s happen to be flyin' overhead. Target practice!"

"That's not a bad idea there, but getting back to what I was talking about – are you serious about burning your kid's tattoo off? How would I go about doing that so everybody doesn't think my kid is a goddam Muslim?"

"You could do it all kinds of ways, man. I was jokin' about the acetylene torch, but you can still burn that fucker off. Just heat up the bottom of a fryin' pan. Of course, he ain't gonna just *let* you do it," he chuckled. "Do you have the guts to do something like that?"

"I don't know. Would you?"

"What kind of daddy would I be if I didn't? You can't be a father and a pussy at the same time." He and Tonto cracked up.

"Not unless you're Bruce Jenner!" Tonto yelled.

"A frying pan, huh? I guess I could do that after he fell asleep. But then I might end up getting burned with it too after he jumps up screaming. That's gonna be tricky."

"Do you let your boy drink?"

"Well, he's in college, so. . ."

"Get him good and drunk till he passes out. That's the way I would do it. I'm serious. He might not even feel it. Me and Billy Ray – I swear, that boy can almost outdrink his daddy already and he ain't even twenty yet. And if he gets that tattoo – well, it won't be the first time I've done something to him after he's done passed out." He looked over at Tonto, laughing. "Did I ever tell you what I did to him that one time? What I did to his dick that time?"

"Yeah! But tell it again – tell *him*! This is funnier than hell."

"Well, we was both drunk as a skunk, but Billy Ray had done passed out and I was gettin' on pretty close to that point myself, I reckon, but I decided I still wanted to have some more fun. So I stumbled around outside just looking for something to get into. It was dark and I was trippin' over everything and I had all these old paint cans up under the trailer where there ain't no underpinnin' and that's when I got the idea into my crazy drunk skull. Most of the paint was black from an old car I was fixin' up so I took one of the cans inside. I pulled Billy Ray's pants down and his underwear and his little ol' pecker was just layin' out there no bigger than a damn popcorn shrimp. I didn't have no paintbrush or anything and I was too damn drunk to go look for one so I just took off my damn shirt and dipped it down in the paint can. I grabbed Billy Ray's dick and there wasn't all that much to hold on to – "

"He takes after his daddy!" Tonto interjected.

"Yeah, well, your mama wasn't complaining about that last night when she had it in her mouth, so you just shut the fuck up and let me finish my story. So anyway, I had my shirt in one hand with black paint drippin' everywhere and I'm trying to *stre-e-etch* Billy Ray's wiener as far out as I can with my other hand and my hand-eye coordination ain't exactly what it should be in this situation since I can barely see straight. But I'm able somehow to stretch Billy Ray's ding dong out to a somewhat respectable length and somehow manage to do a half-decent paint job on the whole thing. Well, I didn't want him to wake up and see his dick like that – I wanted it to be more of a *surprise*. And I couldn't put his pants back on yet because the paint wasn't dry, so then I did something really stupid – yeah, even stupider than paintin' his peter. I pulled out my lighter, thinking that would make it dry faster."

"Real smart," Tonto said. He had been laughing hysterically throughout the whole story and showed no signs of letting up.

"I was drunk, okay? People do stupid things when they're drunk. So I took my lighter and held it down really close to Billy Ray's wing dinger. Man – do you realize how stupid that was? Paint is damn *flammable*! But I was as careful as a shit-faced drunk can be and I made sure the fire didn't actually touch Billy Ray's junk. But it did touch his short and curlies. And I must have dripped some paint into his dick hair 'cause that shit just went up! Damn, talk about your burning bush! So I jump up and just start stomping! Stomping my boot all over Billy Ray down there." To demonstrate he stomped down several times on the air underneath his bar stool, wearing maybe the same boots he had used to extinguish his son's pubic fire. "My boots were all wet and muddy from outside so they put out the fire, but man, Billy Ray was a mess. He groaned and grimaced and reached down to play around with his pecker, but he didn't wake up. Man – his pubes were gone! Incinerated! It looked like someone had done a clear-burn in the woods! Smoke was still rising up and shit, and you could smell where everything had burned – paint, hair, skin. Man, it was disgusting. But besides the fact that he was going to have to grow a new bush there didn't seem to be no permanent damage, so all things considered, I was feeling pretty relieved and lucky that I didn't catch Billy Ray's prick on fire. So I slid his underwear and pants back on and then fell asleep myself.

"I don't know how long I was asleep, but the next thing I know I wake up and hear Billy Ray screamin' in the bathroom. It didn't take me too long to figure out maybe why he's screamin'. I run into the bathroom and Billy Ray screams at me, 'You tried to burn my dick off! You tried to burn my dick off!' I can't help but start laughing at him, he's so freaked out. I try to calm him down and say, 'Nobody tried to burn your dick off. Everything's okay.' 'Then why's it all black!' he screams. 'Why's my dick all black?' I'm cracking up because Billy Ray's being so hysterical and I keep saying, 'Just calm down. Calm down,' trying not to laugh but not doin' such a good job at it. Then he starts in with 'I ain't got no hair! You burned all my hair off!' I say, 'It was just an accident, Billy Ray. Everything's okay. I accidentally caught your dick hair on fire. I'm sorry.' And then he says, 'You burned my dick! Why did you burn my dick?' I said, 'I didn't burn it. It's just paint. That's just black paint.' For some reason, this made Billy Ray even madder than he was when he thought I had actually tried to burn his damn dick off. 'You painted my dick?' he screamed at me. 'Why the fuck would you do that?' 'Calm down,' I said, 'it was just a joke. You're fine. Can't you take a little joke?' He slammed the bathroom door and yelled, 'Leave me alone!' I yelled back, 'It was just a damn joke! Get over it!'

"I was hopin' that was the end of it, but then he starts screamin' again, louder than ever this time. 'I can't pee!' he's screamin'. 'I can't fuckin' pee!' I run into the bathroom and Billy Ray has this scared panicked look all over his face. He ain't mad at me anymore, but he's scared to death. 'I can't pee!' is all he can say, over and over. 'What do you mean you can't pee?' I say. 'I can't fuckin' pee! It won't come out!' So I get down on my knees and look at the kid's pecker and sure enough, the paint's all dried up over his damn pee hole. So I pull out my knife. Billy Ray's cryin' like a goddam baby and he sees my knife and he completely loses his shit. He just starts screamin' like a goddam little girl. 'Calm down!' I yell at him. 'What are you gonna do?' he yells back. 'If you don't shut up I'm gonna cut your goddam dick off!' which probably wasn't the best thing to say at that particular point in time but I was pissed off and still pretty shit-faced and didn't appreciate Billy Ray acting like such a damn pussy, especially when I was trying to help him. So I get back down on the bathroom floor and bring the tip of my knife up to Billy Ray's pee hole and he just starts shakin' – shakin' all over like he's freezin' to death, he's so scared. I'm tryin' to hold on to his peter and it's movin' around and vibratin' and twistin' and slitherin' like a damn fire hose that somebody let go of. I'm like, man, Billy Ray, if you don't keep that thing still this ain't gonna be pretty. But he's still shakin' and quiverin' like he's bein' damn electrocuted, so I ain't got no choice but to squeeze his damn pecker like I'm tryin' to choke it to death just to keep it still and I bring the tip of my knife up to the tip of his dick, and I ain't got my glasses on so it kind of becomes guesswork at this point. Well, I forgot that Billy Ray's been tryin' to pee this whole damn time, so as soon as the tip of my knife made a little headway through that big glop of paint blockin' up his pee hole – well, that was the worst part of the whole night as far as I was concerned. I'm right up close to Billy Ray's pecker because I ain't got my glasses on and then here comes freakin' Niagara Falls right into my fuckin' face. Damn! I ain't never gonna forget that but I wish I could. Billy Ray's been drinkin' half the night and then passed out the other half so he wakes up and you know he has to piss a damn river. I manage not to drown and point his pecker down in the right direction toward the commode and say, 'Here! Hold your own damn dick from now on,' and stand up and hold my breath because I can smell all the damn piss runnin' down my face and go into the kitchen and wash my face for what seemed like a damn hour. After I dried my face I checked on Billy Ray and that bastard's already sound asleep in his bed like nothing even happened and meanwhile I'm gonna smell like piss for three days."

Tonto was still chuckling and asked, "So how long did it take Billy Ray to peel all the paint off his dick?"

"I don't know. I didn't ask. You ready to go?"

Okay. Well. At least I have a greater appreciation now for the fact that Pop never once got drunk and tried to paint either one of our penises. I also realized, listening to this story, how remarkably easy it is to drive around and – without even trying – find someone who has done something so shameful that they are entirely deserving of a ritualistic public humiliation.

The food in this diner may have been excellent but the service was lousy. I had ordered and received a Coke but throughout the preceding narration my waitress had been a no-show. These guys were leaving and I was starving, but I also wanted to know where this pubic pyromaniac lived, so I decided to relinquish my bar stool. "You leavin' before your food gets here?" Smoky the Bear asked.

"Yeah – I gotta run. I'm on a tight schedule today. I can't wait forever."

"Yeah. This place is always packed for lunch."

"You live around here?"

"Yeah, not far. What about you – I don't think I've ever seen you around. I know just about everybody around these parts."

"I travel around a lot on business."

"Yeah, me and Jimmy come here at least once a week. Good food if you don't mind the wait."

"Well, I appreciate the whole frying pan idea. I might have to try that. I don't want everybody to think my son's a terrorist."

"I don't blame you. I don't blame you one bit. That's what I would do if I was you."

I left without paying for my Coke – not because I'm a cheapskate but because I wanted to be in my van ready to follow Smoky when he drove off. I was going to have to rely on my luck once again. Smoky could be headed anywhere after lunch and I wasn't going to spend all day following him around, but if I got lucky he would be headed back to his house to further humiliate poor Billy Ray. Smoky and Tonto soon came out together but each quickly threw up a hand good-bye and headed to their respective pick-up trucks. I wasn't used to driving a big van on curvy mountain roads and Smoky was as accustomed to maneuvering his big truck around these bends as a mountain goat is to scaling rocks, but at least with my struggle to keep him in sight there was no danger of him recognizing me behind him or becoming suspicious that I was following. I followed him for what seemed like several miles. We didn't seem to be headed toward town but rather further out into the countryside, which I took to be a good sign. I rounded one of a hundred curves and could no longer see Smoky up ahead. I didn't worry about this, since I lost sight of him every time he took a curve, but after a half-mile more and still no sign of him I worried that I had lost him. I didn't dare speed up much on this low-shouldered, serpentine two-lane, but I risked a few mph's more and gripped the wheel a little tighter. Even with my acceleration Smoky was nowhere to be seen. I had been passing turn-offs regularly, so if he had taken one of those finding him again would be hopeless. I slowed down to a much safer speed and weighed my options, which were, realistically, only two – I could speed up and continue on, hoping to catch sight of Smoky, or pull over, punch in the address of my hotel and let Siri guide me back to civilization. I decided on the latter. As much as Smoky deserved to receive a token of my disrespect, I also knew that another qualified recipient was just a conversation away.

As I scouted for a good place to pull over I passed a trailer park on my right. I remembered Smoky mentioning a trailer so I thought it worth a shot to drive around for a look-see. I tell you, Will, sometimes my luck amazes me. As I drove through the labyrinthine trailer park, quickly losing my bearings for getting out, there was Smoky leaving his trailer and headed back out to his truck – just a quick trip home to retrieve something before continuing his exciting day. A minute more and I would have missed him. I passed by his truck as he was lifting a leg into the cab. I looked away long enough to prevent him from seeing my face and I noticed a Confederate flag being flown proudly by Smoky's neighbor. (Didn't this idiot know that eastern Tennessee was staunchly Union during the war? That flag would have gotten him hanged.) I looked out my side mirror and saw Smoky backing out. I most definitely didn't want him directly behind me as I looked for a way out of this place. I had no choice but to depend on my luck to lead me back to the highway. I was proceeding very slowly; Smoky was not. He was in a hurry and came up quickly behind me. There was no room for him to pass on what amounted to a mile-long one-lane driveway. I came to an intersection with a trailer on each corner. I stopped only to realize there was no stop sign. The crosstown street, as it were, had the stop signs. Smoky honked and I made a quick decision to turn left – if Smoky followed me it must mean I was headed in the right direction out; if not, I was rid of him. I was relieved when he drove on straight. I completed a square circuit around one block of trailers and found my way out soon enough. Back down the road, I pulled into the same diner as before to give lunch another try. The crowd had thinned; the waitress remembered me from thirty minutes ago – I wasn't a regular so I suppose I stuck out like a sore thumb. I apologized for skipping out earlier, lied about my busy schedule, told her to throw another Coke on my tab if she felt compelled to, and enjoyed a leisurely lunch, my next victim identified and located.

I FELL IN LOVE WITH HER as soon as I saw her but of course I did what's not to love? Woman was put on Earth as man's salvation but most times a man can't be saved. She was holding a small pink bag and waving one arm somewhat frantically as if we wouldn't see her otherwise and of course I insisted we stop, damsel in distress and all, but turns out she didn't need a rescue, just a ride, and I thought about how lucky I was to be at this spot at this moment because a few minutes more and she would be with somebody else most likely and I never would have met her. She sed she was Flop and I guess we all wondered why but Pepper snorted like he already knew why but just to show everyone that he was full of shit I ast where did that name come from? and she sed she had unruly hair as a kid and was called Floppy and it looked like that floppy hair had not been washed in at least a week maybe in some diner sink and it was indeed quite multi-directional. Her dress though still pretty must had been last washed long before her hair, hard to find time for the old tub-and-scrub when you're on the road I know for a fact. Her teeth were bright white or maybe her face was just dirty tough to tell at first in the morning light.

Pepper rolled out making dust behind us with that roadside rumble of gravel in our ears and before Flop had time to adjust herself between Kit and Einstein but not before she had kicked off her sandals and thrown her little pink bag down between her feet. The cats didn't bother introducing themselves trying to be tough guys I guess or maybe just shy but I turned around and quickly pointed out that I was Jeff, just to give myself a head start. I had shotgun but told Kit I needed to switch so I could stretch out more and get better shuteye but I was anything but sleepy after Flop came aboard. I'm not stopping again Pepper sed which I couldn't really blame him for and so we rode on. I turned again in the seat or remained turned which was more like it and out poured the charm full blast while Kit and Einstein dozed and Flop bounced around and looked out the windows like a child who had never been in a car before.

I ast if she was headed anywhere in particular and she sed nowhere special. It wasn't my place to ask why she was hitching her way west but you don't really need a reason the road itself is reason enough compared to what you're leaving behind. But if you want some reasons there are several, from large to small – freedom danger change hope fun id I – all those things you can't indulge back home. Solitude when you want it comradery when you need it. Roll down the window and breathe step on the gas and fly.

Hey hotshot change the station Pepper demanded, too busy turned around with Flop to notice the static creeping in and in full neglect of my primary shotgun duty, had to take my mind for a moment away from Flop's radiant face those sparkling teeth those big round eyes. Nothing much ever near 5^4 worth hearing regardless of where we are. Passing through Missouri now, wise not to expect much beyond honky-tonk crooners, Sagebrush Snotras and Hill-Billie Holidays, not much difference between the pedal steels and the signal squiggles between stations. Always tried to like country music around it so much in the South but for the life of me I can only describe it as music for people who hate the idea of music.

Stopped for Cokes and smokes. A gruff bluesman loosened the gas cap and ast if we wanted to fill it up as we all tumbled out of the car. Flop went in for the washroom key the sign behind the counter sed Restroom For Whites Only! You see, can't even be polite about it they have to scream out their disrespect in exclamation points. Made me notice again the bluesman pumping gas he had to hold it in till he got home or run up into the woods if he couldn't wait. On the lookout for Flop to return from around back of the garage and offered to buy her a Coke. The gentlemanly thing to do. She sed watch this and went inside the waiting area where three grease monkeys in gray overalls gave her the up-and-down and moved in a little closer. She gave the guy at the register a smile and sed something with one hand on her hip and the other twirling a flop of hair though her fingers but might as well have been picking his pockets and tickling his balls. Ol' Rube, in over his head, coughed up a dime and Flop got herself a free Coke. I went in after her to make a more legitimate purchase and noticed root beer hiding down in the bottom hole and pulled one out. I popped off the cap and sed what did she say to you? to Rube at the register. You her boyfriend? he wanted to know. I sed no but it hurt. Rube sed her boyfriend in the car wouldn't give her any change. That figures I sed. He's a stingy son of a bitch I sed nodding more or less toward Einstein Kit or Pepper whichever one Rube preferred. I switched places with Kit and finally got my chance to rub kneecaps with Flop as we bounced back up on the concrete.

I pulled out my notebook not really to write but to show off mostly. What's that? Flop ast. What's it look like? I sed, slick as oil. What's in it? she sed. Ever heard of Ginsberg? I ast. Who? she sed, answering my question well enough but not the way I wanted. I flipped through pages and scanned them up and down even blank ones to make Flop think I must be prolific as hell and eventually I picked out a morsel for her to chew on and recited proudly MEOW – that's the title,

I heard the coolest cats of my generation blow their brains out
    on 52nd Street,
In brownstone basements, speakeasied holes in the ground
    prohibited by no one.
Black cats still slaves to their horns, to their habits, to the
    booze-water white boys
Blowing papa's bread who exit the clubs but never the music,
    who tap tap tap their shoe-toes on the neon saxophone
    street till dawn.

That's interesting she sed, is that all of it? as if I was rapping haiku or sonnets or some such shit. Oh there's a lot more to this one I sed and closed my notebook and slid it back into my satchel because a little bit of poetry goes a long way even if it's good which mine isn't.

Flop fell asleep shortly afterwards but dammit her head leaned over against Einstein who was also asleep and would probably wake up screaming when he looked up and saw a girl. I made sure my knees at least were pushed up against Flop's calico and drifted off pretty deep myself looking out over endless meaningless prairie and listening to Pepper singing running bear loved little white dove with a love big as the sky.

Got a pleasant surprise indeed when half-asleep I felt Flop's head bouncing against my shoulder and thought just keep driving Pepper and Kit and Einstein whatever you're doing please keep doing it I want to keep my eyes closed like this forever. Of course Pepper ruins it by saying hey Flop and then hey Flop again because she was still asleep dam him and hey Flop a third time followed by where you from? She raised her head off my shoulder and sed all over I move around a lot and Pepper though he ast the dam question didn't really care about the answer just wanted to make sure I wasn't too happy I guess kept right on yodeling along with this song in 3/4 full of Spanish guitars singing just for a moment I stood there in silence shocked by the foul evil deed I had done and then sed you ever been to Memphis? but didn't wait for her answer and sed something about Elvis of course but it was hard to hear him over the wind and the radio and his godawful singing made it even worse. I waited for Flop to put her head back on my shoulder but it didn't happen so I pretended to wake up and stretched my arms and my neck was pretty dam stiff so I must have been out a while. I sed hi again like it was the first time I had laid eyes on her and she smiled and ast if I had a cig. You don't say no to a girl asking for a cigarette so I gallantly slipped a smoke between her lips and cupped my hand over my lighter because there was so much air blowing through the car. Flop smoking her cig made me think of Cynthia but then again I thought about Cynthia a lot so it didn't take much. I suppose Cynthia broke my heart if I have a heart to break but here I was falling for Flop so I must be over it whatever it was. When the semester ended I was happy to get away from Cynthia and happy to get away from Columbia so maybe that had something to do with hitting the road I don't know. Flop blew smoke in my face as a joke and I pretended to be mad and blew smoke into her face just like a couple of kids in junior high smoking for the first time hiding out behind the gym or the lunchroom or at somebody's house at a party. I didn't want Pepper asking where she was from or anything else for that matter and I didn't want to know those things either. I didn't want to know if she had a boyfriend or a husband or maybe even a kid though she seemed too young for that but you never know. I didn't want to know if she had a rich daddy or if she was dirt poor and I especially didn't want to know if she had been mistreated in any way because she didn't have to worry about any of that while I was with her and I didn't want to have to worry about it either. I no longer wanted to know where she was headed or how far she wanted me to take her because I didn't want to think about letting her go. I didn't want to know anything about her I just wanted her to stay right here in this backseat with me until we got to California and after that who knows. I didn't want to know any of these things about Flop but I already knew them because why else would she be thumbing all by herself unless she felt safer hitching rides from strangers than staying close to home?

Einstein was awake now and was showing more interest in Flop than I preferred telling her all about his scholarship and the experiment that won him the scholarship which I couldn't follow with a flashlight I was so in the dark. Einstein has a big brain all right but that big brain has gone straight to his head. I couldn't imagine Flop or any other girl taking a serious interest in him but even so if he didn't take it easy I was going to have to remind him that I was his meal ticket but I didn't have to be. Kit was riding shotgun minding his own business which I was happy to see and nodding along to the radio with Pepper singing will my heart be broken when the night meets the morning sun?

8

W,

Please help me. I'm at my lowest ebb. This joke I'm playing on the world and myself is no longer funny. I'm in a Kentucky Best Western, scrimping and saving, no longer in the mood for luxury. I've been such a fool. I miss Jeff terribly. My whole body hurts. One eye is swollen half-shut and both are bloodshot as hell. It hurts to breathe. I don't know how much my injuries are contributing to my despondency, but they're not helping. Mostly I just feel like an idiot. Just one week ago I was entertaining fantasies of my little escapade becoming some sort of worldwide sensation. Why not? It seemed plausible. It was definitely something no one else was doing, so there was the novelty of it all. And with the internet all it would take was one photo being posted by a passerby and in a technological blink of an eye my whole enterprise could have gone viral. I tried not to think too much of such things and to focus on more important rationales, but it was undeniably a driving force and, so I thought, a real possibility. That was one short week ago. Now I understand the pathetic reality of what I have been doing. My lunacy exposed on a syndicated talk show – not exactly the kind of notoriety I had in mind. And now this – to come to such an ignominious pass that I feel lucky to have escaped with my life – though whatever shred of dignity and pride I felt myself to possess has been summarily destroyed. A van crammed full of protesting penises, and I would have made more if I had had the room, because there was no shortage of deserving assholes on whom to bestow them and oh boy think of all the fun I'll have! And after only one week and two measly missions I'm left half-dead and thoroughly chastened. Well, I still have a few penises left but no plans to plant them anywhere unless I erect one to myself. I texted Jeff and told him I hoped to be home soon. I can't go on with this cross-country nonsense. Do you think the pioneers would have traveled like this just to admire the scenery and take in the sights if they had had jet planes? As soon as I get to St. Louis I'm planning to catch the first plane home. Fuck this shit. That's right. When words fail, when poetry is not forthcoming, when music no longer soothes, when you're hurting and homesick and humiliated, when the best part of your life is past and your brother and best friend is dead, when your life is turned upside down with no way to make it right, when there's nothing left to say and you don't feel like talking anyway, there's always *fuck this shit*. Am I a coward? Am I a quitter? Should I stick to the game plan and take those remaining statues and search high and low for those folks who are just screaming out for the proper tribute to their moral vacuity? No, not if all the fun and sense of adventure have been beaten out of it. And even if I still had the will, there's just no way. Not in my condition. If someone wants to meet me at the St. Louis airport or in the parking lot of the Richmond Best Western, then I'll be glad to pass the torch. But I don't have the heart. It seems so foolish now. Pop always threatened us with, "I'm gonna beat some sense into you." And he would do it, too, wouldn't he? With his belt. But why not? It's the Amercian way. Violence has always been America's preferred method of persuasion. And now I know it's literally possible for someone to have sense beaten into them. It's a two-way flow of information and matter. You have sense beaten into you at the same time you're getting shit kicked out of you. Only my gallows humor is left for me to cling to, Will. I hope it will never desert me. But I've gone as far as I can go, brother. I've lost my bearings, my rudder, my compass, and whatever other navigational tools you can think of.

I will be eternally grateful, however, for the existence of this hotel after driving all day through the mountain passes of Kentucky. Those gaps and hollers have been there for centuries to hide men and their moonshine and to provide refuge for any family in need of it who had the desperation and courage to seek it out. For those reasons, at the very least, I don't know if macadamized roads were ever a good idea for that area. If those folks didn't want to be found I say let them be. But instead we have Highway 421, and those 200 miles, as much as anything else, are probably responsible for this foul mood I'm in. Those hills would be a challenge to anyone's emotional and physical fortitude but try negotiating all those sharp turns and sudden brakings with blind eyes and bruised ribs and a broken soul to boot. Just as the van was continually swerving left then right, so was I alternating between wanting to cry and needing to throw up – the latter of which I finally did. I pulled into an old farmer's driveway (I'm assuming this was an old farmer's property – I didn't wait to make the proprietor's acquaintance) and opened my door just in time to heave a week's worth of humiliation and bile onto the old man's dirt tractor path. Not to beat a dead horse, Will, but how quickly all my plans and enthusiasm have been destroyed. And not unlike my whole life since Deb died – a microcosm of a good life turned to dust, or maybe just a fitting finale to that life. There was a moment back in Johnson City when I knew I was going to die. And not only did I know I was going to die at that moment but I was ready to die as well. Things were moving too fast for profound end-of-life ruminations, but I didn't need much time to realize *I am going to die*. I would do what I could to save myself; I would take whatever escape presented itself; but at that moment I was ready to die. Why shouldn't I die? Why shouldn't he shoot me on the spot for doing what I had done, for scrawling the words I had written? I felt no more anger, no more pangs of injustice, no more need to protest. I was ready to receive my just deserts. Is that what you felt? Were you at peace when you pulled the trigger? Or did the thug not give you time to think about anything? Those aren't bad ways to go – either at peace with the world or not knowing what hit you. But please tell me you weren't in agony over something. Please tell me you weren't sobbing in despair or howling with anger at yourself. Please tell me it wasn't my fault. Please, Will, please tell me it wasn't my fault. I think back to those horrible emails I sent you ridiculing your beliefs, or lack thereof, and I'm terrified at how they may have affected you. You're always so sensitive. Why didn't you respond to that last one I sent? I can only hope you were shaking your head at my stupidity and thinking it wasn't worth your time to humor me any longer. What was I thinking? It wasn't like I actually wanted you to change your mind about anything. Why would anyone stand up on a soapbox to ridicule and castigate and argue without any real desire to be listened to? I didn't care what you thought or believed. You were my brother, my best friend, my intellectual equal – as long as you had some belief system that met your requirements – or even if you didn't – I honestly didn't give a flying fuck. Just like all those countless times as kids when I would assert my dominance just because I could, not because I was really angry or threatened or because you had crossed some line I had drawn, but just because it was fun and because I didn't know any other way to tell you I love you. God Will, how could I go my entire life feeling so much love for you and yet never telling you? Not once. Not in a letter, a birthday card, or even in a joke. And ditto for you. Of course I "knew" you loved me and I'm sure you "knew" I loved you, but why couldn't we say it? Why should we have to rely on telepathy and assumptions? And of course it all goes back to Mom and Pop – she didn't mind telling us how much she loved cooking and *I Love Lucy*, but she couldn't bestow those words upon her children? But of course we "knew" she loved us. She showed us in a thousand ways every day how much she loved us, so why should she have to say it? And yes, action speaks louder than words. But what's wrong with the words? Why can't we have both? Why do we treat our love for each other as if it's a crazy uncle in the basement who everyone knows is there but no one wants to mention at the supper table? Are we ashamed of it? Shouldn't we celebrate it at every opportunity? Shouldn't we shout it from the rooftops? And yet we can't even whisper it to each other. Man, if Pop had ever said "I love you" to either one of us it would have been like heaven opening up and Jesus Himself walking down the sky on a staircase of clouds.

Mustn't that be our greatest failing as a species – our refusal to express our love for one another? But is it really a refusal, a choice we make, a reluctance we harbor, a difficulty we struggle with? Or is it an involuntary inability to express our deepest feelings – an emotional or developmental disability of enormous consequence? Maybe it was as impossible for Mom and Pop to tell us they loved us as it was for them to walk through a brick wall. Maybe they wanted to, but were afraid to. Maybe it was a parenting decision. But I imagine it goes all the way back to the steppes of Ethiopia and beyond, where not only cooperation with your neighbors was discovered to be a necessity for survival, but perhaps a basic mistrust of their motives was as well. But whatever perverse, endlessly complicated, unexplainable reasons exist for this inability, or this refusal, it is inevitably catastrophic. Catastrophic for our world, our country, our families, ourselves.

I don't think I need to go on with these missives to the heavens, Will. I think I've said all I have to say. Thousands upon thousands of useless words to finally get around to telling you what I should have told you every day of your life. I'll go home to Portland and pick up the pieces. What else is there to do? I'll do a better job taking care of Mom. I guess Iceland will have to wait. If you receive these messages I'm sure you'll find a way to get in touch with me. My eyes are burning so bad because of all these tears. Please know that I love you. Yeah, you knew that already but it feels good to finally say it. I love you. And I'll miss you forever. Goodbye, sweet William.

One last poem. Call this one "My Greatest Achievement." Sorry I couldn't do it again, Will:

> Riptide in my lungs, flailing wildly,
> Thinking I had to save you first
> Although my strength too was gone.
> But I did it. And I'll never forget how
> Good the sand felt back on the beach.

IT WAS GETTING LATE or at least it felt late my eyelids getting heavy from driving all afternoon but it wasn't even dark yet just starting to turn gray and time maybe to turn on the headlights but instead of asking one of the cats to take over I sed I'm going to find a nice spot to pull over and get some shuteye. Spent the last two nights trying to get to dreamland in a moving car with too much radio too much talk too much shouting too much everything but now with Flop on board I was in no hurry to get to California or anywhere else so let's just make this journey last as long as possible shall we? I saw an old dirt road that looked like no one had been on it for years tall grass between the tire lanes which were just two deep ruts but obvious that it went somewhere or at least used to. Flop sed you're not going up there are you? as I turned into the road my only concern right now getting stuck in these old ruts. I pulled the American as slow as she would go up along the sides of the ruts deciding the best route was to go one tire in the tall grass and straddling one of the ruts and trying not to fall in. I turned a little curve well off the road now and saw an old barn falling in on itself well off in the distance and beside us a tireless tractor rusted through with holes. Off to the other side of us was the rusted-out husk of a car that had been stripped of its parts. I stopped my car beside the tractor where what road there was ended abruptly and it felt wonderful to shut off the engine and relax for a minute before even wanting to get out and walk around. This place is creepy Flop sed and I think we all thought that but only a girl would actually say it. But Flop got out with the rest of us and she and I spent some time just ambulating and circulating our blood and looking down at the ground and through the tall grass on the lookout for snakes and holes and rats and stepping over car parts strewn here and there and dam it felt so good to finally be alone with her. Let's walk over to that barn I sed which seemed maybe a mile away through a big field and when we finally got to it Flop all big-eyed and timid followed me in and when I reached down to hold her hand she seemed glad I did. There was lots of dark brown hay still in the barn wet and compacted from who knows how long ago. It was getting darker by the minute and I sed I guess we better head back feeling a lot sadder than I sounded. We made it back to the car and sat for a few minutes with the doors open Kit ast how long are we going to stay here? not scared of course he sed but wanting to hurry on along to Arizona to see his mom. Pepper and Einstein seemed to enjoy the relaxation as much as me and I could only hope Flop was happy holding my hand and was not thinking too much about her problems. I told Kit I wanted to stay here all night and nobody disagreed so he had no choice but to go along with it. It didn't take long to turn dark though we hardly noticed since there was a full moon out and lots of stars which was a good thing because even I might have been scared spending a pitch-black night in a place like this.

I looked in the glove box for a flashlight didn't find one but did think of something else. Hey Pepper I sed are you going to share any of that big stash you've got? Nobody else knew what I was talking about and Pepper had no plans to share anything but since I let the cat out of the bag he couldn't really say no and I wasn't going to let him off the hook that easy anyway. He took his stash and rolling paper out of his satchel and sed who wants one of these? He knew I did so he looked at Kit and Einstein and they both looked like they had seen a dam ghost. Kit mumbled no thanks but Einstein sed I do but it was obvious he really didn't. Flop sed I want one and I sed you can share mine if you want to.

Even before the grass I was on top of the world with Flop but now with this warm high working into my brain I felt like heartache and troubles were things that only happen to other people and that had never befallen me and never would. I couldn't say the same for Einstein who was clearly smoking his first joint and coughing up one of his already diseased lungs. I sed are you sure you should be doing that? and he nodded through a tremendous scary cough and I ast again are you sure? because I may not save your life this time like I did before and he sed or tried to say you didn't save my life and I sed I beg to differ I believe I most certainly did you were playing that zipper like a xylophone Einstein you would have dropped dead if I hadn't opened your bag for you where's your inhaler thing now you might want to get it back out, all of this through the most horrendous coughing I had ever heard. Flop and I shared a joint as she curled up beside me in the backseat and man oh man how can a cat's life ever be any better than this?

I ast Flop to stroll with me again out to the barn though we could barely make out its shape in the darkness but the grass had given her a little more courage or made her a lot more carefree so we walked out slow in the moonlight holding hands not just romantic but to keep each other from falling on the uneven ground. Outside the barn I kissed her for the first time and we sat together on a bare patch of dirt in front of the barn door barely hanging on a hinge. We kissed slow sweet kisses and I caressed her face and that's all I wanted to do the night was so dam perfect. She sed please treat me nice and I sed of course I'll treat you nice who wouldn't treat you nice? but right away regretting that last part I can be so dam stupid because Flop sed I don't think I'm ready for anything else yet and I sed we have as long as you need.

We kissed more and I sed why don't we sleep out here? and Flop sed I'm not sleeping in that barn and I laughed and sed okay I won't make you sleep in a barn and she ast should we go back to the car? and I sed no no no I'll make us a place right here and even though the barn was pitch dark I sidled my way inside and felt around till I found a hay bale trying not to think what might be scurrying around my feet or away from my fingertips. I dragged the bale out took a deep breath and sed okay let's see what crawls out of this thing and started ripping out handfuls of hay while Flop watched and laughed at me. Nothing jumped out or slithered away and thank God because Flop never would have laid down with me if anything alive or especially if anything dead had been inside that hay bale. There wasn't enough straw to make much of a bed and what there was of it felt damp to the touch but I didn't want to press my luck again inside that barn. I was the luckiest man alive tonight and had been for this whole trip so I thanked whatever lucky star was watching over me and Flop and we took off our shoes and laid down together with nothing but wet hay between us and the hard ground but she put her head on my chest and I stared up at all those lucky dam stars.

I fell asleep after a short while but woke up with my neck

hurting fiercely so I gently woke up Flop and we turned over together. It was summer but still chilly on the wet ground and we hugged tightly and I thought about asking her to make love but I was afraid to not knowing what I didn't want to know about her but knowing how fragile she was so I just hugged her tighter and thought about how beautiful Flop was and how incredible this night was and how despite everything I could never be happier. Regardless of the chilly air and damp straw I took off my shirt and pants and rolled them around my shoes into a ball and gave them to Flop to use as a pillow as I lay my head on her chest listening to her heartbeat. I ast is everything okay? and she sed wordlessly uh huh and then she sed everything is wonderful which made me feel so dam good why couldn't Cynthia have said those words? but I didn't care anymore about Cynthia and once again didn't want to think about what thing or how many things had made Flop so vulnerable and hoped someday she would trust me because I couldn't bear now to think of leaving her or she leaving me once we hit California.

I woke up cold with Flop gently moving my head from off her chest and sitting up beside me in the moonlit dark. She sed go back to sleep sweetheart and slid my shirt-and-pants pillow under my head and sed she was starving and wanted to go back to the car to see if there was anything in it to eat. I tried to wake up and heard myself mutter I'll go with you but my eyelids hurt and wouldn't open and I blindly took my shirt from around the pants-and-shoes pillow and laid it over my bare chest and was immediately back in dreamland. I awoke sometime later with a start thinking I heard Flop's voice but everything was so quiet except for the crickets I must have been dreaming or heard something out on the highway back through the trees.

I slept again and awoke sensing sunshine on my legs and rolled over and felt the warm sun on my face as I opened my eyes and saw that Flop was gone and half-remembered her leaving me during the night. I was so famished my stomach hurt and I could think only about finding a pancake house as soon as we were on the road. It took ten minutes at least to tramp through the tall grass some of it waist-high to get back to my car. I saw Pepper sitting in the car half-in half-out turned facing outside the open door and Einstein was doing the same thing on the other side while Kit was standing away from them beside the old tractor. When I got close enough to see Kit he had a look on his face I can't describe but I could tell something wasn't right. Pepper saw me and stood up and sed look what the cat dragged in and I looked around and ast where's Flop? and Pepper sed gone and I sed gone? where's she gone? thinking she was behind a tree somewhere peeing but became scared when nobody sed anything and Pepper tossed away his cigarette and sed she's just gone Jeff I guess you weren't man enough for her so she just took off walking and he pointed down the rutted road we had come in on. I didn't know whether to believe him or not but I could tell something was wrong and Flop was nowhere to be seen. I panicked and yelled I have to find her! and Pepper laughed and sed you're not gonna find her Jeff she's gone, been gone I don't know since I guess three or four o'clock she's hitched another ride by now man forget about her man she's not worth it. I pushed Pepper and knocked him off balance and yelled fuck you! Why did you let her go! In the dark! What the fuck is wrong with you! Why did you let her go! Pepper yelled back I'm not her goddam daddy and you're not either and if you lay another hand on me motherfucker it'll be the last goddam thing you ever do. I sed did she say why she was leaving? Did she say where she was going? He sed I didn't ask her man we were asleep in the car she woke us up and said she was leaving. He sed man I'm sorry you lost your honey baby sugar pot but man we need to hit the road and you need to forget about that girl. I don't know what happened last night with you two but whatever it was man it made her run to the hills and she's not coming back. I was so furious at Pepper I could have killed him but I held my tongue. My heart was breaking and I could feel tears welling up and all I could do was whimper I can't believe you all just let her leave like that. All this time Einstein was silent facing out the side of the car and Kit had not moved from beside the tractor. I leaned against the car and started crying as quietly as I could and nobody wanted to bother me but Pepper kept milling about picking up rocks and throwing them at nothing. Finally he sed come on man let's go I'm starving and I sed okay and sniffled and started to get in behind the wheel but I felt nauseous and in no frame of mind to drive when all of a sudden Kit who hadn't moved a muscle this whole time ran toward me crying and yelling he raped her! He raped her Jeff! It took a moment for me to understand what Kit sed and then he sed it again and my knees buckled and I wretched and ran toward Pepper and tackled him and we rolled on the ground punching wildly and I was trying with all my strength to kill him. I grabbed his neck but he pushed me away. I scratched at his face and hit him everywhere I could as hard as I could. He hit back and we kept rolling over each other until we both gave out exhausted and hurt. Pepper struggled out from under me and got to his feet and sed I didn't rape her man I didn't touch her. Kit yelled yes you did! so furiously his voice cracked. Shut the fuck up! Pepper yelled. He was leaning over with his hands on his knees blood dripping to the ground from his nose. I was only waiting for enough strength to return to attack Pepper again as I lay panting on the grass. Kit walked angrily to where Pepper and I were and yelled hoarsely Einstein did too! He dared him to and he did it! Pepper lunged toward Kit and sed you fucking choirboy fucking snitch. On the ground with Pepper I had rolled over something large and hard hidden in the grass which now made my back hurt like hell though at the time I didn't even notice. I saw now it was an old carburetor hard to pick up with one hand and very heavy and as Pepper attacked Kit I rose with the carburetor above my head and brought it down hard against Pepper's back which made him scream in pain. It fell from my hands and hit the ground hard, but as Pepper rolled over I picked it up with both hands and crashed it into his face. Blood spurted from his eye and he moaned. As Pepper writhed on the ground I lifted the carburetor and again bashed it against Pepper's face as Kit screamed at me.

 I had been blind with rage but now I was thinking very clearly. I reached into my car and pulled the keys from the ignition and put them in my pocket. Einstein ran quickly away from me. I wanted to bash his head in too but didn't. I heard Kit vomiting at the sight of Pepper's crushed skull or maybe at the realization of what I had done or maybe of what all of us had done. I walked over to Pepper's unconscious body picked his legs up by the feet and began dragging him. Kit was sprawled in the grass dazed and sed meekly where are you going? but I ignored him dragged Pepper further out into the tall grass in the field and headed toward the barn. When I got there Pepper was still lifeless and I didn't care if he was dead or not. I dragged him into the barn and dropped his feet as close to the bales as I could manage. I looked for a pitchfork but didn't find one. I returned to the body and carefully began pulling laying pressing accumulating arranging straw over Pepper until he was buried under three feet of it. Mice squeaked and scrambled away one two three at a time. I walked over to the other end of the barn and dragged bales to the body and arranged them all around the mound covering Pepper. I was soon satisfied that the body was hidden hopefully for eternity and mournfully left the barn. I was covered with sweat and blood both mine and Pepper's and barely had strength enough to walk back to my car.

 Kit and Einstein were gone and I was glad of it. I was near collapse from exhaustion and mostly grief but all I wanted was to find Flop. I tried not to think about Pepper or anything that had happened today but raced along 66 cursing at cars in my way slowing down only as I came into a town and then driving only fast enough to keep moving forward down every street in every small town I came to on 66 coasting through stop lights on corners as I scanned every sidewalk lucky I didn't run over anyone or wasn't crashed into by another car though I felt anything but lucky making sure I didn't miss that little alley here or that backstreet over there or every young face I passed hoping to find Flop. I didn't see Kit and Einstein they had disappeared into some passing car just like Flop but good riddance to them especially Einstein my eyes burning with grief as I thought of poor Flop underneath that sorry sick piece of shit would she have screamed and fought back or just retreated as deep and far back into her shell as she could crawl crying inside screaming too I'm sure oh poor Flop my poor Flop I can't bear these thoughts and Kit thinking he was some kind of hero for ratting them out when he didn't lift a goddam finger to stop them he could have yelled to me for help or pulled them away from Flop or done anything except stand there and watch or go hide somewhere in the woods the coward oh why oh why oh why Kit didn't you do something?

After hours of useless searching my car sputtered and I ran out of gas. I hadn't even noticed I was on empty. It was desert hot and I pulled my torn and bloody shirt off and threw it in the backseat not because of the heat but because of all the blood. I reached into my bag for a clean shirt and remembered I had given one to Einstein but the fucking bastard had taken all of them. Again not feeling the least bit lucky but lucky just the same I had run out of gas not on the open road but in downtown Springfield not half a mile from a service station. When I paid the attendant for the gas can and the gas he saw my bloody hands and sed what the heck happened to you? and laughed not letting on if he suspected I was anything but an innocent victim of some backyard accident. I tried to smile but I doubt if that's what it looked like and didn't try to say anything as I took my change and shuffled sullen and slow away from the gas station. The short walk back to my car with the gas was about all I could do and I decided I needed something on my stomach though I didn't feel like eating. I went into a diner but an old lady sed with a scowl that I couldn't sit down without a shirt on so I ast can I get something to go? and she had to think about it for a minute but she finally let me order something out of the goodness of her shriveled hateful heart.

Feeling a little better after eating I got back on 66 and tried to stop looking for Flop though I know I'll never stop looking for her as long as I live but it was impossible to resist turning off the highway and onto side streets though I tried to. How long can I keep doing this there are hundreds of small towns and thousands of side streets between here and California and I don't have the heart to keep this up forever I just want to bury my head in my hands and cry every time I look and don't see her. There was at least a little hope at first when I drove into a new town but not anymore now there's nothing but desperation and this endless grief. It turned dusky and I had spent all day looking for Flop but I knew I wouldn't find her at night and didn't feel like driving anymore and I was afraid to drive through a town without searching it for Flop so I pulled off the side of the highway thinking I would try to sleep a little until a cop would probably come along and tell me to get a move on. I sat behind the wheel in silence with headlights coming up behind me shining through the car and flashing in my rearview lots of people headed west good luck I thought but you don't know what you're getting yourself into it might not be worth all the trouble after all. My greatgreatgreat Uncle Jeff sure as hell didn't know what he was getting into you start off with so many dreams or maybe just one dream but even that is too many. I couldn't bear to hear the radio all those overexcited asinine deejays doing their damdest to be happy so jarring when your heart is heavy it feels like an assault it is so unbearable. So I sat in silence except for the rattle of tires and the regular *whish whish* of the highway beside me the silence the only thing I had to be grateful for. It's been one hundred years exactly since Uncle Jeff jumped off at Omaha but some things never change out west there's always a need for frontier justice if someone in a wagon train goes off half-cocked and kills someone there aren't any jails for five hundred miles and anyway he deserves to die for what he did everybody knows that and everybody saw him do it so the man in charge does what needs to be done. Jeff killed that man half by accident and half in self-defense I don't think he even realized he had pulled the trigger until it was too late but what I did was just as desperate and just as necessary though sure as hell no accident what was I supposed to do ask Pepper to ride politely with me to the police station so I could turn him in and even after I knocked him out they would have taken him to the hospital first and it would have been his word and Einstein's against Kit's and who was this girl anyway and where was she? You can't arrest a guy for raping a ghost and that's all Flop was now. Maybe her parents were looking for her maybe the cops could track her down in a few weeks a few months a few years and for all that time Pepper gets away with murder if you ask me or Flop so what I did needed to be done.

The cop I expected never came so I woke up with the rising sun in my rearview. I pulled out onto the road wondering what would happen when I hit the next town. A few hours' sleep can work wonders but it's helpless against grief so when I drove through Joplin I turned at every intersection I came to because I didn't know what else to do. I spent all morning driving due west and then driving in circles or actually in rectangles as I scoured every street corner for Flop but destitute of anything like hope.

All the decisions we think we make are really made by circumstances we find ourselves in so there I was stopped at a traffic light facing a Greyhound station across the street from a car lot and before the light turned green I had made up my mind or had my mind made up for me. I turned into the car lot and was offered two fifty for my Rambler which was worth a lot more and he knew it but by taking one look at my bloodied shirtless appearance I guess he also knew I was in no position to haggle. He sed take it or leave it so I took it. I took my trumpet from the trunk grabbed my bag from the backseat then saw for the first time since she was gone that Flop's pink bag was in the backseat floorboard almost stuffed under the front seat. I was overcome anew with anguish as I thought of Flop out on her own again without even the barest of necessities oh Flop where are you who are you with are they taking care of you will you please let me know you're okay? I controlled my tears long enough to sign the paperwork what there was of it and headed across the street carrying Flop's bag along with my stuff the only decision left to make was which way to go east or west but that decision wasn't hard either and I ast if I could buy a one-way ticket to San Francisco and the old man sed not without a shirt on you can't and frustrated by old people I left the station and found a sidewalk vendor selling loud tropical shirts and thought unless Greyhound had a rule against tacky I was in business which was the first drop of humor that seeped into life since I lost Flop.

I found a seat near the front of the bus wishing I could hide away in the back but of course I was the wrong color for that but maybe I could at least ride without anyone sitting beside me I certainly didn't want to talk to anyone and I assumed there was a stench encircling me since I hadn't bathed in days and who knows what kind of strange smell killing a man might give you. For whatever reason maybe that one nobody sat beside me as we pulled out of the station headed to Frisco. We passed through town after town after town and stopped in most of them and at every one I strained my eyes through the glass and through my tears once again hoping to see Flop hoping maybe this bus would catch up to her wherever she was.

My thoughts on the bus eventually turned to California. I didn't know if I could ever play jazz again. Jazz is joyful music and those fast happy runs and playful riffs that had given so much pleasure seemed a million miles away. What I did to Pepper didn't fill me with remorse I still felt only burning anger and a bitter vindication and the memories of Einstein and Kit filled me with disgust and yet more anger, an anger that Pepper's death would do nothing to allay an anger only fueled by thoughts of poor Flop with her dress torn running down 66 and tears running down her face. The only thing stronger than my anger was my anguish at the memory of Flop and knowing I would never see her again and the helplessness of never being able to hold her and soothe her hurt and try as I might to make everything good again but more than that imagining the pain she felt throughout that ordeal and every other unacknowledged ordeal in her sad life and her memories of hardships she had suffered and suffers still every day since the last night she spent with me. I tried hard to imagine a better life for Flop full of helpful people and lucky breaks but I couldn't stop imagining her pain that was real beyond any imagining and such thoughts made my own pain almost unbearable. I felt my life ruined beyond repair, alone, so far from home in more ways than one, without the dreams and joys that had driven my journey west and forsaken by the music that had driven those dreams. But music must be my salvation it is in my heart my veins my blood its healing powers stronger than I will ever be its art more resourceful its beauty more resilient its possibilities more abundant, but not jazz as I know it something else must now speak my pain something from my soul, I have no choice now but to play the blues, what Satchmo Dizzy Miles have been telling me all along but I have not needed to hear. The person who sat behind me was listening to a little transistor radio which I had tried to tune out at first but I began listening through my streaming tears, the soulful voice singing now I find myself wanting to marry you and take you home.

AFTER CHECKING IN TO MY HOTEL ROOM in Johnson City I went back to the parking lot to begin preparations for that night's adventure. The words I chose to inscribe on the body of Smoky's statue were short and direct, no cute rhyming this time: CHILD ABUSER. I had gotten off on the wrong foot with this man as I thought of Jeff and his loving, artistic tattoos and what this cretin would likely do to them if Jeff were his son. And any man with a son, upon hearing Smoky's little lunch-time tale, would wish nothing but similar treatment meted out to him as he had inflicted on poor Billy Ray.

When I had more or less stumbled upon Smoky's lair that afternoon I was so excited finding him again after believing him lost that I didn't give due consideration to the difficulty I was putting myself in. This was no settled community of large spacious lots on wide quiet lanes. Here, trailers were packed tightly with more limited access and with, I assumed, more general chaos and unpredictability swirling around the lives of the inhabitants. Because of this I guessed there would be a lot of flood-lighting overhead and, who knows, maybe even security cameras or guards. I'm afraid I'm unlearned in the ways of trailer parks. I thought about abandoning the plan but decided it was at least worth a trip out in the dark hours of the morning and to make a decision then.

After a twenty-minute drive out of the city I pulled into the trailer park. It was darker than I had expected, which was good. Not much security lighting at all – just a scattering of flood lights, but if one of those lights happened to be installed on

Smoky's lot then I would most likely not go through with it. In the unfamiliar darkness I couldn't find Smoky's lot again. This was a complication I hadn't expected, since I had been here barely twelve hours earlier, and it was as infuriating as it was unwelcome. I screamed obscenities at every intersection and cursed every minute spent parading my van in front of every resident and potential witness in the park. I wasn't sure at this point I would recognize Smoky's trailer if I saw it. Eventually, I drove up to a trailer and pick-up truck that resembled closely enough what I had seen in the daylight to convince me to stop the van and to kill the headlights, but God only knows how many pick-up trucks I had seen already. Also, it was virtually pitch-dark in this part of the park. I strained my eyes and wracked my brain trying to spot or remember something about this location that would verify it as Smoky's. I looked over to my left into nothing but darkness. I couldn't see it but I remembered there should be a rebel flag flying over there. I left my van long enough to walk over closer to investigate. The Stars and Bars was still flying as anachronistically as ever. That was all the proof I needed. There was a small patch of what could be called a yard on which Smoky parked his truck. There was a car beside it, perhaps Billy Ray's. I would need to erect my protest either directly in front of his front door or off to the side of his lot. Most of the surrounding trailers were dark, but others had lights on. There were lights on in Smoky's trailer. I stood beside my van with the engine still running. Was Smoky up at this hour or did he sleep with some lights on? I was indecisive and every second I remained here I felt closer to being found out. I decided to open the back doors of the van, slowly, and hopefully with a minimum of racket. I was taking the opposite approach to what I had done at Jim Bob's. At his house I had executed a *blitzkrieg*, somewhat clumsily but as lightning-quick as I was capable of. Here, I was moving with baby steps and in slow motion, afraid any little sound or movement would call down the trailer-park militia on top of me. I had the van doors open and suddenly I heard the loud rumble, close by, of a souped-up muffler. Someone was definitely up and about. The muffler continued to rumble with short, then long, punctuations. These rednecks can't go anywhere without revving their engines for ten minutes. Whoever it was I was sure Smoky and all his neighbors were used to it so I didn't feel particularly endangered by the noise. In fact, I was emboldened by it because as long as Richard Petty was gunning his engine nobody could hear what I was doing. I grabbed the front piece of my display and quickly set it down on a grassy patch in front of Smoky's tiny front porch. I saw a shadow moving inside the trailer. My heart jumped. The shadow was moving, however, toward the end of the trailer opposite the door. I resisted a strong urge to jump in the van and vamoose – revolutions require courage, even one-man revolutions led by cowards. I grabbed the nail gun and the *piece de resistance* and made quick work of the final step.

The shadow was moving again inside, but I was now back in my van, my mission was accomplished and therefore Smoky could step outside anytime he wished to admire my handiwork. I drove slowly away with no headlights. As I fumbled around for the headlight switch in this unfamiliar cockpit, the loud-muffler'd hotrod came barreling out backwards and smashed into my passenger side. The airbags deployed, smashing into my face and scaring the shit out of me. For a moment I was stunned. Before I realized fully what had happened Richard Petty was banging on my window. "Motherfucker! God dammit!" He stopped banging on my window long enough to go back to the other side of my van to inspect his car. He came back around to my side and tried to open my door, which had automatically locked, thank God. He resumed banging on the window. "You motherfucker!" My eyes were burning and I couldn't see well – because of the airbag dust and also because my headlights were still out. But I tried to drive forward regardless. In my panic I decided that fleeing the scene was preferable to whatever crime or madness would result from stepping out of my van. I punched the accelerator but only succeeded in turning ninety degrees and disengaging the car that had been wedged into the side of the van. Both vehicles were now side by side. But before I could attempt to back around and make a run for it the occupants of various trailers had run out and were beginning to surround my van. Lights were coming on in trailers all around now. "Motherfucker!" Richard Petty said again. "Get the fuck out!" "Did anybody call the cops?" someone else yelled, sounding as if that might not be a good idea. "Don't you have any fuckin' headlights?" "Who the fuck are you?" "Get the fuck out!" "You're gonna fuckin' pay for this!" "We're gonna kick your fuckin' ass!" "No cops! No fuckin' cops!" rained all around me in no particular order. I pressed the window button and lowered the window only far enough to be heard. "Why the fuck should I get out if you all are gonna kill me? I'm calling the police!" At this threat, they started rocking the van. "Get the fuck out!" I reached for my cell to call the police, but then realized that having cops shining flashlights inside my van and onto its cargo wasn't in my best interests, either. The rocking was gaining momentum and the van was in danger of being rolled over, in which case I might never escape. My only choice was to step out of the van. I took a deep breath and opened my door. The rocking ceased and Richard Petty grabbed me and threw me hard against the side of the van. "You're gonna pay for my car, motherfucker!"

"Yes! I'll pay for your fucking car! It was my fault!"

"Fuckin' right it was your fault, motherfucker!"

"Look – just let me get the fuck out of here and I'll make sure I pay for your car. I'll buy you a new fuckin' car if that's what you want."

He laughed. "What kind of dumb stupid motherfucker do you think I am? You ain't leavin' here – not without payin' for my car."

"My insurance will pay for it."

"Like I said, you ain't leavin' here until you pay me for being such a dumb motherfucker and driving around without any fuckin' headlights. My rear end's totaled."

"Are you kidding me? I can't pay for your car tonight. All I've got are credit cards. I don't have my checkbook. Do you have online banking? I'll transfer the money to you."

He laughed so hard he doubled over. "Online banking! What the fuck are you talking about? Online banking! That's funny as shit. What have you got in the van?"

"I don't have anything in the van."

"You lyin' motherfucker. Do you think I'm stupid? I heard all kinds of shit rollin' around in there." He stepped to the back of the van and opened the doors. He pulled a couple of statues out, a front and a back. "What the fuck? What are these fuckin' things?"

"It's nothing. Artwork. They're not worth any money, but you can take them if you want."

"If they ain't worth any money then why the fuck do I want 'em? What kind of faggot are you? Look at this shit." The others were now looking at the statues and getting a good laugh. "You drive around sellin' this shit?"

"Pretty much."

"I thought you said they weren't worth anything."

A little girl ran up and said, "He put one of those things in Bobby's yard, Daddy!"

"What are you doin' out here? Go back to bed! Right now!" She ran away.

I turned around and saw a shadow walking fast toward us. The little girl was running toward this shadow.

"You sold Bobby one of these things? At three fuckin' o'clock in the mornin'? Jesus – is he a homo? What else have you two got goin' on?"

"I think we're about to find out."

Smoky came up to me with the little girl running beside him. He was carrying a rifle.

"I told you to go back to bed! Get out of here!" Richard Petty yelled. She ran away again, but back toward Smoky's trailer.

Smoky took one look at me and said, "Hey – you're the guy from dinner! What the fuck! What kind of fuckin' pervert are you? How do you know where I live?" He leveled his rifle at me. "Give me one good reason why I shouldn't blow your ass away. You were trespassin' on my property."

Someone in the gathering crowd yelled, "We got your back, Bobby. If you want to waste this motherfucker we didn't see a goddam thing."

I said, "Bobby, listen – I got a son the same age as Billy Ray.

He's already lost his mom. Do you want to make him an orphan? I was just playing a little practical joke, that's all. I'm sorry."

The little girl came running back. "There's something wrote on it, too, Bobby!"

"Get your ass in the house, right now! I'm tired of messin' with you," Richard Petty yelled.

Bobby kept his rifle pointed at me but turned his head and shouted in the direction of his trailer, "Billy Ray! Is there something wrote on it somewhere? Get a flashlight if you need to! What does it say?" He turned back to me. "Did you write something on it too? What is your fuckin' problem, man?" He tucked his rifle up into his armpit and fished out a little pen light he had secreted somewhere in his camouflage cargoes. He shone it on the statues that were lying on the ground outside the van and then on the ones still inside. "There ain't nothin' wrote on any of these. Did you write something on the one up there?" I didn't say anything. "You'll be sorry if you did. You don't insult me and my family and get away with it." Just then, someone came running out of the darkness and tackled me, knocking my breath out. He was crying and yelling, but in his rage he was unintelligible. I gasped for air. He slammed his fists into my face. Again. And again. He continued doing so. Bobby, holding his rifle in one hand, reached down with the other and tried to pull the man off me. My assailant kicked me once again in the ribs as he stood up. I was gasping and thought I was going to die. He yelled, "Let me go, Daddy! Let me go! I'm gonna kill him! He called you a child abuser! That's what it says on it! I'll kill you, motherfucker!" Bobby let go of his son's arm and cocked his rifle. I was still on the ground and Billy Ray jumped on top of me and continued his punches, hard and heavy. I could hear all the animalistic noises we were making. I tried to fend him off but was no match for his muscles or his rage. He finally tired of bloodying my face and stood up, only to start kicking me, in the ribs, in the groin, in my face. I lost consciousness.

I came to slowly, hurting all over, and remembered the nightmare I assumed I was still in the middle of. At least the punching and kicking had ceased. I tried to sit up. Bobby said, "You're a lucky man. You have no idea what a lucky son of a bitch you are. You know why? Because if Billy Ray was holdin' this gun right now instead of me you'd be bleedin' a helluva lot more, that's why. But I ain't never shot a man in anger and I don't intend to start now – especially on a no-good piece of shit like you." I could barely see because of the blood in my eyes, but I could make out Billy Ray standing beside his dad, still seething and breathing heavily. "Let's go on back to the house, Billy Ray, and let this scumbag crawl back to wherever it is he came from."

Crawling, indeed, was the only form of locomotion I could manage for the time being. I tried to pick myself up from my knees but it was beyond me. Richard Petty, meanwhile, thought he still had business to conduct with me. "What are you gonna do about my car, man?"

"Fuck you. I'll call the insurance agent first thing tomorrow morning if I'm still alive." I had no way of knowing how much of that came out clearly, but that's what I tried to say. He seemed to understand well enough.

"That's exactly what you're gonna do, asshole." To emphasize his point he put a boot on my back and pushed me face-down back into the gravel. It felt good to lie back down. "Call your insurance, dickface." With that, I was left alone, bleeding, crawling, trying to raise myself high enough to close the back doors of the van and to pull myself up into the driver's seat. I drove around the deserted streets of Johnson City until I saw a sign for a hospital. They checked me in, wrapped my ribs and kept me till morning. Then, against the doctor's advice, I checked myself out. I was ready to go home.

"SO, MOSES, DID ANYONE ever discover the gold delineated by the W?"

"Well, Cunnel, the answer to that question is fraught with difficulties, if for no other reason than the fact that the pusson to whom you have addressed the inquiry is an attunney at law, and we have a way of possing our wuds in such a manna as to renda dottful what may seem to be indisputable fact to a lay pusson. And I say that not to make an honorable profession an object of ridicule – for I have been a proud memba of the bar for more years, I am almost sutton, than you have been alive on this uth – but to bestow upon it the most generous of endossments. Because the truth, Cunnel, is rarely indisputable. And I have been fotchinate many, many toms in my career to demonstrate just how erroneous an assumed fact can be. Often it is a matta of discovering new evidence, which can be entolly dependent on serendipity, but sometoms it's a matta of defonning our tums more precisely, which is entolly within the purview of human intellect to accomplish. The whole history of jurisprudence, in its entirety, can be bolled down to a continuous refonnment of tums until you fond yourself getting closer and closer to the truth. For example, a man is arrested and chodged with cold-blooded mudda, and the state wants to establish that as a fact before the cott, but we have successfully refonned the tums of mudda into various degrees of manslotta and seff-defense so that we can get closer to detummining what crime, if any, this man did indeed commit.

"But now, Cunnel, to get back to the question at hand, if you ask me, 'was that gold ever discovered undaneath that dobble-u?' the whole question tuns on how we defonn *discova*. Was a legal claim recodded by anyone? No, not as far as my knowledge of the matta extends – not since the day the old prospecta stombled into chutch and gave up his soul to God and gave up his gold to whoeva was dun fool enough to look for it. Has anyone made any claims othawise to the land on which the gold is allegedly located? Not to my knowledge, no. Was anyone made aware of the fact that they were within sufficient proximity to the gold to make a claim of discovery? Again, the answer is no. Howeva, if by *discova* you mean, was anyone actually close enough to the dun gold to see it with their own dun eyes? Close enough to smell it if it had been a bear? To drink it if it had been watta? To reach out and pick it if it had been a dun dangleberry? To trip ova it if it had been a tree stomp or to step rot into it if it had been a pile of caribou dung? Well, in that case, the answer would be a definitive dun *yes*. So, Cunnel, to lunn about that dobble-u, I need to tell you about a fella named Duck."

"Duck? Was that a nickname? If so, he must have been an excellent swimmer."

"No – not *duck*. Duck. D-I-R-K. Duck – his given name. It's hodd to make out everything in this gale, isn't it, Cunnel? There's a reason why it's called a hurricun deck. But this fella, Duck Jenkins, he was anotha one of the dun fools who went straight from the loving hands of the Lodd in chutch that Sunday monnin rot into the waiting omms of Mammon. Now, all these other gentlemen I have acquainted you with, Cunnel, in relation to this whole misbegotten scheme, were, by and lodge, men of a fair intelligence. Impulsive, suttonly, and misled by their greed, but smott men, nonetheless. But Duck, unfotchinately, is not a possessa of sotch robust mental alacrity. That's not to say Duck does not possess many other redeeming qualities. I considda him to be a fonn friend and a generous soul. He will give you the shut off his back and will risk his loff just to make you happy. You can't ask anymore from a man than that, nor should you. But poor Duck is fishing with insufficient wumms in his tackle box. He's plowing his fields with a three-legged mule. But since he is a good friend, and considering all the misfotchin and hodship he endured, I'm grateful he made it back from O'gon alive and in one piece. I must tell you, Cunnel, prior to you setting off on your junney across the plains, that, even if O'gon tuns out to be heaven on uth, you must fust pass through the nine dun suckles of Hell to get to it.

"As for Duck, unlock all the others such as Butt Homphrey who couldn't get out to O'gon fast enough, he was content to take his tom, which, despott my statements to the contrary, could be used as evidence to suppott the claim that he was the smottest one of the lot. Duck was the tottise, as opposed to the hare, in that fable. He took a noss, slow showboat up to St. Joe – and, you see now, if Duck had been in sotch a hellfire hurry lock all the rest of 'em, he mott have found hisseff on bodd the *Tennessee* – and we know how that tunned out, don't we? So he had a fonn leisurely rodd on the riva here, then jonned up with a wagon train, and, to hear him tell it, had a grand tom of it too, singing 'round campfires and eating fresh buffalo almost nottly. But once you leave behind the Platte and head up into the mountains, then it becomes motty hodd to sing with your teeth chattering in the cold, and instead of buffalo steak you mott end up having to eat your own dun hoss – which remonds me again of Butt Homphrey. But I've been reluctant to relate that potticularly soddid tale, Cunnel, so let's just remain with Duck for the tom being.

"Lock everybody else dun fool enough to travel by foot across a dun continent, poor Duck had all sotts of bad luck and misadventure once he made it through South Pass, but I know you're eagga to hear about that big gold-plated dobble-u, so I'll just tell you about one potticula incident that is felly indicative of the kond of pusson Duck is and therefore indicative as well of just the sott of trobble Duck invariably found hisseff knee-deep in. By the tom the train had reached the Snake Riva they were ronning out of provisions and pretty dun thusty to boot. And the Snake Riva, to hear Duck tell it, is lock one of those mythological sirens beckoning you, yet remaining just out of reach. It's surrounded by high cliffs and is dun near impossible to get down to most toms, and if you look down from the top of those cliffs, sometoms you can see the riva raging below you and sometoms all you can do is hear it. So if you're hongry and dying of thust, you can perhaps onderstand why Duck mott resort to Greek mythology to get his point across. So the potty that Duck had attached hisseff to desodded to call a halt just long enough to peer down into the canyon and see if there mott be an old mule trail or some other means of getting down to the riva. Duck said that by this tom he was so thusty he would have drunk anything that was just shot of solidification.

"Now, Cunnel, I know Duck very well and I can assure you that what he did next was not undataken melly out of self-interest. The whole potty was famished and Duck would not take any sott of peril to his pussonal safety into consideration for one second if it meant lending a hand to a group of friends in need. So, without any hesitation whatsoeva, Duck throwed hisseff ova the sodd of that canyon, detummined, come what may, to get down to the edge of that riva. Howeva, I must say, that although Duck would neva allow consideration for his own pussonal safety to prevent him from doing anything within his power to hep someone, it suttonly would have benefitted Duck greatly to have taken a little tom to look into other puttinent considerations, sotch as in what manna he intended to arrive at the foot of this canyon and what he intended to do once he got there. But Duck tends to jomp fust, and to look for somewhere to land later. In this case, there was some shrubbery of some sott that he took hold of to hep hisseff down ova the lip of the canyon and then from there he stuck a finga or two into whateva little nook or cranny he could fond in the rock to ease hisseff down slowly to a rock ledge, at which point he reckoned his junney to the riva was about half-way complete. Safely on the ledge, he yelled up to whoeva may have been listening at the top of the canyon, 'Y'all don't have nothin' to worry about! Ol' Duck's gonna get everybody some noss cold riva watta!' Someone yelled down to him, 'You dun fool! You ain't gonna do nothin' but get your dun fool seff killed!' But Duck was not detudd in the least by the lack of confidence displayed by this individual, whoeva he was. So Duck hung hisseff by his omms down ova the edge of this ledge and then continued to stick every dun one of his fingas into every small crevice he could reach ontil he could safely jomp down onto the bank of the motty Snake Riva. 'I made it!' he yelled up at nobody in potticula. 'You dun fool!' somebody yelled back. And it's entolly possible that Duck indeed did feel motty foolish at this point, though he would neva admit to it, because here he was, standing besodd a motty tor'ent of a riva, dying of thust, but now soddenly realizing, I'm shaw, that he had no top of receptacle in which to place a single drop of watta for the benefit of his friends thuddy yodds above him. Afta he hepped hisseff to a noss long quaff from the riva, he did the only thing he could think to do unda the succomstances – he took off his dusty boots and began filling them with watta, up to the brim, as it were, which brought to his immediate attention anotha obstacle he would need to ovacome if were to deliver this life-saving watta to his friends; namely, he was now carrying his watta-filled boots in his hands, which, most lockly, he would need the use of upon his ascent of the sheer canyon wall now facing him.

"But Duck was detummined to slake the thust of his friends, and so, as they say, where there's a will, there's a way. Whereas on his descent, he had the use of his ten fingas, now he would have to rely on his ten toes, which had been liberated from their boots as well as from their socks. To provodd hisseff with at least one free hand, he clenched the top of one of the boots between his teeth as he began his clomb. Filled with watta, howeva, the boot was ratha heavy to be carried in one's mouth, and so threatened to accomplish in a few agonizing moments what it would take a man trained in dentistry several hours to accomplish – that is, the removal of every dun tooth in Duck's head. Howeva, he was not to be detudd. He splayed hisseff out against the rock, lock a lodge lizzudd, or perhaps lock an incredibly lodge spodda, but with several of its legs missing. Duck's toes were precariously insutted into every little crack and hole he could observe in the rock and, in this way, he used his free hand to maintain his balance as he lifted hisseff up a few inches closer each tom to the rock ledge he had paused on ullier, with one boot held fummly in one hand and the other straining every tooth in his dun mouth.

"Now I'm shaw by this tom Duck was looking fo'ward to taking a well-unned break on that little ledge jutting out from the face of the canyon wall, but Cunnel, I tell you, it was not meant to be – at least not yet. And since you are a stranger to the perils of the prairie and the trail, you may be uttaly onfamiliar with one of the foremost dangers you will undottedly have to contend with along the way. Do you have any oddea, sir, as to what Duck may have encountered upon his approach to this ledge?"

"No, I'll admit I don't, and I am reluctant to interrupt your story in order to formulate a guess. Please continue."

"Very well then. By this tom, Duck had been on the trail long enough to recognize the onmistakable sound of a rattlesnake when he hudd it. And he hudd it at precisely the moment he was prepared to place up on the ledge that boot full of watta in his hand. Now, that dun rattlesnake had undottedly wanted to slitha out onto that ledge ullier, but was prevented from doing so by Duck's onexpected arrival on his way down the canyon wall, but as soon as Duck continued on his junney, that suppent came out from its lair behond those rocks and took its rotful place on that ledge. Duck, needless to say, was now in a ratha precarious predicament. That snake was most suttonly aware of Duck's presence, but was onwilling to surrenda its spot on the ledge to this intrepid intruda. And once again, I must give credit where it is most suttonly due, and say that Duck handled this dangerous situation with a calm assurance missing from most of his endeavors. Duck is too impulsive, too eagga to please – that's where he gets into most of his trobble. If he takes a fair amount of tom to think about what he's doing – or what he's about to do – then he will acquit hisseff quott admirably. So he hudd this rattlesnake and became stock still ontil he figured out what he wanted to do. He couldn't see the snake, but he could dettumine from the rattle where it was on the ledge. He slowly raised the boot in his hand up to the ledge, and being very mondful to keep that watta-filled boot at all toms between his omm and the jaws of that dun suppent, he pushed the boot toward the snake – trying, you see, Cunnel, to provoke that rattler to strock his boot and thus hommlessly release its venom into that inanimate object. Well, dun if didn't wuck! That snake strock rot into that approaching shoe leather with a loud *whop!* and then when the boot showed no indication of relenting its attack, the snake tunned tail and retreated rot back from whence it came. Duck poked his head up high enough to make shaw the rattler was gone, then lifted hisseff up onto that ledge. Of coss, that boot had now sprong a copple of leaks the size and shape of snake fangs and was dun near useless as a vessel for holding watta, so he sadly tunned the boot upsod down and poured out what little watta remained, and then tossed the boot back up toward the lip of the canyon. 'I'm coming up!' he yelled, but no one replodd in retunn. He kept the other boot clenched between his teeth to free up both omms for clombing. That boot was now significantly lotter than ullier, since Duck had exutted so motch effutt in his ascent, he had sploshed out nearly half the watta.

Without any futha complications, Duck grabbed hold of those bushes and pulled hisseff back up to safety, but when he looked at what had been accomplished by risking his loff clombing up and down a dun cliff-face and then out-smotting a rattlesnake, he was left holding one dun boot, half-filled with watta, maybe enough to quench the thust of one small yong'un."

"Certainly not enough water to justify the pains suffered in obtaining it."

"No, sir, suttonly not. But what made it ten toms wuss, was this – not fifty yodds from where Duck had risked his loff, there was an ovahanging ledge from which point there were four men from Duck's potty extending *ropes* – with *watta pails* attached to them – rot straight down into the dun riva!"

"The Lord have mercy! What a luckless fellow! But it was he who eventually saw the W, correct?"

"Well, now, Cunnel, keep in mond that you're setting here talking to a lawya, so it all depends on what you mean by *saw*. I'm felly sutton I could argue successfully in cott, were I called upon to do so, that Duck *saw* no sotch thing – but yes, Duck eventually made it out to O'gon and followed the old prospecta's instructions as to where to fond his ustwhile gold claim. And by this tom – rememba, I said that Duck was the tottise, and not the hare – by this tom most everybody else who had been in chutch with me that monnin had now congagated in this same area of a few square molls, with the gold fever pitched so high that these men were besodd themselves with anxiety and all sotts of emotional tubbulence. The whole scenario was a powda keg just waiting for a spock. The old man had said that locating the big dobble-u would not be a simple matta and it appeared that he was being truthful at least in that regodd, assuming, of coss, that this dobble-u existed in the fust place. It was a forested area, covered with bloffs and ravines, and Duck and Butt Homphrey and Joe Clock and Clod Montgomery and the Posson hisseff, and probably thuddy or forty other men I haven't felt compelled to waste your tom even bringing up, they all spent weeks examining every dun mole hill and snake hole and tunning ova every dun rock and dutt clod as if they were sutching for that provubbial needle in a haystack, regoddless of the fact that this dobble-u, as it had been descrobbed, was lodge enough to be seen from quott some distance – yet here they were scrutinizing the ground as if they were sutching for a flea on a hoss's hodd or maybe a dun four-leaf clova. But as I have said on numerous occasions, their brains were so addled with gold fever that not one of them was behaving in any top of rational manna. And I daresay, that if they had all soddenly looked up and seen a golden, glowing dobble-u staring back at them from the sodd of a mountain, then I'm afraid that a scene of bloody violence rarely seen, even in sotch a violent envonment as the gold fields of O'gon, would have suttonly ensued. I'm afraid whoeva was the best shot with a roffle or the best at dodging bullets would be the only one left standing. Fotchinately, that did not happen, owing entolly to the general incompetence of everyone involved.

"But what did happen was that Duck, in his nommal impetuous manna, desodded to clomb a tree to betta survey the landscape, which again shows that he is not nelly as domb as he is made out to be. He scurried up the tallest tree he could fond, lock a squirrel – but Duck isn't a dun squirrel, and to prove it he slipped off a branch up near the top of the tree, lost his grip on the branch he was holding on to and began to plummet to what assuredly would have been his death. But one of his boots – maybe the same one with the rattlesnake bott taken out of it, for all I know – one of his boots caught on a branch, which fotchinately arrested his fall. He dangled upsod down for a moment or two, then managed to rot hisseff and descend the tree unhommed except for a few scratches on his omms and face. The fellows who had been watching him from unda the tree asked him if he had seen the dobble-u. Duck said he had not, and Duck has always been honest to a fault, and everyone knew that, and so no one had reason to dott his wud on the matta. And so eventually afta a few more days of fruitless sutching over all the same ground, a consensus was reached that they had been made dun fools of by the old man in the chutch, and more than one of them vowed swift vengeance if he ever encountered the dun evil vommit again. Some of them desodded to remain out west and continue sutching for gold, but in more promising locations. Butt Homphrey and several others with families back home made the retunn passage down the Columbia and the Missoura. It was a case of fool's gold if ever there was sotch a thing!"

"So, as you suggested earlier, Dirk actually never saw the W?"

"Well, Cunnel, here's how the story ends. Duck comes back into town and I see him and shake his hand and ask him how things went out in O'gon, and he commences telling his story – most of which I haven't bothered to relate to you, but he comes to the pot about clombing the tree and almost falling out of it and so on and so foth, and he says, 'So Moses, I'm dangling by one foot upsodd down in that tree, and I'm thinking, well, since I'm up here I mott as well take a quick look around, but I don't see no dun dobble-u. So I scampa back down and tell everybody we mott as well tun around and head back to Missoura.' So then I said to Duck, 'so, even from the treetops, there was no sonn of a dobble-u?' And the dun fool says, 'No – while I was hanging there all I saw was a goddam M!'"

LEAVING MY KENTUCKY BEST WESTERN, I was no longer interested in the scenic route and hopped on I-75, thankful for all those lanes, which soon led me to 64 West – which in turn would put me in St. Louis well before suppertime. Despite my injuries and heartache I was in much better spirits. My final email to Will had provided a bit of catharsis and I found myself, if not exactly looking forward to the rest of my life, at least feeling more capable of facing it. The van's CD player could store multiple discs so I had loaded it down with all the hard bop I had available – Miles' first great quintet, Lee Morgan, Hank Mobley, Horace Silver – music that could lift the spirits of the undead. First up was Lee Morgan – shot dead by his girlfriend at age 33, the same age as Jesus on the cross – but unfortunately, Lee Morgan isn't coming back. I mourn him anew every time I play his music.

After five hours of the best music ever made, the Arch came into view. Within minutes I had crossed the Mississippi. I asked Siri to take me toward Lambert and she guided me onto

I-70. I had made a motel reservation as close to the airport as possible, within fiscal reason. I checked in and tried to rest my wounded body, but felt antsy and reluctant to spend another afternoon in a carpeted box, so I got back in my van and explored a bit of St. Louis. I always enjoy cruising around, but this part of St. Louis didn't offer anything I hadn't seen elsewhere, only more of it. I looked over to my right at a stoplight and saw a female panhandler. And I must say, she was beautiful. Her black hair, not very long, was combed straight back and shimmered under the sun as if it were wet, or maybe just several days unwashed. But what struck me most powerfully was her skin. From the distance between me in my van and her standing in the grassy median between the curb and sidewalk, I could discern the radiance of it. It could not be called Caucasian, I don't believe, or at least not entirely so. Her skin must have been the result of one of those happy genetic conflations that produces something much greater than the individual constituents. She was holding a sign, neatly lettered, which read, Lost Everything College Educated Please Help. I was intrigued by the combination pleading/resumé quality of it and, to a lesser degree, the lack of deistical blessing that I saw on most homeless signs. A secular panhandler was refreshing. I was feeling unusually friendly, not to mention lonesome. Without any ready cash at hand, I had no way to induce her to talk to me, but I rolled down the passenger window regardless and called out to her before realizing, in addition to being broke, I had nothing whatsoever to say to a beautiful homeless person. She came over eagerly, of course, expecting money. "I like your sign," I said.

"Thanks." She looked at me expectantly, but I had nothing to give her.

"I'm sorry, I don't have any cash. I just wanted to say hello."

"That's okay. Have a nice day!" She walked further down the sidewalk. The light changed. Cars started moving. This street was not on a nice neat grid, where I could easily drive around the corner and back again as I had in Johnson City where I had discussed career opportunities in panhandling. This street was a busy straightaway, and in a small town would have been called "the strip" by the locals. I decided to switch on my emergency blinkers and stay put. I immediately created quite a traffic jam behind me, which I hoped the lady would appreciate. I saw myself in my rearview – my cheeks swollen, my eyes half-shut and bloodshot, fresh cuts on my chin and cheeks. It would be difficult to look more undesirable. I saw her approaching in my side mirror. "Having car trouble?"

"Hey – what's your name?"

"Jesus, you've got to be kidding. Do you know how many guys try to pick me up standing out here? Can you please just leave? You're really fucking up my lanes here."

"I'm trying to help you out. I've got cars lined up back there for half a mile already."

"Yeah, and they're all pissed off. Thanks a lot for your help. Can you please leave now?"

"I'm sorry. I was just trying to help." I switched off my blinkers as the traffic light returned to red. She walked down the sidewalk slowly waving her sign/*curriculum vitae* back and forth. I was determined to talk to her one more time. I was so lonely, and hurting in so many ways. I was fully aware of my temporary insanity and at least partially aware of how crazy I must appear to her, but there was no decision to make, no thoughtful consideration of options to be undertaken. The thought of driving away and never speaking again to this beautiful woman – a woman who obviously had no interest in me – filled me with a dread I couldn't easily explain. The thought, though, of speaking to her and perhaps winning her over – to what end, I wasn't sure – filled me with an equally inexplicable joy.

However, there was one other piece of business I knew I had to take care of first. I was still driving around with the leftover remnants of my public shaming project rattling around the back of my van. Painful as it was to think about – the abject failure of it and the humiliation and drubbing it had brought down on top of me – I was ready to put this particularly wretched episode of my life behind me. I pulled into the parking lot of a large strip mall and drove around behind the stores looking for a dumpster. Luckily, there were no witnesses as I grasped the handle on the side of the dumpster and pulled open the heavy, loudly grating metal door and then, without giving it a second thought, quickly tossed inside the carvings upon which I had lavished so much careful attention and which were the instruments of so much vengeful mayhem in so many recent dreams. I drove around to the front of the mall, parked my van and began walking the half-mile or so back to the intersection, which, with bruised ribs, was neither easy nor fun. I approached her again and said, "Hi there – remember me?"

"Sort of. Maybe."

"I was the guy in the van – holding up traffic."

"Oh yeah." She was paying minimal attention to me as she smiled into passing cars and waved occasionally.

"Do you mind if I ask you your name? I'm not trying to pick you up. Really."

She laughed a bit snidely. "Then what are you trying to do?"

"I'm not sure, to be honest with you. Trying to turn my life around?"

Cars were zooming past, trying to make the green. You don't realize how fast automobiles travel until you're standing by a roadside. The world would be a better place without them. "Why are you standing out here like this? Where's your van?"

"I parked it way up there – at one of your city's fine retail establishments." She walked along the sidewalk, waving. I followed along like a puppy dog. "Would it help if I started waving?" I asked.

"No. Please don't. I don't need any help." Her lights were red, cars were slowing, and she continued her slow walk up and down the median. She stayed on the sidewalk as traffic roared past, but when business opened at each red cycle she moved down into the median and occasionally strolled along the curb with the balance of a tightrope walker. She wasn't having much success at the moment. Every driver ignored her. None of the passengers in any of the cars would make eye contact. Seeing her now up close, her heritage became clearer. She was African-American, by and large. I considered the names our illustrious history has bestowed upon such beautiful people as this: *mulatto* sounds more like a side dish than a human being. Then there's *half-breed* – how must it have felt being lumped in with the cattle? Her skin, which first caught my attention, was even more beautiful the closer I got to it. The only way I can describe it is to say her skin gave me the impression of being more than epidermis, that it went all the way through her body, that's how deep and lush it seemed.

"How long have you been doing this?" I had to speak loudly over the idling traffic, especially one bothersome motorcycle – the smallest vehicle in sight, but also the loudest – as if it had something to prove.

"Look, sir. I can't talk to you and work these cars at the same time. I'm not trying to be rude."

"That's okay, I understand. This isn't the best place to talk. What time do you get off?" I have been unduly influenced by that homeless entrepreneur in Johnson City – I was thinking of this as her job, of schedules and shifts.

She spoke without looking at me, not taking her eyes off the cars and her customers. "Not till after rush hour. Whenever I get tired and hungry."

"Would you like to have dinner with me when you get off work here?"

She stopped waving at cars long enough to look at me. She looked my whole body over up and down and studied my face. "What happened to you?"

"What do you mean?"

"Your face."

"Well – I got into a fight – and lost."

"Look, sir – don't take this the wrong way, but I don't think I really want to go anywhere with you, you know what I mean? I mean, it's hard to trust people."

"I understand." Which I did. I wouldn't go anywhere with me either. "Could we just walk down the street here and find someplace to eat? Close by?"

"Not right now."

"I mean after rush hour. I'll come back here at 5:30 or so."

"Suit yourself."

I took that to be a positive response. "Okay. Sounds good. Thanks for talking to me." I put out my hand for her to shake, which she did, but not before staring down at it briefly as if it were a lizard or a snake or something else that might bite her. I shuffled back to my van, my ribs hurting like hell and my lungs wheezing, but feeling happy.

I drove back to my motel and spent the next hour giddily getting ready for my date. After all the electronically vetted, scientifically selected dates I had procured online – all of which were disappointing and depressing in some way – it was this bizarre encounter I was most excited about. I studied my battered face in the mirror. It was as painful to look at as it was to touch. It was almost enough to make me not want to go through with it. I wasn't going to bring up the "fight," but if she did I was going to have to spin it severely in my favor. Can I please get to a point in my life when I can stop lying? When I no longer have anything I'm so ashamed of? When the reality of my life isn't so fucking ridiculous?

I drove toward our rendezvous as spiffed up as a walking cadaver could be. I approached her intersection and was relieved to see her still there plying her wares. I was in line behind a long row of cars. Lucky for her this light seemed to hold forever, though from what little I saw she wasn't making a penny. I became immediately angry at what I assumed was the reason for this – as Pop would say, niggroes never stop asking for the white man's money. She walked past my van and either didn't recognize me or decided to ignore this crazy man's sudden presence in her life. I lowered my window and greeted her on her return trip to the top of the intersection. "Hey – I'm back."

"Hey."

"Is it quitting time yet?"

"Almost. Give me a few more minutes."

"Sure thing. I'll drive around for a little while and swing by and pick you up."

"No! I'm not getting in with you! You said we were going to walk somewhere to eat."

"Okay, okay. I understand. I don't blame you. But I'm not going to hurt you. I promise." Her eyes darted impatiently. I was monopolizing valuable red-light time. "I'll park my van and we'll walk somewhere, like I promised."

"Okay, that's fine. Give me thirty more minutes."

I had hoped she would trust me enough to let me give her a lift so I could rest my aching ribs, but I drove back to the strip mall, parked, and listened to Hank Mobley for thirty minutes – always time well spent. I was worried on my slow walk back to the intersection. It occurred to me she may have taken the extra time she requested as a good opportunity to skedaddle. A creepy man with a pugilist's face – I couldn't blame her in the least. But there she was – I spotted her long before I got to within hailing distance. When I came round the corner of the intersection she looked right at me but showed no sign of recognition and made no indication that she was going to put down her sign for the day. "Hey – thanks for waiting on me. I was afraid you might be gone."

"Nope. I'm still here."

"Is there any place nearby that you like to go? I'm not from around these parts."

"There are places up the street. I'm not particular."

"Shall we, then? Do you want me to carry your sign?"

"Thanks." The sign was thin cardboard, light as a feather. It was obvious she neither wanted to go anywhere with me nor turn down a free meal. We walked back up the sidewalk I had just come down, across parking lot entrances of an auto-parts store, a hair salon, a boarded-up building that used to be a bank by the looks of it. Looking around, I could have been anywhere in America within the past thirty years. There are streets in Charleston just like this one that have barely changed since before I was born and probably won't change much after I'm gone. This is part of our enduring legacy to the world. Europe has its cobblestone lanes and cathedrals; we have our cruising strips and burger joints.

"You never did tell me your name," I said to her. She hadn't asked for mine.

"Florida."

"Really? That's interesting. If you're going to be named for a state, that's the one to pick. You don't run across too many people named New Hampshire." I was trying too hard but I couldn't help it.

"My mother and father were at the beach when I was conceived, so they said."

"Well, it's a good thing they weren't here then," I said, not even sure myself what I meant by that. Florida gave me a look that I interpreted as annoyance. "I'm sorry – I'm just trying to be funny. My name is Josh, by the way."

"That's okay. I don't have anything to do with my parents anymore – don't even know where they are – don't really care."

"So, tell me about this sign. I've never seen a homeless sign that said College Educated before. It's interesting that you would include that. I mean – is it some kind of political statement? You know, about the severity of the economy, even college-educated people are becoming homeless? Or maybe, I thought it might be a tactic you were using to appeal to the snobbishness of the average person – you know, the American work ethic and all, you wanted to show everyone that you weren't just some lazy homeless person – not that you are or anything, that's not what I'm saying at all."

Florida smiled for the first time. "Nah – it just sucks that I don't have a job, that's all. I don't know why I put that on it." Before we made it back to the mall's parking lot we passed a Subway, which seemed as good a place as any other for two perfect strangers to have dinner. It also gave me a chance to sit down.

Florida ate her sandwich delicately, her chewing deliberate and unrushed. I was happy to see she wasn't famished. If she had eaten ravenishly it would have broken my heart. "Where do you stay when you're not over there?" I asked, nodding back toward the intersection. "I hope you don't have to sleep on the streets."

"No, I stay at the women's shelter. They feed us pretty good there."

"Do you make pretty good money holding up your sign?"

"Nah – nobody wants to help. Well, nobody much. But it beats sitting around the shelter watching TV all day. Keeps me from being a lazy homeless person like you said. I work temp jobs sometimes, so I'm not always on the street begging."

"Where did you go to college? I'm sorry, Florida. Do you feel like you're on a job interview? You don't have to answer all my questions if you don't want to."

"Nah – that's okay. I went to Flo Valley."

"Where's that?"

"Not far. Just get on 270. It's in Ferguson."

"Ferguson? Really? Did you get caught up in all the rioting and stuff?"

"No, but I know people who did. I wasn't there then, but it's always been pretty bad over there."

"Yeah, I imagine it has. Can I ask you kind of a personal question? Actually it's a very personal question."

"Yeah, I guess, but you said I don't have to answer it if I don't want to."

"Of course. Of course. So, you're African-American, right? At least partly." Florida nodded. "The only reason I ask – well, I don't know why I asked it – it doesn't matter. I mean, it's great, actually. But – okay – don't take this the wrong way – I'm still not trying to pick you up, even though this will sound like I am, but you have the most beautiful skin I think I've ever seen – it's just the most amazing – *hue* – the most amazing *hue* I would say."

"Well then, maybe my parents managed to do one thing right."

"Yes! Exactly! The perfect genetic mixture." Still feeling the need, apparently, to display my anti-racist *bona fides*, I eagerly told her about Jerome and the lessons I learned from him. It's been over thirty years but he's still the best teacher I ever had. Telling her about Pop, however, could wait – probably forever.

"I think everybody is pretty much the same," she said. "White people, black people, some are good, some are bad. You just can't always tell which is which."

We finished our sandwiches and I decided to pop the question, as it were. I couldn't tell you when I made that decision – it may have been when I first saw her skin shining gloriously under the St. Louis sun or it may have been the moment the words formed in my mouth. "Let me ask you something, Florida. Maybe I shouldn't ask you this, maybe I'm way off base – but would you like to fly to San Francisco with me tomorrow night?" She showed no reaction. She was sucking her straw as I asked the question, maneuvering past all the ice to vacuum the bottom of her cup, which she continued to do as my query faded away. "I'm only planning to stay a few days. We would be staying with my uncle. He's an incredibly nice guy, he really is. He has a small apartment, but I would let you sleep in the guest bed and I'll be happy to sleep on the couch. And you can leave anytime you want. I'll pay for your flight back. It would just be a chance to see the sights and maybe get to know each other a little bit. Have you ever been out west?"

"Why do you want me to go with you?"

"I don't know, Florida. I just really want to be nice to you. It's been a long time since I've felt like being nice to anybody. Please just let me be nice to you, that's all I'm asking."

"I don't need you to feel sorry for me," she said, her voice rising a little.

"I know, I know, but I feel sorry for everybody," I attempted a small laugh. "It's good to show a little bit of empathy. What do you say? I think it'll be fun. And any time it stops being fun just let me know and I'll put you on the first flight back to St. Louie."

"I don't know. I'm not good at trusting people."

"That's understandable. But look here – we'll be on a plane all the way to California. Nothing can happen to you on a plane. Or in the airport. And we'll take taxis everywhere we go, so if you still think I might be an axe murderer you won't ever have to be in a car alone with me. And we'll be with my Uncle Jeff most of the time too. So I promise that nothing bad will happen to you. I can call Jeff if you want me to. I should probably call him anyway just to make sure it's okay if I bring a guest, but I'm sure he won't mind. I'll call him right now." I reached for my cell.

"No, please don't. I mean, you can if you want to, but it won't do any good. It won't make me believe you." I think she felt she owed me an explanation for the harshness of her comment. She set her cup down and sighed and said, "I was going to sell my car to this guy – for five hundred dollars. This was a long time ago – before I went to Flo Valley. I just needed some cash for something – I don't even remember now why I was selling my car. But anyway – this guy got off the bus and said his brother was coming with the five hundred dollars. We waited about an hour and he never came with the money, so this guy called him – I don't know if it was really his brother or not, who knows – I do remember it was the first time I talked on a cell phone – that's how long ago it was – but he let me talk to him and he said he was held up because he was doing something for his wife, but he said he would be there as soon as he could. So the guy asked if he could take it for a test drive while we were waiting for his brother and I wasn't too sure if I should let him drive it by himself, but I did – and he came back maybe fifteen or twenty minutes later and said he really liked it, so I figured after that I could trust him. I mean, if he wanted to steal my car he wouldn't have come back, right? So then the other guy calls back and says he still couldn't get away from his wife and the guy was totally apologetic and everything. We waited about another hour out in this parking lot and finally the guy says, 'Well, I don't think he's coming and I'm getting tired of waiting on him and I know you are too, but I really want to buy this car.' Then he says, 'is there any way you could drive me to his house?' And he made some joke like, 'if he's not gonna bring the money to us, then we'll just have to go get it from him.' By this point it didn't even occur to me that he might be lying. I drove him way out to this old trailer – it was all the way over in Illinois somewhere and as soon as we got there I got this weird feeling that I had made a big mistake. It was totally deserted and out in the middle of nowhere and totally rundown and everything. I can't explain that feeling – it was so weird. I don't know why I didn't just drop him off and leave. I'll never forgive myself for that. I was so stupid, but I didn't trust my instincts like I should have. I trusted him instead. We went into the trailer and this other guy was there." She picked up her cup, took the lid off and started eating the ice.

"So, they stole your car?"

"They raped me."

Tears came into my eyes and although she said it had been a long time I still felt the anger building inside me so strongly I thought I might throw up. "God, I'm so sorry. I'm so sorry, Florida."

"It's okay. Ancient history." There's no such thing as ancient history. Ask the Shi'ite. Ask the Serb. Ask the Indian on his reservation. Ask the black man. Ancient history is as oxymoronic as old news.

"I don't know what to say, Florida. I'm not like that. I'm nothing like that. Are you having that weird feeling right now? With me?"

"No, I'm not."

"Well, that's good at least." I didn't want to push Florida any further to go to California with me, yet I wanted her to trust me. I started collecting all the wrappers and napkins for the trash. "Well, I guess we've done all the damage to our dinner that we can."

That was meant as a joke, but Florida mistook me. "No – it was nice. I enjoyed it. Thank you so much. Oh my God – I forgot your name. I'm so sorry. I know you told me."

"Josh – much less memorable than Florida." I realized my reluctance to tell her my last name. If she had watched TV during the past year she may have connected me to Pop. "Can I walk you back to your shelter? How far is it?"

"I take the bus if I have enough money."

"I don't want you to have to do that. Why don't we walk? It'll give us more time to talk."

"We can't walk all the way to the shelter. It's way too far."

"How do you get home if you don't have bus fare?"

"I walk if I have to, but I don't want you to have to walk that far."

"Yeah. Maybe not such a good idea after all." My lungs would burst if I had to walk the distance of a bus ride. "I tell you what. Let's start walking and when we've had enough I'll Uber us a cab. You guys do have Uber here, right?"

"I have no earthly idea what you're talking about." She

actually laughed. So did I.

"Trust me."

We started walking, back from whence we came. "What kind of fight were you in?"

"It was in Johnson City, Tennessee, if you've ever heard of that little place. No reason why you should have. But I was in a diner, sitting at the bar – I wasn't drinking, just waiting on my food – and I happened to be sitting next to this guy who started telling me all these horrible things he did to his kid. I'm serious. He thought they were funny. He was laughing about it."

"What kind of things?"

"Well, you wouldn't believe me if I told you – just very disturbing, abusive sorts of things. You see, I have a son – and this kid this guy was telling me about would be about the same age as Jeff, my son – he's named after my Uncle Jeff, you see. And – it gets kind of complicated to talk about – there's a lot of stuff I have to leave out because I've been through so much lately – a lot of pain and grief – this has not been the best time for me to be alive. But anyway, I didn't handle the situation very well, to say the least. I let my temper get the best of me. But I didn't start the fight – well, the first punch thrown wasn't mine, let me put it that way."

"You had a fight inside a restaurant?"

"Well, out in the parking lot. I just told him that I didn't think the way he treated his son was nearly as funny as he thought it was, or words to that effect, and this guy – this mountain redneck, as dumb as he was tall – he dealt with the situation the only way he knew how to. Remind me never to go back to Johnson City, Tennessee."

"I'm sorry. I have a son, too. I never see him though. They took him away. He's with his father. What a joke. He'll end up in jail before I get to see him again. Or dead."

"What's his name?"

"Michael. His father wanted to name him after Michael Jordan – as if that's going to do him any good – worshipping a basketball player. He's ten."

"Jeff's twenty this year. Hey – would you like some ice

cream?" We were walking past a local place with a big flashing neon cone, and another opportunity to sit down. Florida eagerly agreed. I think it must have been the first ice cream for either one of us in quite a while – we used our tongues much more for licking than for talking. The thought of doing any more walking was not pleasant – my ribcage was killing me, but I wasn't looking forward to the end of the evening. "What's the name of this place? I'll get us an Uber."

Florida shook her head. "Uber. You're gonna get me killed."

I wanted to mention California one last time. "Okay – no pressure. But here's the deal." I took a moment to check my email confirmation before speaking again. "Okay, here's the deal. My plane leaves tomorrow night at eleven. I want you to come with me so very much, Florida. I think we would have a lot of fun. But I understand if you don't want to, or if you're afraid to. I'll be sad if you don't come with me, but I'll understand. So what do you think?"

"I have to think about it, Josh. You're asking a lot."

"I know. I know I am. But maybe not as much as you think. It's only for a few days. Then you'll be right back here again."

"I have to think about it."

"Okay. No pressure. Spend some time thinking about it. Whatever you decide to do is fine. Just bear in mind – we'll have so much fun! It'll be great! My Uncle Jeff is such a great guy – he'll take us all around! But seriously, no pressure. I don't want you to do this if you're not going to be totally comfortable." I checked my itinerary. "My plane boards at Gate E20. Will you remember that? Should I write it down? You'll probably need to be there by nine to get through security. Do you have a cell phone?"

"No. I want one but I wouldn't be able to afford the bus."

"That's fine. That's not a problem. You can call me from the shelter, though, right?"

"Yeah, sure. I can find a phone to use."

"Great." I stood up too fast to run over to the counter to ask for a pen and I thought I had been stabbed in the chest. But I suffered in silence and wrote my number down on a napkin for Florida, as well as my gate number and departure time. "Just give me a call if you decide you want to go. Is that a deal?"

"Okay, Josh. I'll think about it. But don't get your hopes up, okay?"

"Too late for that. My hopes are already up. But no pressure." I made our Uber arrangements and the young driver dropped Florida off at the shelter without killing her and then delivered me safely to my van.

I called the airline immediately to make sure the flight wasn't full up and was lucky to be allowed to book another seat. I called Jeff and was overjoyed to hear his voice. He knew I was driving out to see him but didn't know about my change of plans – but if anyone understood aborted travel plans out west it was Uncle Jeff. At least he had made it through most of Missouri before his car kicked the bucket. I explained the situation as much as I was willing to – which is to say I explained damn near nothing. No mention of large wooden penises or Johnson City trailer parks. I did mention my damaged physical appearance just to prepare him for it, but I spun him the same yarn as I had for Florida. I told him I was in too much pain to drive long distances, which wasn't a lie. Jeff, true to form, not thinking of himself, suggested I take a flight home to Portland and go see my doctor rather than come out to San Francisco. I told him I had already bought my tickets and had no intention of not seeing him. He was thrilled to hear about Florida and the possibility she would be with me. Of course he would be at the airport waiting for me, he said. It was nothing for old jazz heads to be up past midnight. Before he hung up he took time to lower his voice and ask solemnly, "So, how are you doing, otherwise?" meaning, of course, Will. "Better," I said, giving this most consequential of questions the least consequential answer I could get away with. Thinking perhaps that one *better* wasn't enough, I waited a moment and gave him another. "Better," I repeated, signaling to him that this was all he was likely to get from me on that particular subject.

I spent the entirety of the next day holed up in my motel room waiting to hear from Florida. The standard movie scene of the poor pining fellow staring at the old land-line as it refuses to ring was now replaced with a new one – the old man pulling his cell out of his pocket every ten minutes on the off-chance he somehow missed her call. I resisted the strong urge to look up the shelter and to check in on her and the stronger urge to drive out to her intersection to see her. As the afternoon turned into early evening the urge became almost insuperable, but I resisted it successfully. This was her call to make and hers alone. I waited as long as I could before leaving for the airport. I was deeply sad driving there alone. I was disappointed for myself, not for Florida. I was sure she made the right decision for herself. I had done a good job of salesmanship but was probably much too hopeful. Who knows what factors played into her decision? Circumstances and people and history impossible to touch upon during a slow walk down the street for sandwiches and ice cream. Maybe she was just playing me for all the sympathy and free food I could provide; maybe she was just as good a storyteller as I was – but no, that wasn't right. She was sincere – I could be sure of that. But why should I think she would be willing to hop on a plane with me or with anyone else? I was an admittedly off-kilter, not-thinking-straight, unpredictable man from out-of-state who had picked a fight with a stranger over something that was none of his business, who drove an empty beat-up van and who had an even more beat-up face. I should be grateful she didn't call the cops. It had been a longshot worth taking, but a longshot nonetheless.

I didn't have much time to dwell on Florida's absence once I arrived at the airport. I had waited too long at the motel for her to call to allow for any leisure prior to boarding and I knew I would have a bureaucracy to contend with at the rental counter after they took one look at the van. Before leaving it behind for the last time I did a quick check of the interior for anything I may have forgotten to pack. I glanced in the floorboard and noticed, peeking out from under the passenger seat, a corner of my wooden childhood map. It had undoubtedly taken much unwarranted abuse as those Johnson City trailerites had rocked and nearly rolled the van. It saddened me to think of relinquishing it, and I gave a moment's thought to taking it with me as a carry-on, but I decided it had outlived its usefulness to me. There's nothing I can do about all these memories I have to carry around, but at least I can attempt to jettison some of their useless symbolism. I placed it gently in the now-empty cargo space behind me and hoped that some resourceful attendant would retrieve it and realize that it would be perfect to take home to his child. Inside the terminal, at the rental counter, there was an incident report to fill out (rather unforthcoming in details) and a Damage Administration Fee to cough up to ensure that proper compensation could be paid to the employee chosen to deal with my wanton carelessness. I was tempted to pick a fight and ask, isn't dealing with damaged vehicles part of your ordinary business operations? Wouldn't this be part of any normal job description in the rental-car business? But I didn't want to waste my breath, since breathing was painful enough already, and I didn't have time to argue with these people. But wouldn't it be nice if I could charge students a Late Paper Fee or an Excessive Questions at the End of Class Fee?

I made it to my gate with a few minutes to spare. I had been given two boarding passes though of course I would need only one, but I shrugged off the wasted ticket purchase as a worthwhile investment in hope and the Late Chance for Love Fee I had to pay for the opportunity of meeting Florida. Money well spent, all the way around. I spent the last few minutes before boarding thinking of Uncle Jeff and began feeling excited about seeing him again. It had been a couple of years. I hadn't seen him since the Time of Troubles began after Pop's arrest, but I was feeling lucky again and starting to look forward to some semblance of a normal life if I could find a job. If not, Portland would be a fine place to hang out a cardboard shingle and start a new business in the panhandling trade. Or maybe I would get up the nerve to move to Iceland after all, with all the other Vikings, if I could convince myself I wouldn't miss Jeff too much, or he me.

I heard the call for first-class boarding, which would never involve me, but I grabbed my carry-on and prepared to queue, hoping to be early in line for regular boarding. As I stood I heard a yelled "Josh!" and instinctively turned around. Florida was walk-running toward me, grinning. I started laughing. Sweet baby Jesus, when was the last time I had felt this happy? Being kissed by a girl, aged eight? The last Christmas morning Santa was real? Will and I breathing heavily on the beach after struggling out of that riptide? I hugged Florida spontaneously and felt like kissing her but maintained enough decorum to hide my giddiness. "Glad you could make it," I said, cool as you please.

On the plane she explained that she had finally made her decision but thought it was too late to call me, so she convinced one of the ladies at the shelter to drive her to Lambert, though having to endure this woman's *this is a really bad idea, this is too weird, you barely know this man, remember what happened in the past, you'll be so much safer here, his eyes are bloodshot?, he was in a fight?, he just came up to you on the street?, you're going to regret this*, on and on all the way to the airport. I thanked her for putting her trust in me and for not listening to that old biddy, who happened to be her best friend at the shelter. "So what made you finally decide to come?" I asked.

"Why not? It's so depressing where I am. I don't feel like I have anything to look forward to or any reason to even be alive. I can't see Michael. I can't get a job. I'm begging on the street. How can going to California with you be any worse than that?"

"That's the spirit." I was smiling so big every bruise on my face hurt.

It seemed like a short flight and I was in no hurry for it to end. But after landing, I grabbed Florida's hand and practically ran through the tunnel off-boarding, bruised ribs be damned. Jeff was waiting for us, as promised, wearing one of his signature Hawaiian shirts. He had chosen not to fly down for Pop's funeral/media circus or for Will's sad send-off, so I was especially happy to see him. He was pushing eighty now, unbelievably, and he seemed to look much older than the last time I saw him. He was balding severely and what hair he had left was pulled back into a long wavy-white ponytail. He gave me a bear hug and said I looked like shit. The bear hug brought tears to my eyes because of my ribcage, but the tears certainly weren't out of place. To Florida, Jeff was as gracious as a southern gentleman could be. He had found another small apartment he could afford in his beloved North Beach. His life in San Francisco had been a series of small apartments, which never bothered him in the least. He had actually been married for a few years back in the 1980s, a marriage which had ended amicably enough according to Jeff. Jazz had been more of a going concern back then, with young lions like the Marsalis brothers igniting a short-lived resurgence for Jeff as a traveling musician. But for most of his life he made a meager happy living gigging locally, doing occasional recording dates when lucky enough to get them, and giving private lessons. He rarely gigged now but he still regularly tutored a handful of lucky students. For a trumpet player, old lips are like arthritis to a pianist. His embouchure was shot. But his was a life lived in the service of his passion and a constant inspiration for me to continually fail to live up to. I was born in the right family but to the wrong father. I would have traded Pop for Jeff faster than your foot could find the downbeat.

It was somewhere between two and three in the morning when we arrived at Jeff's apartment but none of us was ready for sleep. His living room was cluttered as usual, but now, it seemed, even more so. His two cats, Bix and Cootie, used to strangers being around, ignored us and went off to their respective lairs. Released from her mistrust and her depressing life in St. Louis, Florida opened up, laughed, and seemed almost like a different person. Jeff wanted to hear more about my slugfest in Johnson City, but I demurred, unwilling to continue spinning that web of deceit. I simply said, "Jeff, you're such a laid-back cat you have no idea what it's like to be so angry you just want to rare back and beat the holy crap out of somebody." Near dawn, my eyes, the blood finally draining from them, refused to stay open much longer and Florida was already drifting off for stretches at a time. I gently woke her, the touch of her luminous skin thrilling me, and she thanked us both and walked slowly into the guest bedroom where she had put her bag earlier. I took the couch and slept until I heard Jeff stirring around lunchtime. I apologized for temporarily disrupting his existence but of course he was having none of that. These were his normal hours he said. When not staying up all night at a gig, there was nothing as wonderful for him as sitting up till dawn smoking grass and listening softly to Bill Evans or Chet Baker or any number of other geniuses who make life worth living. It had played hell with his marriage, he said, but I imagined he would trade a wife for Bill Evans any night of the week.

After lunch and while Florida was in the shower, Jeff said he wanted to give me something. He walked me to the entrance closet and pulled from the top shelf an old pouch of some sort which appeared to be made of real leather. I had never seen it before. As he held it and began to gently open it, I noticed on the floor of the closet a small, feminine-looking pink bag or satchel. It looked fairly old as well. It struck me as strange that Jeff would have such an odd thing in his closet and I wondered if it had belonged to Stephanie, his ex-wife. Before I could ask him about it, however, he began telling me about the leather pouch he had opened. "I want you to give these to Jeff."

"What are they?"

"I was named after Jefferson Kinninger, who came out west in 1860. These are the letters he wrote back home to Charleston while he was on the wagon trail."

"Are you kidding me?" I was almost afraid to touch them. "Holy shit, Jeff. How long have you had these?"

"I brought them with me when I high-tailed it away from home. Just had 'em stuffed up in closets and in drawers most of the time. I don't look at them anymore. I've got 'em all memorized anyway. I used to read them all the time back when my pop still had them." He paused briefly. "You know, man, there's no telling how many horrible things happen in this world that nobody will ever know about," he said, not a little disturbingly. But then he smiled and said, "We're very lucky these stayed in the family. I don't know what happened to him once he got to Oregon – or even if he got to Oregon, actually. Or what happened to the woman he sent these to. He was planning to bring her out to Oregon, but maybe she decided to stay in Charleston. Or at least the letters did. But I want you to give them to Jeff, okay? They're not for you." He laughed.

"I can't believe this, man. Do you know how fucking valuable these might be? Not that I would ever sell them, but – look at this. You can still read every word. These belong in a library, Jeff. The Portland library would kill to have these."

"Well, Jeff can decide what he wants to do with them. They belong to him now, as far as I'm concerned."

"The Library of Congress would digitize them and put them online. It doesn't matter what they say. It doesn't matter what's actually in the letters. It's just the fact that they still exist. If you stick around long enough, Jeff, all that matters is that you still exist."

"I'll try to keep that in mind."

"I can't believe you never showed these to me."

"Me neither. I never thought of it. Out of sight, out of mind, I guess."

"Jesus. Check out the handwriting. They're beautiful just to look at, aren't they? Man, I don't know if I can hand these over to Jeff or not. At least not until after I read through all of them."

"You two can read them together. It'll be a good father-son activity."

Before I got too carried away with the letters I put them carefully back into the pouch and re-tied the 150-year-old leather strap closing over it. "What's up with this bag, man?" I asked, returning my curiosity to the pink satchel. "Was it Stephanie's? Or is it yours? Maybe it's in the closet for a reason, huh?"

He smiled gently. "No, I need to get rid of that too, I guess. It belonged to a girl I knew once, a long time ago. Don't know why I still have her bag. I don't think she's coming back for it." He shut the closet door.

After all my talk to Florida about what a great time we would have, the fact was, six hours on a lumpy sofa had not done my ribcage any favors. I begged off too much sight-seeing today and Jeff said, "Why don't you just stay in and lick your wounds and I'll show Florida a good time." She looked at me and was clearly angry – I wasn't supposed to leave her alone with strange men, even strange geriatric men, apparently. So we still had a little work to do on the trust issue.

"No no no," I said. "I'll be fine once I stretch my muscles out a little. Where can we go first?" Florida wanted to ride over the Golden Gate Bridge, which I was quick to second since it involved sitting down. I also suggested Lombard Street and anywhere else Jeff's old eyes could see to take us. Jeff drove chauffeur-style while Florida and I sat in the back seat. I held her hand going over the Golden Gate and at several other junctures during our marvelous afternoon.

We enjoyed a late dinner and Florida hung in with us for as long as she could stand it, but was in bed before midnight. Jeff turned out all the lights in the apartment after he had lit a couple of candles. Bix and Cootie took turns jumping on the counters and circling the candles. Jeff seemed unconcerned about the danger of a furry conflagration as their tails swayed over the flames. "They're used to it," was all he said. We sat side-by-side on the couch and Jeff pulled open a small drawer on a nightstand. It contained a smaller case which, as I correctly remembered, contained several rolled joints. "These are getting harder for me to afford," he said, "which makes them all the more wonderful to savor. Let's take our time and enjoy." He lit me up and leaned back further into the couch and we both took in that sweet aroma. My damaged ribs, up to this point, had been a major inconvenience and a minor obstacle, but now, upon trying to take my first deep pull, I realized they were a curse upon my soul. It was hopeless. Jeff rolled over against me with laughter as I struggled to inhale, and his weight against my side only made matters worse. "That's okay, man," Jeff howled, "I'll make sure I blow some over in your general direction!" He stood up and walked over to a bookshelf lined with record albums. There were a few CD cases and even a couple of cassettes scattered about, but by and large Jeff restricted his listening to long-players. I had tried to explain to him the cornucopia of music available online, but he was less than interested. I remembered times I visited him when he had entire walls covered with shelves of LP records. But he had obviously whittled his stupendous collection down to a hundred or so classics he couldn't live without. I imagined a lot of those old records were sold off so he could continue to enjoy his late-night listening sessions in the style to which he had grown accustomed. I had accompanied him more than once to used-record dealers, each of us carrying an armful of beautiful jazz – and not just the music contained in the grooves, but the album sleeves themselves were works of art, gorgeous to hold and to admire. Some of his records were surprisingly valuable; others were surprisingly worthless. The quality of the music was almost irrelevant. We would walk into a record shop in a somber mood, almost funereal, as Jeff prepared to say goodbye to several dozen of his closest friends. But he couldn't remain downcast for long. He would inevitably leave the store with a few new old records he had to have, cutting into the proceeds of his sale but giving him new reasons to live for many months to come. "What would you like to hear?" Jeff asked.

"Anything you got. Host's choice." He had the apartment wired for sound. As soon as the needle dropped I heard, from every corner of the living room, the soothing familiar static of a record beginning to play. A piano began and immediately I recognized Bill Evans. Jeff returned and slid gently into the sofa beside me. He took a deep hit of his joint and closed his eyes. I had to settle for short pulls no different than from a cigarette. "I feel bad that Florida is missing out. Should you wake her and see if she wants to partake?" Jeff asked.

"Nah, she should probably stay away from this. I think she's had some substance issues in the past. It cost her her kid. She's had a rough life."

"Haven't we all."

"If I can just bring some happiness into her life it will make me very happy."

"You're a good guy. I hope she makes you happy, too. Don't be a martyr."

"I haven't felt this happy in a long time, man." I wanted to move the conversation away from me as quickly as possible. It's a most unsavory subject. I thought I should probably ask

Jeff about Pop, another unsavory subject. He was his brother, after all. "I missed you at Pop's funeral."

"Yeah, I'm sorry about that, man. I probably should have been there. It just didn't feel right. Should have been there for you at Will's service, too, but – I'd skip my own funeral if I could."

"Hey – no explanation necessary. I don't blame you a bit." I took as much of a pull as I could stand. "Are you doing okay? Pop left us with a lot of shit to process."

"I hadn't seen your Pop in an awful long time. He had no interest in seeing me. I called him every now and then, but he never called me. Not one single time."

"Really?"

"That's okay. He had no reason to want to call me. I only called him because I felt guilty about leaving like I did."

"But you did the right thing. Nothing to feel guilty about."

"I didn't say I was wrong. I just said I felt guilty." He chuckled. "You don't have to be wrong to feel guilty."

I could have picked Jeff's brain about Pop all night, and I wanted to, but now was not the time. Maybe there never would be a good time for that. Instead, I asked, "Why are you getting rid of those letters now? And so much of this other stuff?" His living room looked like a yard sale.

"It's time, man."

"Are you okay?"

"Oh yeah – for the time being. I'm fine. I'm very lucky I can still get around so well and take care of myself. But who knows how long that'll last? I've never thought too much about the future, but I guess you start thinking about it when you realize you don't have one." He laughed. "At some point, I hope it's still a few years off, but I'm probably gonna have to move into one of those old-folks homes." My eyes were closed but I heard Jeff inhale deeply, slowly over the smooth runs of Bill Evans' piano. It was turning into a melancholy night, but still immensely pleasant and relaxing. We sat silently for several minutes, taking in the music, which was always the primary consideration on these evenings. Eventually, Jeff said, "Assisted living facility. Retirement village. What's with all these damn euphemisms? What are people so fucking afraid of?"

"They're afraid of death, man. Who can blame 'em?"

"Nah, we're not afraid of death. Old people are not afraid of dying. I'm not exactly looking forward to it, but I'm not afraid to think about it. Those euphemisms aren't for the old folks living there. They're for the children who put them there. We don't give a shit what you call the place. Call it the Palace of Death for all we care. Call it Where Geezers Go to Die. It's all the same to me. But the kids don't like to think of their granddaddies being in there. Kids are afraid of death because they still have so much to live for. To them, death's a tragedy, a horrible accident that's not supposed to happen. Old folks know better." He laughed again, the grass working its magic. "But as long as I still have something to live for, I'll keep getting up every morning."

"Or every afternoon."

"There you go. Every day begins at midnight."

So does that mean I'm not really that old? Will's death *was* a tragedy and all I've been thinking about is how my own life seemed to be tragically winding down as well. Jeff handed me the album sleeve to look at. *Time Remembered*. Well yes, that's what you do with time. You remember it, and you waste it. That's all I've really used it for. But I'm so tired of remembering. Just so tired of it. I don't want to forget. I can never forget. But I'm so tired of remembering. I want to think now of the future, where there is no time. And nothing to remember. I haven't had a future worth thinking about for a long time, but maybe Florida can change that. Maybe my son can change that. "Do you miss not having any kids?" I heard myself suddenly say, not even intending to say it aloud.

"Of course I miss it. People who don't have kids are miserable selfish bastards. Jeff is going to be your savior someday, if he isn't already. You're lucky to have such a great kid." We sat in silence until the record finished. "Okay, your turn," Jeff said. I went over to his shelf full of old records and perused them by the candlelight. How was I supposed to choose from so many classics? Well, there was always *Kind of*

Blue, the alpha and omega, where it all started and what it all comes back to, but how many times must Jeff have heard that album and every note on it? Is it still possible to surprise the old man? I pulled out one sleeve after another, without making a decision. Then, what's this? Sinatra? *In the Wee Small Hours*. Alright then. Here we go. I had never known Jeff to be a fan of crooners, but I knew Sinatra was supposed to be a cut above the rest. Just seeing him on Jeff's shelf made me think I should give him more of a listen. I sat down as the music started. "Ah, ol' Blue Eyes. Snotra," Jeff said.

"Is this okay?"

"Oh sure. Definitely. Anything that's up on that shelf is well worth listening to. Snotra's got the greatest phrasing. Impeccable."

So I settled in to listen to Sinatra in the wee hours of this morning, trying not to think about the past even though that's all Frank seemed interested in singing about. Can I stop thinking about Will every minute of every hour? And Pop? And me? Especially me. I closed my eyes and dreamed of caressing Florida's skin and kissing it all over and dreamed of Jeff back home and how he smiles and hugs me when we see each other and I even allowed myself the dream of holding a grandchild laughing with chubby cheeks and sparkling eyes, swaddled in warm clothing, but I guess I was too new at dreaming for what I saw instead was not my grandchild but Will I was holding, quite heavy for my young-boy arms and I have no idea how to hold him the right way and almost drop him once but Mom is smiling and saying you always have to protect him he's your baby brother and I believed her with all my heart.

It's nowhere near January but everything has the feeling of a new start and so I make a resolution, a New Life's resolution, but it'll take practice, like the daily practice I put in on my trumpet as a teen, the only time I ever focused on a dream, playing scales every day until my lips were like rubber. I need an image I can always return to, a mental note that's easy to hit – the middle C of my mind – that will keep me focused on my new dreams and all I have to look forward to. I never realized how lonely Jeff was until tonight, talking of old-folks' homes and dying alone and not having kids of his own. I had only imagined Jeff living the kind of life I had dreamed for myself, chock-full of jazz friends, admiring females and adoring students at all hours. So in my mind I'm driving, not west this time but north-south, straight down Highway 101, Florida beside me and my son in the backseat and we're driving down to visit Jeff every month. It's a long drive but the most beautiful one imaginable. And of course Uncle Jeff will be welcome to ride back with us and spend as much time in Portland as he wants. He can even live with me if he can tear himself away from North Beach. It's a simple image and a simple dream, but those are the best kind, so I resolve to dream again, to push away the past when it intrudes, to dream of love anew and love renewed, of Florida and my two Jeffs, of possibilities winning over uncertainties, and I'll continue to believe I'm the luckiest man on Earth, just as those who have found God believe, through all their adversity and despite a host of life's tragedies, they are still being held in His warm embrace, and, as I drift off to sleep I promise to continue to dream these things and to believe these things, Frank singing the world is lyrical because a miracle has brought my lover to me.

CPSIA information can be obtained
at www.ICGtesting.com
Printed in the USA
BVOW08s1418210118
505358BV00003B/14/P